31.99   7/13/10   31479399

Snyder County Libraries, Inc.
1 N. High St.
Selinsgrove, PA 17870
(570) 374-7163

INVISIBLE BOY

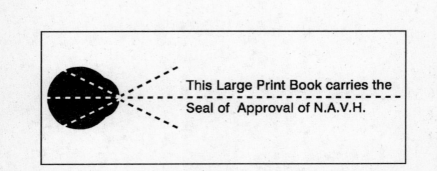

INVISIBLE BOY

CORNELIA READ

THORNDIKE PRESS
A part of Gale, Cengage Learning

Detroit • New York • San Francisco • New Haven, Conn • Waterville, Maine • London

GALE
CENGAGE Learning

Thorndike Press® Large Print Reviewers' Choice.
The text of this Large Print edition is unabridged.
Other aspects of the book may vary from the original edition.
Set in 16 pt. Plantin.

LIBRARY OF CONGRESS CATALOGING-IN-PUBLICATION DATA

Read, Cornelia.
    Invisible boy / by Cornelia Read.
      p. cm. — (Thorndike Press large print reviewers' choice)
    ISBN-13: 978-1-4104-2756-4
    ISBN-10: 1-4104-2756-0
      1. Dare, Madeline (Fictitious character)—Fiction. 2. Cold cases (Criminal investigation)—Fiction. 3. Social conflict—New York (State)—New York—Fiction. 4. New York (N.Y.)—Fiction. 5. Large type books. I. Title.
    PS3618.E22I58 2010b
    813'.6—dc22   2010009504

Published in 2010 by arrangement with Grand Central Publishing, a division of Hachette Book Group, Inc.

Printed in the United States of America
1 2 3 4 5 6 7 14 13 12 11 10

To my cousin, Cate Ludlam,
and my cousin-in-spirit, Eric Rosenbaum

This project was supported in part
by an award from the
National Endowment for the Arts.

NATIONAL
ENDOWMENT
FOR THE ARTS

I looked on my right hand, and beheld, but there was no man that would know me: refuge failed me; no man cared for my soul.

— Psalm 142

■ ■ ■ ■

Manhattan
September 1990

■ ■ ■ ■

1

So here's what I love about New York City: if someone acts like a dumb asshole and you call them on acting like a dumb asshole, the bystanders are happy about it.

Anywhere else I've ever lived they just think I'm a bitch.

Also, in Manhattan the Chinese food is excellent and they deliver, which to me counts as pretty much the acme of human achievement, to date. Especially with free cold sesame noodles.

I'm sorry, but if you pick up your phone and all you can get them to bring you for sustenance is crappy lukewarm national-chain pizza, you do not live in civilization.

Having just spent four years out in what is euphemistically known as "the heartland," I was overjoyed to be back in the city of my birth.

It was an early fall day and totally gorgeous out, and my mother and I were walking down lower Sixth Avenue. We were supposed to be picking up a cake for a party that night, and I was in a most excellent mood.

Mom looked like she'd rather be weeding something or moving piles of rocks around or one of those other kinds of strenuous activities one gets up to out in the country.

"Must be this one," she said, pointing toward a slightly ratty bakery on the opposite side of the street from us, just above Waverly Place.

We sprinted across Sixth against the light, Mom leading the way. She hadn't actually lived in Manhattan since 1965, but some habits die hard.

There was this brittle-looking skinny faux-blonde chick standing next to the bakery's door. Her makeup was kabuki/stewardess, and she teetered atop painfully chic Bergdorf-bitch slingbacks.

I wondered anew why some women were so desperate to wear "fuck-me" shoes. I have long preferred "fuck-*you*" shoes.

Faux-blonde chick pulled the door open but then just stood there, like she was appalled to realize she might for once actually *ingest* something besides diuretics and a half-stalk of celery.

Mom, meanwhile, ran a hand through her

own short, dark hair and breezed in past her.

Stunned at this effrontery, the woman sniped, "So what am I *now,* a doorman?"

Oh for chrissake, lady, get the hell over yourself.

As she was still just standing there, I muttered, "What, you got some problem with doormen?" and strode on inside myself.

The bakery's interior was dark compared to the sidewalk's mellow late-summer bloom of light. It took a few seconds for my eyes to adjust, so I just sucked in the scents of butter and vanilla perfuming the small establishment.

Mom asked about our party cake up at the display counter while a gang of confectionary aficionados sampled tortes and bombes and éclairs at a dozen tiny tables crowded together along the black-and-white-tiled floor.

Just as the proprietress set a pink box on the countertop in front of my mother, I felt a set of Flintstones-pterodactyl claws latch on to my shoulder.

The now-even-more-pissed-off door-lady yanked me around to shriek, "You *bitch!*" right in my face — so close I got nailed with a constellation of spit flecks.

"Um," I said, trying to back off a little, "I

beg your pardon?"

She gripped my shoulder harder and started jabbing me in the chest with a bony finger. "Who. The. Hell." *Poke. Poke. Poke.* "Do you think you *are?*"

The final poke practically broke her french-manicured nail off, right in the middle of the LEFTY'S TATTOO AND PIERCING, CHULA VISTA logo on my best second-hand black T-shirt.

"I think I'm Madeline Ludlam Fabyan Dare," I said, raising my chin to look down my nose at her. "Why?"

"Bitch!" spat my scrawny nemesis, redundantly.

All the people at the little tables were watching now, pastry-loaded forks paused in midair.

Aware of our audience, psycho-babe dropped her hands from my person and just stood there, fists clenched, vibrating like an irate tuning fork.

"Oh, please," I said. "Like it's the end of the fucking world if you held the door for someone?"

Her right hand came back up, finger extended. "You!" *Poke.* "Need!" *Poke.* "To change!" *Poke-poke.* "Your goddamn attitude!" *PokepokePOKEpoke.*

She drove me backwards toward the

14

counter's plate-glass front, behind which rested a stage-lit panorama of buttercream whimsy.

I snapped my hand around her wimpy little calcium-deprived wrist before she could finger-stab me again.

"And *you*," I said, tightening my grip, "need to change your goddamn *medication*."

A couple of onlookers started laughing.

I let go of her wrist. The witch teetered once on those nasty stilettos before dropping her head and scuttling away.

The door banged open, then whooshed closed.

A big rough-looking guy at a tiny corner table raised his foam cup of espresso toward me in appreciation, and the rest of the patrons dropped their forks for a round of applause.

Mom stepped up beside me bearing the pink cake box, now tied shut with red-and-white baker's twine.

"Dude," I said, grinning at her, "I fucking *love* New York."

2

It was Sue who'd found our apartment originally, back when she was still a film student at NYU. I'd known her since boarding school when she'd walked up and introduced herself to me one September morning because we were both class presidents that year — her freshman and me junior, respectively. I'd asked her to look out for my little sister when Pagan came east with me to join Sue's class the following year.

The apartment was a prewar two-bedroom in Chelsea — West Sixteenth between Sixth and Seventh Avenues, no doorman. Sue now hustled her ass off shouting into phones for a production company that made TV commercials, uptown, which taught her how to wring maximum juice from the city on our pooled crappy paychecks.

She briefed us on who had the best Chinese delivery (Empire Szechuan Greenwich, *not* Empire Szechuan Village, though they were a mere block apart), the best bagels (H&H), and the closest place we could get same-day dry-cleaning without paying extra if we showed up by seven and made nice with the counter lady.

Pagan and Sue shared the smaller bedroom, and when they'd needed new roommates in June, my husband, Dean, and I had schlepped down from the Berkshires.

We'd come to New York hoping he'd get into a management-training program with the Transit Authority. He'd done contract work on the subways during his Upstate youth, but to garner a permanent gig it turned out you needed an Uncle Vinnie in the union. So now I was taking book-catalog phone orders while Dean sent out résumés and did odd carpentry jobs for our friends' bosses and parents around the city.

There was money to be made for any likely young man with a power drill, given the stunning proportion of shop-class flunkees amongst Manhattan's well-heeled — one guy even paid him fifty bucks to hook up a VCR — but the gigs weren't exactly leading toward anything Dean wanted to be when he grew up.

And then there was the whole bored-boomer-wives-ogling-the-strapping-young-blond-guy-in-coveralls routine, which didn't sit any too well with me despite my intrepid spouse's continued reassurance that, say, being met at the door of a strange apartment by some fifty-year-old StairMaster-fiend wrapped in nothing but a bedsheet left him rather more embarrassed than titillated.

I was explaining all this to Mom as I followed her into the lobby of our building.

"Not a *fitted* sheet, I hope," she said, as we reached the stairs.

"Dean didn't specify," I said. "Except to say it had cartoon trains on it so he figured it was from her son's room."

"Trains? Good God . . . hardly seems as though she was even trying, does it?"

Mom laughed, but the idea of my marriage being even vaguely at risk made me dizzy with angst. Dean was my refuge, the bulwark of my very sanity.

"That still means it was a *twin* sheet," I said, my voice echoing in the stairwell as we climbed upward. "So she wasn't exactly, like, swamped in fabric."

My mother shrugged. "Probably didn't have the figure for a negligee."

"Way to be maternal, Mom."

Having been raised in a landscape of divorce-shattered families, I considered

18

matrimony a construct of gossamer fragility — equal parts swan's down, lighter fluid, and willing suspension of disbelief.

Mom and I had reached the landing and I opened our apartment's front door, following her into its narrow front hallway.

"I'll just put the cake in your icebox," she said, ducking around a half-dozen trays jammed with the tiny paper cups from Sue's dentist that awaited vodka-spiked liquid for the evening's Jell-O shots.

I thanked her for buying the cake, which I hadn't expected, and wandered toward the living room.

Pagan and Sue were rolling on a second coat of the paint we'd picked out that morning at Janovic, up near Twenty-third, Sue precarious on the top rail of a stepladder, Pague balanced all nonchalant on one thin arm of the hideous seventies-Danish-tweed sofa that had been gleefully abandoned by the previous tenants.

A stranger would've pegged me and Sue as the sisters. We weren't each other's long-lost secret twins or anything, but we both had green eyes, darkish blonde hair, and beaky noses.

My actual sibling, meanwhile, was brunette like Mom and looked straight out of Gauguin, had the man ever happened to paint the girl's All-Tahiti soccer captain carrying her surfboard down the beach.

"I still can't believe we chose this stupid color," said Pagan, pushing a lock of hair off her forehead. " 'Desert Blossom' my ass."

I considered the rancid pink-orange walls. "More like 'St. Joseph's Baby Acid.' "

"Pepto-peach ass-baby," said Sue. "But it looked *totally* apricot back at the store."

"*Ass*-baby?" said Pagan. "What the hell is an *ass*-baby?"

"Fuck off," said Sue.

Mom stepped into the room and squinted at the glare. "Did you guys take the paint chip outside and look at it in the sunshine? They probably had fluorescent lights."

"Maybe it will fade?" I asked.

Mom shook her head. "Reminds me of the time I tried dyeing the turnips blue for Thanksgiving. Complete disaster."

"That *was* nasty," I said. "Crème de la hippo."

"Crème de la hippo *shit,* more like," said Pagan.

Sue stepped down off the ladder for a re-dip in the paint tray just as a car alarm went off outside. The shock of noise made her drop the roller, splattering fat plops of orange up the legs of her jeans.

"Fucking yuppies," she yelled over the flamenco yelps and Bronx cheers. "I'm practically ready to bash in *all* their windshields just to get it over with."

The noise died down and Mom looked around the room. "Keep the lights dim tonight."

"And you'd better put extra vodka in the Jell-O shots," said Pagan, pointing at me. "This is like meeting your hangover before you even start drinking."

Dean rang up from out front, needing help wrangling the keg and a case of Smirnoff upstairs. Sue buzzed him in and propped the front door open.

The elevator dinged a minute later, and Dean walked a hand truck backwards down our narrow entry hall, ducking his golden head a reflexive inch to pass beneath the living-room doorway's lintel.

At six-five, my strapping farmboy spouse was scaled too large for city life. We were lucky to have this much space — a studio apartment would've felt like sharing a starter aquarium with Godzilla.

I trailed my fingers along his hip as he wheeled past, which made him turn toward me and grin.

"Hey, Bunny," he said.

"Hey back."

21

Then he saw the new living-room color and winced. "Don't tell me — All-You-Can-Eat Peyote Day up at the paint store?"

I helped him muscle the keg into a dryish corner. "Nah, we figured it'd be cheaper to shove Oompa Loompas through a wood-chipper."

"Hardy har *har*," said Pagan, climbing down off the sofa.

"I may have just contracted a new disease," said Dean, shading his eyes with one hand.

"What?" I asked.

"Sno-Kone blindness."

"Fuck," said Sue. "We forgot *ice*."

"I should get going," said Mom. "It's a long way back up to Maine."

"You sure we can't convince you to stay for the party?" I asked.

"I've been invited to crew in a regatta tomorrow," she said, "on a Hinckley."

Only those with suicidal tendencies dare stand between my mother and a boat. She'd been, like, the Mario Andretti of sailing — even winning the Women's Nationals immediately after marrying my father.

Dad sat out their honeymoon on the beach at Coronado. Mom made *Sports Illustrated.* The woman is still so psycho-competitive on the water that by fourth grade I'd joined Pony Club in self-defense.

Pagan's the yachty kid, along with our baby half-brother, Trace. But Pague and Mom are the only ones who still routinely bet each other a hundred bucks to see who can tie a bowline faster. I credit this to my sister being named after Mom's first boat, a Snipe she'd sunk off Cooper's Bluff in Oyster Bay trying to ride out a sudden squall in 1957.

Trace had traded in sailing for surfing, now that he was living with his dad on Oahu and trying to graduate from the fourth high school he'd attended in as many years.

I kissed Mom's cheek.

"Wear sunscreen," I said, "and don't scare the lobsters."

Pague and I walked her to the door.

Mom glanced back at us from the top of the stairwell.

"Talk to strangers!" she said, twinkling her fingers in farewell.

Sue and I had just finished pouring the final tray of Jell-O shots when Dean joined us in the kitchen.

"I'm taking dinner votes," he said. "So far we've got one for Benny's Burritos and one for Indian delivery."

"I *hate* Indian!" yelled Pagan from the living room.

"Philistine!" Dean yelled back.

"Let's do pizza," I said. "I'm totally broke."

"I'm down with pizza," said Sue. "We want delivery?"

"Let's walk it," said Dean. "We can just get slices."

"Cool." I picked up the finished Jell-O tray and shouldered the freezer open.

Sue shook her head. "Not enough room in there."

"Sure there is," I said. "Just grab that thing of Bustelo."

She snaked an arm past me to pull the yellow coffee can clear. "Still not gonna fit. No fucking way."

"Way," I said. "Five bucks."

Sue took my wager with a nod. "Sucker bet."

I raised the tray to eye level, then tilted it with care — two inches down toward the right. Syrupy Jell-O flowed toward the lip of each little paper mouthwash-cup, bulging but not spilling over.

I slid the tray slowly home, its upper left edge shaving a pinstripe of whiskered frost from the freezer ceiling.

"Son of a *bitch,*" said Sue.

"Surface tension," I replied, closing the

freezer door. "Kiss my ass and buy me dinner."

I may lack the nautical gene, but don't ever play me for money.

The party was roaring by nine o'clock that night. Somebody'd brought a strobe light, and we had a little vintage Funkadelic cued up on the CD player, "Maggot Brain" throbbing out our open windows into the sultry-for-September night. There was a gaggle of people doing bong hits on the fire escape, and dozens more smashed up against each other in the living room, hallway, kitchen, and both bedrooms.

I'd just made the circuit back from the bathroom and was now stationed next to the front door, cold beer in hand. Not like I had to drive home, but six Jell-O shots was nearing the limit, even for me.

Sue's friend Mike buzzed up from the lobby, and I held the door open for him, sticking my head out into the cooler, quieter air of our second-story hallway.

His blond head soon bobbed up behind the staircase's horizon, and I watched the rest of his skinny frame bounce into view, a foot at a time, until he'd stepped onto the landing's chipped and gritty tiny-hexagonal-tile floor.

"Madeline," he said, "I think I just got mugged in your vestibule."

"Um, Mike? How could you not *know?*"

He smiled up at the ceiling fixture. "This guy at work had some great acid. So it's, like, entirely possible that I just hallucinated the whole thing?"

"Do you still have your wallet?" I asked.

He patted his jacket pockets, then checked his jeans, fore and aft.

"It's gone," he said, grinning even wider. "What a relief!"

"Dude, your pupils are like Frisbees," I said.

He pointed at my red plastic cup. "Hey, is that a beer?"

"Last time I checked."

"Would you share some with me?"

"If you come in, you can have one of your very own."

He patted me on the shoulder. "I'm *so* glad I know you."

I took his hand and led him gently inside.

Sue stood in the kitchen doorway, and the music was even louder.

I leaned toward her, yelling "Mike's tripping and he just got mugged and I think he needs help finding the keg" about a foot away from her ear.

"I'll take care of it," she yelled back.

"Keep him away from the Jell-O," I said, just as the living-room speakers boomed out A Tribe Called Quest chanting "Mr. Dinkins will you please be my May-or?"

Sue gave me a thumbs-up and propelled Mike toward the living room.

The buzzer went off again and I didn't bother trying to identify the persons at the other end of the intercom before pushing the button to let them in.

If it was the muggers, we could all jump them and get Mike's wallet back, worst case.

Luckily, it was instead my college pal Sophia and a friend she'd called about bringing along for the evening.

Scarlet-lipped Sophia leaned forward to hug me hello, her mass of dark curls tickling my cheek.

"This is Cate Ludlam!" she yelled near my ear. "The one I told you about! Your cousin!"

I dragged them both into the kitchen. Cate introduced herself again, holding out her hand to shake. She was a little older and a touch shorter than me, with straight brown hair and eyes that made me think of Edith Piaf.

"Sophia thinks we might be related," I exclaimed over some newly blasting B-52s song.

27

Cate shrugged her shoulders and smiled, pointing to one ear. The B-52s chanted, "*What's* that on your *head?* A *wig!*"

I closed the kitchen door. We could still feel the thump of the bassline, but at least the overall decibel-age had dropped from "skin-blistering" to a mere "painfully loud."

"That's *so* much better," I said, pulling a fresh tray of Jell-O shots from the freezer and offering them around.

I said *L'chaim* and we each tossed one back.

"What were you asking just now?" asked Cate.

"Whether the two of you might be cousins," said Sophia, passing Cate a second little paper cup before taking one herself.

"One of my middle names is Ludlam," I explained. "After my great-great-grandmother."

Cate tossed back her second shot. "We're *all* related. Only three brothers came over from England with that surname."

"But there's Lud*lam* and Lud*lum.* What kind are you?" I asked.

"L-A-M," said Cate. "One brother went to New Jersey and changed the spelling — we call his branch Spawn of Obadiah. Long Island ones kept the 'A.' "

"Same as you, Maddie?" asked Sophia.

"Everyone in my family cemetery spells it with 'A,' " I said. "We probably burned the 'U' people as heretics, unless they were willing to convert — then refused to bury them anyway."

"Where's your cemetery?" Cate asked.

"On Centre Island, in the middle of Oyster Bay."

"I've heard of that one," she said.

"I'd be happy to give you a tour."

"I'd *love* it," she said. "And I'd be happy to show you mine."

"You've got one too? Awesome," I said.

"In Queens," said Cate. "It's called Prospect — the original burial ground for the village of Jamaica, starting in the sixteen hundreds."

"Are you guys still buried there?" I asked.

"Oh, no," she said. "It's been derelict for decades. I only found out about it a year ago."

"Were you researching family history?" asked Sophia.

"No," said Cate. "Someone abandoned a couple of dogs inside the fence and a neighborhood woman rescued them. She saw the name Ludlam on the chapel by the front gate and started calling up any of us she could find listings for."

"What's it like?" asked Sophia.

"At that point it was four acres of jungle," said Cate.

"What about the chapel?" I asked.

"Oh, the chapel . . ." said Cate with a dreamy little smile. "It was a stinking, sorry mess filled with garbage and crack vials, but my God, there's still something about it. . . . The little place just *hooked* me, you know?"

"The addictive poignance of the small, neglected ruin," I said. "I know it well."

Cate laughed. "I've started rounding up volunteers to help with the brush clearing, Wednesday afternoons. Would you like to join us this week?"

"I'd be honored," I said, raising my cup. "And I think we should imbibe another shot in celebration of our newfound genealogical commonality."

"Hear, hear!" said Cate, taking another paper-clad portion from the tray.

"To cousins," added Sophia, lifting her own, "and the lapidary allure of tiny woebegone places."

We knocked back our gelatinous cocktails just as the kitchen door flew open and a half-dozen partiers tumbled into the room, demanding Jell-O themselves as the music blared up to an absolutely depilatory volume.

I looked at Cate and Sophia and shrugged,

pointing toward the living room.

We threaded our way down the crowded hallway, slipping sideways and single file between knots of dancing bodies.

I reached the stereo and eased off on the Velvet Underground's volume, only to have Lou Reed's voice overridden by a street-concerto of car alarms.

Sue was out on the fire escape waving the bong overhead as she conducted a group-stoner cheer of "Die Yuppie Scum! Die Yuppie Scum!"

Her gestural enthusiasm made her tip backwards and I shoved my way toward the window, arms outstretched as my heartbeat went bossa nova, but luck and the thin iron railing kept her from tumbling to the sidewalk below.

"Perfect!" yelled Pagan into my ear. "It's not a party until Sue falls down!"

3

Sunday we were all hungover as shit, stumbling out of bed for coffee well after noon. Dean and Sue and Pagan decided they wanted to go Rollerblading after a long, slow brunch at our local diner, the Hollywood. I decided they were crazy and stayed put.

Some people's bodies say "Go! Go! Go!" Mine counters with "Fuck it, let's lie down with a book on the sofa." And that goes double after a Hollywood bacon-cheeseburger.

It was two hours before the exercise fanatics came home, but I wasn't tired enough to nap. Sunday afternoon has always struck me as a horrible stretch of time to spend solo. If you made it into crayons they'd all turn out burnt sienna.

I picked up the phone to see if I could find Astrid, another boarding-school pal. We were the kind of friends who got in touch once a year or so but always seemed to resume the conversation midsentence.

My own social pretensions were of the shopworn poor-relation Mayflower variety, but there wasn't even a phrase in American to suitably describe Astrid.

You had BCBG in French: *bon chic, bon genre,* but that's rather like "classy" in English. Parisians of Astrid's own ilk would've preferred *comme il faut,* though I figured "living on reds, vitamin C, and cocaine" more accurately described her life amongst that rarefied tribe of brittle-whippet polyglots who traveled by Concorde and gave me the bends.

She was a British/Florentine beauty who hadn't lived anywhere longer than three months since we'd graduated, back in '81 — just kept doing this jagged über-Euro party-girl circuit of London and LA and Palm Beach and the Upper East Side.

It was pointless trying to keep an up-to-date address or phone number for her on hand. I relied on directory-information operators to tell me whether our orbits had aligned whenever I was in New York.

This time I'd put it off for a couple of months, what with moving, looking for work, and stowing my furniture and old Porsche in a friend-of-Mom's barn on Long

Island. You know: life. All the grown-up crap I so royally sucked at.

I dialed 411, gritting my teeth in anticipation of having to spell Astrid's surname for the operator. It was Niro-de-Barile, shortened by Dean to "Nutty Buddy" in the very first phone message he'd written down for me the week he and I moved in together back in Syracuse.

Today's operator indeed had a listing for her — in the East Fifties, no surprise.

I dialed, expecting to get her machine, and was surprised by her live actual "Hello."

"Hey," I said.

"Madissima, how the hell *are* you?"

"Decent," I said. "And at long last actually living in the city, thank God. You?"

"I've been meaning to phone *you,* in fact, but couldn't remember what they call that *last* godforsaken town you were living in, after Syracuse —"

"Pittsfield."

"The aptly named. How *could* one have forgotten?"

"With great pleasure and appalling haste," I said. "What's your news?"

"Darling, it appears I've gotten *married.*"

"Good God."

I heard her blow a stream of cigarette smoke against her phone's mouthpiece.

34

"Last Saturday, actually. Decided I was overdue."

"Who's the lucky winner?"

"Well, Antonini was out of town, so I stuck a pin in my address book and landed on Christoph."

"Was that the polo guy or the one with a Bugatti?"

"The Swiss one."

"There was a Swiss one?"

"I brought him up for drinks the summer you were all crammed into that place on Park and Eighty-ninth? He said he'd never seen a filthier bathroom?"

"I thought you were mad for Prentice that year."

"*Fuck* me, I'd have had to live in Boston. Anathema."

"I'm rather fond of Switzerland," I said. "Hot cheese. Subtitles in three languages. Not much for foreplay, if memory serves, but excellent value overall. Congratulations to him, and best wishes to you."

"We had great fun. Chartered a plane to Southampton."

"My least favorite place on earth, but whatever."

"And how is Dean?" she asked.

"Fine, thank you. Looking for work."

"He's an inventor or something?"

"Or something," I said.

"I told Mummie you'd married a cabinet-maker."

I laughed. "How'd she take it?"

"Oh, she was quite, quite pleased for you. She said, 'How marvelous, just like David *Linley*.'"

I cracked up.

"Don't *laugh*, Madeline," said Astrid. "One has to break these things to Mummie gently. She's not accustomed to reality."

"Oh, please. I mean, admit it, the image of *me* married to anyone even slightly *resembling* the offspring of Princess Margaret is pretty fucking funny."

I heard the click of Astrid's lighter as she lit a fresh Marlboro.

"Oh, and of course *Camilla* was asking after you," she continued.

I'd known the bitch as Cammy at Sarah Lawrence, and had made the mistake of introducing her to Astrid.

"And how *is* darling Chlamydia?" I asked, not caring at all.

"Blonde," said Astrid. "Very, *very* blonde."

"I saw that. Some party shot in *Town and Country,* if memory serves — which just goes to show what an appallingly nouveau-riche rag it's become. *And* she's stolen my nose."

36

"Be generous. Her birth-schnozz was hideous."

"*My* nostrils disporting themselves at B-list Eurotrash galas attached to that odious Nescafé-society cow? She should at least rivet a small plaque to her upper lip crediting the original."

"And Camilla's always so lovely about *you,*" she said, laughing with a touch of smoker's wheeze.

I snorted into the phone.

Astrid was undaunted. "She absolutely *adores* you. Why, just the other day she turned to me and said, 'Isn't it terribly, terribly *sad* about Madeline? She might have been such fun if she weren't *poor.*' "

I sighed. "Festering bitch. Tell her she owes me nose royalties."

"I'll have Christoph give your husband a job instead — how's that? He's got a little company. Out in New Jersey."

"Kiss my shapely ass."

Astrid laughed. "Well, for God's sake let's at least *introduce* them. I mean, who'd ever have believed you and I would be married, and simultaneously? We *must* have drinks — quickly, before one of us fucks it up."

"I demand absinthe."

"Perfect. Wednesday night."

"You gladden my tiny black heart," I said.

"Pitter-clank, pitter-clank."

"Exactly."

"Ciao, bellissima," she purred, hanging up.

4

Wednesday started out Capra and ended
Polanski.

I booked out from beneath the ornate
gateway arch of our building's front courtyard, then turned east on Sixteenth toward
the subway station in Union Square — ten
minutes late, as usual.

My housemates had beaten me out the
door despite having taken showers, which,
in my semiconscious state — what with the
bathroom plumbing running through the
wall right next to my head — I'd considered
a needling passive-aggressive display of
moral superiority.

I'd just kept hitting the snooze bar and
having those short-story dreams between
rounds of cruel clock-radio beeps.

Most mornings I played "Rhapsody in
Blue" on my beat-to-shit Walkman, gentling
the commute uptown with those opening
bars of solo-Deco clarinet. Today required a

mix-tape of slick/vapid eighties cocaine-frenzy anthems: Chaka Khan, Bronski Beat, and "The Dominatrix Sleeps Tonight." Aural Jay McInerney.

A light mist tumbled between the buildings as I walked, white on white, warmed at the edges by bowfront Edith-Wharton brownstones between Sixth and Fifth. The air was still cool this early, but I could feel the day's impending sweaty oppression tapping its foot in the wings.

It certainly wasn't chilly enough to mask the street-stench of vomit and garbage and festering piss. I'd been back here long enough to have once again made mouth breathing my default style of respiration.

I smiled at the sight of my all-time favorite bumper sticker, posted in the Trotskyite bookstore's window: U.S. OUT OF NORTH AMERICA!

I walked faster, slipping through schools of people that grew thicker and thicker as we neared the subway — commuter fish trying to reach the turnstiles so we could spawn and die.

I kept my knees loose on the ride uptown, riding the car's totally fucked suspension like a surfer chick, until we squealed to a halt at Fifty-ninth Street. I bolted out the doors before they were halfway open, first to snake through the exit gate's gnashing teeth — a cotton gin for people.

The Catalog was on the thirteenth floor, straight across from the *Granta* Bitches, with the even-nastier *Review* behind door number three at the end of the hall. We were a triad of money pits loosely conjoined, no doubt the aftermath of some literary-cocktail-napkin Venn diagram. It always felt like that old joke about academia, the one about how the infighting is so vicious because the stakes are so low.

Pagan was already back in editorial by the time I walked into the front office. She was the assistant photo editor and had gotten me a gig taking phone orders, part-time.

I'd been staff writer at a weekly paper in Syracuse for three years, but that counted for exactly dick in Manhattan, a revelation that gave me more compassion for Upstate New York than I'd ever had while living there with Dean.

I parked my take-out coffee next to a vacant computer terminal and sat down, back to the window. We had a cinder-brick air shaft view: the quality of light made it seem like the asshole of February, year-round.

Yong Sun was running the credit-card

41

batch while Yumiko and Karen typed away with phones to their ears.

I booted up my PC and took a sip of coffee, waiting for the third line to ring. The cool part of the job was talking to customers. We had a direct hookup with Baker & Taylor's warehouses in New Jersey and Illinois — wholesalers with instant access to virtually any book in print.

People called from Tucson, Fargo, Bakersfield, Anchorage. They faxed orders from Buenos Aires and Paris and Guam. They sought lost favorite volumes to share with their children. They yearned for obscure absurdist novels, slender poetry collections, meaty anthologies. They thirsted for noir and space opera and Zane Grey, Aeschylus and Kipling and *Hollywood Babylon.* They wanted to tie knots and grow roses and build wooden dinghies, to mend fences and marriages and classic muscle cars.

The phone rang at last. I punched the blinking button for line three and picked up. "Good morning, this is the Catalog, how may I help you?"

At the end of my shift a few hours later, I found Pagan lying sideways on the front-office carpet. She was surrounded by leaning towers of paper trays, her head and arms

42

shoved into the guts of our Xerox machine.

"Fucking jammed again," she said, pushing herself back out. "Not like it matters, since we're out of fucking toner."

The only indication that it was probably ninety degrees and muggy out on West Fifty-seventh by now was the dark tan of Pague's legs, unbroken from her flip-flops to the hem of her raggedy shorts.

You want people to wear stockings and shit, you've gotta pay *way* more than six bucks an hour.

Pagan slotted all the trays back into the machine and tried to push its door closed, but the catch was blown so it took two slams with the side of her fist to make it stay shut.

"Espece de merde," she muttered. *"Ma che cazzo fai."*

I leaned against the edge of the reception desk. "So get Tracy to make the *Granta* Bitches let us use theirs."

"She's stuck in Geoffrey's office with Betty, going over edits for the Fall Bulletin."

"O joy, O rapture."

Betty was the ex-wife of Julian, the owner, and had retained enough post-divorce cred to march down from the *Review* and slap us around whenever she felt like it. On bad days that was pretty much hourly.

A door crashed open against Sheetrock,

43

down the short hallway toward Editorial.

I could hear Betty doing her usual screech-ranting-banshee number: all "congenital *idiocy*" and "how-*dare*-you-fuck-with-me-like-this," and *blah blah* psycho-bipolar-hosebeast *blah.*

Pague and I flinched at the noise of a sudden crack-splash explosion: *Crockery v. Wall.*

"Fucking Betty," said my sister. "She made me bring her that coffee. In *my* mug from home."

"Bitch throws like a champ, though. Especially considering she's missing an arm."

"Don't be evil," said Pagan.

"Compared to *Betty?*"

"You want to be like her when you grow up?"

She narrowed her eyes at me, hands on her hips. No one can shame me like Pagan. Especially when she's right.

"No," I said. "Of course not."

"Go tell the *Granta* Bitches I need to make copies. I don't want to extend Betty's psychotic break du jour."

I checked my watch. "Can't. Late for the cemetery."

"Chickenshit."

"What if I interrupt some *Granta*-Bitch Kill-Toddlers-for-Satan fest?" I asked.

44

"They'll go for my throat like a pack of Dobermans."

She rolled her eyes. "I can't believe I'm related to you."

"Them's the breaks. Gotta run."

I'd never thought of Jamaica as an actual place.

It had always been more transition than geography. Three stops out of Penn Station and you alighted briefly at this celestial concrete expanse carpeted all Jackson Pollock with discarded Kool butts and soda-can tabs and matte-black ovals of chewing gum — a stretch of nowhere to be raced across when exchanging your sleek city train for the big-shouldered cars of the Oyster Bay Line.

I had nothing against Queens, per se, it was just that if you were raised in the milieu I had been, you were reminded of the borough beneath this platform maybe once a year, if that often.

It might happen on your way to the airport, or when a member of your party dismissively remarked upon the "bridge-and-tunnel crowd" still pressed up hopeful against the velvet ropes while a nightclub's bouncer ushered all of *you* inside that particular season's haute meat-market Nirvana (and please understand that such inclusion had always made me feel slightly ashamed and unworthy — whether I'd been granted entrée to Studio or Regine's aged fifteen, Area or Pyramid at twenty — since I can't dance for shit and besides which never had the price of so much as a draft domestic beer in my pocket, even if I was on somebody's guest list and didn't have to pay the cover).

With all of the above in mind on this particular September afternoon, I ventured down Jamaica Station's cast-iron staircases to street level for the very first time.

I consulted my rough sketch of map every few blocks, walking on through a crowded terra incognita of bodegas and boombox stores, newsstands and fruit vendors, feeling very much like the only white chick for miles.

The day had grown hot: air rank with diesel fumes and curry, melting asphalt and the chicken-soup funk of humanity, not to mention the occasional sweet-sour belt of Dumpster leakage wafting out from restaurant alleyways.

I trudged onward, the sidewalk crowds

thinning, the stores fewer and farther between, until I finally turned into a cratered dead-end block in the shadow of some elevated subway tracks. A wall of vines ran down one side of this lane, the occasional snatch of ornate rusted fence peeking out from beneath the leaves.

I spotted a gate sagging open next to a small Romanesque building of golden stone. Its low roof-pitch was more suggestive of synagogue than chapel, and its rose windows were shattered.

I looked across maybe a quarter-acre of cleared lawn inside the gate. There were crooked gravestones poking forth from the hacked weed stubble and a dozen brush-filled black garbage bags lined up at the head of a trail leading into the lot's still-riotous green interior.

I followed the narrow path into a jungle of nettles and vines, towering three times my height in some places.

"Cate?" I called. "It's Madeline. . . ."

I heard soft laughter ahead.

"Cate?"

I found her around the first bend of trail through the brush, with a gaggle of chattering teenaged kids bearing hedge clippers and machetes.

My newfound cousin swiped an arm

across her forehead, then spotted me and waved.

"This is Madeline," she said, rattling off the names of her crew.

It was cooler in the shade, but my face had started pouring sweat now that I'd stopped moving. I took a bandanna out of my pocket and folded it narrow to tie around my forehead, Deadhead style.

"There's a big jug of ice water in the chapel," Cate said. "Let's grab some before I put you to work."

I blinked when we came back out into the glare, following her past an enclosed rectangle of headstones, its shin-high rails held aloft by a squat granite obelisk at each corner.

"Was everything *that* overgrown when you started?" I asked, looking back at the cool wall of green behind us.

"Solid vegetable matter," she said. "It's taken us the whole summer to get this much cleared. The final burial was in nineteen fifty-four — I suspect that's the last time anyone tried weeding."

At the chapel door Cate fished a big wad of keys from her pocket and started sorting through them.

I looked above the iron fence as an elevated train screeched by along its Great-

Wall course of tired concrete.

Kate fitted a key into the padlock, popping it open with a rough twist.

"It must have been beautiful. The whole city," I said, "before there *was* any city."

"You'd have been able to see all the way down to the water from here. The old villagers picked a magnificent place in which to honor their dead."

Impossible to picture: no buildings or asphalt, just foot trails winding through beach plum and shadbush beneath Long Island's great green canopy, connecting sparkling ponds and white beaches, cornfields and oyster beds, wildflower meadows and beaver dams.

We entered the shade inside the chapel, our steps echoing back from its stone walls and floor. Cate poured out two Dixie cups of cold water and handed one to me.

"We just found a headstone the kids are excited about," said Cate. "One of the slave graves."

I told her I'd like to see it too, and we put our cups in a trash bag and headed back outside.

Cate started walking toward the thicker growth and I followed, Indian file, behind her.

Stones peeked out of thinner brush near

the trail, markers for loads of people to whom Cate and I were related: Townsends and Ludlams, Seamans and Underhills.

Beyond that were old New York names I knew only from street signs and arboretums: Lefferts, Wyckoffs, Boerums.

I paused next at the grave of one Elias Baylis:

For his love of liberty he fell a victim to British cruelty and tho' blind was imprisoned in New York in Sep. 1776 and was released only in time to breathe his last in the arms of his daughter while crossing the Brooklyn ferry. During his confinement he was accustomed to sing the 142nd Psalm.

Near that was a smaller, cruder stone, on which was written, *Our Babie.* The two words were so uneven and faint that I pictured a young father incising each letter with his own tools, unable to afford the local gravesmith.

Cate was a few yards ahead. I caught up and we stepped over a pile of vines and a tree's knuckled roots.

She pointed to a white marble headstone centered in the dell beyond, its surface jaded with moss:

> Jane Lyons, a colored woman, who up-
> wards of 65 years was a faithful and
> devoted domestic in the family of James
> Hariman, Sr. of this village, died Dec. 19,
> 1858. Age 75 years

I touched the numerals commemorating her year of death.

"When was slavery abolished in New York, anyway?" I asked.

"Eighteen twenty-seven," answered Cate.

"So they owned her first, and then she stayed on."

"Where else could she have gone?"

I knew better than to think all slave-holding guilt fell on my southern brethren — that *our* racial history was a sweet Underground-Railroad rosebed of "Kumbaya" singalongs with Harriet Tubman waving the conductor's baton — but I hadn't realized it was a mere three decades before Lincoln that Abolition prevailed in my home state.

"At least they had the decency to record her name," I said. "The ones in our cemetery just have blank leaves of slate shoved into the grass — head and foot. Like all that mattered was making sure you didn't dig up a slave by accident."

It made me want to walk up to random

black people on the street and apologize.

"Let me get to work," I said.

Cate led me back up the trail and gave me clippers and a machete.

"There are definitely a few homeless people camping at night in the densest parts," she said, handing me a pair of work gloves, "so look out for that. We try to leave their stuff where we find it."

"Okay."

We started hacking away in separate directions. The dense air around me was soon astringent with the green perfume of sliced grass and the sharp tang of nettle sap.

By the time I'd filled two bags I'd cut into a private lane of tunnel, with no line of sight back to Cate.

My bandanna felt hot and wet against my forehead. I shook off Cate's heavy gloves so I could flip it over to the dry side, then leaned down to pick up a bent tin can and several brown shards of beer bottle with my bare hands.

From that angle I could just make out the edge of another moss-green headstone through the scrim of leaves.

One machete swipe cleared enough space to crawl forward so I could read the stone's inscription, but I shoved over hard into the wall of vines beside me when I realized I'd been about to place my hand on the belly of a bloated dead rat.

I twisted my head away from the sight of its greasy fur seething with ants.

That's when I saw the skull.

6

For just a second I thought I was looking at an ostrich egg, a buttery off-white oval dappled with shifting spangles of green-gold light.

Not egg, bone.

Had someone dug up this forgotten grave? *No.* The ground was flat, the brown carpet of jungle detritus thick and even beneath the skull.

I crawled in farther, cringing when my hand plunged into something warm and wet — a pocket of rainwater trapped in the folds of a plastic grocery sack.

The rat had given off a whiff of decay but back here the air was sweet with damp earth, an autumnal top note of composting leaves.

From this new angle I could make out the skull's sharp cheekbone and the hinge of its jaw. I dropped to my elbows, soldier-crawling beneath the thicket's low edge until

I could look at the face straight on.

Its eye sockets were huge as a Disney fawn's, its seed-pearl teeth tiny and perfect.

A child, then.

In the gloom beneath more tangled foliage, I could make out a delicate birdcage of ribs, smashed in at the solar plexus.

I scrabbled backwards into the hot daylight, yelling for Cate.

Cate dispatched two kids to go call the police.

She and I edged a few feet away from the group so we could talk without freaking anyone out.

"You're shaking," she said.

"I shouldn't have gone into the bushes that far. What if there was any trace evidence? I wasn't thinking straight."

Cate's voice was gentle. "How could you have known that?"

"Well it's a graveyard, right? I mean, if you see something that *looks* like a piece of bone it's not entirely out of the realm of possibility that it might actually *be* a piece of bone."

"And you're *sure* it was a child?"

I nodded, realizing how little else we could divine from skeletal remains in the absence of a pathologist's sad wisdom: no name, no race, no gender.

The tiny being in whose flesh those bones once resided had been rendered invisible.

The child wouldn't have come up higher than my hip standing on tiptoes. Two years old or three or four — entirely too small to be let out of doors alone, much less to have gotten over this spiked iron fence without help, considering Cate's stout locks on the gate.

What toddler would have braved crawling into the depths of this place, even in the wake of an older sibling?

City kids know that any overgrown lot was guaranteed to be teeming with vermin: feral dogs, rats the size of badgers with bent yellow six-penny nails for teeth.

And any stretch of ground this big was likely to harbor equally feral people. City kids would know that, too.

So how *had* such tiny bones arrived at the green-black heart of this pocket wilderness?

I wanted to believe the child had been laid to rest here centuries ago, and that everything else had grown up around it the way briars snaked out of the ground to protect Sleeping Beauty and her dreaming courtiers.

But then I thought of those shattered ribs. Murder was a far more likely scenario. Had the child been killed here?

This was an ideal spot for such darkness: far enough away from the crowded local sidewalks for anyone to hear cries of pain or fear. Even those who camped in these very bushes might not hear a child's voice against the noise of the trains rushing by every few minutes.

But it was also the perfect place to bring a corpse for disposal if one had committed murder elsewhere. A body that small would've fit in a PBS-donor tote bag.

I heard sirens in the distance, growing loud enough to drown out everything else as patrol cars pulled into the tiny dead-end road beside us, one after another.

The noise died out and I heard several car doors open, then the racket of hard-soled cop shoes on the broken asphalt.

A bunch of young guys in blue uniforms pushed through the gate, then headed straight for us.

One of the patrol guys came over to keep an eye on all of us sitting on the lawn. His name tag identified him as Officer Albie, but he seemed uncomfortable with the formality and told us to call him Fergus.

His compatriots, in consultation with Cate, started running yellow plastic marker tape around and through the bushes to keep anyone from stumbling into the child's bones and corrupting their resting place any more than I had.

The kids in our group started getting restless, saying they needed to get home and do chores or schoolwork or take care of younger siblings, or even just run across the street to use the pay phone to tell their families where they were and what was taking so long. The young officer did his best to keep everybody calm and seated, asking the kids to "just simmer down, there" until the arrival of the detectives and whoever else would be needed to check out the whole burgeoning circus officially.

I was pretty out of it in the aftermath of discovering the tiny set of bones, but I still felt for the guy. He looked like he'd graduated himself about two weeks earlier, and high-school kids are about as easy to corral as a bunch of amphetamine-pumped ferrets dipped in Crisco, especially when there's major drama in the offing.

The kids peppered him with questions and demands and objections in between shoving each other and laughing. His voice strained for increasing volume as he struggled to keep a lid on things. Ten minutes in, the guy's hands had achieved an emphatically Sicilian range of motion.

Cate came back and sat down with us. At first the kids grew quiet, but soon the babble started up again, even more overwhelming.

I tried closing my eyes for a minute after swabbing my face with my clammy bandanna.

I couldn't keep them shut, though. I was too intent on checking the gate for plainclothes arrivals.

Then I looked up at the young cop's face. His short hair was dark with sweat, and I worried he'd have a stroke and keel over onto the scrubby brown grass or pitch head-first against the blunt edge of a gravestone.

I leaned over toward Cate. "He's not looking too good," I said.

Cate stood up to place a gentle hand on his arm.

"Would you like to move us into the chapel?" she asked. "It's a great deal cooler inside, and we can all drink some cold water."

The cop gratefully agreed, and the two of them began herding the kids indoors.

I was about to follow them in when I saw a dark sedan pull up alongside the cemetery gate, a chrome-free Crown Vic with a fat antenna sprouting off the lid of its trunk.

We all savored the chapel's cool interior with the young cop as our shepherd, drinking ice water and grateful to be sheltered from the sun.

The kids' restlessness tapered off once we got inside. Maybe it was the dimmer light indoors that made us all settle down, or maybe it was just that we'd all worked ourselves hard on the brush clearing and were now settling into a midafternoon blood-sugar crash exacerbated by post-adrenaline-rush torpor.

The girls all grabbed their school backpacks from the room's back wall and started in on homework assignments. Three of the boys made binder-paper airplanes and lofted them down the nave, competing to see whose craft could drift the farthest before succumbing to gravity.

The sun shifted lower in the sky, sending a thick shaft of light slanting down from the arched western doorway, highlighting the toy planes' wake through whirling motes of dust.

The sounds outside seemed more distant: rush of trains muted by the chapel's pale gold stone walls, mutter and hiss of the cops' radios unintelligible.

High stained-glass windows faced north and south, their intricately fitted cobalt and scarlet and butter-yellow panes interspersed with empty spots that laid bare the place-holding traceries of lead.

"I don't know what to do," said Cate, finally. "I have two packs of Chips Ahoy in one of those bags, but I can't imagine anyone wanting to eat them, considering."

I took another sip of water and swallowed it. "Maybe the kids are hungry?"

Cate stood up. "I'll put them on top of the cooler."

Our young cop Fergus asked if he could grab a couple. Then the kids dove in.

After that there was nothing else for me and Cate to do but wait. We were quiet for ten minutes or so, and I could tell it was making her jittery; my shock passing, her own just settling in.

I figured I'd better keep her talking, keep her mind occupied.

"So who built this place?" I asked.

"Our great-great-great-something-or-other Nicholas commissioned it in 1857, in memory of his three daughters. He named it the Chapel of the Sisters."

I looked across the room toward the weathered mahogany pulpit, its dusty façade graced with overlapping arches.

"When I think about what this *could* be," said Cate, "instead of a place so ignored and abandoned that someone could literally discard a child?"

"Do people break in other than the homeless guys?"

"Some of the monuments have been tipped over and smashed. And the local junkies used the chapel for a shooting gallery before I got decent locks on the doors. I was terrified I'd walk in here and find someone who'd OD'd."

"Has anyone ever messed with the graves *themselves,* though? Dug them up?"

Cate shook her head. "Maybe the parents

couldn't afford a proper funeral?"

"Sure," I said. But I didn't believe it, not for a second.

"A family would have tried to *bury* their child," she said, looking down at her lap.

I traced a finger beneath an inscription carved into the wall beside us: *I will ransom them from the grave. . . .*

"The ground hadn't been disturbed," I said. "There was a thick bed of leaves underneath the bones, and the rib cage was smashed in —"

"Please," said Cate, her eyes clenching shut as she snapped her hand up between us, palm toward me. "I don't think I can handle details."

"I'm sorry," I said. "I'll save it for the detectives."

She touched my kneecap. "*I'm* sorry."

"I know, Cate."

And I did know, too well. I'd seen some awful things the last few years. Been through some shit.

It hadn't made me any tougher or braver. It'd only made me tired and sad.

And inconsiderate sometimes, like now.

Cate was trembling. I put my arm around her shoulders.

"Hey, you know what's good about all this?" I asked.

"God, please tell me," she said, "because I can't think of a single thing."

"The cops are taking it really seriously, you know? Roping off the scene, keeping us all here . . . these guys aren't messing around."

"That *is* good."

"Wanna cookie?" I asked.

Cate shook her head. "Man, who'd've thought the cemetery lady would turn out to be such a wuss, eh?"

"You're not a wuss. You're just sane."

Our young cop's shoulder radio crackled to life, and I heard a gravelly voice say, "Skwarecki's here. Now we're waiting on the ME."

I wondered what Skwarecki would look like. Some beefy guy with a mustache, probably. Grizzled former jock, lots of broken capillaries.

That was the visual average of homicide detectives I'd dealt with before this.

Fergus stiffened up, shoulders thrown back, and I turned to look toward whomever he was staring at.

I was struck by two facts in that instant: I was looking at Skwarecki, and I was an idiot.

She wore a gold badge at the waist of her knife-creased gray trousers, one finger hooked into the collar of a matching jacket slung over her shoulder. Her highlights could've used a little touch-up at the roots, but her loafers were buffed to a twinkle.

My imaginary composite had one detail correct, however. The woman had twenty years on me, but she was still a jock to the bone.

I pegged her for field hockey once upon a time. Good shoulders on her, if a bit slight for defense. Narrow hips and some meat on the back of her thighs: a sprinter.

"Yo, Opie," she said, snapping her fingers at our young cop.

Her voice was fast, clipped Queens, that definitive outer-borough twang, like she had gravel in her sinuses.

"The fuck you waiting on," she said, "second coming of Christ? Get your butt over here."

He hustled to comply, and she was right in his face, cocking one hip as she tapped his badge with her finger.

"Albie," she said, "that what they call you when you're awake?"

He blushed and nodded but she'd made him smile, too.

Neat trick, to bitch someone out and win him over simultaneously.

"So, walk me through this, *Albie,*" she said. "We got a body outside, and we got a bunch of nice people sitting around inside, and you're empty-handed — no clipboard, no pen. As a highly trained detective, this tells me you know exactly what took place here and I can go home already, because you stole the collar right out from under my ass before I even showed up — am I right?"

He shook his head, blushing deeper. But she'd made him laugh.

"So what can you tell me?" she asked. "You got any leads on who's in charge here?"

He pointed at Cate.

"Excellent," she said. "Now, who found the scene?"

He pointed at me.

"Keep this up," she said, "they're gonna make you commissioner."

He smiled, and Skwarecki told him to get the kids' names and contact info, then send them home.

She gave him a friendly punch to the shoulder, turning toward me and Cate.

8

Skwarecki told us her first name was Jayné, pronounced Jen-NAY.

"My mother was some kind of French," she said, and shrugged. "But no one ever calls me that."

She'd brought Cate and me back outside. The medical examiner's van pulled up, and a grim-looking guy climbed out of it with a large black case. Giving Skwarecki a dour wave, he ducked under the crime-scene tape and disappeared into the bushes.

"You gotta be anywhere?" she asked. "I'd like to bring you both down to the precinct."

Cate told her no and I said not really, but that I'd like to call home.

I felt in my pocket for change. "Okay if I run out and find a pay phone?"

Skwarecki was cool with that, so I started toward the cemetery's gate.

Dean picked up when I dialed the apartment.

"Yo," I said, "Intrepid Spouse."

"What's up? You sound kind of bummed."

I sighed. "I might be late for dinner."

"Do tell."

"I'm at the cemetery. With a homicide detective."

"Bunny, you okay?"

Here's the great thing about Dean: he doesn't get freaked out by much. This has proved to be a necessary attribute in a person who finds himself married to me.

"I found a skeleton," I said.

"In a cemetery."

"It's a little kid," I said. "And it doesn't look like it was ever buried, so, you know, we called the cops and stuff."

"You sure you're okay?"

"Kind of."

"You sound shaky," he said.

"More sad," I said. "The kid was *really* little."

"You want me to come out there?"

"That's okay, but I appreciate the offer."

"We're supposed to have dinner with Nutty Buddy."

"Crap," I said. "Astrid."

"Want me to postpone it?"

I looked at my watch: just after five o'clock. "I think I could make it by eight. Can you call her?"

Dean said he would and I thanked him and placed the phone back on the hook.

I'd just stepped onto the sidewalk across from the cemetery when a second dark Crown-Vic-esque sedan pulled in behind the ME's van.

As I crossed the street, the driver's door opened, disgorging a hard-ass-but-elegant-looking African American chick in crimson lipstick and a chalk-striped navy power suit.

The woman wore her hair short, her neck graceful as an egret's. She had feline cheekbones and a complexion the color of strong, clear tea — richly brown and gold and red, all at once.

She glanced around for a nanosecond, fists on her hips, then made the proverbial beeline through the gate for Skwarecki.

I watched the muscles of her long stocking-sheathed calves bunch up as she shifted her weight forward to keep her spike heels from sinking into the crabgrass.

Shoes that expensive, she had to be a lawyer.

I followed her through the gate.

Ten feet in she stopped walking, calves still clenched as she balanced on the balls of her feet.

I ducked past her, trying to act unobtrusive until I pulled up alongside Cate, who was looking down at the clipboard in Skwarecki's hands and nodding while the detective jotted down notes.

The elegant attorney called out, "Yo, Jayné!"

Skwarecki lifted her head. "You get dragged into this *mishegoss* already, Bost?"

The chic stranger shrugged. "Yeah, right?"

"ME hasn't weighed in a hundred percent yet," said Skwarecki.

"You know the drill. Your guys call my guys. My guys call me. I go, 'How high?' "

Skwarecki nodded. "Looking like we maybe got *something*."

"Nice day for it." The woman rested her knuckles back on her hips. "You planning to introduce me?"

"Like you need some engraved invitation?" asked Skwarecki.

The attorney started picking her way across the grass toward the three of us, hands held out a little for balance.

"Behold Louise Wilson Bost," said Skwarecki, "assistant district attorney for the Borough of Queens — top prosecutor in our homicide division, but she dresses way too girly for the job."

Bost-the-Best shot me and Cate a wink and a smile. "Pay no attention to Detective Skwarecki, ladies. She can't hack the competition."

"Hand to God," said Skwarecki. "My next paycheck? I'm buying Louise here a pair of sneakers."

Bost waved a hand in Skwarecki's general direction. "Such a kidder, this one. Laugh? I thought I'd never *stop.*"

She teetered up to us, a little out of breath. "I came straight from court, and I want to look nice for my clients. They've got it hard enough."

Sobering thought: dressing well for her clients was a show of respect for the dead.

Skwarecki said, "This is Cate Ludlam, in charge of the preservation efforts here."

Bost reached to shake Cate's hand.

"And Madeline Dare," Skwarecki continued, "who discovered the child's remains."

"A pleasure, Ms. Bost," I said when she shifted to grip my hand in turn.

"Louise," she replied. "Let's not stand on formality. I'm sure this hasn't been an easy day for the two of you, and if the ME *does* weigh in a hundred percent, we may be spending some time together."

No sooner had she said that than the man himself climbed out of the bushes. He stood up and removed his thin gloves with a snap.

From the grim look on his face, a hundred percent was the least of it.

9

The ME took Skwarecki and Bost aside to talk. They stepped into a spot of shade just inside the chapel's doorway.

We could see their faces again, now, and the conversation was obviously a grim one.

"Those are not happy people," said Cate. "Not by a long shot."

"I wonder what he's telling them," I said.

"I'm pretty sure I don't want to know."

The ME finally peeled off from the trio and climbed into his van.

Bost wasn't worried about her shoes anymore when she and Skwarecki started back toward us.

"Ladies," she said, "we'd like to drive you down to the precinct house now, if that's all right."

"They don't give you guys air-conditioning?" I asked Skwarecki, cranking my window down as she pulled out onto the boulevard.

Bost and Cate followed in separate cars.

Skwarecki snorted at that. "Half the time you're lucky these crates have *wheels.*"

She drummed her fingertips along the top of the steering wheel, already impatient with driving slow enough for the entourage to keep pace.

"Big engine, though, huh?" I asked.

Skwarecki smiled. "Big enough."

"Slap that cherry on the roof, I bet you could haul *serious* ass in this thing."

"Got *that* right."

She checked the rearview mirror, making sure we hadn't lost Cate and Bost.

"Crap," she said, impatient. "Make way for *ducklings.*"

We pulled into the One-Oh-Three and Skwarecki led us upstairs, into a warren of glossy, institutional-green hallways. We wandered down them single file behind her, twisting and turning past windowed door after windowed door.

Most of these bore a department title — FRAUD or SPECIAL VICTIMS or ROBBERY — with butcher paper taped to the back of each glass panel. You couldn't see a god-damn thing beyond them.

Bost obviously knew her way around as

well as Skwarecki did, but I was getting more disoriented by the second, sneakers squeaking against the highly polished linoleum.

We skidded to a halt in front of a door marked HOMICIDE.

Skwarecki ushered us over the threshold and into a bright, noisy bull pen crammed with desks.

I looked at my watch again: just after five.

"You have to be somewhere?" asked Skwarecki, pulling up a couple of chairs for me and Cate.

"I'm supposed to meet people around eight," I said, "but I can blow it off. No biggie."

"We should have you out of here by then," she said.

Bost looked at her own thin watch but didn't sit down. "I need to make a call. May I get anyone some water?"

Cate asked for the ladies' room, and the two of them walked away.

"I take it the ME's news wasn't good?" I asked Skwarecki.

"It wasn't, no."

"Could he tell how old the kid was?"

"Around three."

Three," I said, "Jesus. And you guys think this was a homicide?"

"Skeletal remains, you can have trouble with cause of death, but the ME seems pretty certain in this case."

"Yeah," I said. "Just . . . looking at the rib cage."

Skwarecki nodded. "We'll know more when they finish the postmortem, but there were a number of badly healed fractures."

My throat went all tight. I winced and shook my head, raising my hands up like I could keep the images of suffering at bay.

"You okay?" Skwarecki asked, voice quieter, tough-chick edge fallen away when she saw my eyes tearing up.

"Okay? Yeah," I said. "But really, *really* pissed off."

"Good for you."

I wiped away the incipient tears. "I mean, what the fuck is *wrong* with people, you know?"

"I know," she said.

"A little *kid?*"

"Preaching to the choir," she said.

"Does it get to you?"

"Every damn time."

"I can't imagine what kind of balls this job must take."

"They're not all this bad," she said. "Most times, it's bad guys killing bad guys, you know? But a kid . . ."

76

"Does it get easier?"

She shook her head. "No. Never."

"Does it help if you nail who did it?"

"Sure," she said. "That's what keeps me going. What makes me love this job. I get up every morning and I know I'm going to spend my day trying to do something that *matters,* you know?"

"And this one — you think there's any chance?"

"A kid this age, I doubt we're going to have dental records to go on. And *proving* cause of death . . . ?" She shook her head again.

"Where do you start?" I asked.

"We pull missing-persons reports. Hope we get a hit."

"What are the odds of that?" I asked.

"Crappy," she said. "There's forty thousand sets of unidentified remains in the United States — Jane and John and Baby Does."

"Forty *thousand?*" I tried to get my head around that number: a small city of, literally, lost souls.

"There's no exact figure," she continued. "Not like we've got any national database."

"Even the feds?" I asked.

"Most cases," said Skwarecki, "it's local police. Hell, we've still got a lot of *our* Does filed on index cards, and we've got one of the bigger budgets in the country. Go back a few years, even here, and you gotta cross-check the reports by hand."

"So is there *any* chance of finding out who this kid is?"

Bost stepped up beside me. "We've got one thing in our favor. The remains hadn't been there very long. Six months, give or take."

I couldn't help picturing the species of urban fauna capable of reducing even so tiny a corpse clean down to the bone in half a year.

Rats. Ants. Roaches.

My stomach went sour and I closed my eyes for a second, which only made it worse.

Skwarecki touched my knee. "Hey, that's *good* news. Best we could hope for."

"Okay," I said, still trying *really* hard not to give in to my urge to barf.

"What happens next?" asked Cate, taking the seat beside me.

"First," said Skwarecki, "we pray the victim was local, and that we turn up something at the scene to help with identifi-cation —"

"Second," cut in Bost, "we pray double *someone* cared enough to report this child missing."

78

10

Cate and I didn't have much to say as far as official statements went. We'd already told Skwarecki and Bost the times we'd arrived at the cemetery, respectively.

I described finding the bones, said I hadn't actually touched them before I backed out of the bushes again and started yelling. We gave our addresses and our phone numbers, work and home.

We both asked to be kept in the loop on any further information they might turn up at the cemetery, and Cate asked if it would be all right if she continued work on the brush clearing once the police had finished with the scene.

"Maybe we can find something else," she said. "Something to help with identification."

Skwarecki agreed to that, but asked that Cate not return until she'd called with the official all clear.

79

"We've got a new group of volunteers scheduled for next Wednesday," Cate said. "Do you think that would be enough time?"

"Probably," said Skwarecki, "but wait until I let you know for certain, all right?"

"Absolutely," said Cate. "I wouldn't think of doing anything otherwise."

Bost and Skwarecki gave both of us their business cards.

"If you find *anything* when you go back in," said Skwarecki, "don't touch it. I want you to call me from that pay phone immediately, day or night. My beeper number's on there, okay?"

Cate and I assured her that we'd follow her instructions to the letter, and that we wouldn't ever be in the cemetery at night anyway, especially now.

Bost still looked concerned. "Is the next group going to be from the high school as well?"

"No," said Cate. "They're members of a Quaker meeting in Matinecock. Mostly retirees. They come twice a year — wonderful people. I can promise you that they'll be careful, respectful."

Bost nodded. "I'm certainly fine with it, then. You strike me as a woman with good judgment."

"Thank you," said Cate.

"Cate," I said, "I'd like to come back too, if that's cool with you?"

She smiled. "Absolutely. I'd love it."

The four of us stood up and shook one another's hands.

Cate and I started to leave, but after a few steps she stopped. She turned back toward the other two women, so I did too.

"Prospect has come to mean a great deal to me," she said. "Maddie and I have family there. I don't know how else to describe it other than to say that for me, it's a *sacred* place. And when I think — when I *know* — that a child suffered there . . . Well, I want to do the very utmost I'm capable of, to make up for it."

Amen to that.

I followed her toward the door, wondering how the hell we were ever going to find our way back to the outside world through all those shiny green Lewis Carroll hallways.

The clock in Cate's dashboard read 6:17 as we drove away from the precinct house.

"I can give you a ride back into the city," she said, "if you'd like."

"I'd hate to make you come all the way in then turn right around again to go home."

"What time's your dinner?"

"We're supposed to meet up at eight," I

said. "Somewhere in Chinatown. I'd love to get home for a quick shower first."

"My guilt is assuaged, then. This time of day the subway's your best bet."

"Sounds perfect," I said.

After that we drove in silence for a minute, thinking our thoughts.

"I liked what you said back at the precinct," I said finally. "I feel the same way, even though I don't have anywhere near your connection with Prospect, you know?"

Cate nodded. "I can't explain it, but I feel responsible."

"I'm all about the guilt. God knows we killed enough Indians. Not to mention the slave graves."

"Jesus," said Cate, "we really *are* related!"

As the subway sped me back into Manhattan I pondered the events of the day.

Maybe it was a blessing the child had been killed and was no longer in pain? But that was a hideous solution. The worst possible.

I'd had too much experience, in my own life, of being powerless to help fellow children when it mattered most. The only thing that had changed was me being in a grown-up body now. I still felt like a kid inside, a fierce little tomboy who wanted to defend those preyed upon at the playground or at home with my fists and feet.

I'd grown up in a time and place that left children appallingly vulnerable to the predations of grown-ups: California in the late sixties and early seventies. The adults were so busy playing at Peter-Pan self-actualization that most of us kids would've fared better being raised in a cave by LSD-dropping wolves.

By third grade I'd built a sturdy fort in the woods near our house, just in case any of my friends needed to run away from home. I'd stocked it with charcoal and matches and a saucepan and five cans of shoplifted chili, all of it safe in a waterproof underground cache I'd copied from my garage-sale *Girl Scout Handbook.*

There were just too goddamn many bad stepfathers and mentally-absent-moms' psycho boyfriends out there.

I'd wanted to be prepared for all of us.

I still did.

Dean was already dressed by the time I screeched into the apartment, out of breath.

He had on crisp khakis and a Brooks Brothers shirt, his hair still wet from the shower.

He took one look at me, all sweaty in my grass-stained jeans and grimy T-shirt, bandanna tied around my neck. "I feel so underdressed."

I stood on tiptoe to kiss his cheek. "Shut it, tall boy. I bet you didn't even leave me a clean towel."

He tilted my chin up to kiss my mouth. "I left you two, folded up on the sink. Figured you'd be in a big fat hurry."

"Thank you," I said, racing past him.

I took the world's shortest shower, then threw on makeup and clean jeans, followed by a white T-shirt, a string of fake pearls, and the least fucked-up pair of my dead great-grandmother's Belgian shoes I could find in our closet, feeling the need to one-up Astrid's ubiquitous Ferragamos.

My hair would probably dry on the way there.

I walked back out into the living room, earrings in hand.

"You know where we're going?" I asked.

"Yeah," said Dean. "Some Vietnamese place."

"Subway or cabbing it?"

"Cab," he said. "You know we're both useless below Fourteenth."

"Sue and Pagan?"

"At that Chino-Latino diner on Ninth. Might meet us later for drinks."

"Cool," I said. "Let's hit it."

We sprint-walked west on Sixteenth to grab a taxi on Seventh Avenue. Our neighborhood wasn't much — sort of a no-man's-land above the Village — but we were stuck with Barneys at that end of the block.

There was something about the multistoried emporium that annoyed me profusely, not least that it was the homeland of hundred-dollar socks and thirty-dollar bath soap. My mother always joked that she remembered old radio advertisements for it back when the original Barney had offered two pairs of pants with every cheap suit jacket.

It now drew in the sort of hideously snippy Eurotrash Poser-*riche* I'd spent the majority of my urban life avoiding: stringy little people like that bitch at the bakery.

On the bright side, the place was a magnet for taxis.

Dean hailed one, and we tumbled gratefully into a backseat reeking of artificial pine and stale cigars.

"So tell me about the cemetery," said Dean when we'd rolled down the windows.

He lifted his arm so I could lean in against him, then wrapped his hand around my shoulder.

"They figure the kid was about three years old. Beaten to death," I said.

"How could they tell?"

"Well, the rib cage was all smashed in."

His hand tightened around my shoulder when I told him about the other fractures.

"A three-year-old," said Dean, shaking his head slowly. "And you and Cate went down to the cop station?"

"We couldn't tell them much, and it sounds like it's going to be pretty near impossible to figure out who it was."

I explained about the dental records and the 40,000 unidentified dead people and everything.

I stared at the yellow NO SMOKING — DRIVER ALLERGIC sticker on the scratched Plexiglas barrier between us and the front seat, just zoning out while I thought about all that.

"This is going to stick with you," he said, "isn't it?"

"You know me too well."

"You don't have to get involved with it. More than you are already."

"Yeah. Sure."

"Bunny . . ."

I looked up at him.

He wrapped his hand gently around the back of my head, then kissed me.

"They play hardball here," he said. "And the cops know what they're doing, okay?"

"Okay," I said.

"So let them take the risks. I want you safe. Promise?"

"Promise."

He kissed me again even though we both knew I was lying.

The cab pulled up to the curb in front of a grubby-looking building on Mott Street. Dean handed the driver ten bucks, asking for three back while I did my best to shake off the day's morbid events and switch into cocktail-party-chatter mode.

This was not a transition I'd ever made easily without the dedicated consumption of numerous actual cocktails. Especially with the moneyed Euro crowd.

I looked at my watch again: eight-fifteen. Perfect.

"Please, God," I said, steeling myself as I stepped out of the cab and clutched Dean's arm, "let this place have a fucking bar."

We descended half a floor from street level, down a curving set of steps with cheesy fake wrought-iron curlicues supporting its flimsy banisters. Coupled with the dining room's flocked scarlet wallpaper, I figured some ill-advised past owner had meant to invoke Ye Olde Bourbon Street circa *The Partridge Family*.

The place had a promising Indochinese tang of anchovy and lime, but I wondered whether Astrid had suggested meeting here because the food was decent, or because it matched some quaint conception she'd formed concerning my piteously impover-ished circumstances.

Darling, you'll adore Madeline; she's so very . . . bohemian.

Maybe I should have arrived wearing a beret while coughing blood gamely into some threadbare-but-impeccably-starched handkerchief edged in convent lace.

Then Astrid herself waved from across the room and gave me her old wicked grin and I was instantly only deeply glad to see my dear friend, no longer fearful that the grotty choice of restaurant had meant she wanted to avoid being seen with *us*.

And, as always, every pair of eyes in the suddenly quiet restaurant was drawn to her.

I could tell you that Astrid's thick, straight curtain of hair had the sheen of french-polished mahogany, that her skin was heavy cream with a hint of coffee and her dark eyes compelling as a doe's, that she possessed a heroic brow, a lush mouth, cheekbones to melt your heart — but it's all beside the point.

Here's what people remember about Astrid: She was the single most exquisite human being they'd ever seen.

I don't mean merely beautiful, I mean that she was quite literally *stunning,* and that I'd watched strangers go pale and stumble in the street on catching sight of her.

It was my friend's tragedy that she was also brilliant.

Had she been either plain or stupid, she might have had a chance of being happy.

Astrid and spouse stood up as we reached

their table. She was wearing a diamond-quilted black velvet jacket with a big hood. Very Chanel.

She gave me a hug and said, "*Che bella,* Madeline, I thought you'd *never* fucking get here."

We shook hands all around and took our seats. The freshly minted husband pressed a cocktail menu on me and Dean, then miraculously caused a waitress to appear with our drinks.

I leaned back in my chair and felt — for the first time in a very long while — that all was right with the world.

A fist-sized cockroach climbed up over the baseboard, proceeding up onto the fuzzy red wallpaper.

"Charming little place," I said. "You guys come here often?"

12

Christoph actually seemed like a decent guy, and interesting, both of which came as a surprise to me. He was probably twenty years older than us: slender, with the last of a summer tan warming his face and longish pale brown hair swept back to curl a bit just behind his ears.

The waitress placed a couple of plates of summer rolls on the table, their thin rice-paper wrapping aglow with the hues of shrimp and cilantro and chopped peanuts inside, and we were well into our second round of drinks.

"So we are importing these wonderful machines from Europe," Christoph was saying to Dean, "but it is very difficult to teach the Americans to use them properly."

My husband nodded, putting a roll on his plate. The rest of the food just sat there, more set decoration than sustenance.

Astrid, growing bored, laid a hand on her

husband's wrist.

"Darling," she said, "Maddie's a *liberal*."

Christoph looked over at me with a wry smile, eyes crinkling up at the corners. "Really? How astonishing. You seem like such an *intelligent* woman."

"Astrid has always considered my political worldview a sad flaw of moral fiber," I said.

"I don't think I've ever shared a meal with one of you before," said Christoph. "Are you, in fact, one of these 'Democrats'?"

"Quite so," I assured him.

"This is remarkable! You must explain to me what this means. Do you, for instance, run about and plot to blow things up?"

"Mostly the patriarchy," I said.

He nodded to Dean, grinning. "And you *allow* this?"

My husband shrugged. "These days one finds it necessary to foster the illusion of free will in women."

Christoph laughed. "You Americans, really — such an *amusing* people."

"And you Swiss," I said, "so very . . . *Swiss*."

"Cuckoo clocks and chocolate?" he asked.

"I was thinking more of the memorial in this little park in Saanen, near Gstaad — a cannon, with a plaque on it commemorating an uprising throughout the countryside in the thirteen hundreds protesting the fact that the government in Berne had grown too liberal."

"You know Saanen?" Christoph asked, surprised.

"My sister and little brother went to school there," I said. "Charming village."

Okay, so I wasn't above trying to claim a bit of Euro cred as protective coloring. Pagan and Trace had gotten to ski the Alps daily; I figured I should end up with *something* as a consolation prize.

Christoph turned to Astrid. "Really, my dear, you have the most *remarkable* friends."

She touched her throat. "Of course."

He nodded to Dean. "You must come out to New Jersey with me sometime, to see my little company."

We all shared a cab uptown, Christoph and Dean chatting about scientific stuff while Astrid pressed me to continue on with them to some new nightclub.

"Sadly, I have work in the morning," I said.

"You're *writing,* of course?" asked Astrid. "Forging the uncreated conscience of your race in the smithy of your soul?"

"Actually, at the moment I'm answering phones."

She shook her head, face stern. "Maddie, for God's sake, you're an *artist.* I insist that you stop *indulging* in such distractions."

I shrugged. "And our landlord insists on the rent."

"A peasant," she said.

"Bien sûr."

Astrid gave my knee a consoling pat. *"Courage,* my sweet . . . *ne désespères pas."*

She leaned forward toward Christoph, who'd claimed it was his pleasure, as the evening's host, to ride up front beside our driver.

"Darling?" She snaked her hand through the little divider window, touching his hair. "Why don't you bring this marvelous Dean out to New Jersey with you *tomorrow?* There's really no point in our leaving for Southampton until Friday morning."

Ten o'clock was agreed upon all around, as the cab pulled up in front of our building.

The four of us climbed out into the sultry evening for a round of doubled air-kisses — that display of affection Dostoyevsky described as the "gesture Russians tend to make when they are really famous."

Astrid and I exchanged ours last, and she held on to my shoulders for a moment, whispering, "I *do* love you, Madissima."

She'd let her guard down, just for that instant, and I realized I'd never heard anyone sound so fragile and alone.

Leaning in, I kissed her cheek for real.

"Do they *ever* eat?" asked Dean.

We were in our kitchen dipping fat broken pretzels into a jar of Nutella.

"Biennially," I said. "Tiny little salads, dressing on the side."

He examined his pretzel. "So they're like, what, *air* ferns?"

"Or vampires."

"Should I wear a suit tomorrow, you think?"

"God no," I said. "He'd find it distressingly plebeian."

Dean laughed, pushing the Nutella toward me.

13

I was at the Catalog early the following Wednesday morning. By nine o'clock there were four of us manning the lines.

"I started out *so* excited this morning," said my fellow order-taker chick Yong Sun, stepping into the phone room.

"What about?" I said.

"Well, I was running late, so I caught a taxi to my subway station, and the driver asked if I was Korean." She took a sip of her coffee.

"White guy?" asked Karen, who was at the desk next to mine.

Yong Sun nodded. "I thought, '*Finally,* one of you people got a clue!' you know?"

"I'm so proud, on behalf of my ignorant race," I said.

"So I asked him how he could tell," she continued, "and he shrugs and goes, 'You smell like garlic.' "

"Fucking white people," said Yumiko,

across from us. "So fucking stupid."

We'd had variations of this conversation before, but I still found it morbidly fascinating.

Yumiko's parents had come from Japan, Karen's from China, Yong Sun's, obviously, from Korea.

The three of them spent a lot of time ranking on each other's respective heritage, explaining the hierarchy to me as Japan first, then Korea, then China, in order of current economic supremacy.

Karen would always snap back in response to that that everyone in the room could kiss her American-born ass, because if it weren't for China, "*your* stupid countries wouldn't know how to read or write, and we'd all be out of a damn job."

I always made a point of thanking her for our employment, not to mention fireworks, dim sum, and pasta while we were at it.

Yumiko glanced at an old copy of *Vogue* someone had left on her desk. "So how come rich fucking white people dress like such shit all the time?"

She was barely five feet tall — a graceful slip of a girl who might have just stepped from the mists of an ukiyo-e woodblock print — but she was equipped with the most superbly atrocious vocabulary I'd ever encountered. Seriously, the chick made *me* sound like a repressed Mormon.

"Rich white people dress like shit to show they don't have to care," I said.

Yumiko gave my crap T-shirt and frayed khaki Bermudas a how-the-hell-would-*you*-know smirk. "Fucking stupid. You're all, like, a bunch of fucking *freaks*."

"I've always thought so," I said, booting up my computer.

"I mean," she continued, "how could anyone even fucking *kiss* a white guy? They've got those *eyes*, you know? All *blue* and weird shit. Like they're fucking *dead*. It's disgusting."

"More for me, then," said Karen.

Yumiko waved this off. "Banana bitch — only yellow on the outside."

"So, what, you like Japan better than here?" I asked her.

"That's all bullshit, back there," she said. "They won't let you do fucking anything, you know? Like, my cousin used a curling iron on her hair once, for school? The teacher stuck her head in a bucket of water in front of the whole class. Said they had to make sure she wasn't *Korean* or some shit."

"Tasteless fool," said Yong Sun, bouncing the palm of one hand under her own natu-rally curly tresses, the gesture of Frieda in a

Peanuts special.

"Plus, they think I'm ugly," said Yumiko.

"You're a total babe," I said. "What are they, crazy?"

"My eyes are too big, and I have dark skin — my grandfather calls me Indian Girl. You're supposed to be all squinty and pale and shit. *Fuck* that."

"Well, over here, you're *gorgeous,*" I said.

"Over here I have no tits. They think I look like a fucking twelve-year-old boy."

"Trade you," I said, pointing at my own abundance of boobulage.

She ignored that. "I go to Victoria's Secret, they can't even sell me underpants — both legs fit in one hole. I try on jeans at the Gap, they're all size zero — like, not even big enough to get a real *number.* Fucked up."

"Whine, whine, whine," said Karen, smiling. "Just like some stupid FOB."

I knew from previous Yumiko-rants that this acronym stood for Fresh Off the Boat.

Yumiko said, "Shut the fuck up and give me a Marlboro."

Karen drew a red-and-white soft-pack from her purse, extracted a smoke, and tossed it onto the carpet.

Yumiko stuck it behind her ear, filter forward.

"Pussy chink-ass bitch can't even *throw* right," she said. "No wonder your grandma's still slopping around rice paddies behind a water buffalo — dog-eating communist motherfuckers."

"*Koreans* eat dogs," said Karen.

"Do *not*," said Yong Sun.

"With *garlic*," said Yumiko.

Yong Sun stood up. "With that attitude, I think it's *your* turn to do the credit-card batch."

"I did the fucking credit-card batch *Friday*," said Yumiko. "It's your turn."

Yong Sun shook her head. "I'm the manager. And I'm busy."

"Doing *what?*" asked Yumiko.

"Putting more garlic in this damn coffee," said Yong Sun, walking out the door.

"Kiss my ass!" Yumiko yelled after her.

"In your dreams, bitch," echoed Yong Sun's voice back up the hall.

The phone rang, lighting up line two.

I pounced on it, beating Karen by a nanosecond. "Good morning, this is the Catalog, how may I help you?"

When line three lit up, Karen slapped the button down so fast the phone didn't have time to chirp, much less ring.

She smugly flipped off Yumiko, then pointed her still-extended middle finger toward the credit-card terminal.

Yumiko pursed her lips to make a wet kissy noise, then slapped her unrepentant size-zero butt.

Cate called around ten, saying we had the all clear from Skwarecki to go back inside Prospect.

"I'm out of here at noon," I said. "When are you meeting your Quakers?"

"One o'clock, so your timing's perfect."

"Cool."

"You're *sure* you want to do this, Madeline?"

"Course I'm sure. I've been thinking about it all week."

"Me too," she said. "And I'm so glad you're coming."

We said good-bye and I clicked open another line, dialing Dean in New Jersey. He'd started working for Christoph Monday morning, the pair of them commuting back and forth across the George Washington Bridge in Christoph's Jeep.

The secretary put me through to Dean's extension, and I said, "How's it goin', ya goddamn genius?" when he picked up.

"Decent," he said. "Nice day out here."

I looked out the window at the Catalog's air shaft. "I wouldn't know — thanks for the heads-up."

"You going back to the cemetery?" he asked.

"Cate just called. I figured I'd grab a sandwich or something and jump on the subway."

"What time'll you get home?"

"Way sooner than last week."

"Famous last words," he said.

"Really and truly. Even if we find any-thing, Skwarecki's said she's coming to us, you know?"

"Just be careful, Bunny. Get a ride to the subway if you guys stay later than four, all right?"

"Scout's honor," I said. "Pinkie swear."

"Hey, you talked to Nutty Buddy?"

"Astrid? Not since they called to hire you. Why?"

I heard him exhale. "Probably nothing."

Dean had spent enough time with my pals to have pretty decent girly-radar. Plus he had two sisters.

"What flavor of probably nothing?" I asked.

"She's been out here to the office a couple of times —"

"They *are* newlyweds. I'm sure the novelty will wear off. No offense —"

"Bunny, I mean she's driven out here a

couple of times a *day* since Monday. She's got Christoph's other Jeep."

I had a hard time picturing Astrid voluntarily venturing out to New Jersey pretty much *ever*, even under heavy sedation.

"Okay. That is kind of weird," I said.

"She seems shaky. Like she could use a friend."

"Astrid's got a *bazillion* friends."

"Yeah," he said, "but how many of them aren't assholes?"

"Good point," I said.

We were both quiet for a second.

"Look, Bunny?" said Dean. "There's something else."

"Tell me."

"She hasn't taken off that black jacket she had on the other night. She just wanders around the office with the hood up. In sunglasses."

"Shit," I said.

"Just give her a call sometime."

"I will."

"I should get back to it," said Dean.

"Cool. Catch you après-graveyard."

"You bet."

I was just about to hang up but instead said, "Hey, Dean?"

"Yeah?"

"If Astrid does come out there again, try

and get her to fucking eat something, okay? Bitch needs a cheeseburger."

I put down the phone and Yumiko blew a plume of Marlboro smoke across my desk. "You going *back* there, after you already found that dead kid?"

"Yeah," I said. "We're going to try and help figure out who it was."

"Fucking white people," she said, stubbing out her smoke in a brimming ashtray. "All of you — *crazy.*"

I shrugged.

So many cities, all mashed into each other on one tiny island.

On the train to Queens I pondered Dean's concern for Astrid and started thinking back to what she was like as I'd first known her.

There was one Sunday night in particular when I was sitting in the Ford Smoker bumming Marlboro Lights off Joan Appelbaum.

Whenever I'd had cash enough to buy my own, I walked down to the Dobbs Ferry Grand Union and purchased something off-puttingly bizarre like Philip Morris Commanders. These tasted like burnt sneakers marinated in Guinness, but since that meant only the truly desperate cadged them off me, each pack lasted twice as long.

That no classmate ever begrudged me a

cigarette despite this all-too-transparent strategy spoke to a tribal generosity of spirit I'd never once experienced in nine years of public school, go figure. Here sportsmanship counted: humility trumped money, wit meant nothing without courtesy, and our loyalty to one another was both absolute and fierce — no matter what.

Ford was one of the "new dorms," an abrupt trio of skinny, cedar-shingled seventies-ski-lodge towers. It was down the hill from my own digs in stately Cushing, whose fin-de-siècle stucco had once also housed my mother.

At 9:55 P.M. the green vinyl common-room sofas were still packed with Tab-swilling nicotine-junkies attired in standard girls'-boarding-school winter leisure wear: Bean duck boots and long underwear beneath prim-necked calico-flannel Lanz nighties.

I, meanwhile — sockless in flat orange espadrilles — sported a duct-tape-repaired down jacket, somebody's older brother's madras-plaid pants (sold to me cheap for weed money), and a hideously clashing aloha shirt scored over Christmas break from the St. Vincent de Paul in Salinas.

"You study for Hindley's bullshit poetry-thing yet?" asked Joan, spotting me a third cigarette.

I leaned in toward the flame of her lighter. "I'm waiting on Astrid. Bitch is late getting back from the city."

"All-nighter, then." Joan squinted up at the smoke-wreathed clock.

"How the hell does Hindley expect us to memorize sixty-nine poems in a single weekend?"

"More to the point," said Joan, "why the hell would you wait until the very last possible *night* to open the damn book?"

"Because I'm an idiot?"

She blew a smoke ring. "You'll fucking ace it anyway. Like always."

"Which doesn't mean tonight won't utterly *suck*. . . . I'd pawn my left ass-cheek for a hit of speed."

"That sophomore chick up in Strong has a whole bottle of her mother's diet shit."

"Too broke," I said. "Story of my life."

"Boo fucking hoo," Joan replied, tapping ash into someone else's abandoned fuchsia Tab can.

"Where the hell is Astrid?" I asked, eyeing the clock again.

"Why do you care? Start without her."

"That would be the prudent course of action, but it would require knowing where my copy of the actual fucking anthology was."

"You really *are* an idiot."

"Indeed," I said. "The merit of your hypothesis — as cogent summation of my native character — has long since been firmly established."

"Nobody likes a smart-ass."

"*Au contraire,* my always-thoroughly-prepared-for-class friend," I said. "Everyone likes a smart-ass; especially when we fail our stupid poetry-bullshit English tests so they get to wag their fingers and say, 'I told you so.' "

Joan tilted her head to peer out the window behind me. "Bet that's her pulling up right now."

"Taxi?"

"Limo," she said. "Stretch."

I blew a smoke ring of my own. "*Definitely* Astrid. The Venezuelans all signed in early."

Joan dragged a finger through my vaporous O as it wobbled past. "Lucky bitch. How the hell can she afford limos?"

"Flocks of smitten stockbrokers," I said, "desperate to have her stay on for just one more vodka-tonic at Doubles, or the Yale Club."

No sooner had I spoken than Astrid herself danced through the smoker's doorway: whip-lean in slender khakis, white tails of her beau-trophy shirt flaring wide with each twirl.

She was trailing what appeared to be a sable coat along the ash-foul carpet behind her, and high as a ribbon-tailed kite: Ray-Bans still on, Walkman turned up so loud everyone in the room could hear David Byrne's tinny "*This* ain't no party/*This* ain't no disco" plaint bleeding out from under the headphones.

"*Darlings,*" she said, flashing a red box of Dunhills, "who's got a light?"

"*Whose woods these are I think I know . . .*" read Astrid from her beat-to-shit orange copy of *Understanding Poetry*.

" 'Stopping by Woods on a Snowy Evening,' " I said.

"By?"

"Frost, *duh.* Like anything else with trees or winter."

I sat cross-legged on her dorm-room floor holding a Dunhill out the window; she was draped sideways across her bed, now wearing the goddamn fur over ice-blue pajamas.

A rush of frigid breeze ruffled the Indian-print bedspread nailed to the wall at my elbow, the stereo needle starting over again fresh on the same Beatles album we'd been

108

listening to for the last two hours.

"Hail to thee, blithe spirit —" she read.

"bird thou never wert. Keats."

"Shelley." Astrid flopped over onto her back, making the mattress shiver, then stretched her long legs up the wall beside her, crossing her ankles in the middle of Jim Morrison's poster-forehead. "Title?"

" 'Ode on a Piece-of-Shit Something-Something I Can't Remember Because It's Four in the Goddamn Morning'?"

"Actually, it's 'Ode *to* the Roundly Celebrated Demise of His Whiny Iambic Ass,' " she said.

"*Bien sûr.* And by the way, nice fucking coat."

"Mummie's."

"She's not going to miss it?"

Astrid shrugged. "She's away for three months. And you're dressed like shit again."

"Satire," I said. "Besides which, I'm out of quarters for laundry."

"Madeline, one must make an *effort.* All that overbred bone structure wasting its sweetness on the desert air."

"Thomas Gray," I said. " 'Elegy Written in a Country Churchyard.' And who'm I going to impress on a Sunday night — the security guards?"

Astrid snapped the book shut, then lolled

her head off the end of the bed, looking at me upside down. "Shall we do another line?"

By that she meant coke, not poetry: Swain-of-the-Hour's parting gift as he'd tucked her into the limo that evening — two grams, all told, which we'd already put quite a dent in.

I flicked my cigarette out the window, watching the glow of its orange ember arc high and then plummet, three stories down toward the snow. "That would be lovely, if you can spare it."

"Lots more where this came from," she said, reaching for her hand mirror and razor blade. "So we might as well do *all* of it."

"Your generosity is greatly appreciated, even so."

I gave the room an aerosol spritz of Ozium before shutting the window. This was a spray billing itself as air-freshener, but which actually worked by deadening anyone-who-inhaled-it's sense of smell for several minutes — essential camouflage in the dorm-parent wars since we weren't allowed cigarettes upstairs.

You'd find a blue-and-white can of it atop the brown school-issued bureau of every partier on campus, alongside her requisite bottle of Visine.

Astrid laid out two fat lines on the mirror and handed it to me along with a rolled-up twenty.

I snorted them up, then put the mirror on the floor and pinched each nostril shut in turn, inhaling sharply to get it all down.

"Thank you for that," I said, licking my finger to swipe the last granules off the mirror, rubbing the slick of white into my gums.

"Straight-arrow Maddie Dare giving herself a freeze," said Astrid. "Who'd believe it?"

"Fuck off."

For the most part I didn't indulge. My own bureau-top was Ozium-free, my closet filled with nothing but dirty clothes. I valued my scholarship far too much to mess around, profoundly grateful to have escaped my then-stepfather Pierce's needling daily assholery.

Besides which, both my parents were stoners, so bong hits had never felt like much in the way of rebellion.

Coke, I reasoned, was different. It wasn't like there was ever a ton of it on offer, and it was so easy to hide, so hard to detect once ingested. No harm, no foul.

Who'd believe it, indeed?

Not the dorm parents, nor even the Disciplinary Committee. Lucky me.

I gave Astrid the mirror back, then opened *Understanding Poetry* at a random page while she laid out a fresh brace of lines for herself.

Maybe we'd bonded because she had even less of a home to count on than I did, and effectively the same lack of cash. My parents actually didn't have any, and hers just kept spending it all trying to look like they had even more. As such, we'd learned early to elicit the kindness of strangers.

"Here is Belladonna," I intoned, *"the Lady of the Rocks/The lady of situations."*

She did one line, muttered "Byron," and snorted up the next.

"Try harder, Veruca."

Astrid rolled off the bed and walked over to her stereo. "If I have to listen to one more *second* of fucking 'Norwegian Wood' I'm going to shoot myself. Read me another couplet."

"What are you putting on?"

"Vivaldi."

"What the hell's Vivaldi?"

"Your people have no *culture,* Madeline. If ever there were a race whose conscience remains woefully uncreated —"

"I am *highly* conversant in the greatest hits of Puccini," I said. "Mozart . . . Beethoven . . . And by the way, eat me raw."

She dropped the needle onto *The Four Seasons,* Side A, then opened the window and lit a Dunhill.

"Not bad," I said when the first violin started in, soaring above the string-section pack. "Got a good beat — you can dance to it."

"Read me another couplet, ungrateful bitch. That last one was a lousy hint."

I cleared my throat. " 'HURRY UP PLEASE IT'S TIME —' "

"Eliot!" she crowed, triumphant.

"Title?"

Looking back over her shoulder, she threw me a smirk. " 'Teenage Wasteland'?"

"*Exactemente,* you goddamn genius."

"We're going to rule the world, you and I."

"Of course," I said. "No question."

"Say that like you *mean* it."

I picked at my jacket's duct tape. "Sure."

At fifteen I'd discovered this small slice of world in which my natural impulses suddenly marked me not outcast, but leader. I'd seen my life come shining, from the west down to the east.

I was now three years older, and reluctant as hell to leave this safe haven.

I looked up at her. "I must admit to an increasing sense of panic that I'm doomed

113

to become one of those awful little people who peaked in high school."

"Goddamn it, Madeline, we are the *balls,*" said Astrid, kicking me in the thigh. "Now and forever."

"Look," I said, "in this place, you and I own any goddamn room we walk into. We can get up onstage and play the entire school like a fucking violin, conjuring forth any nuance of emotion we want — teachers, classmates, administration — off the cuff, pitch-perfect every time. Either one of us could snap our fingers and start a riot, or stop one dead in its tracks."

She nodded. "Absolute power."

It's why we were friends. I mean, who the hell else could we have admitted this to?

"Absolutely," I said, then pointed at the window. "Out there, however, it's a goddamn crap shoot. Entropy . . . chaos."

She crossed her arms, impatient. "Don't be such a pussy."

"I'm not a pussy, I'm a realist. Our main ingredient is just charisma, Astrid, the very quintessence of ephemerality. 'One shade the more, one ray the less . . .' and *hey presto,* it's gone."

"Bullshit," she said. "The only thing that can take it away is allowing yourself to doubt it."

"Well, there you go, then. I'm dead meat."

Astrid blew a stream of smoke out the window, then turned back to me. "Take off your jacket."

"Why?"

"So you can give it to me."

"I don't want to fucking give you my jacket. The window's open and it's god-damn freezing in here. Besides which you're already *wearing* a coat."

"Yeah, but we're trading." She stuck the Dunhill in the corner of her mouth and shook off her mother's sable, holding it out toward me.

"Fuck off. I like mine better."

"The hell you do," she said. "It's an ugly piece of shit with duct tape all over it."

"I happen to *enjoy* duct tape."

"Cocky bitch."

"Damn right," I said.

She took another drag and put her coat back on. "You know how many people would've traded?"

I shrugged.

"All of them," she said. "Everyone but you, Madissima. So *fuck* doubt. The only thing you need to do is *arise, go forth, and conquer.*"

"Tennyson. 'The Passing of Arthur.' "

"We are the best fucking minds of our

115

generation," said Astrid. "And I will *never* let you forget it."

She leaned out the window, blowing a plume of smoke into the frosty air before extending her sable-draped arms in a gesture of sublime grace, a benediction over those still asleep in the waning darkness.

"Hear this," she said into the night, "from Astrid and Madeline: We. Are. The. *Balls*."

She declaimed Eliot's second-stanza blessing, then — softly — across all the campus below:

"Good night, ladies, good night, sweet ladies, good night, good night."

Then the sun came up, and, four hours later, the pair of us aced Hindley's bullshit poetry test: ninety-eight apiece.

It was hard, now, to remember the two of us — me and Astrid, as children — but harder still to recall the people she'd believed we would become.

14

I got from Jamaica Station to Prospect faster this time around. Not just because I knew my way, but also because the air felt a little crisper — there was a nice snap to it, heralding fall. Not enough to make me wish I'd brought a sweater, just adequate to walk at a brisker pace, freed from summer's soggy oppression.

Cate was just unloading her car when I turned into the little dead-end lane.

She looked up and smiled. "You're the first one here."

The other volunteers arrived moments later — half a dozen mellow-looking older folk wearing sturdy shoes and floppy hats. They might've just returned from an Elderhostel rafting trip down the Colorado: no-nonsense, ready for anything.

Cate jumped right into describing the parameters of today's mission.

"All we know so far is that the child was

three years old," she said. "So we're looking for anything that might help to identify him or her . . . clothing especially. Let's work in pairs this week, and go slowly."

The Quakers nodded.

"If you uncover *anything* other than plant matter," she continued, "even if it looks like run-of-the-mill garbage, bring it out to the edges of the cleared trail and leave it next to the little railings, here." She pointed to the granite corner-marker of a family plot.

"Didn't Skwarecki say we shouldn't touch anything we found?" I asked her, once the Quakers had paired off and moved away.

"Her crew's spent some time here since," said Cate, "and she thinks if we do turn anything up, the stuff will most likely have been moved by animals. She's coming by later to look over whatever we do find."

I tied a newly laundered bandanna around my forehead.

"Nice," she said, handing me a machete, gloves, and a garbage bag. "Makes you look like a pirate."

"Damn, and here I was going for Hendrix."

Cate laughed, picking up a set of clippers, and the pair of us headed off into the bushes.

Ninety minutes on, we'd filled ten bags and lined up a five-foot, single-file parade of worthless-looking objets-du-garbage alongside the central trail.

Cate topped up one more load, then spun the bag closed and retrieved a toothed plastic closure from her shorts pocket. I reached over to keep the bag's neck shut with my fist so she didn't have to cinch it one handed.

She hoisted the load over her shoulder, Santa-style. "Ready for a break?"

"Thought you'd never ask."

I gathered up our tools, slowly scoping out the hacked weeds underfoot as I walked back toward the trail edge. All I turned up was a root-beer bottle and a wad of disintegrating newsprint.

There was nothing obviously connected to a child — no little toys, no tiny sweaters with name tags sewn in, no laminated photo-ID cards reading, MY NAME IS _____, AND SKWARECKI SHOULD ARREST _____.

We hadn't found a thing that required a second thought: bent cans and grimy bottles, the rusty blade of a garden trowel, a tangle of kite-string with silver Christmas tinsel inexplicably wound in — pointless, all of it.

I placed my latest finds at the back of the sad little line of crap and sighed, shaking my head.

Maybe the Quakers were having better luck, or maybe there hadn't been anything to find in the first place.

I wiped my hands on the back of my shorts and started trudging up toward the chapel, only slightly cheered by the promise of ice water.

When I stepped inside the chapel I found Cate deep in discussion with Detective Skwarecki.

Cate was looking at the floor and nodding, cup of water in hand, while Skwarecki gesticulated with what looked like the remaining half of a Chips Ahoy.

I grabbed some water myself before walking over to join them.

Cate looked up at me. "We may have a bit of good news."

"The Quakers got lucky?"

"We've turned up a missing-persons report that could be relevant," said Skwarecki. "It was filed last April here in Queens, by the mother of a three-year-old boy."

"So, right age," I said.

120

"The pathologist thinks the child we found was African American," added Cate. "Which fits."

I looked at Skwarecki. "You can tell someone's ethnicity from their bones?"

"Broadly speaking," she said. "You get different features distinguishing Caucasoid, Mongoloid, and Africanoid skulls, even in children."

"Like what?" I asked.

"The shape of the nose holes, proportions of any nasal bones, whether the zygomatic bones — cheekbones — are curved or square. Even the chin's angle means something. Our guy's pretty confident that this child's ancestry is African."

"Is there any way to tell for *sure* whether the woman who filed the report is the mother?" I asked. "Some kind of test?"

Skwarecki shook her head. "Not with skeletal remains. With a blood sample we can at least establish the likelihood of two individuals being closely related."

"Sure," I said. "Blood typing."

"Serology, or HLA," she said, "but again, with these remains . . ."

"What about DNA?" I asked.

I'd read about it in the *Times*, but it was still pretty new.

Skwarecki shook her head. "That takes a

big sample of blood or saliva or semen from both individuals. And there's a lot of argument on whether the results really even stack up forensically."

"I thought it was foolproof," I said.

She shrugged. "This guy Castro almost got off last year, killed a pregnant woman and her daughter. They thought they had him on DNA — blood on his watch — but his lawyer convinced the judge it was a lab screwup, not a match. That's got everybody's panties in a knot over guidelines, chain of evidence."

I slugged back the last of my water, discouraged.

Cate asked, "So, in a case like this, how *do* you establish someone's identity? You said there probably wouldn't be dental records."

"It's tough," said Skwarecki. "Skeletal structure can't even confirm gender, before puberty."

I peered into my now-empty water cup for a moment, like I'd find some useful advice printed at the bottom.

Nope.

I raised my eyes to meet Skwarecki's. "Did the missing boy have any dental records?"

"No," she said. "I asked his mother this morning."

I thought about "our" child's smashed rib cage and all the other fractures the ME said had never been set so they could heal properly. If he was the missing boy, it didn't sound like he'd ever been taken to a doctor, either. Skwarecki had to be thinking about all of that too.

"So how did this lady manage to lose her son?" I asked. "Were they, like, at the beach? In a department store?"

I wanted to give this woman I'd never seen the benefit of the doubt. Maybe she had no connection to the battered bones we'd found. Maybe she was honestly grieving the most horrifying kind of loss life could throw at any parent. For a minute I sure as shit hoped so, even if it meant we'd never know whom the Prospect child belonged to.

But then I thought it would be better to know, better to make sure Skwarecki got who did it.

"She said she was out looking for work," said Skwarecki.

"Please tell us that this woman didn't leave her three-year-old home alone," said Cate.

"She didn't," said Skwarecki, shutting her eyes for just a moment and looking very, very tired when she opened them again. "She told me she'd left him with someone she trusts, absolutely."

I felt cold, suddenly, like the ice water in my stomach had suddenly leaked out into the veins snaking up through my rib cage, coursing onward into my lungs and heart.

I looked at Skwarecki. "Boyfriend or stepfather?"

She closed her eyes again, for longer this time. "Boyfriend. A guy named Albert Williams."

15

"And this Albert Williams boyfriend says what?" I asked. "A toddler ran to the corner deli for cigarettes?"

Cate put her hand on my forearm. "Madeline, we don't *know* these people are to blame."

I looked down at my sneakers.

Cate removed her hand. "Detective Skwarecki, what did the man say had happened?"

"Williams's version is they were sitting on a bed watching TV together and he fell asleep. When he woke up, the door was open and the boy was gone."

I shook my head, breathing out through my nose.

"The *front* door?" asked Cate.

"Motel-room door," said Skwarecki. "A place the county's using for temp housing, out by LaGuardia. The mother'd been there maybe a month."

"That's where you spoke with her today?" asked Cate.

"No," said Skwarecki. "She gave her grandmother's address and phone number on the report. I met her there."

"And where does the grandmother live?" I asked.

"Maybe ten blocks from here," said Skwarecki. "Two-family house — the grandmother owns half."

She smiled a little, for the first time that day. "That is one *very* tough little old lady, let me tell you. She's kicking some major butt on the little boy's behalf."

"More than his mother?" asked Cate.

"His mother . . . well . . ." Skwarecki looked up at the ceiling. "Let's just say she's not gonna get hired by IBM anytime soon. Or Seven-Eleven."

"How do you mean?" asked Cate.

Skwarecki shrugged. "Work homicide? You know from crack-hounds."

"This just breaks my *heart,*" said Cate.

I put my arm around her shoulders and turned to Skwarecki. "Do you think we found her little boy?"

"How she looked this morning? You gotta wonder how she even knew he was gone."

"But the woman filed a missing-person's report, didn't she?" asked Cate. "For all we know, she turned to drugs out of grief — *after* she lost her son."

"Sure," said Skwarecki, humoring Cate. "But it was the grandmother made sure that got filed. Dollars to doughnuts."

"She came down to the station, the grandmother?" I asked.

"With his mother, the first time," said Skwarecki. "She's been back a lot since, solo. That's how I got the report so fast. Desk sergeant says everyone knows her downstairs. She brings cookies."

"And was there anything in the report that could help us identify the little boy?" I asked.

"What he was last seen wearing," said Skwarecki.

Cate looked up. "Given your description of his mother, do you trust her account of what he had on?"

"The grandmother confirmed it," Skwarecki said. "She'd just bought him new clothes, and checked to see what was missing: little red overalls, blue-and-white striped T-shirt, white socks, and a pair of sneakers with ALF on them."

"That puppet on TV?" asked Cate.

Skwarecki nodded.

The sneakers got to me. I looked down and started blinking really fast, but I could still feel tears welling up in the corners of my eyes.

"*Crap,*" I said as fat plops of salty wet started dropping straight down from my face to the stone floor.

Now it was Cate's turn to put her arm around me, which she did with great gentleness.

"Yeah, right?" said Skwarecki. "Should've seen me when the grandmother said *ALF* was his favorite show. Then she brings out a photograph, him sitting on Santa's lap last Christmas? I just about broke down and bawled right there in her living room."

"That is so sad," I said, gulping as my nose filled and my throat started to ache. "Jesus Christ."

"Tell me about it," said Skwarecki. "And then she hands me this tin of cookies, a thank-you for the guys back at the One-Oh-Three."

"Skwarecki," I said, "you're *killing* me here."

I pulled my bandanna out of my pocket and blew my nose.

"At the risk of starting Madeline up again," said Cate, "may I ask if you can tell us the little boy's name?"

"Edward," said Skwarecki, grave once more. "But they call him Teddy."

128

■ ■ ■ ■

We led Skwarecki outside, and the three of us walked down the trail to see if the Quakers had found anything useful during the course of the afternoon. They started coming out of the bushes when they heard us, and Cate urged everyone to take a break.

No one had found even a scrap of fabric so far — just little piles of garbage as useless as Cate's and mine.

"Detective?" A woman stepped forward from the group. Cate introduced her to Skwarecki as Mrs. Van Nostrand.

"I found something that I didn't want to risk picking up," the woman continued, "without your having seen it first."

Skwarecki followed her into the bushes. They emerged moments later, looking grim. Skwarecki, now wearing latex gloves, tucked a large rolled-up plastic bag into her jacket pocket.

She and Mrs. Van Nostrand spoke briefly before the woman made her way back to the chapel.

"What is it?" asked Cate, when we were alone.

"A vertebra," said Skwarecki. "Small. Looks human."

Cate blanched.

Skwarecki touched her arm. "I should run this down to the ME. You two sticking around?"

"While it's still light," said Cate.

"Maybe an hour, I'll swing back," said Skwarecki. She strode away toward her car, across the dead grass.

Cate and I got in another hour of vine-hacking after that, filling a further half-dozen bags without finding anything of consequence.

The Quakers called it a day around five, and we walked them to the front gate, thanking them for their hard work.

There must have been four dozen bags of trimmings piled in a neat row along the sidewalk.

We sat on the ground outside the chapel, leaning back against the sun-warmed stones of its exterior.

"Let's just wait here for Swarecki," I said. "Take a load off."

"Twist my aching rubber back," said Cate.

Both of us were pretty drowsy, judging by the amount of yawning we did.

"Do you think we'll ever find out who this child really is?" she asked.

"I hope so."

I shivered, wondering which would be worse: knowing your son was dead or having no idea where he was and whether or not he was in pain.

"If it *is* Teddy," said Cate, "do you think the grandmother knew he was being abused?"

"She doesn't sound like she would have stood for it from Skwarecki's description," I said.

I watched the sun slip westward, edging down behind the vine-decked trees. Their branches stirred, dancing light across the grass.

"I wonder where Teddy's grandmother is, in all of this?" asked Cate.

"How do you mean?"

"The cookie lady's his great-grandmother. We're missing a generation."

I pondered that. "Good question."

"I'm so tired."

"I can't imagine getting up to go bag the last of that garbage," I said.

"God," replied Cate, "what a hideous prospect. I could sleep the whole night through right here."

"I'll go do it in another minute," I said. "We didn't clear too much ground after the first pass."

I pressed back against the chapel's

warmth, relishing the loose tiredness in my shoulders.

The wind came up again. I listened to it coursing through the trees, like a rush of creek water along polished stones.

Then I thought I heard a woman's voice.

"What was that?" I asked Cate.

"What?"

"It sounded like 'Hello,' " I said. "Maybe someone at the gate?"

I stood up to walk around the chapel's south end.

A tiny, white-haired African American lady peered in through the fence, her prim gray suit's skirt-hem revealing calves thin and straight as wood split narrow for kindling.

I moved toward her across the grass, charmed by the sparrow of hat she'd pinned atop her regiment of beauty-parlor curls.

"Good afternoon, young lady," she said.

"Good afternoon, ma'am. May I help you with something?"

"The letters on this sign are so small, dear, and I don't see as well as I used to," she said. "Can you tell me whether this is Prospect Cemetery?"

"Yes it is, ma'am," said Cate, stepping up beside me. "What can we do for you?"

"I'm Mrs. Elsie Underhill," the woman

132

said, "and I understand that someone here may have found my Teddy."

I didn't say anything. Cate cleared her throat.

"Are you police officers?" asked Mrs. Underhill.

"No, ma'am," said Cate. "I'm in charge of coordinating the volunteers here."

Mrs. Underhill shifted her purse to shake our hands after we introduced ourselves, then asked, "Were either of you here when the child was found?"

"Yes, ma'am," I said. "We both were."

"We're expecting Detective Skwarecki back shortly," said Cate.

"Oh, I don't want to interfere. I just wanted to see the place Teddy might have been laid to rest."

"The detective told us about your loss this afternoon, Mrs. Underhill," I said. "We're both so very sorry."

"Thank you, dear," she said. "Thank you kindly."

She opened her purse and pulled out a sheet of notepaper. "I've written my number down, just here. Could you make sure the detective receives it? And I hope, if you find anything else, it might be possible for you to let me know directly?"

"Of course we will," said Cate, taking the

133

note. "This must be such a difficult time for you and your family. My heart goes out to you."

"If the child you found *is* Teddy," said Mrs. Underhill, "I'd very much like to speak with the person who discovered him. Might there be any way to arrange that?"

"It was I, Mrs. Underhill," I said. "I'd be happy to tell you anything I can."

"I'd appreciate that so much, but I don't want to trouble you now. Just please, keep us in your prayers."

"Of course," I said. "Of course we will."

"Please let us know if there's anything we can do for you, Mrs. Underhill," said Cate. "Do you have a pen? I'd like you to have my number, as well."

When Cate finished writing, I added my name and numbers, home and work, then tore the sheet of paper in half.

Mrs. Underhill took the pen and paper back from me and put them in her purse, then touched my arm. "I don't live far away. Maybe you could come by sometime, for a cup of tea? It would be such a comfort to me."

"Yes, ma'am," I said. "Whenever you'd like."

"May we give you a lift home?" asked Cate.

"No thank you, dear," said Mrs. Underhill. "The walk will do me good."

We all shook hands again.

Cate and I stood quiet, watching that gentle woman move away down the sidewalk. Head high, back straight, Mrs. Underhill shouldered the yoke of grief with tacit dignity.

When she'd disappeared around the corner, my cousin turned to look at me.

"Underhill . . ." Cate's voice trailed off.

We both knew there were headstones bearing that name among the graves behind us, and what it meant.

"Yeah," I said, "Teddy is family."

Cate and I returned to our seats on the ground, leaning back against the chapel wall. The sun had inched down a little lower, its angle backlighting the tree trunks and everything in front of them.

I saw something I hadn't noticed before, beside the main path. A tiny object, balanced atop the squat granite obelisk marking one corner of a family plot.

"Cate?" I said, sitting up straighter.

"What?"

"I think somebody found a shoe."

16

Cate and I leaped up and bolted across the dry grass.

I'd been right: the backlit object was a tiny white sneaker, but neither of us wanted to touch it before Skwarecki's return.

Cate stepped slowly around the granite post on which the shoe had been placed.

"It's got writing on it, down this side," she said, pointing.

I edged around the post in the other direction to stand beside her, but half the shoe's swirly lettering was obscured by the shadows of some caked-on mud.

I squatted down and grabbed a twig off the ground, using it to poke the sneaker's little snub toe gently toward the western light.

I read the words aloud, "Club Melmac."

"What's that, some kind of brand name?"

"No." I dropped my twig and stood up. "Skwarecki should be back by now, shouldn't she?"

"Madeline, please tell me what Melmac means."

I kept staring at the gate, not wanting to blink. "It's the name of ALF's home planet."

Cate inhaled sharply, and then, for what seemed like ages, I didn't hear the sound of her breath again.

Finally, she exhaled with a raggedy moan, like she'd been punched.

"Oh, Maddie, that poor woman. This is just so damn *awful*."

"I know," I said. "It sucks."

I'd gone cold again, despite the sun's continued warmth on my back. I wrapped my arms tight around my rib cage but couldn't seem to stop shivering.

We'd been staring across the grass before Mrs. Underhill showed up and hadn't seen the shoe. Could she have put it there?

No, that was ridiculous. It was just the different angle of the sunlight.

And Mrs. Underhill hadn't come inside, past the gate. Had anyone come up behind us while we were talking to her to deposit the shoe, we'd have heard them crunching through the dry weeds.

Besides which, what good would it possibly do this woman to falsify a connection between her missing great-grandson and the child we'd found?

Paranoia. Get over yourself before you start babbling about Zapruder footage and the grassy knoll.

"Are you all right?" Cate touched my shoulder, gently. "You're shaking."

"I'm just cold," I said.

"I'll get my jacket out of the car."

"I'm okay."

"I'll get my jacket," she said again.

She crossed my field of vision, taking a dozen long strides to reach her car.

"Okay," I said, though she was out of earshot.

Skwarecki's dark sedan coasted to a halt just shy of the gate.

Skwarecki crouched down beside the tiny shoe. "You guys did good today."

Latex gloves back on, she used my same twig to lift the sneaker by its still-tied laces, lowering it gently into the brown paper bag she'd taken out of her trunk.

"It doesn't *feel* good," said Cate. "Just awful and sad."

Skwarecki closed the top of the bag. "You've gotta concentrate on the positive. This little boy can be laid to rest now. His family can have some peace."

"I'm trying," said Cate.

She wandered a little distance away, kicking at stray gravel with the toe of her shoe.

"You think they *all* deserve that?" I asked Skwarecki. "It's hard to believe Mrs. Underhill had anything to do with this — from how she acted today, and the way you described her — but, you know, his mother? You think us identifying her son is going to bring *her* any peace?"

She glanced up at me, lips pursed, then tilted her head an inch to the side with an upward twitch of her corresponding shoulder.

No, she didn't think so. Not for a second.

I nodded and Skwarecki dropped her eyes, extracting a pen from her jacket pocket to jot words and numbers into underscored blank fields on a tag already stapled to the bag's brown paper.

"How come you're not using a ziplock this time?" I asked, remembering the plastic bag into which she'd placed the vertebra.

"Certain kinds of trace evidence, you need paper."

I glanced toward Cate, making sure she was out of earshot.

"Blood," I said.

Skwarecki nodded. "Any dried fluids."

Urine. Semen.

"Seal something like that in plastic, you

get humidity," she said. "Contaminates everything."

"That makes sense."

Skwarecki stood up. "You got cops in your family or something, Madeline?"

"Or something," I said.

She cracked a little smile. "It just seems like you know the drill."

I twitched my shoulders.

"And you're wishing you didn't know," she said.

"Damn straight."

"Yeah," she said, shaking her head. "Kind of shit like this-here?"

"Fucked up."

"Tell me about it. Fucking assholes."

"No shit."

"I mean, a little *kid?*"

"His little *shoe?*" I pointed at the paper bag.

"What the *fuck,* am I right?"

"Shitheads."

"Yo," said Skwarecki, "fucking *exactly.*"

And then we shoulder-bumped each other. I felt much better.

Having bonded, the two of us rested our hands on our hips, standing side by side and looking over toward Cate.

"Skwarecki?" I asked.

"Yo."

"What're the chances of actually nailing someone for this?"

"Like I told you before, close to bubkes."

"Promise me you'll go for it anyway."

"That's what we do."

"Cool."

"Fuckin' ay," said Skwarecki.

Cate turned around, looking calmer, and started walking back over to us.

"What happens next?" I asked Skwarecki.

"Paperwork. See if little Teddy was in the system."

"Which system?" asked Cate.

"He was a battered child," said Skwarecki. "We need to know if anyone reported the abuse."

"How can we help?" asked Cate.

Skwarecki tucked the evidence bag under her arm. "If we build any kind of a case, Bost'll need you and Madeline to testify."

"Detective," said Cate, "we have to *get* the fucker who did this."

"Amen," said Skwarecki.

"I don't see how I'm going to stop thinking about all this, after today," said Cate.

She was driving me back to Jamaica Station, the light already fading around us: early dusk, that thin blade-edge of winter.

"Don't you wish you could *do* something about it, right now?" she continued.

"Of course," I said, "because I have absolutely no patience."

"And that poor Mrs. Underhill. Do you think she knew?"

"That Teddy was being abused? She had to."

"But Madeline, she obviously cared a great deal about him. I can't believe she would have stood by if she knew he was being hurt."

"How do you ignore broken bones?" I asked. "We're not talking bruises here."

"Why would she bring cookies to the cop station all the time if she knew — without ever bringing up the abuse?"

"Could she miss spotting multiple fractures in a three-year-old? I can't even imagine how his mother tried to explain them away. I mean, what — she just kept saying, 'Teddy jumped off the roof again, guess he didn't learn his lesson the first three or four times,' and Mrs. Underhill went, 'That's nice, dear, maybe you should buy him a crash helmet'? I don't buy it. That lady is *not* stupid."

"It's not about stupidity," said Cate. "Sometimes people can't allow themselves to know. They're overwhelmed by everything else at stake."

"I don't buy *that,* either."

"Maybe she didn't see him often enough to realize he was being beaten. Or she didn't want to risk losing any contact at all with him."

"Then she's a coward."

"That's harsh," said Cate.

"Harsher than how Teddy died?"

"No, of course not, but we still can't know who killed him. Maybe his mother's boyfriend was telling the truth."

"Someone beat Teddy so hard they broke his bones — on at least one occasion before his death, because the fractures had time to heal — but a stranger killed him?"

She was quiet, digesting that.

"Cate, how far is it to LaGuardia from here?"

"Nine miles, give or take."

"So they're living in a welfare hotel that far away, but we found Teddy's body ten blocks from his great-grandmother's apartment?"

"Now you think she did it?"

"No," I said. "But you'd have to be pretty damn local to know Prospect even existed. The sign is tiny — Mrs. Underhill wasn't sure she'd found it today, even when she was standing right at the gate."

Or so she said.

Cate sighed. "Good point."

"I hate this," I said. "All of it."

"But we're both coming back tomorrow, aren't we?"

"Of course."

She pulled up to the curb to let me out. "Call me from work. I'll pick you up at the station."

I leaned back in through the passenger window before she'd put the car back in gear. "Anybody halfway normal would consider us total freaks, you know?"

Cate smiled at me, a little sadly. "This is one of those weeks when 'normal' seems like a delusion of grandeur."

■ ■ ■ ■

I came up out of the subway station in Union Square and hooked a right at the Gandhi statue.

I couldn't see all the way to the Hudson, but it still seemed as though the clear, warm western light spilling toward me had bounced sparkling across the river on its way.

I turned up the volume on my Walkman, the mournful second movement of Beethoven's Seventh in Teddy's honor.

I zoned out for the next few blocks, trying to think of nothing but the music until I'd turned into our building's courtyard — no damaged children, no evil grown-ups.

I hit the tape's Stop button and pushed the headphones down around my neck once I'd crossed the threshold into our apartment, calling out, "Hi, honey, I'm home!" to whomever might be kicking back in the living room's brazen apricot glare.

This was greeted by a lackluster chorus soon revealed as Sue, Pagan, and Astrid herself — all sprawled on the sofa.

Sue and Pague were in post-work shorts-and-flip-flops mufti, but Astrid was still wearing her quilted black jacket, with sunglasses on top of her head.

"What do you, sleep in that thing?" I asked her.

Astrid looked up at me with those limpid eyes, the circles beneath them stained coffee-dark with fatigue.

She shivered inside the coat, drawing it closer around her too-slender frame. The problem wasn't what she slept in, but whether she'd slept at all.

"Maddie," she said, "do you think I should go to Rome?"

It turned out she'd already been there for over an hour, asking that question over and over of Pagan and Sue while they gritted their teeth, waiting for my return. Astrid overwhelmed me inside ten minutes, and I'd excused myself to the kitchen for a fortifying beer.

Pagan ducked in behind me seconds later, while I was still rattling through drawers in search of a bottle opener.

"Nutty Buddy's gotten kind of, um, *nuttier*," she said.

"I'm worried about her," I said, popping the cap off my Rolling Rock.

"What's the deal with Rome?"

"I think it has to do with the guy she didn't marry."

146

"You should ask her. Or maybe just stick her in a cab for the airport. She's exhausting."

"You think it's too much coke?" I asked.

"Too much something."

"It's not like she's got a runny nose or anything."

"Maybe she's shooting it," said Pagan.

"You think she'd seem this tired?"

"Heroin, then? Who the hell knows."

"What do I do?" I said. "She's my friend, and I don't know how to fucking *help*."

"I'm not sure you can."

"That's so fucked up. Just . . . wrong."

"Maybe you should call her husband."

"I don't know him at all. And the whole thing's so weird because now he's Dean's boss."

"How 'bout her mother?"

I'd only met the woman once, and she hadn't struck me as the kind of person with much of a shoulder to cry on — if she were even in the country, which she seldom was. At most she might begrudge her daughter another sable coat.

I looked at Pagan. "It's like I'm watching somebody who really matters drifting out to sea, and I'm standing here on the beach doing nothing."

"You have to talk to her."

"What do I even *say?*" I asked.

"I don't know," said Pagan. "Maybe that part doesn't matter."

The pair of us walked back down the dark hallway.

"So, Astrid," I said, "what's with the sudden desire to switch continents?"

"Do you think Christoph loves me?" she asked.

"A man charters a plane to Southampton two weeks ago so he can marry you," I said. "I think that's evidence of high regard, don't you?"

"I can't tell if he *really* loves me, Madeline," she said.

"Astrid, how could he *help* but love you?"

She pulled down her sunglasses to cover her eyes, slumping back into her dark velvet cocoon.

"Astrid," I said, "you're the most beautiful woman in every room you've ever walked into, and you're great fun, and you're very, very smart. If the man doesn't love you, he's an idiot."

"So you think he doesn't?"

"I didn't say that," I said. "In fact I think he seems absolutely smitten with you, from what I saw at dinner."

"What does Dean say?"

"I'm sure he'd say the same thing. It just

seems so obvious, you know? Your husband loves you."

Sue rolled her eyes and edged out of the room.

"Should I go to Rome?" Astrid asked again.

"What's in Rome, Antonini?" I asked.

"He hasn't called."

"Which is not exactly surprising considering you married someone else the minute he was out of town."

"I could fly there this weekend," she said.

"What would you tell Christoph?" I asked.

"I don't know if I'd tell him anything."

I couldn't discern whether this was buyer's remorse or merely a bid for general reassurance. The fact that my husband now worked for hers made the whole thing even more fucked up to navigate.

"Astrid, what do you want me to tell you? I don't know what you want."

"I want to know whether you think I should go to Rome," she said.

Pagan stood up.

"I have a song for you," she said, patting Astrid on the shoulder.

She walked over to the stereo and cued up a CD. Seconds later the B-52s were singing "Roam If You Want To" at very high volume.

Astrid smiled but didn't look very re-assured.

"Look," I said, "it's getting dark out. Why don't I get you a taxi home? I bet Christoph's home by now, and you can call me in the morning at work, okay?"

"Okay," she said, pulling her hood up and getting creakily to her feet.

I walked her downstairs and was relieved to find a cab pulling up to the curb right outside.

I bundled Astrid into the backseat and told her everything would be okay, hoping I was telling the truth.

"Do you think I should go to Rome?" she asked again as I was about to close the door.

"I think you should sleep on it. If you still don't know in the morning, we can talk about it some more."

I shut the door and patted the cab's roof, then watched it whisk her away down the darkening street.

I raised my bottle of Rolling Rock in salute, wishing her safety in whatever journey she'd embarked upon.

"Toasting the city, Bunny?"

I turned to find Dean walking toward me down the sidewalk.

"Thank God," I said, hugging him. "I thought you'd never get here."

"You have some really fucked-up friends," said Sue when we were all back splayed out across the living room, having called Mykonos for delivery of baba ghanoush and hummus and souvlaki, agreeing we were all too communally exhausted to consider walking anywhere.

"I can't believe she was *here,* too," said Dean. "She drove out to the office in New Jersey twice today."

"After you called me this morning?" I asked.

He nodded.

"That woman needs a fucking job," said Sue.

"Or a fucking *life,*" added Pagan. "I mean, *go* to fucking Rome already. Who fucking cares?"

"I'm worried about her," I said.

"Why don't you worry about world peace or something, Maddie?" asked Sue. "I mean, use your energy wisely."

"Oh, right, because the pursuit of world peace is such a historically non-frustrating endeavor," I said.

Pagan laid her head down on the arm of the sofa and closed her eyes. "What. *Ever.* I'm just so happy she isn't talking at me anymore."

We heard the rattle-and-clink of someone wrapping heavy chains around a bicycle.

"Hark," said Dean, "the dinner bell."

It wasn't until we'd paid the delivery guy and opened up all the various containers across the coffee table that I started relating my adventures out in Queens that day.

"I wouldn't have known what Melmac even *was*," said Pagan, scooping up a bite of lamb and tzatziki with a wedge of pita bread.

"I don't know why I did," I said. "It's not like I really watched that show. I mean, maybe a couple of times when I had the flu or something. I don't even remember."

"It's your photogenic memory," she said. "Only this time there was some purpose to the useless trivia your brain is flypaper for."

"Photogenic?" asked Dean.

"Old joke," said Pagan. "Long boring explanation."

"Who's got the salt?" I asked.

Pagan picked up the shaker from down the table and set it on the napkin beside my plate.

I started shaking the white gold generously over my food.

"You haven't even tasted it," said Sue.

"Why ruin the first bite?" I replied.

Sue said, "I want to know more about the cemetery. Who do you think killed the little boy, his mother?"

Pague and I said "Boyfriend" simultaneously.

"But if he'd been beaten up a lot before?" asked Sue. "I mean, does anyone even know how long his mother'd been with the boyfriend?"

"I have a hard time picturing a woman doing that much damage, just from the upper-body-strength perspective. His rib cage was totally —"

"We're *eating,* here," said Pagan.

I shrugged. "Sue asked."

Pagan pointed her pita at me. "Funny, I didn't hear her say, 'Could you please cause me to be overcome with extreme nausea.' "

"Sorry," I said.

"You should be."

Ah, sisters.

Sue turned to Dean. "So how's the new job?"

"Interesting," he said. "I'm liking it so far."

"What do these machines do, anyway?" asked Pagan.

"Tell you how much shit there is in a sample of water. Microbes have to breathe, so you measure their respiration and figure out your level of contaminant."

"I'm so glad I went to film school," said Sue. "I have no idea what you just said."

"They don't seem to work. Christoph keeps blaming the ignorant American workforce lacking proper respect for holy Swiss inventors in lab coats. I'll find out next week."

"Next week?" I asked.

"They're sending me to Houston on a service call Sunday night. Looks like it's time for a fresh set of coveralls."

"Pinstripe or herringbone?" I asked.

"Herringbone," he said. "More slimming."

Sue went out for a game of pool with some pals, and Dean wandered off to bed.

Pague and I decided to have one more beer before we went to sleep ourselves, after turning off the lights in the living room to stop the evil orange from searing further into our eyeballs.

Our lone streetlamp threw a soft glow in through the room's two windows, the fire escape's locked gate casting long skinny shadows across the ceiling.

"Tell me more about the kid," said Pagan, taking a sip of beer.

"His name was Teddy Underhill."

"So he's a distant cousin or something, right?"

"Might be. I mean, he's black."

"Which means maybe our family owned his family," she said. "Ouch."

"Doesn't rule out being related."

"Of course not. How'd he end up in the cemetery?"

"We don't know." I took a sip of my beer, then told her about the hotel by LaGuardia and how close Mrs. Underhill lived to Prospect.

"His mother told the cops she'd been out on a job interview," I said, "but Skwarecki doesn't believe it."

"Skwarecki?" asked Pague.

"The homicide detective chick."

"Why doesn't she believe the mother?"

"Says she looked like a crackhound."

"How big was the kid?"

I held my hand about six inches above the surface of the coffee table, and Pague shivered.

"I'm kind of struck by something," I said.

"What?"

"How you and I immediately blamed the boyfriend. Nobody else did — Sue and Dean, Cate this afternoon."

"How 'bout the cop?"

"Skwarecki's totally down with the boyfriend angle. I could just tell. But it being my default response freaked her out a little."

Pagan shrugged. "That's just our life."

"Stepfathers, sure," I said. "But I got spanked *once.* Mom and Michael were having a dinner party and I kept stomping my feet on the mattress and chanting 'Fee fi fo fum' really loudly for an hour after they'd put me to bed."

"I would've thrown you out the window."

"Right? I mean, it's not like we were beaten, ever."

"No."

"Or, you know, *molested.*"

Pagan didn't say anything.

After a few seconds the quiet took on a scary gravity.

My little sister took another swallow of beer.

I was cold all of a sudden. That creeping chill I'd felt back in the cemetery, when Skwarecki described the last time Teddy had been seen alive. I looked down to see all the little hairs on my forearms standing straight up.

"Pague?"

"That whole thing with Pierce," she said.

"*What* whole thing with Pierce?"

"I told you about it."

"I'd totally remember you telling me anything to do with that stupid pompous arrogant sorry-ass piece-of-shit skeevy *butt-*head," I said.

My sister scootched her back down against the sofa, nestling her head into the top of a nubby-tweed pillow. She hooked a big toe under the coffee table to pull it closer, then stretched her bare feet across its surface.

A lone car swept past in the street below.

I turned sideways to face her, hugging my knees to my chest.

She looked up at the ceiling. "It's weird."

"What's weird?"

"That you don't know," she said. "I could've sworn I told you years ago."

19

I could've sworn I told you years ago.

Maybe thirty seconds elapsed after my sister said that — half a minute during which pretty much every nuance of Pagan's and my entire childhood crashed through my head.

I was eleven when Pierce moved into our house. Pagan was nine and a half. Mom split up with our dad in 1967, and with our brother Trace's father in '72.

Pierce came on the scene following her yearish-long stints dating a very sweet seventeen-year-old guy, then a newly divorced South African mathematician whose kids we played with on the weekends he had custody.

We were pretty cool with it all, frankly. The only still-married parents we knew were Mr. and Mrs. Neare, who knocked back highball glasses of vodka-spiked green Hi-C from 7 A.M. onward, every day.

By the time the schoolbus returned their kids they could barely maneuver the Victrola's needle onto their next bullshit-Republican Mantovani record.

All the other moms hung out in each other's kitchens, half of them with toddlers in their laps. They laughed over coffee or glasses of wine, comparing notes on the vagaries of vanished men and the fifties myths they'd been raised believing the worth of: monogamy or the rhythm method or the Stock Exchange.

That was the surface of things. The version Mom told at cocktail parties back east, illustrating how much better everything was now that we'd abandoned Long Island for California.

Mom didn't talk about how there was never enough money, or how bright the kitchen lights seemed in the middle of the night as she emptied ice trays into a dishtowel to soothe some other mother's black eye or bruised throat.

They'd tiptoe back outside to lift sleeping children tenderly from some broken-down station wagon's backseat, the blankies still clutched in tiny fists, fat cheeks flushed with the warmth of footie pajamas.

Like I said, most of the time we were pretty cool with that life, me and Pagan.

But we got out as early as we could. I scored a scholarship to Mom's boarding school, and Pagan was treated to a year in Switzerland by her godmother.

I was fleeing the miserable daily grind of Pierce in our house, but I never imagined he had anything to do with my sister's exodus.

I was the kid he hated: the bitch, the smart-ass, the "put-down queen."

The man enjoyed playing favorites, telling me I was fat and ugly compared to my lithe, dark-haired mother and sister.

I'd envied my sister, the beloved child: Pagan-the-graceful, Pagan-the-good. The kid who'd never blurt out a sharp phrase, unable to resist the sheer snapping delight of the words in her mouth.

She was not a constant, involuntary, green-eyed-blonde reminder of Mom's first husband and his utter indifference to our financial upkeep.

Pierce lived in our house for five years. He gave Mom $150 a month, and pointedly begrudged every single lightbulb, chicken thigh, paper towel, bowl of cereal, or gallon of gas that money purchased.

He'd paid goddamn child support to two goddamn ex-wives, and he was goddamned if he'd pick up the slack for any deadbeat asshole who didn't fucking care enough about his own goddamn kids to make sure they went to school with goddamn shoes on their goddamn feet.

Unless it was something for Pagan.

But I'd gotten it totally, utterly wrong: the premise underlying everything I remembered.

And I should have known,
I should have known,
I should have fucking well <u>known</u>.

I flashed on an afternoon when I was thirteen or so, sitting in the backseat of Mom's car.

She was up front behind the wheel, Pierce riding shotgun beside her.

We were parked in someone's driveway, picking Pagan up after a friend's slumber party.

The three of us watched a dozen ten-year-old girls stumble out of the house one by one, clutching rolled-up pastel sleeping bags and little pink or purple overnight cases.

And as each downy-armed, bare-legged child walked past us to climb into a parent's car, Pierce pronounced judgment, in his plummy community-theater drawl, on whether or not she was a nymphette.

I just kept seeing that afternoon in my head while Pagan spoke on the sofa, next to

161

me in the present.

She told me about the time he'd French-kissed her when she was eleven, the time he'd pressed his hard-on against her leg and asked her if she liked the way a real man felt.

I asked her if she'd told Mom about that, or about the time we got left with him for a long weekend, when Pagan said she'd fallen asleep in their bed after we'd all been watching TV together, and Pierce woke her up by sticking his hands between her legs.

"I told her all of it," she said, taking another sip of beer.

"What the hell did she say?"

"It was a pretty bizarre conversation, actually."

"Like how?"

"Well, she started out being all Mama-Bear protective, but only right at first, then it felt like she was tuning in and out, changing her mind."

"Changing her mind about what?"

"About whether what I told her had actually happened," said Pagan.

"Wait a minute. Mom thought you made this *up?*"

"It was a long conversation."

"I don't care how fucking long it was — that's completely insane. I mean, your kid

162

comes to you and tells you something this awful . . . *Jesus.*"

"I don't mean she accused me of lying, more like I had to keep trying to convince her, and the longer we talked, the more she didn't believe me. Or maybe didn't want to believe me? It got . . . slippery. She was sliding away from it, in her head. From me. By the end of the conversation I felt like she was completely gone, and I still wanted to pin her down, make her say 'Yes, I understand that this really happened, and it was wrong and I'm angry enough to do something about it.' "

"Did she?" I asked.

"No."

"So what happened? How did it end?"

"She got pissed at me, asked why I had to be such a drag and concentrate on the negative stuff, and then she wouldn't talk about it anymore."

I gripped my empty beer bottle tighter, wanting to throw it across the room. Or at our mother. "When was this?"

"A few years ago," she said. "I was in college."

"Have you guys talked about it since?"

"I've tried a couple of times, but it seems pointless. Besides being painful. The fact that she's so squirrelly about it is horrible."

"Squirrelly how?" I asked.

"Like, she's actively choosing not to believe it, but won't say 'You're lying' to my face, because then I could call her on it."

"And she still hangs out with him," I said. "Every time she goes back to California."

"Right. And then she's gotta *tell* me about it, you know? All bubbly about how much fun it was, having dinner with Pierce and his new wife or whatever, and expecting me to be chipper and shit. I mean, this is like — if somebody had *stabbed* me, would she still be going to *parties* with him?"

I scooted my feet over to her, pressing my toes against her hip.

I'd spent vast amounts of time and energy despising Pierce Capwell, never once realizing how tremendously fortunate I was that he'd loathed me from the moment we met.

"Pagan, I am so goddamn sorry," I said, my anger on her behalf so fierce that I burst into tears.

20

We hugged each other good night around one, and I lay in bed for hours wondering whether I owned anything worth pawning for a plane ticket west so I could bludgeon Pierce into a flat bloody slick of pulp with the rounded end of a ball-peen hammer.

I remembered him needling Mom about how spoiled we were until he'd coerced her into giving us more household chores. In any other household that would have in and of itself been perfectly fair.

It was the way he gloated about it, sitting on at the kitchen table every night during my week to do the dishes, long after everyone else had left to go watch TV, for instance. He'd take a seat out of my direct line of sight, drawling on and on about "what a tiger your mother is in bed," then have the gall to complain when I rushed through the task, neglecting to clean bits of food out of the strainer in the bottom of the sink.

He'd fish the slimy dregs out with his fingers, calling Mom back into the room so he could shove them in her face to underscore my brazen disrespect for the moral worth of a job well done.

But as vain and cruel and depraved as he'd been — with his ridiculous pompadour and his skinny legs and his too-carefully-kept Vandyke beard — we kids were still better off than Teddy Underhill.

Pierce had splashed me with constant vitriol, he had molested my sister, but he hadn't killed us.

I thought of Teddy's shattered bones, and I knew that in the greater scheme of things my siblings and I could count ourselves lucky.

Our mother had chosen a lover who was merely vicious, repellent, and morally bankrupt. She hadn't trusted our welfare to a man who wanted us dead.

It took every ounce of moral fiber in my being to drag my ass out of bed the following morning. Dean had already sprinted uptown to meet Christoph. I was still on the early shift at the Catalog, which meant I was supposed to be in midtown by seven-fifteen.

Sue had another hour to sleep in, and Pagan more than that because she wasn't on the work roster that day.

The inhumanity of the hour struck me as supremely sucky vindictiveness on the part of the entire universe. I tossed back pint-the-second of my signature "light sweet crude" Café Bustelo following a blistering shower that had done nothing to resurrect so much as a shred of my mental acuity.

I slapped on my Walkman headphones and cued up some Mozart, hoping to quell the sour burn of unrequited rage in my belly. Maybe if Astrid didn't go to Rome she could spot me a ticket to California. I wouldn't need any luggage, just a nice fat Louisville Slugger as a carry-on.

I was not now nor had I ever been a morning person, but I was even more grateful than usual that Manhattan so rarely called upon me to endure extemporaneous gouts of A.M. chirpiness from my fellow commuters. Had any cheerful misguided tourists offered me so much as a flicker of cornfed-Rotarian eye contact on the Fourteenth Street uptown 4-5-6 platform that morning, I would've gripped them firmly by the necks of their *EVITA/CATS/MISS SAIGON* sweatshirts and body-slammed them headfirst onto the third rail, then pissed on their respective

167

pointy green souvenir-foam-rubber-Statue-of-Liberty halos to ensure adequate electrical conductivity.

It was, in short, already shaping up to be what Pagan's Greek college flatmate, Marilli, referred to as "one of those don't-fuck-me days."

Yong Sun was the only other person in our half of the office for the initial two hours, and as we were backed up in Fulfillment with a humongous new shipment of books from Baker & Taylor, I manned the phones solo.

This turned out to be a good thing. Barring one pissed-off Quebecois who deeply resented my having suggested the works of Robertson Davies in response to her request for a reading list of "Canadian literature," the people calling in that morning were universally hip and funny and courteous.

By nine o'clock the Bustelo had fully kicked in and I was yakking it up with a noir-fan insomniac on Maui.

I'd just talked the guy into a copy of Charles Willeford's *Cockfighter.*

"What else should I get?" asked my new sleep-deprived buddy in Lahaina.

"Have you tried any Jim Thompson?" I asked.

"Throw me a couple of titles," he said. "I

never remember authors."

"Well, off the top of my head: *Pop. 1280, The Killer Inside Me, Texas by the Tail, A Hell of a Woman* —"

"And you like this guy, ya?"

"Pinkie swear," I said. "Thompson kicks *major* pulp ass."

My Maui pal and I settled on five Black Lizard reissues.

"You're gonna love this guy, I promise," I said, closing out the order. "He's 'the Dimestore Dostoyevsky.' "

Not to mention the perfect guy to emcee my next family reunion.

Around eleven-thirty I called Cate about meeting up that afternoon.

When we'd hung up, Yumiko pointed at my phone. "Some *other* psycho white bitch wants you. Line two."

She lit a Marlboro, fairly dripping with disdain.

I picked up, only to get an earful of same from the other end.

"Madeline," said Astrid, "what sort of *odious* persons have you been forced to consort with at your horrible little job?"

"Ruffians. Trollops."

"That snippy little bitch put me on *hold*."

"And are we having a jolly time this morning, on the H.M.S. *Feudalism*?"

"Oh, bugger *off*," she said.

"Cool," I said, hanging up.

Line one lit up again, instantly.

"Don't fucking look at *me*," said Yumiko.

I lifted the receiver. "You've reached the offices of *honi soit qui mal y pense.* How may I abase myself indulging your slightest imperial whim?"

"Kiss my ass," said Astrid.

"Oh, like you *have* one, scrawny bitch."

That made her laugh. "Chrissy wanted me to invite you and Dean out to Southampton this weekend."

I crossed my fingers behind my back, having despised all things Hampton since toddlerhood. "And we're so very pleased to accept your kind invitation."

"You *do* have a car somewhere?"

"In Locust Valley."

"How the mighty are fallen."

"Ah," I said, "but how the tiny are risen."

"Camilla says kiss-kiss."

"Goody gumdrops. Tell her I want my fucking nose back."

"You'll have the whole weekend to tell her yourself, Madeline. We're driving out together right now."

O joy. O rapture.

"Please God," I said, "let me have some

170

Percodan left."

"What?"

"I merely said, '*Poor* Antonini, all by himself in Rome.' "

"Mad. Uh. *Line.*"

"Sweetie, please," I said. "You *know* my lips are sealed."

Astrid didn't seem to find comfort in this assertion.

"Some things are sacred," I continued. "I mean, good *God,* woman, we *prepped* together."

This time she hung up on me.

Southampton. *Fuck.*

Cate had copied out Mrs. Underhill's home number for me. I pulled the slip of paper from my pocket and started dialing.

21

Two hours later, I was on a sidewalk outside Jamaica Station scrutinizing the passing traffic for Cate's car, still thinking about the coming weekend with Astrid.

I had been *so* not kidding about the Percodan.

Here's how much I hate all things Hampton: if someone told me "You're getting five root canals, followed by lunch at the Maidstone Club," I'd hoard the anesthesia so I could shoot it up all at once in the ladies' room, hoping to black out face-first into my lobster salad.

And Southampton specifically? The place was downright feral, an overpriced Trump-skanky trailer park peopled exclusively by Dobermans with the Hapsburg lip.

The prospect of girding my social loins for two full days of *The Astrid and Cammy Show* would've been excruciating in the happiest of times: forty-eight hours of gossip about people I didn't know and places I couldn't afford, larded with inside-joke punchlines in all the latest slang of languages I didn't happen to speak.

Coming right on top of the one-two-punch revelations about Teddy and Pierce, it might just kill me. And I'd have to gut my way through it with a smile on my face because Dean needed the job, and we both needed his fucking paycheck.

I stepped back from the edge of the curb when a car that wasn't Cate's pulled up right in front of me.

The passenger window slid down and I heard a woman call out, "Yo, Madeline."

My ride was Skwarecki.

"Is Cate okay?" I asked, worried.

"She's fine, I just thought she looked a little busy so I offered to come instead."

Skwarecki's radio kept bleeping and squawking as we drove toward Prospect, interspersed with rough voices speaking in snatches of numerical code.

"How's tricks?" I asked.

"Mrs. Underhill identified Teddy's sneaker this morning."

"I know," I said. "She invited me over for tea, later."

"That poor woman," said Skwarecki.

"It's hard to tell whether finally knowing a child is dead would be even sadder, or come as a relief, you know?"

Skwarecki slowed for a red light. "From what I've seen it's both. A *lot* of both."

"Does she know about Teddy's life, what happened before he died?" I asked.

"We haven't discussed it with her yet. It's hard to predict what will happen once she knows — if she doesn't already."

"She had to know."

Skwarecki shrugged. "Even if she did, the question is what she's willing to do about it. Sometimes a death like this fractures a family's loyalties; sometimes it makes them pull closer together."

"And sometimes it makes everyone go *la-la-la-la-la* with their fingers stuck in their ears."

Skwarecki looked over at me and raised an eyebrow, not saying a thing.

Smart woman.

Had Mom really not suspected anything about Pierce back when Pagan and I were kids?

I crossed my arms. "But so far do you think she had any idea?"

"Doesn't sound like it. But Teddy's mother came to live with her when she was nine years old. Mrs. Underhill raised her

174

after that."

"What's his mother's name?"

"Angela," said Skwarecki.

"And what happened to Angela's mother?"

"Shot to death," said Skwarecki. "By a boyfriend."

"Jesus."

"Bad shit. Angela'd seen her mother get the crap beat out of her for years by a string of different guys, then had to watch her die."

"Were most child abusers abused themselves?" I asked.

"Sure," she said.

"I mean, you guys see a lot of this, right?"

"But you know what? *Not* everyone who was hurt as a kid grows up to hurt other children. Most people don't — even the ones who suffered the most appalling, scariest kinds of physical damage imaginable."

Skwarecki hit the turn signal and checked her mirrors, then pushed the wheel left to cut across traffic. "I'm not saying personal history won't fuck with your head, but you raise your hand to a child? That's on *you*. It's *not* inevitable. It's *not* a virus that gets handed down. It's a *choice*."

She slowed down, waiting for a gap in the oncoming cars, then gunned it for the shade of Prospect's shattered lane.

"I think it's worse to do it if you've known pain yourself," I said. "I have no fucking sympathy for the people who grow up to pass it on."

She nodded, and we pulled to a stop in front of the gate.

I played with the door handle but didn't move to get out.

Skwarecki put the car in Park and stepped on the emergency brake. She rested both hands back on top of the steering wheel.

"Like I said yesterday, you seem to know the drill," she said.

"Compared to a kid like Teddy? I know *nothing*."

Skwarecki turned her head toward me. "There's a lotta territory between *Father Knows Best* and 'beat to death by a crack junkie.' "

"No shit," I said.

"Maybe we've both got reasons why this hits home."

"It's, like, I saw cracks in the surface of things when I was a kid. The kind that get bigger and bigger until really bad shit starts leaking in, filling the void."

"Sure," she said.

"Not just in my family," I continued, "but everyone's around me, growing up. I wanted to fix it. I wanted to make it *stop*."

176

She opened her door but didn't get out. "A lot of people decide to be cops out of feeling like that."

" 'Protect and serve.' "

"You ever think about it, going on the job when you grew up?"

"Nope." I opened my door and we both climbed out of her car.

Skwarecki looked at me across its roof. "So what *did* you want to be?"

"Same thing as now," I said. "Batman."

She cracked up. "How's that working out?"

"Three more boxtops, they're mailing my cape."

We helped Cate drag some more brush-filled bags out to the sidewalk.

"Dude," I said, "you cut all this yourself? You're a *machine*."

"It's the steroids," she said. "And possibly the Geritol."

"Sign me up," said Skwarecki. "I could use a good boot in the ass."

We stood in the shade surveying Cate's handiwork.

"Find anything else?" asked Skwarecki.

"Six bottles," said Cate. "Five Olde English 800s and a pint of nasty-looking bourbon."

"You have the sneaker," I said to Skwarecki. "What else are we looking for?"

"I wish I knew," she said.

"What if there *is* nothing else?" asked Cate. "What happens then?"

Skwarecki looked toward the chapel. "You got any more of those Chips Ahoy rattling around?"

"Half a package, out in my car," said Cate, but she didn't look like she was in any big hurry to go fetch them.

"You mind if I take a few?" asked Skwarecki. "I missed lunch and I'm starting to feel a little peaky."

Cate said, "Detective," and paused, looking like she was about to say something serious.

"Yes ma'am?"

Cate exhaled. "Nothing. I'll get the cookies."

We followed her out to the street.

Cate opened the back door of her car and reached inside to pull a Foodtown bag across the seat toward us. She stood up, blue package in hand. "Would either of you like any water?"

Skwarecki said no and I added, "I'm good, thanks."

Cate closed the door and handed over the Chips Ahoy.

Skwarecki dove in and Cate watched, brow furrowed.

"Cate," said Skwarecki through a mouthful of cookie, "something's bugging you."

"I just can't stop thinking about that poor little boy."

Skwarecki swallowed. "Understandable."

"The idea that whoever did this is going to get away with causing his death . . . ?" said Cate, her voice trailing off.

Skwarecki took another bite.

I waited until she'd finished chewing. "It's going to be the mother's word against the boyfriend's, isn't it?"

"Is there *any* way to tell which of them did this?" asked Cate.

Skwarecki shook her head and folded the top of the bag carefully closed. "With what we have now? No."

"If we'd found him sooner?" asked Cate.

"There might have been something pointing to one of them, with an autopsy. But even so, best we can hope for now is the pathologist estimating Teddy's age at the time of a specific fracture, based on the way the bones healed. Maybe that rules out the boyfriend. Maybe not."

"But there's no way to tell who broke them in the first place," I said.

"Madeline," said Skwarecki, "we may not

179

even be able to establish the cause of death."

"His rib cage . . ." I said.

Skwarecki shook her head. "All we know is he didn't live long enough for those bones to heal. But the ribs might have been broken postmortem."

"Is there enough evidence to arrest someone?" asked Cate. "The mother, or the boyfriend, or both?"

"Getting there," said Skwarecki. "I'm waiting on one more thing."

There was a strange little *Star Wars*–sounding warble from her general vicinity.

"Beeper," she said, moving her jacket aside to peer down at her hip. "I have to go back to the station for a bit."

By the way Cate was gnawing on her bottom lip, we both wanted to grab Skwarecki by her beige-clad shoulders and start screaming "What? What 'one more thing'?" while shaking her back and forth hard enough to make her eyes rattle.

"Skwarecki," I said, *"spill."*

The detective gazed down at the sidewalk. "Look, I need to get my tail to the One-Oh-Three. How long'll you guys be here?"

Cate checked her watch. "Two hours."

"I told Mrs. Underhill I'd come over," I said. "But could I hitch a ride with you out to Locust Valley, Cate?"

Cate nodded and Skwarecki wolf-whistled. "Locust Valley. Aren't *we* fancy with the schmancy."

"I need to see a barn about a car," I said.

It didn't seem like the appropriate moment to mention that the car was a Porsche, that I needed it to drive to Southampton for the weekend, or what had happened between me and its previous owner before I discovered that he'd willed it to me.

I mean, I felt like Skwarecki was only just starting to like me, and it was, indeed, a *very* long story.

Skwarecki got into her own car and took off.

"Would you like to come with me, to Mrs. Underhill's?" I asked Cate.

"That poor woman, Madeline. I don't know if I could bear it."

"I'm sorry to ditch you. Will you be okay alone?"

"It's fine, really," she said. "I've already been here all morning. Please tell Mrs. Underhill how sorry I am, and I'll see you in a couple of hours, all right?"

"Sure," I said, not wanting to go either.

22

Mrs. Underhill lived in the brick-faced left half of a two-family house on the kind of Archie Bunker block where each residence paired the neighbor's incongruous architectural whims side by side: Tudor versus Spanish, Flintstones versus Jetsons.

The cars on her street were old but proud: stalwart American models in tired colors, avocado and copper-fleck and harvest gold. Not a Honda in sight, just Big Three sedans and wagons so seventies-huge they seemed more suited to ship channels than parkways.

I slipped between the chrome bumpers of a gold Lincoln and a black Cadillac, thinking they must have required the aid of tugboats to park.

Mrs. Underhill's bricks were trapped in a loveless marriage with her neighbor's lumpy swirls of mouthwash-green stucco, but their shared front lawn was trimmed crew-cut neat. At the squeak of the gate latch, both sets of parlor curtains twitched: synchronized vigilance.

I rang the left-hand bell and waited while Mrs. Underhill disengaged what sounded like half a dozen dead bolts. She opened the still-chained door to peer out at me.

"Well hello, young lady," she said.

Her voice was warm and soft, but I could tell she'd been crying.

"Have I come at a bad time?"

"Not at all, dear," she said. "Just give me a second to get this chain off."

It was warm out, but she wore a thin cardigan over her housecoat, buttoned at the neck.

I heard a kettle's whistle from down the hall behind her. "There's my tea, ready. Would you like a cup?"

"That would be lovely," I said, following her into the kitchen.

She padded slowly toward the stove and turned off the burner. Her feet were tiny, shod in little pink slippers with satin bows on them.

Her kitchen floor gleamed, and there wasn't so much as a fingerprint on the old Wedgewood stove.

The room smelled of lemon Mr. Clean, the baking sheet of cookies set to cool atop a wire rack. Half the alphabet danced across the bottom of her icebox door: colorful plastic magnets scattered at toddler height.

How could a child have been harmed here? How could this place, this woman, have produced someone who'd do that, or even allow it?

She reached into a lower cabinet for a wicker-handled tray, placing it on the countertop. The effort made her breathe hard for a moment, hand pressed over her heart.

"Mrs. Underhill, are you all right?" I asked.

"It's the emphysema. Terrible thing — don't you ever mess with those cigarettes."

"I used to, but I quit."

"Do your best to *stay* quit, then," she said. "You don't want to get like this when you're my age. Hard enough to be an old lady when you *can* breathe."

She was so tiny, so thin.

"You look pretty good to me," I said. "A glamorous thirty-nine."

Mrs. Underhill smiled. "I like a bit of sweet talk. You may just get invited back here."

"In that case," I said, "now that I get a better look at you, you can't possibly be a day over thirty-*four*."

She smiled again, patting the tray. "I'll fix everything up on this, then we can go sit

184

down in the front room."

I didn't know how the hell to ask her whether she'd known about the abuse, but whatever Teddy had suffered, the damage couldn't have been inflicted by those frail, palsied hands.

Would Skwarecki even want me to ask?

This wasn't some podunk town, and NYPD territory didn't strike me as any kind of place for amateurs.

While our tea steeped in its rose-adorned pot, she placed a doily on a matching plate before piling it high with warm cookies. "Do you take cream or sugar?"

I said, "No, thank you," because her hands were already tired enough to make the teacups chatter against their saucers.

"Let me carry that for you, please," I said. "You just lead the way."

I followed her into the living room, placing the tray on her coffee table alongside a bowl brimming with cellophane-wrapped hard candy.

Mrs. Underhill turned on the lamps at either end of her camelback sofa, their frilly-tutu shades perched atop ceramic ballerinas. She sat down slowly on the center cushion, knees creaking a bit.

I didn't know how to restart the conversation, not wanting to mention what she must have been told by the police this morning.

There was a honey-colored upright piano in the corner with a book of hymns in its music rack and a row of framed photos across the top. I walked over to look at them, still at a loss for something to say.

I touched the first frame, gold-leaf with clusters of grapes at each corner. It held a wedding portrait: Mrs. Underhill in a froth of veil and a square-shouldered white satin dress, hair rolled Andrews Sisters–high above her forehead. She was smiling up at a slender man in uniform, her hand resting gracefully against his left breast pocket, just beneath a row of medal ribbons.

"That's my Edward," she said. "One week home from the war."

"You look wonderful together — so happy."

"We *were* happy, for all the years we had. I lost him very young."

"I'm so sorry."

The next two portraits were of young women in mortarboards and graduation robes, one hairdo sixties Jackie-Camelot, the next eighties Jheri curl.

Smiling. Full of promise.

"My daughter and granddaughter — Alicia and Angela."

"Angela is Teddy's mother?" I wasn't even

186

sure what tense to use.

"She is. When my Alicia passed, Angela came to live with me."

The final frame held another color portrait, a chubby little boy grinning as he sat on Santa's lap.

Teddy, named for Edward.

"Come sit down now," she said, "before your tea gets cold."

I perched on the edge of a velvet side chair and reached for my cup.

Mrs. Underhill sat demurely, thin legs crossed at the ankles.

I missed my mother suddenly, knowing she would have brightened the room with pleasing chatter.

Mrs. Underhill lifted her own tea, cup trembling. She took one dainty sip and brought it to rest in her lap again.

I cleared my throat. "Your house is lovely. Have you lived here a long time?"

"Forty years," she said.

"Did you get to pick out the brick, on the outside?"

"The family before us did. I've always liked it, though."

"I have to admit I like it better than your neighbor's choice."

"That *green!* Can you imagine?"

"Minty fresh," I said, and she smiled at me.

"That was Gladys, all over — she liked things lively. Her two boys live there now."

"It must be nice, knowing your neighbors."

"Sometimes they play their music a mite loud," she said, "but they keep the yard so neat, and always shovel the walk in winter. They're fine young men."

"Did you grow up in Queens?"

"Born and raised. My family has been in New York for a long time."

"Mine too," I said.

"Which part of the state?"

"Here on Long Island, a little further out."

"The way you speak, I wouldn't have picked you for Queens."

"I grew up in California, mostly," I said, "but I was born here. My mother's family settled in Oyster Bay. My father's started out in Brooklyn, I think."

"Edward's people were from Brooklyn. Well, of course we were cousins, somehow. *My* grandmother's maiden name was Underhill, too."

I looked down into my teacup. "It's an old name, on Long Island."

"You're interested in local history?" she asked.

"My sister and I used to spend part of the summer back here every year. My grandfather loved talking about that kind of thing."

"So he shared his knowledge with you. That must have been wonderful."

Actually, I'd written him off as a snob with a death fetish, fonder of expired relatives than those above ground. But he'd planted a morbid note in me, all the same, one that ramped up to full Bach-gothic fugue when during high school and college my history teachers started outlining our ancestors' specific exploits.

"Is that what brought you to the cemetery?" asked Mrs. Underhill. "An interest in genealogy?"

I nodded, not wanting to burden her with my guilt over familial Indian massacres, slave-holding, and the possibility that she and I were cousins.

In pondering that, I'd let the conversation coast to a speechless halt again.

"Please, have a cookie," she said.

I glanced at Teddy's picture and couldn't imagine eating anything, but it would've been rude to refuse so I picked the smallest one.

"You're very kind to have invited me here," I said. "This can't be an easy time."

189

I took a bite of cookie. It was delicious — brown sugar and butter crumbling on my tongue.

Mrs. Underhill looked down at her tea. "The police called me this morning. With the news."

"Yes ma'am." The cookie broke in my hand. "Detective Skwarecki told me. I'm so very sorry."

"It's better to know. Hard as it is, it's better I don't have to wonder anymore."

I examined my shards of cookie, wishing I could produce words of comfort.

"You're married, dear?" she asked.

"Yes."

"Any children of your own?"

"Not yet."

"It changes you, having a child," she said. "When I married Edward, it was as though he and I shared the same heart. But when you have a child . . . ? A little piece of your heart — the most important part — ventures out into the world."

"That sounds scary," I said.

"Yes, but at the same time *wonderful*."

Mrs. Underhill's assertion was belied by her lingering glance down the piano's row of photos.

"About what happened," I said. "Mrs. Underhill, I wanted to ask . . ."

190

But I couldn't finish the question. Those picture frames contained three pieces of heart she'd never get back: her husband, her daughter, and Teddy. Skwarecki was even now drawing a bead on the fourth piece, the last: Teddy's mother, the only living member of Mrs. Underhill's family.

She looked from the photographs to me. "Yes, dear?"

"I'm sorry."

I slipped the bits of cookie into my pocket. I didn't want to offend my hostess, but there was no way I could have swallowed anything else.

I looked into her haunted eyes and then away, afraid I might start crying.

"Miss Dare," she said, "Madeline . . ."

"Yes ma'am?"

She raised one quivering hand to her throat. "There's something I want to ask *you*. A favor."

"Please. Anything."

"I hoped you might tell me anything you can remember about finding Teddy. Anything at all."

I was quiet, not sure what exactly she wanted to know.

"If it's too much for you, talking about it . . ." she said.

"No ma'am. It's just that I don't know if I

can tell you anything that would be helpful."

"I don't mean about the investigation. I just mean how he *was,* when you found him. I've been lying awake so many nights now, worried about him being lost and alone. Scared. Hurt."

She was sitting up so straight, tears gathering against her lower lashes.

I understood, then, what she wanted.

"He was tucked inside a little thicket," I said, "resting on a bed of soft leaves, right next to another child's gravestone."

She closed her eyes and brought a fist up to her mouth, shoulders hunched forward.

"There was an angel carved into that stone," I said. "A little cherub with the sweetest face."

I slipped down out of my chair and moved across the floor toward her, on my knees. "Teddy was at peace, Mrs. Underhill. I know he was."

She lifted her head, tears sliding down her cheeks.

"Thank you," she said.

I sat down at her feet and gave her a napkin from the tea tray before taking her hand lightly in mine.

We stayed like that for a long time. Everything quiet but for the rasp of her breathing, the echoing tick of her front-hall clock.

"You had a question," she said at last. "What was it?"

"It wouldn't be right of me to ask you, not today."

"Today's grief will last as long as I do, undiminished. I won't take it as any unkindness if you speak your mind."

She wrapped my hand in both of hers.

I dropped my eyes, still trying to find the words.

This woman brought you here. She came to Prospect and found you because she wants this conversation to happen. She wants you to ask what she knew, so she can finally tell someone.

"Mrs. Underhill," I said, "I want to ask about Teddy."

Her hands tightened around mine.

"You had to know he was being abused."

"I knew," she said.

"Did you try to stop it?"

"Yes," she said, tears coursing down her tiny face. "I tried so hard."

She closed her eyes and took in a sharp, shallow breath, all the slender volume her lungs could bear. When she exhaled this wisp of air, her grief shaped it into a threnody of devastation. It was the most pitiable, pain-stricken sound I'd ever heard, and one I hope never to hear again.

"He was just a *baby,* and he suffered so," she said.

I wrapped my arms around her fragile torso, feeling her go slack against my chest as she wept.

"God forgive me," she whispered. "I didn't try hard *enough.*"

I stroked her hair, pressing her head gently down onto my shoulder.

Eyes closed, I thought of Pagan, and Mom, and the time I'd cradled a drowned pheasant chick in my hands, warming its down while it died.

I was standing halfway down Mrs. Underhill's front three steps, the tin of cookies she'd packed for me tucked under my left arm, my right hand still cradled gently in both of hers.

"I hope you'll come back," she said, giving me a peck on the cheek, our height made even by the step between us.

"I will. And please call me if you need anything. Or to talk."

"Thank you, dear," she said, releasing my hand.

She shivered once and pulled the thin cardigan closer around her shoulders, buttoning it down to the hem before turning to walk back inside.

I listened to all her locks being clicked and slid carefully back into place between us, then turned toward the street.

I let myself out through the little gate in the yard's hip-high chain-link fence and latched it securely behind me.

Just in case Mrs. Underhill was looking, I waved one more good-bye toward her living-room window.

The spyhole-gap in her neighbor's lace curtains twitched shut behind glass grown milky with a watcher's breath.

23

"Teddy Underhill was already in the system," said Skwarecki back at Prospect.

"*Which* system?" asked Cate.

"Child Welfare," said Skwarecki. "There was a report of abuse three months before he was killed."

"By Mrs. Underhill?" I asked.

She shook her head. "A neighbor."

A stranger.

I looked down at the brown grass, weary and disappointed.

"Someone out by LaGuardia?" asked Cate.

"Brooklyn," said Skwarecki. "Angela Underhill and her boyfriend had an apartment in East New York — third-floor walk-up in a brownstone. They moved in together when Teddy was around six months old."

"So how did they end up in a welfare motel in Queens?" asked Cate.

"My best guess is they were avoiding Teddy's caseworker."

"*And* the neighbor?" I asked.

Skwarecki nodded. "They knew who'd called it in. Ms. Keller."

"Who?" asked Cate.

"She lived directly below them. Keller called SCR, and SCR called ACS."

"Which stand for what?" I asked.

"Sorry," said Skwarecki. "First one's the Statewide Central Register of Child Abuse and Neglect. They run the hotlines, decide which reports get handed on to the Administration for Children's Services. If that happens, ACS sends someone out to the family within twenty-four hours."

"So did SCR hand it on?" I asked.

"Keller called the line for mandated reporters, so they took her seriously. She used to be an ER nurse."

"What's she doing now?" asked Cate.

"Chemo."

From Skwarecki's expression I knew she wasn't talking about a change in the woman's medical specialty. "How bad?"

"She had a double mastectomy two years ago. Last fall they found tumors in her lungs. Now it's her liver."

"So this is not only a woman who's professionally up to speed on the signs of abuse," I said, "but also one spending a great deal of time in her apartment."

Skwarecki nodded.

"Have you met with her yet?" asked Cate.

"By phone," said Skwarecki. "I'm going out to see her tomorrow. You guys remember Louise Bost?"

"The ADA chick with the girly shoes," said Cate.

"She'll be coming with me, to take Ms. Keller's statement."

"And her statement's the thing you need before you can consider making an arrest?" I asked.

"There's also a larger question of timing," said Skwarecki.

I leaned back against Cate's car. "How so?"

"Ms. Keller's in hospice."

Cate winced. "That ill, and she tried to save Teddy."

"This is one tough cookie," said Skwarecki. "She won't let them start her on a morphine drip until after she's given her statement. Said there was no way she wanted any question about whether she was compos mentis."

"How old is she?" I asked.

"My age," said Skwarecki. "Just turned forty-three."

"What about the caseworker?" I asked.

Skwarecki's eyes shifted back to mine. "I've spoken with her, too."

"And?"

She didn't answer me.

"Skwarecki," I said, "the woman gets a credible report that a little kid's getting the shit beaten out of him and she doesn't do *anything?*"

"She closed his file."

"She did *what?*" said Cate.

"Not immediately. She went to the apartment. Met with Teddy's mother, saw his injuries — old and new. Wrote it all up as a case of a child at 'High Risk.' "

"Which means?" I asked.

"It means the child protective specialist thought that Teddy's situation merited court involvement."

"That was the best she could do?" I asked.

"It's the secondary rating. If she'd written it up as 'Immediate Danger' he would have automatically been recommended for foster care," said Skwarecki.

"And why didn't she?" I asked.

Skwarecki shrugged. "Who knows. Her caseload, the wait for foster-care placements? There's a good chance it wouldn't have made any difference. The specialist may have had the best intentions in the world, but there's a sixty-day window —

they'd left the apartment before she came back."

I shook my head. "And she closed the fucking file."

"She couldn't track them down, so, yes, she closed the file," said Skwarecki.

I was livid. "When they were all of, what, ten miles away? In subsidized goddamn *housing?*"

Swarecki leaned back against her car, eyes closed.

"Come on," I said. "*Somebody* working for the City of New York in an official capacity had Angela's name. She wouldn't have had that motel room otherwise."

Skwarecki raised her hands up alongside her forehead so she could press the heel of each palm into its corresponding temple — hard. Her fingers stuck straight up, like antlers.

"Did anyone try contacting Mrs. Underhill?" I asked.

"ACS?" said Skwarecki, pissed off. "Don't get me fucking *started.*"

"I'm sorry," I said.

"My fault. I'm bitchy 'cause I missed lunch."

I put my hand on her arm. "Want a cookie?"

"What I'd *really* like's a couple aspirin,"

she said. "Maybe a boilermaker to wash them down."

"There's Excedrin in my glove compartment," said Cate. "But you're on your own for the booze."

Skwarecki gratefully swallowed two of the fat white pills with ice water instead.

"Listen," she said, "you guys are great. I appreciate all your help. Sorry I got pissy."

I shook my head. "You're working your ass off, Skwarecki, and I'm sitting here pestering you like I question your judgment."

"Thanks." The detective looked at her watch. "You guys need to hit the road, right?"

Cate consulted her own. "We do, yes. Especially if I need to drop you first, Maddie."

Before I climbed into the car I looked back at Skwarecki. "Hey, have you talked to Mrs. Underhill again since she ID'd the sneaker?"

"Not yet," she said.

"I'm thinking now might be a good time."

"What, you got her warmed up for me — good cop/bad cop?"

"Maybe good cop/good cop? She's a nice lady."

Skwarecki laughed, snapping me a salute.

201

■ ■ ■ ■

"A *Porsche?*" said Cate an hour later.

I'd just pulled the tarp off my car, and the low western sun was warming up its black exterior, winking yellow off the chrome.

We were standing inside my mother's friend Polly's old barn, just off Skunk's Misery Road in Locust Valley. There probably hadn't been so much as a Shetland pony stabled there since Kennedy Airport was called Idlewild, but it still smelled faintly of alfalfa and horse shit.

Not, in my opinion, bad smells.

Cate had her hands on her hips, a tad slack-jawed. "How much *do* they pay you at that catalog?"

"It was kind of free," I said.

"You were just minding your own business one day when you stumbled across an old brass lamp lying on the beach?"

"I, um, inherited it."

"*Still,*" she said. "The most I ever got was six fish forks and a chafing dish, from my great-aunt Julia."

"Cate, I can't even afford a full tank of gas for the damn thing."

"But you haven't sold it."

I shrugged. "I'd miss being able to come

out and visit."

"Do you ever actually drive it?"

"Mostly just run the engine. Check the tire pressure and the fluids."

"That's *all?*" she asked.

"Okay, so I confess to strewing the occasional handful of rose petals around. Lighting some incense."

"Good for you," she said. "It's beautiful. It deserves a little worship."

"It does, doesn't it?"

"So who left it to you? Any chance I'm related?"

"Just this guy," I said.

"Well, he obviously thought well of you."

"It's complicated," I said. "He was kind of an asshole, actually."

"You're driving it back into the city?"

"Yeah. We have to go to this work thing for my husband over the weekend, way the hell out on the island."

"Madeline, *promise* me you'll put it in a garage tonight."

"Cross my heart and hope to die, stick a needle in my eye."

"Can we just sit in it for a minute?" she asked.

"I bet the traffic still sucks on the expressway," I said. "Wanna go for a ride?"

I hadn't been out here for a month, but

the machine started right up with my favorite throaty growl, and I'd left some Allman Brothers cued up in the tape deck.

I turned to Cate. "Hey, d'you remember if there were any cars parked in front of the big house when we drove in?"

"Not a one," she said. "And I think there were dust-sheets over the furniture inside."

"Cool."

I turned up Duane and the boys as loud as they'd go and we hit seventy by the time we were halfway back down Polly's driveway.

It had just been that kind of day. And week.

We cut across Ludlam Lane and rocketed over to Bayville.

I sprang for a couple of ice-cold Manhattan Specials at the souvlaki place next to the mini-golf down on the strip before we swung back to Polly's barn via Shore Road and Mill Hill.

Cate climbed out, then leaned back in through the passenger window. "If I hear from Skwarecki I'll call you."

I said, "Back atcha," and watched her get behind the wheel of her own car. Her hair was sticking up and she still had a big dazed grin on her face.

I followed her sedately down the driveway, then waved and blew past her at the end, heading back for the city.

It was close to seven, but there must have been an accident on the LIE because even westbound 25A was still a nightmare. I switched over to the radio's AM band for a 1010 WINS traffic report, but turned it off when Tom Carvel's pitch for Fudgie the Whale ice-cream cakes segued into a Radio Shack ad so boring it made me yearn for Crazy Eddy shrieking about prices so low he was practically *giving* it all away.

I was stuck in second gear behind a truck full of lawn mowers. At every stoplight a chorus of late-season crickets rose above the grumble of our idling engines.

I didn't want to think about people dying of cancer or beating children to death, but my alternative was contemplating the abyss of Mom's having remained so nauseatingly chummy with Pierce Capwell.

Hard as that had been for me over the years, I couldn't begin to imagine how exponentially much more pain it must've caused Pagan.

I wondered whether she'd talked about what happened with anyone other than me and Mom — if Sue knew, or if Pague'd be

205

okay with me telling Dean.

And for the rest of the drive into the city I thought about this one summer afternoon in California, back when I was sixteen, a couple of months after Mom and Pierce had broken up while Pague and I were away at school.

Mom had started tentatively dating Fassett, a guy I rather liked, and she and I were doing the lunch dishes in the tiny kitchen of his condo while Pagan taught seven-year-old Trace how to play tennis on the complex's courts out back.

All of a sudden Pierce came bursting through the other man's front door and started running from room to room, screaming all kinds of horrible bullshit about Mom and how she'd betrayed him, which struck me as especially outrageous and pathetic since it turned out he'd been balling this ugly intern chick at the Forest Theater for at least a year before Mom had finally told him to move out.

She turned from the stove to face Pierce as he barreled through the kitchen doorway.

He hit her in the mouth once — hard — and everything seemed to slow way, way down.

I picked up a big-ass carving knife out of the sink, then turned around.

I raised it in my fist until he could see that I'd aimed the tip of its twelve-inch blade at his throat, then quietly suggested he get the hell away from my mother.

Pierce backpedaled out of the room on his little banty legs, then swiveled to sprint for the front door.

He must have known I'd walked out of the kitchen behind him, because he couldn't resist stopping for a moment on the welcome mat outside.

Hand on the doorknob, he turned back and looked me in the eye while he got in one last dig:

"If it wasn't for that knife, you little cunt, I would've knocked you flat."

24

Sue and Dean and Pagan were halfway through dinner by the time I'd found a cheap enough parking lot in the meat-packing district, but the burrito they'd brought me from Benny's was still warm.

Christoph had driven Dean back early from New Jersey, trying to beat the traffic out onto the Island so he'd make Southampton in time for dinner with Astrid and Cammy.

"Do you think we could drive out Saturday instead of tomorrow?" I asked. "The LIE was just a total fucking nightmare coming *this* way."

"Check with Astrid, I guess," he said.

I called her Upper East Side machine and made our excuses, knowing she was probably checking for messages hourly, as usual.

Sue looked at her watch. "Funny, she hasn't called *once* tonight — not even to interrupt dinner."

"She's hanging with this other friend," I said.

"I thought we'd successfully palmed her off on *La Bella Città Roma,*" said Pagan.

Dean shook his head. "Alas, Nutty Buddy didn't make it past the eastern tip of Lawn Guyland."

"Still," said Sue, "I live in hope."

"She's having a rough time, you guys," I said.

"My heart bleeds," said Pagan.

"I know," I said, "but she's still my friend."

"Madeline, why are you always friends with the crazy bitches?" asked Sue.

"Um, because I am one?"

"Right," she said. "I keep forgetting."

Pagan snapped her fingers and looked at me. "Hey, that reminds me. Your mother called."

"*My* mother?" I said. "I had her *last* month."

Pagan wadded up her burrito tinfoil and chucked it at my head. "She's driving down from Maine on Monday. With some new guy she wants us to meet."

"Gee," I said, "won't *that* be just fucking ducky?"

Pagan shrugged. "He's taking us to lunch at 'Twenty-one.' "

"Just you and me?" I asked.

209

Pagan waved a hand at Sue and Dean. "These guys, too, if they can get off work."

"I'll be in Houston," said Dean. "Shucks."

Sue said, "What are you, chicken?" and I made a couple of *bawk-bawk* noises at him.

"Definitely," said Dean, completely unfazed.

Saturday morning Dean and I ransomed the Porsche from the slaughterhouse garage and hit the road for the dreaded Hamptons. Even with the seat all the way back his knees were still up around his ears.

"So how bad is it out there?" asked Dean. "My experience is limited to Binghampton."

"It's heinous," I replied as we dropped down into the Midtown Tunnel. "Want a Percodan?"

"Maybe after lunch."

The traffic was totally fucked until practically Commack, which was a new low, even for me.

"Ah, Exit Fifty-two," said Dean. "Such memories . . ."

Having had twenty-four après-reception hours to kill before our wedding-trip flight for Switzerland two years earlier, we'd grabbed a bag of hamburgers at White Castle and spent our first married night on a freezing-cold waterbed at the Commack

Motor Inn.

"I still can't believe they gypped us out of that heart-shaped bathtub," I said, taking my hand from the gearshift to give him a couple of fond pats on the knee.

"If it gets really bad this weekend we can come back here for a late second-anniversary celebration."

"Fuck it," I said, "let's bail now. I bet they wouldn't even miss us."

"Can't," he said. "Christoph and I still have some technical shit to go over before Houston."

I sighed. Dean had been raised on a farm Upstate. Trust me, you do *not* want to get between a Methodist and his work ethic.

It had taken me three years to talk him into leaving his hometown. The fact that he was now pushing *me* to spend a weekend in the nether-belly of my own geographical heritage was a bit off-putting.

"We should go visit your parents," I said. "It's been months since they've seen you."

Dean laughed. "Good *God,* Bunny, they don't even have Szechuan."

"Pinko," I said as the traffic finally melted away before us.

Dean laughed harder.

I shifted up into fifth and floored it.

I hadn't told him about Teddy and Mrs.

Underhill, nor had he asked.

We wrestled with Christoph's directions, making several U-turns before finally stumbling upon a hedge-constricted dirt lane with a name that bore some passing resemblance to the actual word we'd been told to look out for.

I threaded the Porsche down it with care, trying to skirt the worst of the potholes without scraping against the branches on either side.

The house was a stark, thumpingly graceless mid-seventies saltbox pastiche clad in cedar shakes and plopped at the edge of a treeless meadow.

The new dorms all over again.

I turned off the engine just as Christoph appeared in the front doorway, looking genuinely pleased to see us.

Dean unraveled himself from the passenger seat. I reached into the backseat for our bags, setting them down in the driveway to retrieve a gift-offering of wine.

Christoph had come outside, so I stood up with the bottle in my hand to thank him so very much for his most kind invitation, et cetera, while we did the whole kiss-kiss routine.

The only thing I know about wine is that

it's a good idea to proffer all the cash in my pocket to a liquor store's most asymmetrically coiffed, Off Broadway–ready employee while humbly beseeching him or her to rescue my ignorant Rolling Rock–swilling American ass from potential Continental derision.

Christoph looked at the bottle in my hand and smiled. "How thoughtful of you, dear Maddie. Shall we have a glass once we've gotten you settled?"

He picked up our bags, overriding all protest on Dean's part. "Don't be silly — you must allow me the pleasure, as your host."

Christoph switched the bags to his left hand to give Dean a welcoming clap on the shoulder before leading us inside the house.

"I will just show you where you are to be sleeping," he said. "After which I should no doubt awaken Astrid and Camilla."

A large market clock in the front hallway gave the time as five minutes past two.

Christoph and Dean started up the stairs.

I dry-swallowed a Percodan and followed them.

25

"Camilla had these pills," said Astrid. "From some photographer in London. We weren't sure what they were."

"And you took them anyway," I said.

"Well, of course," she said.

She had nicotine-stain circles under her eyes and *still* looked like a Florentine Catherine Deneuve.

"Were they like, speed, or tranquilizers, or what?" I asked.

"They were blue," she said. "And we had some champagne, and then we got in the Jeep and drove out here. I don't remember much after the tunnel."

Cammy wandered into the front hall wearing very short shorts and a little tiny pink tank top and these stupid-ass knee-high Aspen-hooker cave-girl boots with shaggy blond fur on the outside. The rest of her pillow-creased face looked like haggard shit, but her plastic surgeon's homage to my nose was perfect.

"Did we go to a Chinese restaurant yesterday?" she asked Astrid, walking past me without a flicker of recognition.

Astrid pulled a crushed soft-pack of Marlboros out of her jeans. "You're hallucinating."

Cammy lifted a heavy silver lighter from the sideboard next to us, then took a cigarette from Astrid. They both lit up.

"Wait a minute," said Astrid, "did we have a scorpion bowl? I seem to remember floating gardenias and long straws."

Cammy shuffled away into the living room and fell into a chair, the motion tumbling ashes down the front of her shirt. "I can't *stand* scorpion bowls."

"Chrissy, did we come home with gardenias?" asked Astrid.

Christoph shook his head. "You were both sound asleep in the living room when I arrived."

"And what time was that?" she asked.

"Four o'clock, a little after."

Astrid turned toward Cammy. "Where's my coat?"

Cammy squinted. "It's over here, wadded up."

Astrid stalked across the room, saying "Aha!" when she picked up a football-sized jumble of rather fine tweed.

She shook it out and put it on. Though it was big on her and now looked like something a wet dog had slept in, the jacket was beautifully cut. I presumed it belonged to Christoph.

Astrid patted herself down, producing a crumpled piece of paper from her vest pocket.

"A receipt?" asked Christoph, amused.

Astrid arrayed herself along the sofa and turned on the nearest side-table lamp. Cammy winced at the light, flicking ashes onto the carpet at her feet.

Astrid smoothed out the piece of paper against her thigh, peered at it, then said, "Jesus *Christ!*"

"S'matter?" asked Cammy.

"We tipped those Chinese people four hundred and fifty-seven *bucks.*"

Cammy shrugged.

"On a forty-dollar *check,*" added Astrid.

Cammy stood and padded into the kitchen, returning with a bottle of mineral water.

I tried willing my stomach acid to get with the program and dissolve the damn Percodan, already.

"With a credit card?" asked Christoph.

"Sweetie," said Astrid, stroking his arm,

"your Amex."

He cleared his throat. "Perhaps you might ask them to reduce the charge."

She lowered her lashes to half-mast. "Darling, won't *you* do it? You're so good at that sort of thing."

"I'm afraid I have some business to discuss with Dean this afternoon," her husband replied, smiling but unmoved.

He led my spouse outside onto the living-room terrace.

Cammy yawned and looked at Astrid. "Let's just go. Get it over with."

Astrid pulled her sunglasses out of the tweed jacket's left pocket and put them on.

She and Cammy brushed past me and out the door as though I were the front-hall coat rack or something.

Still holding the stupid bottle of wine in my hand, I watched them climb into the smaller of the two Jeeps outside and speed away.

"Great to be here," I said. "And always such a pleasure to see both of *you.*"

Dean and Christoph appeared to be having a great time outside, so I set to work locating a corkscrew, a tray, and three wine-glasses.

I opened the bottle, put two glasses on

the tray and filled them halfway, celebrating my accomplishment by consuming a generously medicinal allotment of Côtes-du-Who-the-Fuck-Cares from glass number three.

"Trenchant," I decreed, "yet surprisingly perky-nippled."

I poured myself a refill, plopped it on the tray, and headed outside.

"Of course," Christoph was saying, "I suppose we must allow for the fact that these Americans whom one finds working in factories, and so on, they are not very well educated."

"One might find it impolitic to insist on that point, however," said Dean. "Particularly while in the field attempting to convince them that one's product has technical merit."

"Even so," said Christoph, "the people . . . they need a strong hand."

I polished off my second glass of wine.

Christoph turned to me. "Your husband, Maddie, he is *really* very smart about these things."

"Oh, yes," I said. "Quite."

I tried to sound nonchalant about it when what I really wanted to do was grab him by the shoulders and insist that my husband

218

was the smartest, most principled, hardest-working man he was ever likely to meet, much less employ — that Dean could build a house or a train car from scratch, had fixed my old VW Rabbit's dead engine with a Swiss Army knife and a Bic lighter when we got stranded in the rain the night of our second date, and that he was, moreover, equally at home discussing Goethe, the psychological function of shamans in rural Nepal, and the continuing impact of FDR's agricultural policy.

Instead I bit my tongue, trying to look intrigued with their discussion of biological oxygen demand and Teutonic lab protocols until enough time had passed that I could courteously excuse myself.

I rattled around inside the house, desperate for something to read. The only printed matter in the entire place was the previous July's *Town & Country,* which I took upstairs to our guest room.

In the old days I'd usually found a couple of people I knew in this publication, albeit vaguely: friends of my grandparents, or names that were familiar from my parents' tales of boarding school and deb parties back in the fifties. Now it might just as well have been the society gazette of Madagascar, or Pluto. Who the fuck were these people? And how the hell could they afford all the crap in these advertisements?

I didn't want to be them; I didn't even covet their stuff. I just couldn't compute the vertiginous gulf between these Jaguar and Bulgari and Harry Winston ads and my own continuing struggle to chip in on communal baba ghanoush delivery from Fourteenth Street.

My mother still danced on the verge of magazine world whenever the spirit moved her, but I lived in terror that the middle class's lowest rungs had long since been yanked up and away from her children: a rope ladder dangled from the basket of some hot-air balloon, above our reach, now gliding seaward.

How would the generations after me turn out if I couldn't scratch my way to safety in this one? Would my failure spawn another Teddy Underhill, or, worse yet, his mother?

Seven bucks an hour and my pompous ancestry felt like precious little armor against the abyss of either contingency.

But was money any protection when you got right down to it?

Of course not. Just look at the fucking Hamptons, not to mention the abundance of dangerous psychos still extant amongst my wealthier relatives.

It was another two hours before Astrid and her Sancho-Panzer returned from shaking down the Chinese restaurant, by which point I was standing at the kitchen counter poking the armful of meadow flowers I'd gathered into the neck of an empty milk bottle, stem by stem.

It had been either that or lighting the house copy of *Town & Country* on fire so I could stomp its ashes into the driveway gravel, shrieking with boredom.

All the Percodan in America could not sweeten this little weekend. And besides which, we'd run out of wine.

I'd turned on the kitchen lights, the sky long since tipped violet by burgeoning dusk, but Astrid still wore her sunglasses.

"Madeline Dare with a talent for the arrangement of *flowers*," she said. "Not something I'd ever have imagined."

"How'd it go with rescinding your tip?"

"They would *not* listen to reason," she said.

"Gee," I replied. "Bummer."

She twined a stem of Queen Anne's lace through her fingers. "I shouldn't have said anything in front of Chrissy. He hates it when I borrow his credit card."

"Actually, he seemed okay with it," I said.

She yawned, ignoring that. "I must go get changed."

"You look fine. The sunglasses are a tad over the top, but other than that —"

"For a *dinner* party."

"Here?"

"A friend's place, up the road."

"Well that's lucky," I said. "You're down to cocktail onions and Grey Poupon."

"Don't worry," she said. "The *real* season is over, of course, but I'm sure you and Dean can still find someplace to eat in town."

I stared at her, struck dumb as a cow.

"It would've been so awkward to have you tag along," she said. "They're not the sort of people you'd fit *in* with."

I wondered whether my old friend could've hurt me more had she just smashed my head through the kitchen wall, for sport.

The answer was a big fat no.

Her eyebrows rose from behind the dark glasses. "Oh, for God's sake . . . you're not going to *cry*, are you?"

Not for a second, if it fucking kills me.

"Maddie, don't be ridiculous."

"Jesus, Astrid." I looked away from her, crossing my arms. "I haven't been ditched since, like, fifth grade."

"The hostess was *already* upset because we're bringing Camilla."

I wanted to bolt from the room, to bury my head in my mother's lap, or, better yet, to hide behind winter coats and tennis racquets in a dark, distant closet, arms wrapped tight around my knees.

Cammy came back downstairs in a little black dress, trailing Marlboro ribbon clouds.

At least she'd changed out of the Flintstones footwear.

I pointed at her feet. "Much better."

She stared into space somewhere past my right shoulder, pupils dilated as hubcaps. "Better than what?"

"The boots," I said. "They looked like you'd skinned a litter of golden-retriever puppies. Way too Cruella De Vil."

"De Vil," said Cammy. "She does shoes?"

She sucked in a drag, cheeks hollow, then French-inhaled.

I shook my head. "Coats."

Cammy rounded her lips to exhale, wreathing my head in smoke. "Never heard of her."

"Quelle surprise."

She looked past me to Astrid. "Let's take that Porsche tonight. I *hate* Jeeps."

"The Porsche belongs to Maddie," said Astrid.

Cammy blinked, twice. "Who?"

Astrid hooked a thumb at me.

The nose-plagiarist bitch tapped ashes onto my toe. "How did *you* get a car like that?"

"I shot a man in Reno," I said, "just to watch him die."

Cammy blinked again. "You bore me. Tell Christoph we left."

She let her cigarette fall into the sink. I watched its ember hiss and go black.

26

Dean and I had finally found a pizza place after driving around for half an hour.

"God," I said as we took our seats inside, "that fucking *bitch.*"

Dean glanced around the room. "Given our current geographic coordinates, Bunny, I'm afraid you'll have to be more specific."

Our waiter glided to a halt well away from the table as though worried that some random observer might presume we were known to him.

"Have you reached a decision?" he asked.

"We have," I said.

He appeared to be fighting a rather powerful fluctuation in local gravity. Or just the inexorable magnetism of Caroline Kennedy, three tables over.

Under normal circumstances I have an abhorrence of taking out my shitty day on waitstaff, having worked too many horrible restaurant jobs myself over the years. The work is grinding, and thankless, and the kitchen floors are always so goddamn sticky. But I was so tired of this town and all the people in it, and besides which it was a *pizza* joint, for chrissake.

"Excuse me, sir?" I said.

He crossed his arms. "Yes?"

"Would you prefer to have us shout into the kitchen from here, or shall I just commence hoisting a string of code-flags?"

"My apologies, madam," he said, inching closer with palpable reluctance — a mime in a wind tunnel.

Dean fluttered his lashes at me over the top of his menu. "Why don't you order for both of us?"

"Why don't I stick a fork in your eye?" I muttered.

He grinned. "Because our waiter neglected to bring cutlery?"

"You are *so* dead," I said.

"Shall I give you a few more minutes?" asked the waiter.

"No thank you," I said. "We'd like a large escargot pizza, please. With goat cheese but not the raspberry coulis."

"Foie gras?" asked the waiter.

I closed my eyes. "Let us *both* pretend that you refrained from uttering such an entirely *de trop* suggestion aloud."

Chastened, he transcribed the order to his little pad, a task that apparently necessitated the employment of jazz hands.

"What sort of beer do you have?" I asked.

He tapped the wine list beside me with his little gold pen. "We have an extensive *cellar,* madam."

"And might one hope to stumble across a martini therein?"

He confessed that one might indeed.

"Please bring me two, then," I said. "Very dry, very cold, small olives."

"I'm not really a huge martini fan," said Dean.

"Yeah right," I said. "Like I'm planning to share."

Dean's eyes went wide. "You're ordering two martinis for yourself?"

"I am," I said. "Because that stupid whore Cammy stole my fucking Percodan."

"Madam," said the waiter, sympathetic at last, "you have my sincerest condolences."

"Thank you," I said. "And could you please bring my husband a glass of whatever ridiculous sort of wine a person is expected to drink with escargot pizza?"

The man bobbed his head and scuttled away.

Dean nudged my foot under the table. "The people . . . they need a strong *hand.*"

"The Hamptons," I replied, "they could use a little *napalm.*"

"Look," I said, as we turned back onto Job's Lane, toward Chateau Butthead, "are you *sure* you want to work for Christoph?"

"You're the one who introduced me to the guy, Bunny."

"Mea fucking culpa," I said. "I take it back."

"And besides, what about Nutty Buddy?"

"Nutty Buddy's affection for me appears to have fallen down through the grate of a neglected storm drain."

"You're in kind of a pissy mood," he said.

"Ya *think?*"

"Is it just getting ditched tonight?" he asked.

"Let's see . . . in the past ten days I've discovered the bones of a three-year-old kid who was beaten to death, learned that not *only* did my most-despised 'stepfather' molest my sister but *also* that my mother finds it socially inconvenient to believe her, and — bonus! — I'm expected to make nice to Mom's *newest* boyfriend this Monday, over lunch, while you're in Texas doing errands for my newly *former* friend's husband. Pinch me, honey, because I just couldn't *be* more thrilled with my fabulous life!"

"I'm not sure martinis should remain among your cocktails of choice."

"You want to walk back to Manhattan?"

"Is there some kind of bus?"

"I believe they call it a jitney," I said.

"Of course. How too-too silly of me."

Dean moved his hand to my knee. I put mine on top of it.

"I'm sorry," I said.

"Astrid really hurt your feelings, didn't she?"

"*So* much."

"Bunny, how can you take someone like that seriously? And you know the dinner party would have been excruciating. Chock-full of vapid Cammy-trash."

"If you'd known Astrid, back at Dobbs, she was just . . . damn. I don't even know how to explain it."

He squeezed my knee. "You outgrew each other."

"Dean," I said, "did you ever have a friend who made you believe there was not a shred of doubt you were going to accomplish something, like, I don't know . . . splendid, or even heroic?"

"Every time I dropped acid."

"Okay, look," I said. "Whatever kind of shit happened in my life? Astrid always remembered who I was *meant* to be. And I remembered the same for her. It wasn't that she had my back, or we'd exchange Hallmark cards every cheesy holiday. It was just, like, I had *someone* out in the world who'd keep a little ember of my mojo safely banked in the ashes."

"Until tonight," he said.

I didn't answer.

This would have been an optimum moment for my husband to look me square in the eye and proclaim, "Fear not, Bunny, for *I* cherish the eternal flame of your inner Batman."

Not least because I had exactly that kind of deep and abiding faith in *him.*

Instead he gave my knee a final pat and said, "Teen-angst romanticism. You can't expect that kind of thing to last."

He was a guy, after all. And also a grown-up, unlike his wife.

We drove on in silence until I turned into the narrow lane with the hedges.

It was nine o'clock. The house was dark, and both Jeeps were still gone.

I turned off my car and pulled the key from its ignition.

You're twenty-seven years old, Madeline. Maybe it's time to stop clapping for Tinkerbell.

27

Dean pled exhaustion and wandered up to bed. I kicked off my shoes in the living room and did a back layout onto the sofa. It was only nine-fifteen, but I didn't see any point in turning on the lights. It wasn't like there was a single book in the house, or even a television.

I couldn't stomach the idea of *Town & Country* again, but was getting just about desperate enough to check the upstairs bathrooms for shampoo bottles so I'd at least have marketing copy to read off their backs: *Are you Limp and Unmanageable? Lather, rinse, repeat.*

The martinis were wearing off. I followed Dean upstairs and crawled into bed beside him, but he was already asleep.

"What," I asked, "no hot monkey love?"

He snored a little and turned over onto his side.

I tried burrowing under the covers and

closing my eyes, but after a few minutes it became patently obvious that the sandman wasn't coming by anytime soon.

There are few things more lonely than lying awake in the darkness thirsting after the contented sleep of the person beside you.

I got up again, walking softly downstairs to the kitchen for a lukewarm glass of tap water, then another — talismans against waking up to Astrid and Cammy with a hangover. The morning promised to suck plentifully enough.

There was a bit of light from the numbered face of a phone on the kitchen wall. I dialed our apartment in the hope of conversational redemption, hanging up just before the machine kicked in on the seventh ring.

Mom was beyond reach in Connecticut or something, on her way down from Maine. I wasn't feeling ready to talk to her, anyway, and couldn't think of a number for anyone else likely to be home in the city on a Saturday night.

It was ten o'clock now. I reached into the front pocket of my jeans and pulled out my wallet, then cracked the icebox door open so I had enough light to read the number off Skwarecki's business card.

I dialed 7-1-8 and then a string of num-

232

bers, getting patched through to her extension.

It rang once. I sat on the floor, Indian-style.

"Homicide. Skwarecki."

I could hear the rumble of voices in the background, the clatter of a typewriter.

"Hey, it's Madeline. This a bad time?"

"It's slow. Mostly just me and the boys getting warmed up — swing a few bats around, knock the mud out of our cleats."

"Cool," I said.

"You're sounding bummed."

"Bored. I don't know."

"Where you at?"

"Suffolk County. I got dragged out for the Asshole Telethon."

She laughed. "That an annual thing?"

"Year-round, I think."

"Sucks to be you, huh?"

"Could be worse," I said. "Could be dying in a famine, flies crawling over my eyelids."

"Yo! Get a load of Little Miss Perky Sparkles."

"Sorry. I totally didn't mean to call you up and go Eeyore on your ass."

"Not like you dialed 1-800-Sunnybrook-Fucking-Farm over here. This could well be the most uplifting chat I'll have tonight. You aren't dead, *and* you're not calling about someone who is. Hey, win-win."

"That doesn't freak you out every time you pick up the phone at work?"

"Beats typing reports," she said.

"So how'd you end up in Homicide, anyway?"

"Fate, maybe," she said. "The eeny-meeny-miny-mo of the universe or some shit."

"What're you, from California now, Skwarecki?"

"Yeah, right — 'Have a nice day'? I don't fucking think so."

"So how'd it happen, then?" I asked.

"Me in Homicide? Babe, I'm telling you, *fate*. No question."

"And?" I said. "Once upon a time —"

"In a galaxy way the hell far, far away . . ."

I could hear the creak of her chair as she leaned back. "It was my first day on the job, right? I'm fresh out of the academy, nineteen sixty-seven, and they send me to Bed-Stuy, for chrissake. I'm twenty years old, in stockings and this dumpy little skirt, and they give me a purse with a holster in it and a fucking 'Police Matron' hat that makes me look like I'm working for Pan Am or some shit, right?"

"Ouch."

"Besides which," she said, "this is *waaaaay* before Angie Dickinson made the world safe for female cops, okay? So I show up early for my very first eight-o'clock shift on the job, and the desk sergeant takes one look at me in this getup — all sweet-cheeked and dewy-eyed — and starts screaming about who's the joker trying to fuck him in the ass by sending a goddamn *girl* over there, and how he doesn't have enough shit to eat already without he's gotta babysit Barbie and *Skipper.*"

"Okay, I *so* would have burst into tears, at that point."

"Let me tell you, I'd already been through months of this shit, even before the academy. Shoulda heard my dad — and my *brothers?* You just get numb after a while if you're lucky. And this jerk behind the desk, he doesn't drag it out for too long. Just throws up his hands after maybe five minutes and tells me, 'Stay out of fucking trouble, don't do *anything,* just go walk up and down the sidewalk in front of the station house so I don't have to fucking *look* at you, honey, because I've got actual *work* to do here this morning.' "

"What time of year? I mean, is he throwing you out to wander around in the snow or something?"

"October," she said, "piece of cake."

"So you're outside, walking back and forth on the sidewalk all day?"

"This is what I'm led to believe. And at first it's really busy — eight A.M., so you got the night shift leaving, morning guys coming in — a ton of people shoving around, right? In and out. And I'm just trying not to get run down, minding my business, down the fucking sidewalk, turn around, back *up* the fucking sidewalk. . . ."

I hear her take a sip of coffee or something on the other end of the line.

"And after a while," Skwarecki continued, "I notice there's this guy sitting on the curb, maybe twenty feet from the front door? He's got his head in his hands, knees pulled up, looking beat to shit, like the cat dragged him around the block all night."

"A cop?"

"Nah," she said. "Just some guy. I'm walking past him thinking maybe Hispanic: two-tone shoes, little porkpie hat pushed back on his head, one of those Cuban shirts — regular Mambo-King son of a bitch, except rumpled. Like he went out the night before dressed pretty sharp but now it's the next morning, right?"

"Just sitting there?" My butt was starting to fall asleep, so I stood up and refilled my water glass at the sink.

"I'm telling you, Madeline, the crowd thins out and the guy doesn't *move*. Not like he's a stiff or anything, but he just sits there — doesn't look up, nothing. Every once in a while I think maybe he's *crying* a little, into his hands. But I'm supposed to stay out of trouble, right? So I just keep walking back and forth past him, bored out of my freaking mind, nothing else to look at."

"For how long?" I ask.

"Three fucking *hours*, Madeline, until finally I can't stand it anymore. He's sobbing by this point. Shoulders jerking around, all that."

"So you talk to him?"

"I try to, except he looks up and he's got snot running out of his nose, eyes all red, and he tells me *'No habla inglés,'* right? But straight across the street there's a bodega, so I go over there and try to find someone bilingual, could maybe help me out with this guy."

I swallow some water. "Mm-hmm . . ."

"And there's this little boy, twelve years old, speaks a little English? So I drag *him* back over to this guy, and say 'Ask him what's the matter,' and he goes *bi-bi-bip* and the guy tells him *bi-bi-bip* right back, and then the kid looks up at me and goes, 'Hey, Missus, he sad 'cause he kill his *girlfriend*.' "

"Skwarecki, you are fucking *kidding* me," I said.

"Hand to God, Madeline. So I go, 'Ask him *when*,' and it's all *bi-bi-bi, bi-bi-bi* again — back and forth, the two of them — and the kid looks up and says, 'Three o'clock this morning.' "

Her chair creaks in the background. "And I say, '*How* did he kill her?' so the kid asks him, and then he looks up and tells me, 'Missus, he shoot her.' So I say to this kid, 'Ask him, where's the gun?' and when the kid does, Ricky Ricardo on the curb there reaches down the front of his pants and pulls out a chrome-plated fucking thirty-eight, which he then holds out to *me,* barrel-first."

"*Awesome,*" I said.

"Yeah, right? And I have a handkerchief in my pocket, so I pick the damn gun up with that — all dainty and shit — and shove it in my purse-holster thing, and then say to the boy, 'Ask him, where's his dead girlfriend now?' So the kid does and the guy points across the street, and the kid tells me, 'In that car right there, in the backseat under some blankets.' So I go, 'Ask him will he come inside with me,' and the guy listens to the kid and then he nods and stands up and trots right into the station house with me, no problemo."

"Dude, *Skwarecki*," I said, sitting there in the dark and shaking my head in wonder.

"Maddie, you should've seen that desk sergeant. Pissed *off?* I'm *telling* you, fucking red in the face, jumping up and down, all, 'I told you to stay out of *trouble*, not *talk* to anyone, and here you are, ya *stupid* bitch, dragging some nightclub *spick* into the station house — what's your fucking *problem?* You fucking *deaf?*' "

I started laughing.

"And so of course I go, '*No*, sir, it's just that this man committed a homicide late last night, and I've got the murder weapon in my purse and the vic's parked across the street in a Buick, and I thought you might want to take him into custody, *sir.*' "

I said, "You weren't kidding about the whole fate thing. Jesus H. *Christ.*"

"Ach," she said. "You wanna know from fate? The detectives upstairs stole the collar right out from under me."

"Even so, that's the best story I've heard in just about forever. You totally cheered me up."

"You want me to *really* cheer you up?"

"Absolutely," I said.

"They're going under."

"Huh?"

"The two-bagger," she said.

"Skwarecki, what is that, *golf?*"

"Madeline, your *perps* — Teddy's mother and the boyfriend."

"Oh," I said, comprehension dawning. "The two-bagger."

"*Now* you're cookin' with gas," she said.

"Wow," I said. "I can't believe they're dead."

"Whaddaya — *dead?* Jeez, you want to give me a heart attack?"

"They're *not* dead?"

Skwarecki started laughing. "Where do you come *up* with this shit?"

"Hey," I said, "you tell me 'bags' and 'under,' I think funeral."

"Funeral?" She cracked up.

"What?" I said.

She struggled for breath. "Listen to you, over here — regular fucking laugh riot, I swear."

"Yeah, yeah, me and Phyllis Diller. We have a goddamn *gift.*"

She snickered again. *"Under . . ."*

"Skwarecki, I still have no idea what the hell you're talking about. Under *what?*"

"Arrest."

"Oh," I said. "Duh."

"Yeah, well. Took you long enough."

"So when does this happen?" I asked.

"Tonight," she said. "We'll bring 'em down here, get 'em in the box."

"Skwarecki, that is the *best* news. Thank you for telling me."

"Hey, I would've been trying to get ahold of you, anyway, give you a heads-up."

"About what?" I asked.

"Bost is gonna need you to testify for the grand jury."

"When?"

"Sometime this week, probably. The arraignment's Monday, then she's got about six days to go after an indictment."

"So does she need me for the arraignment, too?"

"That's just about bail. No point in you coming out for that."

"Cool," I said.

"You want to meet up maybe Tuesday morning, we can walk you through the rest of it."

"I'll give you a call from work first thing Monday, when I know my schedule for the week. Then I've gotta go meet my mother for lunch or some shit."

"Sounds good," she said. "So we got you cheered up, now, or what?"

"Just like a whole new world," I said, "all

241

shiny and lemon scented."

"Night, then. I gotta hit it."

"Hey, can I ask one more question?"

"Sure thing."

"Any idea which one of them killed Teddy?"

"We like the boyfriend, but we'll charge Angela, too."

"Did you talk to Mrs. Underhill?"

"Couple nights ago, right after I saw you."

"How'd it go?"

"We're thinking she'll testify," she said. "You did good."

"God willing."

"Yeah, right?"

28

I finally slept okay, considering.

Dean woke up at dawn, his circadian rhythm still governed by some lingering neurochemical trace of childhood heifers and cornfields. He went for a long walk but was back downstairs with Christoph by the time I'd stumbled out of bed myself.

Our host pressed us to stay on through lunch at the very least, but we extricated ourselves by pleading the onus of nonspecific untended responsibilities back on Sixteenth Street, not to mention the time-suck logistics of returning my car to its barn before catching a train into the city from Locust Valley.

"If you'd ever like to park it behind the office in New Jersey, you're welcome to," said Christoph. "It might be more convenient."

He smiled at me, eyes crinkling up.

I thanked him for the offer just as Astrid

wandered downstairs, wine-stale and bleary-eyed.

"You're leaving?" she asked, taking in our little pair of bags perched stoutly by the front door.

"Needs must," I said.

"Kiss-kiss." She leaned in to assail me with a rank blast of ashtray and soured perfume.

I spoke into her ear. "Best to Cammy, and she owes me six Percodan."

She pulled back, blinking at me. "Darling, no hard feelings? It was entirely necessary. We'd never have *survived* that wretched dinner otherwise."

"Mmm . . . God knows we *all* have friends whose company one must be drugged to endure."

Astrid clapped her hands. "That reminds me, I got you a present."

She tripped lightly upstairs, returning moments later with a hefty and rather worn paperback book.

"I ran across this the other day and immediately thought of you," she said, passing the volume to me.

I looked down to read its title. "This is quite . . . unexpected. I don't know how to thank you."

I wasn't kidding. The book in my hands

was *Mein Kampf.*

I peeled back its cover, hoping she'd inscribed some sort of punchline, or at least an explanation.

The book's first page was blank but for an anonymous *$2.00,* scrawled in pencil across its upper right-hand corner.

"I have no idea what it's supposed to mean," I said, tucking the repulsive tome under my arm, "but I'll certainly remember our weekend here every time I see this."

"What was *that* all about?" asked Dean as we drove away.

"I was hoping you might clue me in," I said.

He shook his head, hands thrown up in dismay.

"Dean, I mean, *Mein Kampf?* What the *fuck?*"

I stopped at the end of their road, looking left for oncoming traffic. "Was that intended as, like, an expression of her marital manifesto, or just some garbled-but-massive 'Fuck you'?"

"Maybe it's a cry for help," he said.

"Like what? 'Lassie! I'm trapped in a mineshaft! Run home and get the SS'?"

" 'Help me, Obersturmbannführer Kenobi! You're my only hope!' " replied

Dean, raising a fist to each ear for the full Princess Leia.

"I just don't get it," I said. "I really, really don't."

"Bunny, there's nothing *to* get. The woman's just fucking nuts."

He was right, not that it made me any happier. "You want to stop for breakfast?"

"Let's wait for the Commack exit," he said. "These people would put escargot in *oatmeal*."

It took us five hours to get home, all told, what with Sunday traffic and the vagaries of the Long Island Rail Road, but I'd rarely been so happy to be safely back in our tiny second-floor commune.

"Home, Sweet DayGlo Home." I said and plopped down on the sofa, cheered by its very hideousness.

There was a note on the coffee table, pinned down under Sue's bong and a lighter:

We're out mocking the nouveau-riche at Barney's. Sam Chinita's for dinner?
— mwah mwah, S & P

Dean saw that the bong's bowl was filled and flicked it alive with the lighter. After taking a long gurgling hit, he offered it to me.

"No thanks," I said. "I'm happy enough just having escaped the social carnage."

"I need a haircut," he said, before exhaling. "Don't want to scare any Texans tomorrow."

I patted my duffel bag. "No problem. I'll just curl up right here with my close personal friend Adolf."

Dean leaned down to kiss me on the forehead. *"Auf wiedersehen, meine kleine Hasenpfeffer."*

I made myself an iced coffee, ditching Adolf for F. Scott. I'd just gotten to the part where Tom and Nick and the gang were driving through the Valley of Ashes, bound for Manhattan, when I started drifting off.

I wondered whether that had been part of Queens, between East Egg and the city, before succumbing to sleep entirely, duffel bag mashed under my head for a pillow.

I woke up to the racket of our front-door locks twisting over. My ashy dreams frittered away, leaving only the vague recollection of Astrid cast as Jordan Baker, languidly duplicitous about having improved her lie in a golf game.

Sue and Pagan swept down the hall in

their Rollerblades, spinning to crash butt-first into the chairs beside me.

"Fun weekend?" asked Pague.

"Hideous," I said. "They ditched us last night, *and* stole my Percodan."

"Typical," said Sue, reaching for the bong. She reloaded the bowl and lit it, then pointed at my discarded book.

"The fuck is this?" she said, voice pinched as she held the smoke in her lungs.

"Present from Astrid," I said. "You believe that shit?"

"Nazi fucking hosebeast," she said, exhaling a rush of blue cloud all over it.

Pagan reached for the bong. "Why the hell would Astrid give you *that* as a present?"

"Search me," I said. "Dean thinks it might have been a cry for help."

"Help *this*," said Sue, flipping Hitler the bird.

"No shit," I said. "And don't get me started on Christoph."

"Dean really wants to work for the guy?" asked Pagan.

"Dean wants to work," I said. "I don't think he's committed to anything beyond that."

"Bummer for you," said Sue. "Means you're pretty much stuck kissing Astrid's ass for as long as the checks clear."

"Just close your eyes and think of England," said Pagan.

"I can handle the ass-kissing," I said, "as long as I don't *ever* have to go back to those fucking Hamptons."

"Ramen to that," said Pagan, raising the bong in toast.

We heard the front door open again.

Sue leaned back in her chair to call, "Hi, honey, you're home" down the hallway.

Dean strode in, sporting the shortest haircut I'd ever seen on him.

"Dude," said Sue, "you look like a fucking marine."

Pagan tossed off a salute, holding the bong out toward him. "Semper Fry."

29

Sam Chinita's was an old-school diner on Ninth Avenue, at least as far as the building itself went. Time-worn Moderne stainless and linoleum, a no-nonsense kind of place that probably once had *Steaks and Chops* blinking out front in neon script.

Now the menu was Chino-Latino: half Cantonese, half Cuban. You could get egg rolls or fried plantains, hot-and-sour soup or *cafe con leche*. I always wondered if the old waiters with their shiny black pompadours had successfully fled Mao only to find themselves desperate to escape Castro's Havana.

"I'm not really looking forward to this lunch tomorrow," I said over my plate of black beans and yellow rice.

"Because of Mom, or because of the new beau?" asked Pagan.

"Both, I guess." I reached for the platter of fried *platanos maduros*. "This whole thing with Pierce — I want to bitch her out, but not in front of some random-preppy-stranger dude."

"Maybe that's why she's bringing him," said Sue. "Like, for a little social Kevlar."

I shook my head. "She doesn't know I know. Or she *thinks* I've known for a long time. Either way, she'd have no idea it's this high on my agenda."

"Are you sure she's even going out with this guy?" asked Dean.

I rolled my eyes.

He turned to Pagan. "I mean, did she say 'I want you to meet the new love of my life' on the phone? Maybe he's just some pal she's splitting gas and tolls with on the trip down."

"Dean, this is *Constance*," said Pague. "It's not what she says, it's how giddily she says it."

"But what *did* she say?" asked Dean. "About the guy, specifically?"

My sister shrugged. "He's the one with the boat."

"So?" said Dean. "Some guy with a boat's giving your mother a ride to New York. You'd think it was Defcon Ninety-seven."

"Don't be an idiot," I said. "He's treating her *kids* to lunch at 'Twenty-One.'"

"Not to mention the spouse and the

roommate," added Sue.

Pagan patted my husband on the hand.

"Poor guy's in it for the nookie," she said. "*Big* time."

After Dean went to sleep that night I cut the alligator off an old Lacoste shirt and stitched it onto the breast of his new coveralls. It looked good with the herringbone.

I went into our bedroom and kissed him on the forehead before folding them up and tucking them back into his duffel bag.

I called Skwarecki from the Catalog late the next morning as soon as the phones calmed down.

"Things are starting to get under way," she said. "Bost wants to go over the process, let you know what to expect."

"Just tell me where and when."

"Can you make tomorrow, about eleven?"

"I don't have to be at work until three in the afternoon. You think that's enough time?"

Skwarecki said she figured it was, then gave me directions via subway.

"You want to ride in the front car to Union Turnpike and come up the last set of stairs on the platform, onto Queens Boulevard," she said. "There's a big bronze statue right there, next to the sidewalk — guy with a sword standing on a pile of bodies. Keep Fat Boy on your left and about a block down you'll come to these two big ugly gray buildings. You want the one closest to the boulevard. I'll meet you in the lobby."

I jotted all that down. "So how's it going, otherwise?"

"I'll be happy to see the last of nineteen ninety, let me tell you. Twenty-three hundred homicides already. My first year we didn't quite break a thousand."

"So, what, the population's bigger?"

"Same number of people, double the murders. And the robberies? Maybe four times as many."

"What the hell happened?"

"Jobs went away and the drugs got harder."

"You think it'll ever go back to how it was?"

"Dinkins's balls ain't big enough, for damn sure."

I glanced at the clock on the office wall. *"Fuck."*

"What?" she said.

"Gotta meet my mother for lunch," I said. "New boyfriend."

"I thought you were married."

"Not mine, hers. Mom's oh-for-three on the marital front."

"Geez. Good luck with that."

"Your lips to God's ears," I said, hanging up.

30

"So what's this new guy's name?" asked Sue.

She was wedged between me and Pagan in the backseat of an old Checker cab on the way to '21.'

"Larry or something," said Pague. "Tony. I don't know."

"I wonder if he's married," said Sue. "Like Bonwit."

I looked out the window. "I wonder if he'll make us order off the children's menu, like Bonwit."

Sue laughed. "He was a piece of work."

"Feh," I said. "Scathing dickhead."

"He had a few nice moments," said Pagan.

"Bonwit, nice?" asked Sue.

"When he was dying," said Pagan. "For a couple of days, right before."

I shook my head. "Doesn't count."

"He was scared," said Pagan. "It actually made him kind of sweet."

"I'm sorry he was scared," I said. "But he was still an asshole."

"Yeah," said Pagan, "but it's too bad you didn't see him in the hospital. He was really happy you'd sent him that book about the Tall Ships taking wheat to Australia. I was even a little sad when he died, you know? Surprised the hell out of me."

"I was sad for Mom," I said. "She really loved the guy."

"Maybe the new one will cheer her up," said Sue. "Maybe *he'll* turn out to be a decent human being."

My sister and I groaned.

"What?" asked Sue.

Pagan said, "The nice ones *never* last —"

"Because Mom gets bored," I said. "And we always end up feeling so damn *sorry* for them."

"Thank God I'm not a fucking goy," said Sue. "You people are crazy."

"We're here to meet our mother," I said to the maître d'.

"Under which name was the reservation made?"

"Constance Jones?" I said, Mom having reverted to her maiden name in recent years.

He consulted the day's page in a large

leather book. "I'm sorry, I don't see a Jones."

"Um, maybe Constance Capwell?" I asked.

He looked up at me, shaking his head.

"Dare?" I said, not really believing she'd have supplied Dad's surname.

Another head shake.

"Dougherty?" asked Pagan, citing the last name of our first stepfather.

"Are you certain the luncheon was meant to be today?" asked the maître d', not unkindly. "I'd be happy to check tomorrow's reservations."

Mom breezed in just then, thank God, on the arm of a rather large gray-haired man in glasses and full Brooks Brothers kit.

"Larry McCormack," he said. "Table for five, downstairs."

The maître d' gave him a tiny bow, from the neck. "Very good, sir."

The Larry-person turned toward me, Sue, and Pagan, of such good cheer that he was verging on downright goofy.

The man's blue blazer was unbuttoned. It swung open to reveal a bit of a gut hanging over his Nantucket Reds, nearly obscuring the whales embroidered on his belt. His loafers were down at the heel and revealed a suitably Yankee disdain for polish.

Serious money.

Mom introduced us, and Pagan and I each looked him in the eye while shaking his hand and saying "How do you *do?*"

Sue went next, saying she was pleased to meet him, thanking him for allowing her to be included.

We were shown to a crisp white table in the downstairs bar, its ceiling hung, as ever, with toy planes and trucks and wagons, most bearing what I'd always presumed were the corporate logos of regular customers.

The maître d' pulled out our chairs and dispensed menus, then disappeared with a virtual puff of well-oiled smoke.

Larry pulled out Mom's chair, then claimed the seat next to her. He was still grinning at the three of us. It was rather unnerving.

"Who'll join me in a shrimp cocktail?" he asked, rubbing his very large paws in glee.

I nudged Pagan's ankle, muttering, "Six months. Tops."

She raised her fist to her mouth and faux-coughed. "Hundred bucks he won't see Thanksgiving."

We dropped our napkins into our laps and shook on it, under the table.

"How was the drive?" asked Sue.

258

"Not bad," answered Mom. "We came down the Taconic this morning."

Larry pursed his lips. "It's about time somebody *managed* that forest. I've never seen a stretch of trees more in need of a good paper company's stewardship."

"The Berkshires?" I said.

Mom giggled, and he swallowed her hand in his.

"What line of work are you in, Mr. Mc-Cormack?" asked Pagan.

"Energy," he said. "I'm retired now, of course. But it was absolutely terrific — wonderful people, wonderful business."

"And did you have any particular specialty within the field?"

"I gave my heart to the cleanest power in the world," he said. "Nuclear."

Pagan choked on her ice water. Sue tried to give her a couple of strong claps to the back without making a huge deal out of it.

The waiter purred up to take our drink orders.

Presuming they didn't stock methadone, I settled for gin.

"You drove down the Taconic, from Maine?" asked Pagan. "I would've thought Ninety-five was the most direct route to Manhattan. Weren't you staying in Hartford?"

"We spent the weekend with Larry's youngest son, out in Litchfield," said Mom. "*Such* fun!"

"I hope you girls won't mind that we told *my* kids first," said Larry.

Pagan tipped her head closer to mine, hissing "You have *so* got to be fucking kidding me" through clenched teeth.

Mom brushed the fingertips of her free hand lightly across the inside of Larry's wrist, with a sidelong-glance bonus.

He cleared his throat, cheeks going pink.

Be still, gag reflex.

"We hope you girls don't have any plans for Valentine's Day," said Mom.

"February?" I asked. "In *Maine?*"

She ignored that, showing us her gumball-machine engagement ring. "Larry had this made by the most *charming* little man in Bar Harbor. I've always adored dark sapphires."

The waiter returned with our cocktails.

Should've held out for the methadone.

The only time I got Mom alone was when she tailed me to the ladies' room, in the lull before dessert.

I didn't have the balls to give her shit about Pierce in front of the aproned little-old-lady attendant, not least since I didn't

260

really have cash to spare for the tip saucer unless I planned to walk home.

"Well? What do you think?" asked Mom, eyes crinkling up adorably as she smiled at me via the mirror over the sinks.

I think this guy's ball four, coming in high-and-outside and not worth a twitch of your shoulders. And we both know you're gonna swing for it anyway.

The attendant turned on the taps in front of Mom, then unveiled a fresh bar of soap.

I twisted my own faucets quickly on. Feudalism creeps me out, no matter how vestigial.

"He seems like a very kind man," I said. "And he obviously adores you."

My mother lifted her dripping hands from the sink. The silent attendant draped them with a starched piqué towel, turning off the taps in lieu of a curtsy.

Mom was going to feel like shit when she bolted this time. Because he was nice enough, and she really never meant any harm.

"Larry sat me down to go over his portfolio last week," she said, spritzing her wrists with the house bottle of Joy, "so I'd know you children would always be taken care of."

"That's touching, Mom."

261

Too bad my mother was no gold digger.

Bet she even gives back the ring.

I dried my hands, watching her breeze out the ladies'-room door.

Smiling weakly at the aproned old lady, I dug out my last five bucks, trying to smooth out the bill's wrinkles before I laid it gently across her little white plate.

We burst into our apartment an hour later, sans midlife lovebirds.

"Fucking *Maine?*" said Pagan. "In fucking *February?*"

"I don't even want to *think* about it," I said.

"What is she, nuts?" asked Pagan.

"Oh, right," I said, "*news* flash."

She flopped onto the sofa. "Right out of her head."

"Twisted," I said. "Oobie-shoobie."

Sue drew a pack of '21' matches out of her pocket and held them up. "*Fuck* shrimp cocktail. Who'll join me in a bong hit?"

Dean called from Texas that night, around eleven.

"You got in okay?" I asked.

"Piece of cake, and all the guys at Chevron were impressed with my preppy coveralls."

"Where're you staying?"

"A Holiday Inn out by the refinery," he said. "King Leisure Suite."

"Ooooo . . . swanky."

"Bed's too big without you."

"Same here," I said, patting his empty pillow in the dark.

"How'd lunch go?"

"Mom's getting married."

"Again?"

"Who knows," I said. "Maybe the fourth time will be the charm."

31

Tuesday morning I came up the subway stairs into a biting rain. The sky was low and gray, and everyone around me kept their heads ducked against the sooty blast of wet.

Fall, already.

Skwarecki's statue loomed beside me: a smugly chubby guy, knee-deep in naked dead chicks but draped in a Tarzan diaper to protect his own modesty.

Fat Boy's right hand rested loose on the hilt of his sword, blade casually balanced across the top of his shoulder. Gripped in his left fist was a skein of hair, at the bottom of which a woman's severed head dangled like a purse.

I bulled my way forward into the slanting rain, shoulders hunched. I could see the twinned concrete hulks Skwarecki had described in the distance. There was another sculpture out front, stainless steel and a lot more modern. The rainy wind made it whirl like a giant cheese grater.

The floor inside was dirty and wet. I got in line for the metal detector, scanning the crowd beyond until I saw Skwarecki waving at me.

"No raincoat?" she asked when I'd made it through. "What do you, wanna to catch pneumonia?"

We were in a tall atrium jammed with people. Dozens of voices bounced off the walls. Skwarecki walked point through the crowd, me trotting close behind. We passed several courtrooms. All I could see as we rushed alongside each set of glass-paneled doors was IN GOD WE TRUST writ huge on the far wall inside, above the head of a judge.

Skwarecki flashed her badge to some guy in a beige uniform and said, "She's with me," before he waved us ahead into a long hallway. The names on the office doors we passed were a global mishmash: Tsangarakis, Seide, Murphy, Chu, Lapautre.

We finally arrived at a reception area manned by a phalanx of no-nonsense-looking women whom my mother would have described as "salty old broads."

The one in the middle held up one finger until she'd finished transferring a phone call, then grinned up at Skwarecki. "What brings you down here this fine morning?"

"Hey, Rosemary," said Skwarecki. "We've got an appointment with Bost."

"I'll let her know you're here." Rosemary handed me a register to sign and gave me a bar-coded GUEST sticker for the front of my coat, then buzzed us in past another sturdy set of doors.

The hallway beyond was painted a shiny institutional green from the floor to waist level, with grimy white above. We passed a row of head shots, former DAs in sequence, from the twenties onward. I watched stiff celluloid collars give way to soft fabric, while bow ties morphed into Windsor-knotted four-in-hands.

Bost's office was right next to a group shot from the mid-seventies, judging by the stunning width of the attorneys' lapels.

Skwarecki rapped a quick "shave and a haircut," then opened the ADA's door. I followed her inside.

Bost stood and reintroduced herself, hand stretched out across her desk to shake mine.

"Detective," she said, "thanks so much for bringing Ms. Dare down today."

Skwarecki nodded. "No problem. I figured she'd need a little help navigating — maybe we'd all get some lunch later."

We sat down in the visitors' chairs. There were some snapshots and Xeroxed cartoons pinned to a corkboard behind Bost's head, the window to her left giving a depressing view of the day outside. Next to me was a framed black-and-white shot of the old steel globe left over from the 1964 World's Fair, in Flushing Meadows.

"I see you're admiring the Unisphere," said Bost, "unofficial icon of Queens."

"It was always one of the first things I recognized outside the airport as a kid whenever I came east," I said, "along with those towers that looked like they had a stack of pancakes on top."

"I've always loved that thing," said Bost. "I remember my dad taking me right up into its shadow, all excited about the coming wonders of the Space Age."

"I've never seen it up close," I said.

"It's huge — twelve stories tall. There were jets of water shooting up all around it back then. Spectacular."

"What are the rings for?" I asked, pointing at the three silvery trails circumnavigating the central globe.

"Orbits," said Bost. "They're supposed to mark the paths of Gagarin, Glenn, and the Telstar satellite."

"Cool," I said, turning from the photograph to look across the desk at her.

"Aw, *Christ,*" she said, staring up at the ceiling.

I raised my eyes to the same spot, where a patch of yellowed damp was leaking through from above. Two fat drops plummeted to the surface of her desk, inches away from a fat manila file folder.

Bost snatched the file out of the way as more yellow drops started plopping down, thick and fast. "Swear to *God,* this building . . ."

Skwarecki stood up. "What say the three of us grab an early lunch?"

"Brilliant plan," said Bost, reaching for her coat.

We got a booth by the window at an Italian place halfway up the block on the other side of the boulevard.

"What *was* that?" I asked as we scootched in across the red vinyl. "Are the pipes backed up or something?"

Skwarecki laughed.

"The prisoners are backed up," said Bost.

"How?" I asked.

Skwarecki reached for her menu. "The floor above the prosecutors' offices — it runs from the jail to the courthouse. The guards hate having to process the inmates twice, so if things get behind schedule they just lock the hall at both ends and let them all stew up there."

"You have fifty guys sitting around for five, six hours," explained Bost, "eventually they gotta use the facilities."

"Problem is, there aren't any," added Skwarecki. "I mean, it's a hallway."

I stared at the two of them. "That was piss?"

They nodded.

"Leaking through the goddamn ceiling?"

Bost gave me a thumbs-up in confirmation. "Not like they don't know we're right under."

"Dude," I said. "That is *completely* repulsive."

She shrugged. "My world, and welcome to it."

Skwarecki gave me a little punch to the shoulder. "You just gotta heart New York, am I right?"

We were picking over our lunch plates, initial hunger sated.

Skwarecki'd ordered the manicotti, Bost a Caesar salad. I was staring down at a platter of eggplant parm, hoping I could negate the image of felonious urine given enough red sauce.

"The first step is the grand jury," Bost said. "I'll let you know when we'll need you to testify as soon as it's calendared."

"Will Teddy's mother and the boyfriend be there?" I asked.

"The proceedings are considered secret," she said. "The defendants and their attorneys won't be told what you said, or even that you testified. You won't be cross-examined. The only people in the room with you will be myself and the grand jurors."

"No judge?"

"Only very rarely, if there's a procedural question. This isn't a trial. I'm just asking the grand jury to decide whether or not it's *possible* the defendants might have committed a crime. If the answer is yes — a 'true bill' — I have permission to prosecute the case. The jurors draw up an indictment, listing the charges I'm allowed to file against the defendants."

"Is the answer ever no?" I asked.

"I've never had that happen," said Bost, "but we make a point of having a solid case before anything goes to a grand jury. Waste of time, otherwise."

"And you're charging them both?" I asked.

"We like the boyfriend for it," she said, "but the mother saw what was going on.

270

She didn't step in. From a legal standpoint, that makes her equally responsible for her son's death."

"She was there?" I asked.

"When Teddy died?" replied Bost. "Yeah, she was in the room. She saw the whole thing."

"And she didn't try to stop it?"

Skwarecki nodded. "We've got her on video saying she didn't lift a finger."

"*Jesus,*" I said.

"But she's got a *very* good lawyer," said Bost. "Marty Hetzler. He'll try to get the charges against her dropped."

Skwarecki nodded again.

"Marty's right across the room, in fact," said Bost. "Over at that big table. Snappy dresser, white hair."

I turned my head to check out the guy she'd described. He had on one of those striped shirts with white collar and cuffs, a thick gold bar-pin making the knot of his tie pop. His blue suit was double-breasted and nipped at the waist, peaked lapels sharp enough to inflict paper cuts.

The guy started laughing like he'd just heard the best joke in the world, head thrown back so a thick piece of blue-white hair fell across his forehead.

When he threw his arm across the shoulders of the fellow diner on his left, in apparent appreciation, I flinched in my seat and said, "Holy *shit.*"

Skwarecki said, "What, you know Marty?"

"I know Kyle," I said. "The guy sitting right next to him."

32

"You know Kyle West?" asked Bost.

"Jesus," I said. "What's he doing *here?* I mean, he used to talk about going to law school, but this is ridiculous. What is he, working for Hetzler?"

"Kyle's an ADA," said Bost.

"With you guys?" I asked.

She nodded.

"Thank God," I said. "It would've been way too weird if it turned out he was working for Teddy's mother."

Bost looked at Skwarecki. "He's been a prosecutor in Special Victims for what, two years now?"

"Just about," said Skwarecki.

"What's Special Victims?" I asked.

"Sex crimes," said Bost. "He's done a lot of good work, especially with kids."

"Our little Kyle?" I said.

"Good people," said Skwarecki. "*Seriously* good people."

"Always was," I said. "Haven't seen him since college. And let me tell you, me and Kyle and our buddy Ellis? We used to *drink*."

Skwarecki slid around to the edge of the booth and stood up. "So let's drag his ass over, already."

I watched Skwarecki walk across the room. Kyle looked up at her with a big smile on his face, and then she pointed over to our table. He saw me and slapped a hand over his heart, grinning even wider as he feigned cardiac trauma. He said something to Hetzler and then bounced up out of his seat.

"Maddie Dare! What the hell brings you to fashionable Queens?" He slid in beside me and gave me a huge hug.

"We're getting her prepped for the grand jury," said Bost.

"Sweetheart," he said, "tell me everything!"

So I did.

"And now you have to tell *me* why you're yakking it up with that guy Hetzler," I said.

"The jury just came back on a case of mine," said Kyle. "I kicked Marty's ass — client got twenty-five to life."

"Awesome," I said.

"This was Garcia?" asked Skwarecki.

Kyle nodded, turning to me. "Maddie, the most adorable little girl, and so brave on the stand — I can't even tell you."

"The father wouldn't cop to it?" asked Skwarecki.

"Total dirtbag," said Kyle. "He dragged it out and dragged it out until he'd made her testify."

Skwarecki shook her head slowly. "You had him admitting to *everything*. Right off the bat."

"On video, no less," said Kyle. "Bad enough, what he'd already put her through."

He shook his head. "Five *years,* Maddie. The most horrific abuse, and she's only twelve now. Imagine?"

"But you got the guy?" I asked.

"*Nailed* him," he said. "Marty didn't have a prayer."

I invited Kyle to dinner on Sixteenth Street that night, since he'd offered to drive me back to the city — or at least what he and I called "the city." Skwarecki would've no doubt given us a ton of shit for making any such distinction between Queens and Manhattan.

As Kyle slowed to make the turn onto our block in the dusky light, I saw a fat unconscious guy leaned up against a parking-sign pole. He was canted forward from the waist, belly mashed against thighs, knuckles nearly grazing the sidewalk, head hanging lower than his ass.

Actually, it was his ass I noticed first. The guy's pants were shoved down around his knees, baring a floating visual non sequitur of giant beige harvest-moon butt cheeks.

"Did the Thanksgiving parade start early," asked Kyle, "or did we just drive by an enormous naked ass?"

"An enormous naked homeless ass. There was a paper cup by his foot with dollar bills sticking out the top. Kind of amazing it hasn't been stolen."

"I'll be sure to mention that next time anyone gives me shit about how Dinkins hasn't brought crime rates down."

Kyle clicked on his hazard lights and double-parked behind a guy loading suit-cases into the back of a station wagon.

"How bad are they?" I asked.

"Crime rates?"

"You're on the front lines. Are things getting worse, or has it always been this bad?"

The station wagon pulled out and Kyle maneuvered into its spot.

"It started out bad," he said, pulling up the emergency brake, "and it's been getting worse for thirty years."

We got out of his car and headed into the courtyard of One-Thirty-Five.

I let us into the vestibule and stuck my key in the inner door's lock. "You know, when I first came east for school — in seventy-eight, seventy-nine — there weren't homeless people everywhere. There were, like, occasional bums, you know? But even in Grand Central there were only bag ladies — crazy old women in ratty fur coats. We could still use the bathrooms there. You didn't see people begging everywhere, passed out on the sidewalks, all of that."

"You didn't see giant asses on every street corner," said Kyle.

"Was it just Reagan, or what?"

"It's complicated," he said.

"I read some old essay about living in Manhattan, E. B. White or something," I said as we started up the stairs. "And he was talking about how they had wicker seats on the subways. Fucking wicker, can you imagine? But then you read about gangs in Five Points, back in the day — people getting garroted in hansom cabs, race riots in Astor Place a hundred years ago — and I just wonder if it's all because there are too many people smashed in together here. If it's always been this ugly."

We walked into the apartment and I

turned on the hallway's light. No one else was home yet.

"The homeless stuff was partly Reagan and partly Koch," said Kyle. "Reagan cut federal funding right and left, but it was Koch's decision to shut down mental wards around the city. You'd see people walking down the street still wearing their hospital ID bracelets. And then a lot of SROs shut down — hundreds of hotels where you used to be able to get a cheap room by the week."

"Want a beer?" I asked, stepping into the kitchen.

"Sure."

I opened the fridge and grabbed two Rolling Rocks. "And the actual crime stats?"

"Worse. Like I said, a thirty-year upswing. But that's complicated, too."

I twisted off the beer caps and handed him a bottle. "So is it about drugs? I mean, maybe this is really stupid, but I always think of *The French Connection* and then that scene in *The Godfather* where they discuss the Mafia getting serious about heroin — so that's the seventies."

"Absolutely," he said. "And God knows you and I were up close and personal with the influx of coke in the eighties."

"No shit. I watched that wave build from Studio Fifty-four on up through the advent of freebasing, at which point I drew the line."

"So to speak," he said.

"Sorry," I said, and we clinked our beers together. "Let's go grab the sofa before everyone else gets home."

The whole gang was in residence, still talking about drugs and crime over a fine dinner of Szechuan.

"Swear to God," said Sue, spearing a potsticker. "It was a whole year before I realized 'bodega' wasn't Spanish for 'crime scene.'"

"Crack made everything worse," I said.

"It's been fucking horrible here," said Kyle.

"Not just here," I said, thinking of Syracuse.

"Thank God for the War on Drugs, right?" said Pagan. "Because *that's* been fucking brilliant."

"Fucking morons," I said. "Nancy-goddamn-Reagan-'Just Say No' Buttheads."

"Your tax dollars at work," said Sue.

I nodded. "Partnership for a fucking Drug-Free America. It's all just the same old shit."

"Same as what?" asked Kyle.

"I don't know," I said. "Like the crap

brochures they used to have lying around in the back of my middle-school library back in California? All this *Reefer Madness* 'It leads to harder stuff!' scare-tactic crap, mixed in with bullshit like 'Here are some names that criminals use for Marihuana' — spelled with an 'h,' mind you —"

"Like 'tea' and 'maryjane,' " said Kyle.

"Exactly. I mean, slang last current when used by jazz musicians in nineteen fifteen?" I said.

"We had those brochures too," he said.

"And now we just have the fried-egg TV ads with 'This is your brain, this is your brain on drugs,' " said Pagan. "It's just flailing. A flailure."

Sue scooped some dry-fried string beans onto her bowl of rice. "Thank you, George Bush."

"Look, the only thing the War on Drugs has done is made it harder to buy weed," said Pagan.

I added, "And then made coke tacky and ubiquitous, before fueling the innovation of crack."

"It's still just coke," said Sue. "It's just cut less and doled out in cheaper portions."

Kyle shook his head. "Except the mandatory minimum sentence is different for crack versus powder. Which is not a good thing."

"Why?" asked Pagan.

"Because powder is suburban and crack is urban," said Kyle. "So you get poorer people doing a lot more jail time for a far smaller quantity of the same drug, since nineteen eighty-six."

"How much smaller?" she asked.

"They call it the hundred-to-one drug-quantity ratio. Five grams of crack gets you a mandatory five years in prison. And that's just for possession. You'd need to get busted with five-*hundred* grams of powder before you'd be looking at that same five years."

"And five grams of powder?" I asked.

"Misdemeanor," he said. "One year, max."

"Like *that's* gonna help," said Pagan. "I mean, don't get me wrong, it's not like I think crack is God's gift to humanity, guaranteed to build strong bodies in twelve ways and get the crabgrass out of your lawn, but even so —"

"Supply-side economics," I said. "Only thing you can do is legalize everything. Make it bonded, like bourbon. Generate some tax revenue."

"Why the hell not?" asked Pagan. "When the drinking age was twenty-one in California, we could get anything illegal we wanted, even in middle school — mushrooms, coke, LSD, mescaline, sinsemilla that'd knock you flat on your ass — but no booze."

"I'm not sure Seagram's wants the competition," said Sue.

"Seagram's already has the competition," I said. "But maybe fewer people would die fighting over the profits and distribution. Maybe it's time to take Al Capone out of the equation across the board."

"Madeline, there's a lot more to it," said Kyle. "It's not that easy."

"I know. But still —"

"It's *not.* Look at the case you're involved with, what happened to Teddy Underhill. What's happened to this city, all the violence — it's not just strictly some offshoot of misguided prohibition."

"You're right," I said. "But is there a higher rate of crack addiction than alcoholism in this country? And aren't more kids beaten to death by parents that're just plain drunk?"

"Yes," he said, "and the majority of drug-related homicides are dealer-on-dealer, not committed by users."

"So what *do* we do?" I asked. "How do we protect children? Prohibition doesn't work. What else is there?"

"I don't know, Maddie," he replied.

"There's nothing I can do about the big picture. I just try to make sure the bad guys go down so they stop hurting kids."

"One day at a time," I said.

Sue looked at Kyle. "What's going to happen with the people who killed the little boy Madeline found? Will you guys get *them?*"

"We're doing everything we can," he said. "I just hope it's enough."

"And it's not the only case any of you guys are dealing with," I said. "It's not even officially yours at all. You must have a ton of other things on your plate."

"Today I've got a guy who burned his kid to death with an iron," said Kyle. "I think Skwarecki caught the little girl left in a Dumpster."

The rest of us put our chopsticks down, our interest in dinner officially finished as we contemplated those images.

"Sorry," he said, looking at our pale faces around the table.

"Thank you for what you do," said Sue, raising her beer toward Kyle. "I couldn't handle your job for five minutes. I really couldn't."

We all joined her in toasting him.

"Nightmare," said Pagan. "The whole thing is a fucking nightmare."

■ ■ ■ ■

Dean called at midnight, his time, just after I'd drifted off to sleep.

" 'Lo?" I croaked.

"Hey, Bunny, I wake you up?"

"No problem."

"It's an hour earlier here, but I figured you'd be awake." His voice was soft, a little drunk.

I checked out the clock-radio: quarter after one. "How's Houston?"

"Flat and wide, with shitty Chinese food."

"I can meet you at the airport, with sesame noodles."

"Naked?"

"Not sure how that'd go over on the PATH train."

He laughed. "Wear my trench coat."

"You don't *own* a trench coat."

"My old coveralls, then."

"In public? Dream on."

"In private, then. Don't bother with the airport."

"You're on."

"In that case, I'll spring for a taxi home."

"I miss you," I said.

"See you at eight. Don't forget the noodles."

33

Wednesday morning I'd put on the only suit I owned for the grand jury, a college pal's castoff first-interview getup in navy gabardine. The stiff double-breasted jacket and pleated skirt made me look like a stumpy maiden aunt on alumnae day.

I thanked God Dean wasn't back yet; he would've given me no end of grief.

Bost was pretty sharp by comparison, in tailored gray with a skirt that hit above the knee.

The grand-jury venue was smaller than the courtrooms I'd walked past Tuesday on the way to Bost's office.

There were two doors, both solid wood with no glass panels. I'd been shown in through one of them from a little waiting area. I presumed the second door led out to the main hallway.

I took my seat and glanced over at the jurors, maybe twenty faces. Everybody looked like they were my parents' age and up.

Bost stepped forward and nodded at me. "Could you please state your full name for the record, please?"

"Madeline Ludlam Fabyan Dare," I replied.

One of the jurors' eyebrows shot up, an older Irish-looking guy in a brown cardigan.

Who could blame him? It was a mouthful.

"Ms. Dare," said Bost, "to begin with, I'd like to ask you about the events of September nineteenth."

"Certainly," I said.

And we were off. I described meeting Cate, the cemetery, the whole nine yards.

Bost paused for a moment.

I looked around the room while she consulted her paperwork. It was a stark little place, with one wall paneled in unrelieved teak as testament to the enduring banality of Bauhaus: "Mid-Century," though that wasn't what anyone would have called it in 1990.

I would've just called it motel-ugly, then and now, being the sort of person who considers Danish Modern the Velveeta of furniture.

"Can you describe what happened next?" asked Bost.

"Cate gave me a machete and some big clippers, and some garbage bags. And then I went to work."

"Can you describe the area you were working on?"

"I was hacking into a pretty thick section of vines and bushes. I think I filled up two bags, and then hit a bit of a tunnel, low to the ground."

I described crawling into the thicket.

"What happened then?" asked Bost.

"I could see something round and white lying on top of the leaves," I said.

"Did you know what it was?"

"I'd crawled in a little further before I realized it was a skull. By that point I could see the rib cage and everything. I realized the bones were a child's."

"And after that?"

"I backed out and ran to find Cate," I said, then related what happened up until Skwarecki's and her own arrival at Prospect.

"And did you return the following week?"

"Detective Skwarecki got in touch with Cate a few days later, and gave her the go-ahead to bring in the next scheduled group of volunteers."

"Had Detective Skwarecki asked you to be on the lookout for anything in particular?"

I looked at the jurors and described the clothes in the missing-persons report.

"Did you find any objects of that sort?" asked Bost

"We found a shoe," I said. "A little sneaker."

A few of the jurors nodded.

"Can you describe the sneaker?" asked Bost.

"It was white, and there were two words written on it."

"And what were those?"

" 'Club Melmac,' " I said.

I expected her to ask me whether I knew the significance of that, but she didn't. Or maybe she did and it would have been hearsay or something, unless the details in the missing-persons report were related by Skwarecki directly.

"What did you do then?"

"We waited for Detective Skwarecki to come back."

"The detective had been there already that day?" asked Bost.

I explained about the vertebra.

"And when the detective returned," said Bost, "you and Ms. Ludlam showed her the sneaker?"

"We did, yes," I said, "and she bagged that as well."

"Thank you, Ms. Dare," said Bost. "I'm going to ask now whether the jurors have any questions for you."

She and I both turned toward them.

A silver-haired African American woman leaned forward. "I have a question."

Bost said, "Yes ma'am?"

The woman raised a pair of glasses, suspended around her neck by a fine chain dotted with tiny pearls. "May I ask who *found* the sneaker?"

Bost looked at me. "Ms. Dare?"

"One of the other volunteers," I said.

The juror nodded. "And do you know *which* one?"

Bost relayed the question to me. "Did you know at that time which of the volunteers had discovered the sneaker?"

"I didn't," I said, looking from her to the juror. "Someone left it sitting on this little granite post, near the central path."

"So you don't know where, exactly, the shoe was first discovered?" asked the juror.

"Did you know its original location, Ms. Dare?" relayed Bost.

I spoke directly to the juror. "No ma'am. I only saw it after it had been placed on the post. The other volunteers had gone home by then. Cate and I left it right there until the detective arrived."

I left out the part about poking it with a stick.

"I see. Thank you," said the juror, settling back in her seat.

Bost waited a moment. "Are there any further questions?"

The jurors shook their heads.

Bost turned toward me.

"All right, Ms. Dare," she said. "Thank you."

I stood up to walk back out through the waiting room.

Kyle had asked me to find him once I was finished.

The security guy let me through into the DA's offices. Rosemary the receptionist had me sign in again before handing me a GUEST sticker. This one was blue.

She called Kyle and he came to the desk to get me.

"Do I need an umbrella this time?" I asked as I followed him back down a different hallway, away from the one leading to Bost's office.

"You should be safe," he said. "Things seem to be moving along today. And we don't get as much leakage on my side."

His office was a little white cubby with a view of the parking lot. Where Bost had had her photo of the Unisphere he had a bulletin board jammed with Kyle-at-the-beach-with-friends photos and a dozen shots of a little beige dog with a mushed-in face.

"That's Mason," Kyle explained. "Is he not the *most* adorable thing ever?"

I peered at the photos, squinting. "That guy in the Speedo?"

"My *dog,* Madeline."

I am not the hugest dog person who ever lived, but I agreed that Mason looked precious and well behaved and remarkably brilliant, for a non-human.

Satisfied with my level of Mason worship, Kyle asked, "So how'd it go with the grand jury?"

"Okay, I guess. Bost just asked me about finding the skeleton, and then the sneaker, a week later."

"That makes sense," he said. "She'll want to show the basis on which Skwarecki established the victim's identity."

"So if the jurors come back with a true bill, what happens next?"

"This is the hurry-up-and-wait part of things. They have to do another arraignment, first of all."

"The same as the first one?" I asked.

"This will be the 'arraignment on indictment.' " And then he got into the details, explaining why I didn't really need to show up for anything until the actual trial.

"And they'll definitely plead 'not guilty'?" I asked.

"We'd know by now, otherwise."

"No plea bargains?"

"We don't really do that in Queens, after the indictment," he said. "Safe to say that your guys are going to trial."

"Even if they change their minds?"

"Sometimes," he said. "Like that case I just had with Marty? I was *begging* the defendant to change his plea to guilty the whole time."

"Why?"

"So his daughter wouldn't have to testify. There was no reason to put her through it."

"Skwarecki said you had the guy confessing to everything beforehand."

"Exactly," he said, "and that asshole knew we had him, but he made her get up on the stand anyway."

"I can't imagine," I said.

"I tell you, Maddie, this little girl? She was *magnificent*. She showed up the day she had to testify wearing this fuzzy pink hat with a kitten on the front, and underneath the kitten it said 'Fabulous' in hot-pink sequins. So she looks up at me and says, 'Kyle, I know you're going to make me take my hat off, but I just wanted to wear it as long as I could.' "

He was making me get all teary-eyed.

"And did you make her take it off?" I asked.

"Are you *kidding?* I knelt down right next to her and I said, 'Honey, if you hadn't shown up in that hat today, I would have had to go out and buy it for you, because if the people on that jury need to know *anything,* they need to know *You. Are. Fabulous.*"

"Oh, crap," I said, reaching for the box of Kleenex on his desk because now my eyes were brimming, ready to spill over.

"I'm telling you, Madwoman, that little girl climbed up into the box and she didn't flinch once, just spoke into the microphone with all the guts in the world and told us exactly what happened. Horrible, explicit, *evil* things she'd already been forced to live through once."

"So you got him? The father?"

"He changed his plea then and there, the bastard."

I blew my nose.

"Good," I said. "And I hope he has a really shitty time for the *entire* rest of his life."

Kyle shrugged. "Twenty-five years. I bet

he's out in fifteen."

"Maybe he'll get killed in prison."

"Sure," he said. "If we're lucky."

I thought about Pierce, wishing him the same fate.

I looked at Kyle. "Is it *ever* the creepy-drifter guy with free candy — this kind of stuff?"

"Stranger Danger," he said. "The last great myth."

"Yeah. I mean, your little girl with the hat, that kid Lisa Steinberg getting beaten to death by her adoptive father, Teddy . . ."

Pagan . . .

"Don't get me wrong, it happens," he said, "but it's an infinitesimal percentage overall. Ninety-nine out of a hundred, the kind of abuse you're talking about? It's the nonbiological male in the family orbit. The stepfather, the mother's boyfriend . . ."

"And the mothers?"

"Sometimes they don't know. Sometimes they're too scared to do anything about it. Maybe they're financially dependent on the guy."

"Fuck *that*."

"My sentiments exactly," said Kyle.

I tossed my Kleenex into the wastepaper basket next to his desk. "Wanna go get some lunch?"

34

Kyle and I planned to dawdle over lunch.

"I'm working late tonight anyway," he said. "I might as well take a decent break now."

We had a window booth at the same Italian restaurant where I'd run into him days earlier with Skwarecki and Bost.

"There's really nowhere else to eat around here," Kyle explained. "Sooner or later you run into everyone — cops, defense attorneys, everyone in the DA's office. I guess it keeps us all honest. Or at least polite."

The minute he said that I saw Skwarecki and Cate standing in the main dining room's arched doorway and waved them over.

I introduced Kyle and Cate to one another, and we ordered a round of iced teas and sodas while perusing our menus for more solid fare.

"Are you guys done with your stuff for

the day?" I asked Skwarecki and Cate.

Cate nodded.

Skwarecki said, "Should be another hour or so. Bost said she'd beep me."

"So will we know today about the indictment?" I asked.

"Sure," she said. "Late afternoon, probably."

"I think it's so interesting that they'll both be tried at once," said Cate. "It seems a bit counterintuitive, to me."

"Well, you really want the codefendants in the room at the same time," said Kyle. "Nothing creates more doubt in a jury than an empty chair. The defense has a field day with that. And then it's a lot more time and expense to have to go through the process more than once."

Skwarecki traced an index-fingertip line through the beads of condensation on her water glass. "Not to mention that when you have witnesses testifying in separate cases, they might remember slightly different details each time. Even if it's something small — 'He was wearing a gray suit,' 'He was wearing a blue jacket,' the defense'll use the contradictions to make a jury question the entire statement."

I said, "They'll have separate lawyers, though, won't they? Albert Williams and

Teddy's mother."

"With codefendants," said Kyle, "having both defense attorneys working for the public defender's office would be a conflict of interest. That's how the mother ended up with Marty as counsel."

"I was wondering about that," I said. "I mean, judging from his tailor alone the guy doesn't look exactly affordable."

Kyle took a sip of his ice water. "There's a rotation of local criminal defense attorneys who are called upon to step in. She got lucky."

"Marty's going to milk this thing for airtime," said Skwarecki. "Mark my fucking words."

"Our Mr. Hetzler has been called many things," agreed Kyle, "but shrinking violet is not among them."

An hour later we were debating the merits of coffee and/or dessert when a group of young gang-affiliated-looking guys took over the table beside us: pants hung low, thick gold chains weighed down with medallions the size of hood ornaments.

Kyle and Skwarecki gave them a solid once-over, eyes hooded. The boys glared right back, bristling.

So the perps ate here too.

Or maybe they're just tourists.

"Dessert?" asked Cate. "Good God, I feel like I just ate an entire Zamboni drowning in marinara."

"I'm having a cannoli," said Skwarecki. "It's just been that kind of day."

"You don't have to get back to work?" I asked.

She shook her head. "I'm RDO."

I must have looked confused.

"Regular day off, Maddie," Kyle explained. "Our pal here's getting paid overtime to testify."

Skwarecki grinned. "Your tax dollars at work."

"Hey," I said. "Any job where they shoot at you should be worth at least a million bucks a year, net."

"Your lips to God's ears," said Skwarecki, clinking my glass of Diet Coke with her own.

There was a trilling noise from under the table, like R2-D2 had gotten lost down there.

Skwarecki consulted the beeper hooked onto her belt. "They must be finished."

She got up and walked into the entrance to use the pay phone. I could see the lump of a gun at her hip under the blazer.

Our waiter returned to the table. Kyle told

298

him we wanted a cannoli and four espressos.

Skwarecki came back in and sat down.

"True bill?" asked Kyle.

"Better than that," she said. "Eight counts each."

Cate and I high-fived.

I dropped my stinging palm back down to my lap. "So eight is good?"

"Eight is excellent," said Skwarecki, "but she wants to talk to us about the sneaker."

"What about it?" asked Cate.

"The grand jury had a lot of questions about the way it turned up. Bost needs the other one safe in hand before this thing goes to trial. One of you want to play tour guide for me tomorrow morning?"

The boys at the next table ignored us, laughing.

"Does it have to be tomorrow?" asked Cate. "I'm up to my neck at work for the next few days."

Skwarecki crossed her arms and swiveled toward me.

Bost stepped into the room's arched doorway, scanning the crowd until she spotted our table.

"Sign me up," I said. "What the hell."

Bost pulled up a chair.

"Good work today," said Skwarecki.

"Not enough," said Bost.

She looked at me and Cate. "Has Detective Skwarecki told you about the necessity of finding the second shoe?"

"Yes," I said. "I'm going back to Prospect with her tomorrow morning."

"And you understand that any further evidence-hunting requires the detective's official presence and oversight — start to finish — if we want a chance in hell of nailing these assholes at trial?"

"Yes," I said again.

She lifted her right hand, palm up, to count off a list of further directives slowly on her fingers, each successive digit extended and then bent farther back beneath the downbeat of her fist: manual bullet points.

"You do not *move* anything, Ms. Dare," she said. "You do not *touch* anything. You do not *think* about touching anything — and I mean not even a gum wrapper."

Only the index finger to go. Bost raised her hand to eye level.

"In fact," she continued, that last finger now a pistol barrel aimed dead-center at the bridge of my nose, "you will not so much as *consider* the act of thinking about touching anything."

She dropped her hand and leaned forward,

right in my face and drill-sergeant close. "Are we *clear?*"

"Dude," I said, "back off."

I was on the brink of giving her a Three-Stooges *doink* to the eyes when the flare of her nostrils died down and she dropped her shoulders, resuming a civilized distance.

"Ms. Bost," I said, "if you'd prefer that I not accompany Detective Skwarecki to the cemetery tomorrow, just tell me so. I'd be more than happy to bow out."

She looked at the floor, her voice quiet. "We'd appreciate your help, but it's essential that you understand how crucial maintaining a proper chain of evidence is right now."

"Of course," I said.

Bost stood up, saying good-byes around the table as she gathered up her purse and briefcase.

Skwarecki watched her stride away. "Fucking lawyers."

Kyle laughed.

"No offense," added Skwarecki.

"Not exactly a team player, is she?" asked Cate.

Skwarecki snorted. "You could suit us all up for the World Series at Shea and Bost still wouldn't admit we're walking to bat from the same dugout, you know?"

"Of course not," I said. "She thinks it's

Wimbledon."

"I gotta hit it," said Kyle, standing up. "See you ladies round the campus."

Skwarecki made her excuses and followed him out once they'd both chipped in for the check.

One of our neighbor boys pulled out a Polaroid camera, standing up to take pictures of his pals. The other guys started goofing around, shoving each other and laughing, making bunny ears behind each other's heads.

Tourists, then. Or maybe a field trip.

I blinked when the flash went off again, straight into my eyes.

Dean got home that night at eight on the dot. I'd blown off wearing his coveralls, but Pagan and Sue were out playing pool, so we didn't have to share the noodles.

35

The rain had blown through by Thursday morning, but the sky was still heavy with dryer-lint rafts of cloud, sunlight distilled to a squinty dim glare that made my teeth hurt.

Skwarecki had told me eight o'clock, and I was pissed about having made it to Prospect's front gate on time just so I could spend the subsequent twenty-five minutes pacing alone on the broken sidewalk, shivering and undercaffeinated.

"Bitch better show up with doughnuts," I said, my words unheeded by a passing squirrel.

I had Cate's gate key in my coat pocket, but no pen or paper with which to write my detective pal a note explaining how I'd gotten sick enough of waiting to embark upon our Quest for Sneaker-Grail without her, Bost or no Bost.

Skwarecki was now half an hour late, and I wanted to get started — or at least get off the damn sidewalk and behind the chapel.

There was a low passageway under the train tracks, and the post-rush-hour stragglers coming through it kept giving me the hairy eyeball.

I couldn't tell whether they were sizing me up for a mugging or just presuming, pissed off, that I was some crack-harpie suburban skank looking to score cheap rock and generally taint the neighborhood.

Door Number One made me a paranoid racist asshole; Door Number Two scrawled "kick my guilty liberal ass" across a piece of binder paper and Scotch-taped it to the back of my coat.

Either way, I doubted I could endear myself by humming a few bars of "Don't Mind Me — I'm Just Waiting On a Cop."

Two young guys sauntered by and then slowed to establish an observation post twenty feet away. They were in watch caps and down jackets, jeans riding so low the denim hems puddled atop their slack-laced sneakers.

It was time to move my Skwarecki vigil to a better-trafficked location, so I started walking slowly down my side of the block, trying to keep it loose.

Eye contact or not?

Still undecided by the time I'd reached

visual-acknowledgment range, I avoided the question entirely by squinching my eyes shut and yawning, then speeded up to join the crowd at a bus stop.

Skwarecki was forty-five minutes late now. I thought about finding a pay phone, but didn't want to miss her if she did finally show.

A bus rolled up to the curb and everyone else got on it. It pulled away and I stood alone, traffic whipping by. Five more minutes, then ten. Still no sign of her.

I looked down the block for a pay phone — no such luck. I checked back over my shoulder to see if the pair of gate-sentry dudes had moved on yet.

There was only one now, and he smiled at me.

I heard the gun of an engine behind my back, followed by what I hoped to hell wasn't the *whump-ump* of fast tires jumping a curb.

Just when I thought about turning to look, something slammed into my legs.

First I was airborne, and then I wasn't anywhere at all.

". . . Head wound . . . possible fracture to . . ."

Skwarecki's voice, tuning in and out.

I opened one eye to find her face blurry above me, then twitched my hand with the intention of checking my scalp for blood, only somebody had shoved a whole bunch of big fat pointy railroad spikes into the flesh of my right forearm.

"Get me a bus down here right god-damned *now*," she said.

I tried saying, *Fuck the bus, how 'bout a goddamned ambulance?* but all that came out was *"Aaaamn . . ."*

"She's coming around." A man's voice.

I lifted my head, saw stars, and blacked out again.

A bump and a swerve and then my eyes were open. Siren going and a guy leaning across me in a paramedic jacket. Something stiff around my neck so I couldn't move my head.

"Skwarecki?" Talking made my throat hurt.

The guy looked down at me. "Right be-hind us."

"My arm."

"You're okay. Almost there."

We pitched to the side one more time and the siren wound down.

The guy moved out of my field of sight, everything bumping as they shoved me out the back, then the sound of hydraulic doors and after that strips of light rolling by overhead.

Somebody yanked a curtain back, and then it all stopped moving.

A hairy hand moved a flashlight across my eyes, and I felt the snick of scissors along my left sleeve.

It's the right *arm that hurts.*

The curtain slid wider on its rails and I heard Skwarecki say "Jesus Christ" down by my feet.

"Can't take me anywhere," I mumbled, hoarse.

"Yeah, right?" She was trying for cocky but just came off scared.

Which, frankly, scared the hell out of me.

The scissors kept going on my shirt until I was lying there pretty much starko from the waist up, and then the guy with the hairy hands started poking and prodding, making me whimper with pain.

Please let me not have worn the bra with safety pins where that strap unraveled.

"You're gonna be okay," said Skwarecki.

"Absolutely," said Hairy-Hand Guy. "We'll get that arm set in a jiffy."

"I don't have to be awake for that part, right?"

No response. *Great.*

307

Skwarecki gave my right instep a squeeze, the significance of which took a second to register.

"I'm barefoot?"

Jesus, who'd want a pair of five-year-old high-tops I'd scored at a Goodwill in the first place?

"I've got your sneaks bagged up right here," said Skwarecki.

Maybe my amputated feet were still in them only I didn't know it yet.

Except I'd just felt the squeeze of her hand.

I tried wiggling both sets of toes — was that really the gurney's surface behind each heel, or some kind of phantom-limb thing? Fuck feet — did I even have legs?

I screwed my eyes shut, fingers crossed at the end of my non-excruciating arm. "Skwarecki, please tell me why you have my shoes in a bag."

"I figured you'd want 'em," she said.

Okay, so presumably they weren't soaked in blood with my shinbones sticking out the top. "Um, why'd you take them off me?"

"I didn't," she said. "That's just what happens when you get hit by a car hard as you were. The force'll knock you right out of your shoes."

"Out of a pair of laced-up Converse? How

is that even possible?"

"Basic laws of physics," said Hairy Hands. "Let's cut those pants off, too. I want a look at her knee."

I tried to shake my head. "Why can't I move my head?"

"You're strapped into a neckboard," said Skwarecki. "It's okay."

The cold scissor-blade slid along my belly. "This is such bullshit," I said. "And I'm freezing."

Dr. Hairy draped a sheet over my torso. "Now let's get you up to X-ray."

"This is really starting to hurt," I said, tears leaking sideways out of my eyes and down my temples as I stared up from my gurney at a different hallway ceiling.

The pain was worst in my arm, but the rest of me throbbed in concert. We'd been sitting outside the X-ray room for what felt like weeks.

"Shock's wearing off," said Skwarecki. "You still feel cold?"

"Now that you mention it."

"I'll ask that guy for a blanket or some shit when he gets back."

"Oh, like he's *coming* back. *Ever.*"

"He will if he doesn't want his ass shot off by yours truly," she said.

My teeth started chattering. "I love having

a friend with a g-gun. Cuts through so much paperwork."

"Speaking of that, I'm going to need a statement from you."

"L-later?"

"Sure," she said. "But did you see anything? Get a look at the car?"

"Skwarecki, I'm so c-cold. . . ."

"Hey," she called out. "Somebody got a blanket around here?"

I heard squeaky footsteps approaching, then felt something soft settle over my legs.

Better.

She waited a moment until my teeth came to rest. "You remember anything about the car? Get any kind of look at it?"

I started to shake my head, then remembered the neckboard. "I got a look at the air. After that I don't remember anything. Even hitting the ground."

Skwarecki didn't say anything. The noise of everyone else rushing through the hallway filled in the silence.

"There were these two guys hanging around, though," I said. "Across from me when I was out front at Prospect. That's why I walked out to the bus stop. When I looked back, one of them had left and the other one was staring at me, smiling. Freaked me out."

"What do you mean?" she asked.

"Well, maybe the other guy went off to call somebody, you know? Like, say, a friend with a car."

"I'm figuring this for a random hit-and-run," she said. "Fucked up, but random."

I thought back to the smiling guy. "It kind of felt like he knew . . ."

"Knew what?"

"Jesus, *I* don't know. He was smiling at me and it gave me the creeps."

"Maybe he liked the view of your ass."

"I'm serious."

"Fine," she said. "What'd these guys look like?"

"Watch caps," I said, "big down jackets, sloppy jeans, and very white sneakers."

"You just described ninety percent of the male population between the ages of ten and thirty. In all five boroughs."

"African American."

"Narrows it down to twenty-six percent. That all you got?"

"Yeah," I said, "pretty much."

The truth was, I had no idea what the two guys looked like because I'd been doing my best *not* to look at them, and Skwarecki was no doubt totally right about it all just being random.

"You're going back, right?" I asked.

"Where you got hit? I've already sent out a couple of uniforms, doing a canvass — see if anybody got a plate number."

"Not that," I said. "Back to the cemetery. I'm really glad you guys are checking whether anyone saw me get hit, but Bost is right — we need the other shoe."

"Don't worry about it."

"Why the fuck not?"

"Because you're bleeding and your arm is broken and you're working up to a helluva shiner on that left eye?"

"So?"

"So take a load off."

"Skwarecki, what're you, gonna make me *guilt* you into this?"

"Into what?"

"I'd like to have something to show for having gotten run down by a car this morning, okay? If it weren't for the damn shoe, I wouldn't have been there."

I didn't mention the part about how I'd been out on that corner waiting for her to show up.

"Of course I'm going back," she said, in this cheesy soothing voice. "Soon as they get you squared away."

"You're just waiting around to see if I cry once they start yanking on this arm to get the bones set, so you can tease me later for

312

being a total pussy."

"Oh, like you're not already crying?"

"Fuck yourself. Showed up an hour late and you didn't bring doughnuts?"

"There was some shit going down at the precinct. We gotta get you a beeper or something."

"Yeah, maybe it would have taken the impact."

"Jesus, if I'd *known* . . . ?"

"It's not like you ran me over, Skwarecki. And I'm grateful as all hell you showed up when you did, but I still want you to get your tits out of my face and go find that shoe."

"And you're planning to, what, take a taxi home?"

"Subway," I said.

"I don't fucking *think* so."

"Try and stop me."

"I handcuff your good wrist to the gurney here, Madeline? Not like you'll be breezing through any turnstiles. In your underwear."

"Fine. I'll call my husband. Ask him to take off early."

"He's at work?"

"Yeah. North Jersey."

"Got a car?" she asked.

"Might be able to borrow one."

"Better leave now, even still. What's his

number?"

I recited it. "Ask him to bring me some pants, will you?"

"I've got a pair of sweats out in the car."

I said "Great," then waited to hear her footsteps fading well away down the noisy hall before I closed my eyes against the pain and started crying for real, which only made everything hurt worse. Plus which now my nose was all runny and I didn't want to wipe it on my blanket.

"Here's a tissue," said Skwarecki, leaning into view as she pressed a Kleenex gently against my upper lip.

"Oh, perfect," I said, "you're still here?"

"Shut up and blow."

"Not unless you promise first that you'll go find that shoe . . . with someone along who's got your back."

"Or what? You gonna snot me to death?"

"Damn straight."

36

Three hours later I had a spiffy air cast and sling, seven stitches in a newly shaved oval on the side of my head, a fully realized black eye, and a bellyful of painkillers.

Skwarecki was gone, and I lay propped up on my gurney back in the ER, waiting for Dean to arrive with Christoph's Jeep. I couldn't feel a goddamn thing except for a velvet opiate glow floating around and through my entire body.

I had on cop-issue sweatpants and a hospital smock. A nurse had tucked a pillow under my damaged arm to help the swelling go down, explaining that I couldn't have a real cast for at least twenty-four hours.

My fat, bruise-dark fingers seemed adequate proof of that thesis, sticking straight out from the end of the whole splint shebang like stiff little breakfast links.

I didn't care. I was in fact wasted to the

point of being awed by the soulful beauty emanating from each person whom fate had contrived into ER with me: Dr. Hairy Hands, all the nurses, the little boy puking into a green plastic pan next bed over — even the homeless-looking dude with blood gushing from his flattened nose.

One love, Jah guide.

"Bunny?"

I looked up at my husband's stricken face and smiled. "Hey, it's so great to see you."

"What happened?"

"I got hit by a car," I said.

"I know. Your friend Skwarecki told me on the phone. Are you okay?"

"I'm really, really good. Really."

"You're on really, really good drugs right now."

"Mm. *Yes!* Innnnndubitably."

"Not to harsh your buzz," he said, "but you also look like you got beaten to shit."

"I fought the car and the car won. Doobie-do."

I closed my eyes, grooving on how the fluorescent lights made the inside of my eyelids glow pretty and scarlet. *"Wow."*

"I'm going to go see how I sign you out. Then we'll get you home."

"You're amazing. Thank you so much for being so amazing . . . all the, like, *time.*"

He smoothed a strand of hair off my forehead. "Bunny, have you eaten today?"

"Food," I said, *"wow."*

I dozed off until he came back with a nurse. They put my high-tops back on, then helped me sit up before gently swinging my legs over the side of the gurney.

They'd parked a wheelchair right next to me, but just leaning a few inches to port so I could reach for the floor with my right sneaker's toe loosed a retinal cascade of hot, sharp little stars.

Dean bent down to brace me, his mouth close to my ear. "Bunny?"

"Can't," I said, eyes shut again.

I felt him wrap one arm around my waist and snake the other beneath my knees. "Okay?"

I leaned into him. "Feel sick."

"I got you," he said, lifting me gently off the gurney. "Don't worry."

I remember Dean fastening my seat belt, and then the sun glittering on the East River when we drove across a bridge.

"Look," I said. "All those girders. All that sky."

His hand was light on my knee. "Home soon. Go back to sleep."

■ ■ ■ ■

"Wakey-wakey," chirped Pagan. "We got you a cheeseburger."

I was on the sofa, adrift in a bay of pillows.

Pagan and Sue and Dean were seated around the coffee table next to me, prising lids off a bunch of crimped-foil take-out containers.

"You guys rule," I said, voice croaky. "Anything to drink?"

Sue slid a tall paper cup across the table. "Pepsi — not diet. Dean figured you could use the sugar."

I pulled it closer with my left hand, then tried to lift my head toward the straw.

No luck, and my mouth felt like a coal scuttle.

"Here." Sue bent the straw at its crinkled hinge, picked up the whole vessel, and tucked it into my armpit. "Can you reach?"

"Think so." I craned my head up a couple of inches and managed to get the straw between my teeth.

The cup shifted, ice sloshing, and a tide of sweet effervescence flooded my mouth.

Heaven.

"Big excitement today, huh?" asked Pagan.

"I guess." I sucked down another sip of cola bliss.

She dipped a french fry in catsup. "What were you, wandering around in the middle of the road?"

"Sidewalk," I said. "I heard the tires hit the curb."

"Before the actual car hit *you?*" she asked.

"Pretty much."

Sue took a bite of her own fry, examining my sling and air cast. "Fucked you right the hell up —"

"But thank you for not dying," added Pagan.

"No shit," I said, grazing the coffee table's wooden edge with my knuckles in gratitude.

Dean had a burger in his hand, but he didn't raise it to his mouth. "Bunny, do you think this had anything to do with the little cemetery kid?"

"Skwarecki doesn't think so," I said. "I mean, maybe in a small town the whole thing would be fishy, but it's Queens — couple of million people?"

"Rush hour," said Sue. "Everybody driving like maniacs?"

"Exactly. What are the odds, right?" I got the straw in my teeth again.

Dean took a bite of burger, chewed, and swallowed. "You mentioned two guys,

319

though, when we were coming home from the hospital. And one of them left?"

"Prospect is off the main drag," I said. "The front gate's on this little unpaved lane across from a college, and there were some people walking by. Skwarecki was way late. These two guys came out from the subway — a little walkway under the tracks — and then they were hanging out in the campus gate across from me. Not like they were sharpening machetes or anything, but I figured I should move out to the street. There was a bus stop, more people around."

"And then you got run over?" asked Pagan.

"Run *under,* really. That car had me airborne like a bull with a rodeo clown."

"You landed on your arm?" asked Sue.

"I don't know. I hit my head on the roof and then bounced."

"That explains the stitches," said Pagan.

I shrugged and then winced. "We got any more painkillers? Everything's starting to throb again."

"In the kitchen," said Dean, taking one more quick bite of his burger before standing up to go get them.

"You are a young bronzed god," I called after him.

"You're high," his voice echoed back down

the hallway.

"So what happened with the two guys?" asked Pagan.

"Nothing, really," I said. "Just . . . when I looked back over my shoulder, one of them was gone, and the other one was kind of smiling at me."

"Smiling, like 'creepy grin of foreboding' or just 'have a nice day'?" she asked.

"Pagan," said Sue, "when's the last time some strange guy smiled at you without whipping out a box cutter and demanding your wallet?"

"Last month, on the subway," answered my sister.

"You mean the one who whipped out his dick and then barfed on you?" I asked.

Sue settled back into her chair, arms crossed. "My point exactly."

"He didn't really barf on *me*," said Pagan. "His briefcase got the worst of it."

Dean came back in, white paper bag in hand. "Want me to unscrew the cap for you?"

"Please," I said.

He shook out a pair of tablets into the palm of my left hand. "Got enough soda left to swallow those?"

"Sure." I dumped them into my mouth and washed them down.

"Now eat some burger," he said.

"Fries first, okay?"

He picked up a few and held them to my lips.

I bit off half and started chewing, mumbling "Need salt" through my mouthful of potato.

Dean shook his head. "No they don't."

I started to call him a rat bastard and he shoved the fry-ends into my open mouth.

"No fair," I said once I'd swallowed.

"Eat," he said.

The phone rang and Sue grabbed it.

I turned away from the piece of cheeseburger Dean was swooping toward my mouth.

"Actually," said Sue, "this is her roommate, but she's right here next to me on the sofa."

I looked at her, mouthing, "Who?"

Dean plucked the Pepsi cup out of my armpit so Sue could hand me the phone.

"What's-her-name," she said. "The cop."

I raised the receiver to my ear, straining its piglet-tail of cord. "Skwarecki?"

"The one and only. How's that shiner?"

"I'm avoiding mirrors, like a vampire."

"Excellent plan."

"Hey," I said, "thank you for taking such good care of me today. I owe your ass, big-time."

"Fuck that noise. Least I could do — I mean, if I'd shown up when I was supposed to . . . ?"

"Not your fault," I said.

She sighed. "At least I'm gonna end your day on a better note."

I glanced at my blackened fingers, now swollen to the point of being shiny. "That wouldn't be hard, but do tell."

"I got it, Madeline."

"Got what?"

"The fucking shoe," she said. "Right here in front of me on my fucking desk — ALF's face on it and everything."

I felt light-headed. "The rest of today was worth it, then."

"I may have something about that, too," she said.

"What?"

"Partial plate number, and a description of the car. I can't promise you anything, but my guys're trying to narrow it down, okay?"

I gave the coffee table another tap for luck. "God love you, Skwarecki — tits and all."

Dean coaxed half the burger down me before I started drifting from shore on a riptide of sleep.

I woke up in the dark when a sanitation crew rolled east up Sixteenth Street, slamming each building's metal cans empty against the lip of their truck's hopper.

The stereo's green LEDs read 4:02. I still couldn't open my left eye, and my bones hurt like I was getting crushed and compacted right along with the garbage.

Two notes of sharp whistle from below and the driver eased off the clutch, lumbering on toward Sixth Avenue. In the streetlight's orange glow I saw that someone had left me more painkillers laid out on the table beside a coffee mug.

I fumbled for the pills, so stiff and sore I had to rest the cup on my chest and tip it toward me without lifting my head. Lukewarm rivulets of tap water coursed down both sides of my neck, soaking the back of my collar before I got enough in my mouth for a decent swallow.

The streetlight snapped off and the brick buildings across from us looked gray in the predawn quiet. The pills were starting to kick in by the time Dean padded out into the living room, around four thirty.

He yawned, glancing at the empty coffee mug. "You found that smack I left out for you?"

"Right after the garbage truck woke me up. Thank you — much needed."

"Think you can get to Saint Vincent's by

yourself today?"

"Saint Vinnie's? For what?"

"To get your real cast on," he said. "Sue got the doctor from yesterday to switch your appointment, save you a trip to Queens."

"Cool," I said, grateful for her foresight. St. Vincent's was just a few blocks down Seventh Avenue.

He sat down on the sofa's edge just below my hip. "I have to pick up Christoph this morning, early. Will you really be okay on your own?"

"It's fine," I said. "Don't worry."

"Bunny, are you sure this doesn't have anything to do with the cemetery?"

"Yes," I lied. "Absolutely."

Dean reached for my good hand, weaving his fingers with mine.

"Bullshit," he said, giving my digits a squeeze.

I squeezed back. "You making coffee or what?"

They'd wanted more X-rays at St. Vincent's.

I'd spent most of the morning drifting in and out of sleep on the sofa, then hauled myself up an hour before my two o'clock appointment, not sure how I was going to get dressed. In the end I'd stuck with Skwarecki's sweats and found an old T-shirt

325

of Dean's. I drew one sleeve carefully up over my damaged arm before trying to get my head in through the neckhole, but the effort made me so dizzy I had to feel for the edge of our bed and sit down for a minute, the gray cotton still wrapped around my face like a bank robber's stocking mask.

After that it took me half an hour to shuffle a mere three blocks down Seventh Avenue.

I'd been waiting two hours since getting my arm irradiated, cooling my heels on a plastic hallway chair.

A young Indian guy walked toward me, folder in hand, white coat hanging loose over his green scrubs. He looked exhausted.

"Miss Dare? Can you come with me?"

I stood up and followed him down the hall to a small examining room.

"This is quite a bad break," he said when I'd scooted up onto the vinyl-upholstered exam table.

"Are there good ones?"

He held up an X-ray. "I'm just saying it could have been cleaner."

"What does that mean?" I asked.

"Well, we'll get you into a cast today. The swelling's gone down enough for that. And they did as good a job of setting the bones yesterday as possible. But I'll want you back here in a week for another look to see if everything's knitting up properly. Then get those stitches out of your scalp."

He checked the X-ray again. I wouldn't describe him as looking pleased with it.

"What if it's not?" I asked.

"Hm?"

"What happens if everything doesn't knit properly?"

"Oh," he said. "Well, then we just have to break the bones again and reset them. Maybe throw a pin in there."

Just?

"Let's get that cast on, then, shall we?" he said.

37

Mom came down again from Maine the following Tuesday, alone this time. Larry was off at some reunion through the weekend — college or nuclear, I didn't quite catch which.

I'd gone downstairs to the street after she buzzed from the lobby, okay enough to help schlep a load of stuff from the back of her double-parked car despite my cast.

It was getting cold out. Mid-October and the leaves on our street's little trees were turning colors and falling into the gutters.

I stepped outside, over the milk crate of rummage-sale oddments Mom had used to jam the lobby door open.

She bustled across the courtyard toward me with two brimming brown-paper grocery bags.

"Can you take this one, you think?" she asked. "It's just noodles and a bottle of lemon juice."

"Sure."

"It goes in the kitchen," she said. "I'm making dinner tonight."

She dropped the other bag on the floor and went back out to her car.

Picking my way blind back over the milk-crate doorstop, I tried to gain some purchase underneath the bag. There was a rip starting down the side.

A ball of iceberg lettuce sat on top of everything else and I tried to hold it in place with my chin, but it got away from me and bounced across the dirty floor, smack into the door of the elevator.

I waddled over and gave the lettuce a sharp side kick, hoping it would ricochet into the baby strollers behind the stairs so we wouldn't be forced to eat it.

Some people employ a five-second rule to gauge the edibility of food that's touched floor. Mom prefers more flexibility, like "November."

The errant globe of iceberg banked off the bottom step's outer corner and rolled right back to the center of the room, just to mock me.

I heard the click of my mother's shoes against tile as she entered the lobby.

Though laden with a trio of canvas ice bags, she swooped to recapture the battered lettuce with a graceful curtsy.

"Can you press the elevator button for me?" I asked.

"Of course," she said.

I waited for the doors to open while she bounded up the stairs like a freaking gazelle.

I mashed my cast into the floor buttons, not knowing whether I'd managed to press "Two" in there somewhere until the conveyance wheezed to a halt at our level.

The doors opened and I stepped into the hallway just in time for the grocery bag to blow out.

A ReaLemon bottle smashed into acidic green shards at my feet, closely followed by a hard rain of pasta boxes, one of which tripped down the stairs, back toward the lobby.

"This broom is a piece of shit," said Mom. "You should throw it away."

She squatted down and began sweeping broken glass and lemon juice into our dustpan with the edge of her hand.

"*Stop,*" I said. "Jesus Christ."

She ignored me.

I stepped into the puddle. "Do you not recall the time you stuck your hand underwater in the kitchen sink to grab the broken wineglass?"

Mom looked up. "That was *years* ago, Madeline."

"Nineteen sixty-seven," I said, "in Jericho."

"How do you even *remember* this shit?" she asked.

"The kitchen wallpaper was gray, with orange windmills. And you bled all over the fucking place and had to get five stitches."

"Four," she said.

"Use the dustpan. It's not like I'm in any shape to apply a tourniquet."

"Now I don't know how I'm going to make dinner," said Mom.

We were in the kitchen, with everything stowed away except the remaining ingredients for her meal.

"What were you planning to cook?" I asked.

"Angel hair with parsley and smoked mussels and soy sauce and lemon juice, but of course I no longer have lemon juice."

Despite my abhorrence of all mushy bivalves residing in flat oblong tins, I resisted the urge to suggest that we order a couple of pizzas.

"We just happen to have a few of these fancy new citrus things," I said, gesturing with my cast toward a bowl of fruit next to the dish strainer. "I'm told they're called lemons."

"Wonderful," said Mom.

She pulled a quart Mason jar of straw-yellow liquid out of her purse and unscrewed its lid. "Would you like a glass of wine?"

"Thanks, Mom, but I'm still on antibiotics."

"Everybody think like me, everybody want my squaw," she said, filling a glass with ice cubes before pouring the vino in.

Mom lifted her drink in my direction. "To the revolution, wherever it may be."

"Sure," I said. "Why the hell not."

"Oh! I almost forgot!" She put down her glass on the counter.

Reaching into her bag again, she produced a pair of flat wooden implements and handed them to me.

The things were squarish with tapered handles, made of unfinished blond wood and grooved on one side, tied together with a jaunty bow.

They resembled ill-conceived salad tongs, or possibly something with which Aztecs might once have played Ping-Pong.

"Um, wow," I said. "Thank you."

"They're butter paddles," she said.

"In case your dairy products, like, misbe-have?"

"To make butter balls with. For dinner parties."

"Butter balls," I said.

"You take hunks of butter and roll them around between these, then put them in a bowl of ice water. The grooves make a pattern."

She seemed so disappointed by my lack of enthusiasm that I said, "You're very thoughtful to have brought them. Why don't we try them out tonight?"

She *was* thoughtful, not just for bringing them, but for driving down to look after me in the first place.

It was just that she had a sort of archaeological fondness for the culinary implements of her youth: potato ricers and sturdy meat grinders that clamped to the edges of tables, rust-speckled eggbeaters with red-painted wooden handles, matte-black picnic Thermoses lined in spidery silver glass and stoppered with actual corks under their dented tin cups.

She'd find them at rummage sales and church bazaars and then give them to us for Christmas and birthdays, or just present them excitedly when she came to visit. Despite the general inutility of these items, not to mention the microscopic dimensions of our urban galley kitchen, we never had the heart to dispose of her artifacts.

That Mom had most often seen such objects wielded by her family's cook perhaps deepened the perfume of nostalgia they held for her, but I still found it touching that she wanted so powerfully to outfit us with all the modern conveniences of the World War Two gourmet.

If nothing else, it served as a reminder that I was not the sole person in our bloodline to be plagued by memory.

I laid down the paddles on the counter and opened the icebox door. "We're out of butter. I can call Pagan and ask her to pick some up on the way home from work."

"We don't have to use them tonight. I just thought you'd find them amusing."

"I do. I think they're wonderful."

Mom filled a large stockpot with water and lifted it onto the stove to cook the pasta in. "Dean's out of town?"

"Louisiana, until Saturday."

"So just the four of us for dinner. When do Sue and Pagan get home?"

I looked up at the Elvis clock nailed above the doorway. "Another hour, probably."

Here the two of us were again, in a tiny

kitchen, me by the sink and Mom at the stove.

I watched her put the lid on the pot and crank up the rear burner's flame beneath it.

"Are you lonely when Dean goes away, or do you like having a little space?" she asked.

"Both, I think."

If I wanted to confront her about Pierce I knew that this next hour would be the time to do it, but everything was so twisted up with my obligation and her generosity and all the thousand-tendriled vines of nuance that snaked around and between us.

It would be so much easier just to go for the kind of light chatter she liked best — ask her about Larry and why she'd decided to get married a fourth time all of a sudden, and maybe joke around about how long the line of her initials would be now for any sort of monogram.

We'd all been through this "Mom's new guy" shit before. She'd be lost to us for at least a year, busied with stroking some male ego, pretending she couldn't open jars for herself and that she'd never held a political opinion. Or maybe not even pretending, but actually not *remembering*.

Of course it wouldn't be as bad as when we were kids. We wouldn't have to live with the guy, first of all. We wouldn't have to shift places around our own dinner table — again — to accommodate his preferred mealtime location, or eat whatever fucked-up health food he was into, or learn which seemingly innocuous conversational topics would end up bringing on scattered showers of Y-chromosome petulance *this* time.

And we wouldn't have to watch our mother's loyalty grow paler with every challenge, withering with atrophy like my arm in its cast. At least not every day.

"Hey, Mom," I said, "you want to come sit in the living room for a minute?"

38

I sat with my back against one arm of the sofa, cast resting on a pillow in my lap, cross-legged and barefoot.

Mom was perched at the other end. "Would you like me to put on a little music?"

"I want to ask you about something," I said.

Her right hand gripped the wineglass, half-empty now. "Maybe a bit of opera? Or that nice classical station?"

"How 'bout *The Weavers at Carnegie Hall*?" I said, needing some cozy old McCarthy-can-kiss-my-blacklisted-pinko-ass solidarity.

Mom's left thumb sneaked beneath her middle and index fingers to fiddle with the new engagement ring. "Wonderful."

"It should be in that pile of CDs," I said. "Next to the stereo."

"What's your opinion of Larry?" she asked.

"He's pro-nuke *and* thinks a forest without Boise Cascade is like a day without sunshine. *Mazel tov.*"

"He's very kind," said Mom. "Do I just press Eject?"

"Push Power first," I said. "Hey, the man obviously *adores* you. And it was lovely of him to spring for the big shpendy lunch."

She nodded. "He was nervous about making a good impression."

"Refreshing and much appreciated. I give it six months."

"Six months until what?"

"You're bored enough to bolt or he turns out to be a flaming asshole."

Mom sat back down.

"Pagan says you won't make Thanksgiving, by the way," I continued. "Though of course if it's 'B: asshole,' we both give it five years."

"Well, after five years I've heard all their *stories,*" she said.

"We know."

She stood up. "That water's probably boiling by now."

"Angel hair takes three minutes."

"So should I go start it now?"

"Turn off the stove and come back."

338

Mom stopped fiddling with her ring and clutched a fistful of sweater, rubbing the side of her thumb back and forth against the wool.

We figured this tic had been spawned when her parents endorsed a brief 1939 fad for encasing babies' elbows in tiny plaster casts to deny them the comfort of thumbsucking.

"I'm tired of sitting," she said. "I've been in the car all day."

"We need to talk," I said. "About Pierce."

"Oh for God's sake, Madeline, why do you *always* want to drag up old shit?"

"This is actually *new* shit. At least to me."

"Over and done with."

"It isn't, Mom."

"Don't be *ridiculous.*"

"Look," I said, "I didn't know he'd molested Pagan. She told me last week. Because of the little boy I found."

Mom's thumb moved faster, almost a blur.

"She also told me that you don't believe her," I said.

"I asked Pierce about it."

"Oh, gee, let me guess what he said — why did you even bother?"

"It was only fair to hear both sides."

"No, Mom," I said, "it's only fair to believe your *daughter.*"

339

"I'm sure the truth is somewhere between their two versions."

"We'll just say Pagan's *partially* lying about having been dry-humped repeatedly by your sack-of-shit boyfriend back when she was ten years old?"

Mom's mouth went grim and tight, giving her an uncanny resemblance to her dead father.

"Which I guess would mean you're only *partially* betraying her," I said. "I mean, at the very least, ask yourself, why would she make it up if it didn't happen? What *possible* purpose could that serve?"

"I am *not* betraying Pagan. Or anyone."

"Right," I said. "That's why you can't *wait* to tell us what a good time you've had seeing Pierce every time you go back to California."

"Pierce is my friend. So is his wife."

"And does his wife have any daughters, Mom?"

"One."

"How old?"

Mom shrugged. "She's a troublemaker. They sent her to live with the father a couple of years ago."

"How old?"

"I don't know . . . thirteen? Why the hell does it possibly matter?"

I covered my eyes with my left hand.

"You are such a fucking *idiot,*" I said. "Jesus Christ."

Mom was silent for a long beat.

When she spoke again, her voice was appallingly perky: "I'm going to cook dinner now. Before all that water boils away."

Just after Mom left the next day, I discovered two more vintage gifts arranged sweetly atop my bed: an embroidered cashmere cardigan and a Luneville luncheon plate.

She'd folded the sweater's arms inward at each elbow, to look as though some shyly invisible two-dimensional friend were offering up the French-porcelain artifact, hoping for my approval.

I stared down at the bed. This was no hastily assembled peace offering, but something my mother had thought up well ahead of her long drive down from Maine: sweater a perfect fit and the exact green of my eyes, plate's cottage-nosegay motif my favorite since early childhood.

Having too little money for last-minute extravagance, Mom kept us ever in mind, scouting out small treasures to bestow on each of her children, sweetening our way through the world.

Nothing between us was simple, or ever

had been.

Two days later I got my stitches out. Then they rebroke my arm.

39

I made Pagan pay me the hundred bucks on Thanksgiving Day. It's not like she could really argue.

We were in Maine, after all, at Larry's house.

Taped to his icebox was a group shot Mom had cut out of the *Carmel Pine Cone,* the newspaper we'd grown up with in California.

Mom was standing between Pierce and his wife at a party, and all three of them were laughing.

40

"What do you *mean,* wives can't come to the Christmas party?" I asked.

It was a Sunday in mid-December and Dean and I were out in New Jersey, ostensibly taking care of some paperwork in his office.

I'd been surprised by the building Christoph housed his business in. It was right next to a weed-choked set of railroad tracks, your basic bad-sixties plantation homage: cheap fake bricks with a pair of two-story white columns framing the entrance: *Gone With Bad Taste.*

"*Spouses* aren't invited," said Dean. "Don't ask me why."

I perched on the edge of his desk. "Why?"

He ignored me, raising his thousand-page Xerox of an incomprehensibly Swiss-German biological-oxygen-demand-quantification-device-thingie repair manual higher between us.

I nudged the pages with my still-plaster-encased arm. "Like, so your colleagues can get all the secretaries drunk enough to fuck out in the parking lot?"

A choking sound emanated from behind my husband's Teutonic-pulp rampart.

"Duh," I said.

No response.

I swung my legs, making syncopated heel-thuds against the kettle drum of his file drawer.

"Will there be tons of coke," I continued, "or just grain alcohol in the punch?"

"Bunny, I *have* to finish this."

"So maybe I'll crash it. With Astrid. I should have this thing off my arm by then."

More choking.

"We could jump out of a giant cake wearing fishnets or something," I continued. "Freak the shit out of everyone."

Dean lowered his reading matter. "If I buy you lunch will you stop *talking?*"

"Briefly," I said, leaning over to stroke his hair, left-handed.

"Give me ten minutes."

"I bet you say that to all the girls."

"All what girls?" asked a man's voice from behind me, husky and debauch-battered.

I turned to find Captain Kangaroo's evil twin lounging against the door frame: thick-

345

wristed, broken-nosed, and in no kind of hurry to raise his eyes from my tits despite the sling and cast that framed them.

My pectoral equipage rated a slow nod of approval. He loosened the knot of his tie, tongue-tip sliding across his front teeth in pink salute.

I got the feeling he'd been standing there long enough to have overheard my drunk-secretarial-parking-lot-sex comment. And that he was less a drunk-secretarial-sex-in-the-parking-lot than a drunk-secretarial-blowjob-in-the-men's-room-stall kind of guy.

"You must be Mrs. Bauer," he said, his voice a wooden spoon dragged through pea-gravel.

"It's Dare, actually." I slid off the desk and stepped toward him, left hand stuck out in front of me. "Madeline."

Captain K had one of those slow, crawly handshakes — like he was asking Helen Keller if she knew the one about the salesman and the farmer's daughter.

He shot my husband a smirk, not letting me go. "Jesus, Dean, you married a feminazi?"

I smiled sweetly. "Beats a Republicunt."

He dropped my hand and I smiled wider. *Dick.*

"Got a hell of a mouth on her," he said, squinting back at me.

Dean shrugged. "You know these debutantes . . ."

"Oh, right. She's *Astrid's* friend."

"Bunny," said Dean, "this is Vincent Taliaferro. My boss."

"Bunny?" That rated another smirk.

"So, *Vinnie,*" I said, "you had lunch yet?"

Right when Taliaferro was locking up out front, Christoph drove into the office parking lot, Astrid riding shotgun beside him.

Because the patriarchy didn't already suck *enough.*

From across the restaurant table Taliaferro pointed his butter-smeared knife at me.

"Why the hell do you care what a bunch of moolies get up to?" he said through a mouthful of dinner roll.

Dean had brought up the investigation despite my shin-kick of under-the-table admonition.

I draped my napkin across my lap. Taliaferro's spilled down wide from his collar, a waterfall of snowy bib.

He took another big bite of roll, chewed once, and knocked it back with a slug of ice water. "You even know what a moolie is, Madeline?"

I gave him a curt nod. Sure I did: slang abbreviation of the Italian for "eggplant."

"Do yourself a favor," he said. "Look around this restaurant."

It was a dark green room with a Burger-King solarium tacked on: lots of framed one-red-rose-on-a-piano-keyboard posters, two big ESPN-tuned TVs hanging above the bar.

Taliaferro brandished the knife. "Nice place, am I right?"

"Lovely," I replied.

He put down the knife, handle-tip at rest on the tablecloth, blade balanced against his butter plate's edge. "You wanna know why?"

"Enlighten me."

Taliaferro rubbed the pad of a thumb to and fro against the thin skin on the back of his other hand. "Because it's all one color, *that's* why."

Christoph smiled. Astrid was still on Planet Chanel behind her sunglasses.

Dean reached into the bread basket, handily avoiding having to look me in the eye.

I leaned forward, mashing my cast against the edge of the table. "A little kid got beaten to death, Vinnie. I found his bones. It has literally *nothing* to do with skin color."

Taliaferro reached past the oil-and-vinegar

cruets to pat my free wrist, his face screwed up with a sympathy I wanted no part of.

"Fucking animals, hon," he said. "Look what they did to Newark."

Christoph nodded. "I find these conversations so helpful because I must admit to being still confused by certain aspects of your national culture."

"Really?" I said. "Which ones?"

"More wine?" asked Dean.

Christoph waved a hand over his glass, declining.

"Perhaps we can help," I said, "by throwing light on any particularly troubling nuance of American life?"

Dean stepped on my foot.

I took a swallow of beer, then smiled across the table at Christoph *and* whacked the side-edge of my kneecap hard against my husband's thigh.

"Well, Madeline," said Christoph, smiling back, "I must say that I find it astonishing, for instance, that you put up with all of these *niggers*."

I nearly choked on my Heineken. "*Excuse* me?"

"I mean, really," he went on, "why don't you just send them all *back?*"

Jesus, maybe Astrid's gift of Hitleriana really had been a cry for help.

I looked to Dean, who appeared to have developed a sudden penchant for bird-watching out the restaurant window.

"*Christoph,*" I said.

"Maddie?"

"I'm astonished."

"How so?" He smiled again, eyes all crinkly.

"Well, haven't you forgotten something?"

"Forgotten what?" he asked.

I leaned across the table to pat his hand. "I could have sworn this is the part where you're supposed to leap up out of your chair for a rousing chorus of '*Deutschland Über Alles.*'"

Christoph pursed his lips, brow furrowed. "Certainly not," he said. "I am Swiss."

Back at the office I kicked a bottle cap off the parking-lot asphalt into the border of scrubby weeds.

"*That* went well," said Dean.

"I'm sorry."

He sighed.

"Look," I said, "I was raised by feral hippies in California. The only pointers I got on how to act wifely at a business lunch came from *Bewitched* reruns."

I elided over the summers with my grandparents. It's not like I picked up many

350

important safety tips at the yacht club. They never mentioned money, much less actual work. Mealtime conversation consisted mainly of Jew-bashing and requests for more cocktails; thankfully, children weren't expected to weigh in on either topic. Or on any other.

And besides which, am I the only one here who was nauseated by today's *lunchtime conversation?*

"For God's sake, Dean, you didn't even speak up when Christoph announced he could always spot someone Jewish because their *ears* are lower."

Dean looked away from me. "I'm not asking for Samantha twitching her nose here, Bunny. I just wish you'd dial down the Jane Fonda routine a bit."

"Jane *Fonda?*"

"Whatever."

"Are you fucking *kidding* me?"

"Look, I'm just as much behind the whole 'I am Woman, hear me roar' thing as the next emasculated liberal-arts guy, but why do you even care what someone like Taliaferro thinks? So he's a north-Jersey redneck misogynist. Big fucking deal."

"And what about Christoph's contribution? I didn't exactly see him soliciting contributions for UNICEF."

"I still don't see the point in you going all mano a mano over the antipasto platter."

"The *point?*"

"You heard me," he said.

"How can you even *work* with these people, Dean? You've got Christoph blathering on about how we should ship all the 'niggers' back to Africa, and his henchman Vinnie ready to push everybody onto the boat with German shepherds and a firehose."

"Bunny, it's cold out."

"What d'you guys do for office meetings?" I asked. "Break out the white sheets and big pointy hoods and do a kickline?"

"Exactly. Then we gang-rape the secretaries and go burn a cross down by the river."

"That's not funny."

"Oh, please. It's fucking hilarious. Let's go inside."

He put a hand on my shoulder.

I shrugged it off. "Dean, do you even get why this matters to me?"

"Right now? What I get is that I'm standing in a parking lot freezing my ass off."

"I'm serious."

"Me too."

"Don't fuck with me," I said.

"I'm too fucking *cold* to fuck with you. Or anyone."

"Dean, for chrissake," I said. "Christoph and Taliaferro back up to me, rain down an entire dump-truck load of shit on my head, and you don't say one *word?*"

He looked away, jaw clenched.

"I mean, what the *fuck?*" I continued. "Did they, like, hide some psycho-alien Reagan-pod under your desk and suck your brains out?"

He lifted his chin. "It's a job, all right? It's a fucking job. With a fucking paycheck. Not to mention the health insurance."

He looked at my cast but was nice enough not to mention that I'd been doing even less to augment his salary lately, given all those hours I hadn't been on anybody's clock for out in Queens — or down at St. Vincent's so they could keep breaking my damn arm.

And I was the one who'd talked him into moving down here in the first place, not to mention meeting up with Christoph.

But these guys are still assholes.

I shivered.

"Dean, look," I said, "I'm sorry —"

He shook off *my* hand this time. "Here's an idea: the next time you want to go all Angela *Davis* on my ass, all oppressed by the patriarchy? *You* pay the rent —"

"I *said* I'm sorry. Jesus —"

"Because on *your* pay we can live in a

353

cardboard *box,* on top of a fucking *subway* grate."

We stared at each other, livid.

I dropped my eyes first.

The wind picked up, making dead leaves skitter across the asphalt.

The rush of air was cold and dry, and we were both standing here in this stupid parking lot because I'd asked for it — because I'd thought it was what I wanted.

Maybe he could work here for a year or something and then move on. Preferably without requiring denazification.

"I *am* sorry, Dean. Really. Look, we've both been under a lot of pressure —"

"*Some* of us have work to do," he said, cutting off my attempt at conciliation.

"Hey, I just wanted to —"

But he'd turned away and started walking toward the building's front door.

I followed three paces behind, willing his silent back to rot in hell.

41

"You'd tell me if Christoph were sleeping with other women, wouldn't you?"

Astrid and I were sitting in an empty office on the first floor. I could hear Dean and Christoph talking, upstairs, apparently having a fine old time.

"I think he is," she said. "I think he's cheating on me."

"Maybe we should crash the Christmas party. In disguise."

"I'm not joking."

"Astrid, it's not like Christoph would tell me if he were sleeping around. I mean, he knows I'm your friend."

She still hadn't taken off her dark glasses. Or the hooded coat.

She smelled perfectly fine so I figured she at least had to launder it occasionally — unless she had six of the things and just rotated.

"He hasn't said anything to Dean?" she asked.

"Why would he tell Dean? That would be incredibly stupid."

"Because you think Dean would tell you?"

She was sitting in a desk chair on wheels, twisting it back and forth slowly. I don't think she'd even noticed my broken arm.

"Dean *would* tell me," I said. "And Christoph knows that, so he wouldn't tell Dean."

"So you *do* think he's cheating on me but hiding it from Dean."

"Astrid. I will say this one more time: I do not think your husband is cheating on you, nor does *my* husband think your husband is cheating on you. End of story."

"But Maddie —"

"And if you ask me again I'm going to walk upstairs and invite Christoph over for brunch and a threesome tomorrow morning just to get this the hell *over* with."

She rocked the chair faster, but at least that had made her smile a little bit.

Okay, so it was more of an "Oh please, like he'd sleep with you?" smirk.

Well I'd rather blow Eichmann, honey, so I guess it all evens out.

"Take your sunglasses off," I said.

"What?"

"Your shades," I said. "They're giving me

the creeps. 'Madeline, I am your father. . . .' "

She put them on top of the desk.

"Way better."

She started rocking the chair again. "He's cheating on me, Maddie. I know it."

"Astrid, look," I said. "Can I be honest here?"

"Of course."

"You're sounding a little crazy. Like, the *DSM-III Revised* kind of crazy."

She stopped rocking. "How do you mean?"

"We've known each other since we were fifteen, right?"

She nodded. "Yes."

"You remember the first night we got to be friends?"

She looked away.

"It was around the end of November," I said. "Sophomore year. A bunch of us were hanging out in Randy and Pauline's room, even though they were both away for the weekend. Just a random Saturday afternoon, a while after lunch — I forget why we were all there. You guys were probably doing bong hits in the closet or something, hiding from the dorm parents."

"You never partied with us back then," she said. "You were such a straight arrow.

357

Didn't even smoke cigarettes yet."

"Randy and Pauline's beds were shoved together, like a gigantic sofa with piles of pillows. Typical dorm room: Indian-print tapestries on the walls, big posters from Fiorucci. All of us just lazing around on our stomachs talking shit, you know? What boys we liked and did they like us back, and which of us had lost our virginity already, how much school sucked, and how there was never anything to do on the weekends."

Astrid didn't say anything, but she'd slowed the chair's motion, listening to me like I was soothing her fears with a bedtime story.

Maybe I was.

"Everyone else kind of drifted out of the room, eventually," I continued, "wandered down to the common room to smoke a butt, or to the dining hall for dinner, but you and I stayed, just kicking back, still talking. We didn't even turn on the lights when it started getting dark outside. We had too much to say, couldn't be bothered to walk across the room."

"We must have left to sign in by ten, but I don't remember getting up, even then."

"The Lewises were on duty," I said. "Two doors away, right at the end of the hall. We ran there and back, babbling the entire time. You never even went downstairs to smoke, just leaned out the window with a Marlboro in your mouth every hour or so, fanning the smoke away, insisting nobody'd be able to see you through the trees."

"You were terrified of getting busted, but I was right."

"We were still talking when the sun came up."

Astrid put her feet up on the desk and leaned her chair back on its axis. "Our first all-nighter."

"Of many," I said.

"We must've talked for eighteen hours straight."

"At *least,* before we finally passed out from sheer exhaustion."

"And we didn't even have a term paper to blow off writing, at the time."

"It made me really happy, that night. I think it was the first time I ever truly felt like I belonged there. Like maybe it was going to turn out okay."

She poked me in the thigh with her toe. "Like *what* was going to turn out okay?"

"My life? I don't know."

"Bullshit," she said. "We had the world by the balls and you knew it, even then."

"*You* did. You were this cool kid, and suddenly out of the blue we had all this crap in common, and after that, everything was just easy."

"Bullshit," she said again.

"Whatever, okay? That's not what matters right now."

"And what does?" She sounded so tired, so lost.

"*You* do. Shut your eyes and forget about Southampton and Christoph and Cammy and all the bullshit whirling around your head right now."

"I can't."

"None of it means shit," I said. "None of it changes the fact that you, Astrid, fucking well *matter.*"

She shook her head.

"Have I *ever* lied to you?" I asked.

"That I know of?"

"In twelve years, have I ever fucking said even *one thing* to you that contained so much as a single iota of bullshit when it was about something important?"

She didn't answer.

"I haven't," I said. "Ever. So when I say that there's no fucking way in the universe that Christoph is fucking around on you, you should believe me, okay?"

"Mad —"

"Shut up. You are the most beautiful woman I've ever met. And damn close to the smartest. And we're still the balls, okay? We are the fucking *balls*."

I looked up and saw Dean standing in the doorway.

"Can I talk to you for a minute?" he asked.

I followed him out into the hallway. "What's up?"

"I think we should leave your car here."

"How 'bout we just *leave?*" I whispered.

"I still have a lot of work to do. Christoph will give us a ride back into the city."

"I'll wait. I don't think I could handle being trapped in a Jeep with the two of them."

"I still think you should keep the Porsche out here."

"Maybe you can drive it back out tomorrow morning?"

"Sure," he said.

"I owe you big-time."

"You sure as hell do," he said, grinning as he snaked an arm around my waist and leaned down to kiss me.

"All is forgiven?"

His breath tickled my ear. "If you really want to leave now, Bunny, I can catch a ride with them solo."

"No way," I whispered back. "I wouldn't wish that on a *dog*."

I drove Dean back into the city myself, long

after dark. He went to bed right away but when the phone rang just after midnight, I was still lying alone on the living room sofa, wide awake in the urban semidark.

I grabbed it up quickly, before it could ring a second time. Everyone else in the apartment was asleep.

"Mad?" Astrid's voice.

Oh great.

It's not that I wasn't concerned about her, it was just hard having the same conversation over and over again. My reassurances never seemed to stick.

"Yeah, it's me," I said.

"I don't know what to do."

She sounded horrible. "Hey, are you crying?"

"Christoph pushed me down the stairs."

"Jesus . . . *what?*"

"At the office," she said. "In New Jersey."

"It's like, midnight. You're still out there?"

"No. It all happened this afternoon. After you and Dean left."

"All *what* happened? Are you okay?"

I heard her take a drag off a cigarette, then exhale.

"Astrid? Talk to me here, for fuck's sake —"

"I called the police."

"Did he hurt you?" I sat up. "Where are you?"

"They came and I filed a report and everything and now I'm back in the city."

"*Where* in the city?"

She took another drag. "You believe me, don't you?"

"Of course I do," I said, but the fact that she had to ask left me feeling uneasy. "Has anything like this happened before?"

"Maddie, should I leave him?" She was whispering now.

"Where *are* you?" I whispered back.

"The apartment. Our apartment."

"Is Christoph there *with* you?" I asked, a little shocked.

"Of course. But I don't want him to hear me." She coughed into the phone.

"Do you want to come spend the night here?"

"It's all right now. I just have to go to court next week."

"I can come right now and get you if you want. Really."

"I'll call you later," she said, and hung up on me.

Staring at the dead phone in my hand, I half wanted to call the police and send them racing to her apartment, and half didn't believe a word she'd just said.

Dean padded out into the living room rubbing his eyes. "Who was that?"

"Astrid."

He yawned. "What'd she want?"

"She said Christoph pushed her down the stairs today after we left your office."

He sat on the sofa at my feet. "On purpose?"

"She told me she called the cops."

"You talk to him?"

"Are you kidding?"

"Astrid's okay, though?"

"I guess. I mean, it didn't sound like she was bleeding to death or anything. She said she'd call me later and hung up on me."

"I don't want to cast aspersions," said Dean, "but Christoph just doesn't seem like that kind of guy."

"I know, but still."

"Astrid," he said, shaking his head. "Nutty *Buddy.*"

"No, I can't *believe* she'd make something like that up. I mean, Jesus, Dean — what the hell should I do?"

"Not much you can do. Besides coming to bed and getting some sleep."

"You sure?"

"I think it will all blow over by tomorrow."

Dean stood up and started tugging on my hand.

"Let it go," he said. "It's after midnight. Call her in the morning."

"Okay, just promise you'll call *me,* from work."

"I solemnly swear you'll get the full report on whether or not Christoph's acting like a mad wifebeater and/or foaming at the mouth."

I let him pull me up off the sofa. "First thing?"

"Cross my heart."

"Listen, I'm sorry I was acting like a bitch today."

"That's all right. You're probably just getting the monthlies."

I punched him in the arm. "Don't be a dick."

"You *love* it," he whispered. "You know you do."

I phoned Astrid three times before I left for work the next morning, but no one picked up.

The whole thing seemed unreal after a good night's sleep. Not just her midnight call, but Taliaferro being so obnoxious, Christoph going all *sieg heil,* and my parking-lot fight with Dean on top of everything else.

I pulled on my coat, which still took some doing, one-armed, and wondered whether it was worth dialing her number one more time before I left for work.

Maybe she was just sleeping in.

And why the hell shouldn't she? It's not like she has a job she's got to show up for, right?

All the same, there was a flicker of uneasiness in my belly.

Or maybe she's dead. And wouldn't you feel like a creepy bitch for dissing her in your head then, *Maddie Dare?*

I went back into the living room and punched in her phone number one more time.

The machine picked up again, her voice saying, "You've reached Astrid and Christoph. Please leave a message."

"Astrid, listen, it's Maddie. I just wanted to see how you were doing this morning. Give me a call at work."

I was just about to start reciting the Catalog's 800 number when she picked up, groggy.

"Hey," I said. "You all right? I was worried."

"Maddie?" she said, coughing. "What the hell time is it?"

"Early."

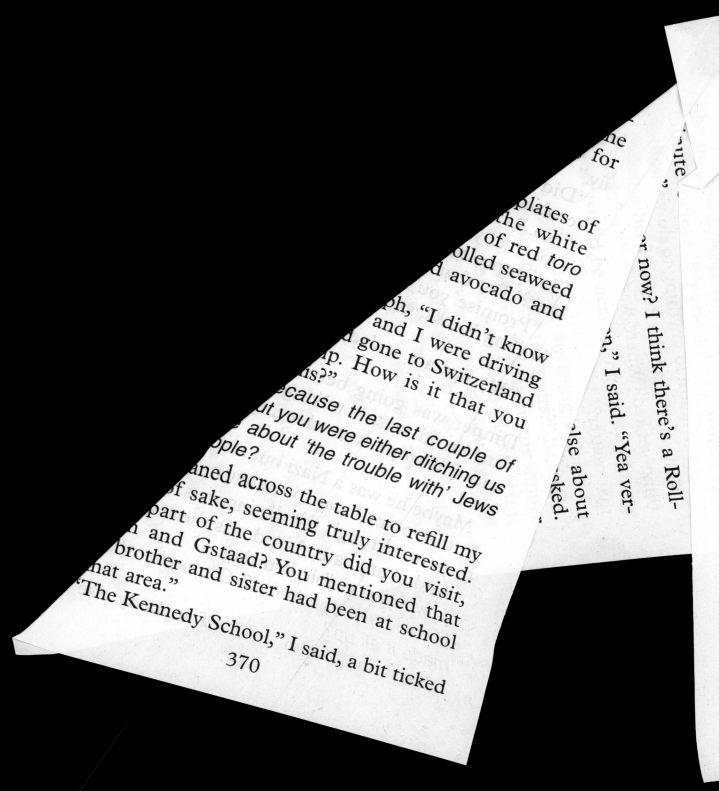

I heard the rasp of a lighter. "You woke me up."

"Sorry. I just wanted to make sure you were okay before I left for work."

"I'm fine," she said. "Really. I just need more sleep."

"Okay. I'll let you go, then. Call me later."

"Yeah. Sure."

She coughed again and hung up.

We were slammed that week at work: phone and fax orders already picking up for the holidays, and Betty ran through every hour on the hour to throw things in Editorial while shrieking about how we were all lazy, incompetent pieces of shit.

At one point she even made Yumiko cry, though of course Yumiko got all tough again a minute later and swore it wasn't anything That Crazy One-Arm White Bitch had said, it was just that she'd caught some shrapnel when Betty missed her with the stapler, smashing a fresh pot of Sanka with it instead.

Even so, I left Astrid a message every day on my lunch hour, saying I hoped she was doing okay.

She didn't call back.

Dean saw her a couple of times out at the office with Christoph. He said she seemed

plates of
the white
of red *toro*
rolled seaweed
avocado and

...ph, "I didn't know
and I were driving
gone to Switzerland
up. How is it that you

because the last couple of
you were either ditching us
about 'the trouble with' Jews

leaned across the table to refill my
sake, seeming truly interested.
part of the country did you visit,
and Gstaad? You mentioned that
brother and sister had been at school
that area."

"The Kennedy School," I said, a bit ticked

fine. That they both did.

"Want to have dinner with Astrid an
Christoph?" asked Dean, when I walke
the door Friday night. "He just called
minute ago."

"Is it a command performance?" I wall
into our room and tossed my coat acr
the bed, then sat down at the end of
mattress to take off my boots.

I didn't feel up for double-dating, not
ing heard from Astrid since her midr
phone call about getting pushed dowr
stairs.

"More like a bon voyage," said Dean.
kicked off early because he's coming
me to Houston tomorrow. I said we
him know when you got home."

"They want us to slog uptown?"

"He suggested Meriken."

This was a sushi joint just a few blo
from us, on Seventh.

"Sounds okay, actually," I said, surprised
to find this was true. "Especially if the offer
includes some beer. What time?"

"Whenever. He said they'd cab it."

I flopped backwards onto the bed, cast
thunking against my ribs. The arm inside
didn't ache anymore, but it itched like hell.

"Will you call him back?" I asked. "I feel

368

the restaurant was scoping out our table for
outward signs of domestic strife, after all —
not that that had anything to do with Dean.
Why was I only the friend for when every
thing sucked? Where was Cammy when t
going got tough? Or Astrid's mother
that matter?

I reached for the sake.

Our waiter placed tiny oblong
sushi and sashimi gently on
tablecloth, artful arrangements
and pale gold hamachi, hand-r
cones brimming with fanne
shreds of crabmeat.

"Maddie," said Christo
until today when Dean
home that you two ha
on your wedding tri
never mentioned t
Well, maybe be
times we hung o
or lecturing me
and black pe
But he le
thimble
"What
Saane
your
in

And
ily, with n
Stockholm sym
made it all up?
I was the one in a cast,

369

I heard the rasp of a lighter. "You woke me up."

"Sorry. I just wanted to make sure you were okay before I left for work."

"I'm fine," she said. "Really. I just need more sleep."

"Okay. I'll let you go, then. Call me later."

"Yeah. Sure."

She coughed again and hung up.

We were slammed that week at work: phone and fax orders already picking up for the holidays, and Betty ran through every hour on the hour to throw things in Editorial while shrieking about how we were all lazy, incompetent pieces of shit.

At one point she even made Yumiko cry, though of course Yumiko got all tough again a minute later and swore it wasn't anything That Crazy One-Arm White Bitch had said, it was just that she'd caught some shrapnel when Betty missed her with the stapler, smashing a fresh pot of Sanka with it instead.

Even so, I left Astrid a message every day on my lunch hour, saying I hoped she was doing okay.

She didn't call back.

Dean saw her a couple of times out at the office with Christoph. He said she seemed fine. That they both did.

"Want to have dinner with Astrid and Christoph?" asked Dean, when I walked in the door Friday night. "He just called a minute ago."

"Is it a command performance?" I walked into our room and tossed my coat across the bed, then sat down at the end of the mattress to take off my boots.

I didn't feel up for double-dating, not having heard from Astrid since her midnight phone call about getting pushed down the stairs.

"More like a bon voyage," said Dean. "We kicked off early because he's coming with me to Houston tomorrow. I said we'd let him know when you got home."

"They want us to slog uptown?"

"He suggested Meriken."

This was a sushi joint just a few blocks up from us, on Seventh.

"Sounds okay, actually," I said, surprised to find this was true. "Especially if the offer includes some beer. What time?"

"Whenever. He said they'd cab it."

I flopped backwards onto the bed, cast thunking against my ribs. The arm inside didn't ache anymore, but it itched like hell.

"Will *you* call him back?" I asked. "I feel

the need to lie here stupidly horizontal for a minute before I peel off my work-crap clothes."

"Want a beer now? I think there's a Rolling Rock."

"That would be heaven," I said. "Yea verily."

"Did you ever hear anything else about the whole episode with the stairs?" he asked.

"No. I could ask them both during dinner — be really subtle, you know? Like, 'Hey, Christoph, have you stopped beating your wife?' Bet that would go over big."

"Promise you won't and I'll make it *two* Rolling Rocks, even if it means a run to the deli."

"My lips are sealed," I said.

Dinner was going better than expected so far. Astrid wasn't talking much, but Dean and Christoph were chatting about Switzerland.

Maybe he was a Nazi but not a wifebeater? At that point I was too exhausted from work to parse through the distinctions.

And at any rate, Astrid was there voluntarily, with no visible bruising.

Stockholm syndrome? Or maybe she just made it all up?

I was the one in a cast, if anybody else in

the restaurant was scoping out our table for outward signs of domestic strife, after all — not that that had anything to do with Dean.

Why was I only the friend for when everything sucked? Where was Cammy when the going got tough? Or Astrid's mother, for that matter?

I reached for the sake.

Our waiter placed tiny oblong plates of sushi and sashimi gently on the white tablecloth, artful arrangements of red *toro* and pale gold *hamachi,* hand-rolled seaweed cones brimming with fanned avocado and shreds of crabmeat.

"Maddie," said Christoph, "I didn't know until today when Dean and I were driving home that you two had gone to Switzerland on your wedding trip. How is it that you never mentioned this?"

Well, maybe because the last couple of times we hung out you were either ditching us or lecturing me about 'the trouble with' Jews and black people?

But he leaned across the table to refill my thimble of sake, seeming truly interested. "What part of the country did you visit, Saanen and Gstaad? You mentioned that your brother and sister had been at school in that area."

"The Kennedy School," I said, a bit ticked

at myself for being quite so pleased that he'd remembered. "Pagan was there for eighth grade, Trace for seventh and eighth."

"Did they enjoy it?"

"Very much," I said. "And I admit to being quite envious. They're both excellent skiers now."

"You wanted to stay at home in California, then?" he asked.

I drank my sake and he filled it again. "I started at Dobbs the year Pagan went to Saanen, with her godmother's daughter Arabella."

"They're the same age?" he asked.

"Pals since they were babies, too. Actually, there's a favorite story of mine about Arabella. One of the youngest boarders that year was Roger Moore's son. I think he was five or six —"

"And they sent him away to *boarding* school?" asked Dean.

Astrid started casing the room like she was plotting to bail on us for a cooler table.

Fuck off, it's a good story.

"He and Arabella got put on the T-bar together," I said. "And you're supposed to tuck it under your butt, but not actually *sit,* you know?"

Christoph reached for a piece of *toro* with his chopsticks and nodded, smiling.

371

I picked up a piece myself, eschewing left-handed chopsticks for my fingers.

"Except he's in kindergarten and she's tall for twelve," I continued, "so their ride up was pretty sketchy."

Astrid yawned, her plate still empty before her.

"At the top the kid looks Arabella up and down once, *slowly,* then says, '*Husky* bitch,' and shoots away down the Eggli."

Christoph and Dean started laughing.

Astrid leaned forward, her face contorted with anger as she growled, "Don't you *dare* laugh at me."

And before anyone could respond to that, she stuck both arms out straight and dragged them across the table, growling with effort as she shoved everything over the edge — our soup bowls and sushi plates, bottles of soy sauce and sake, even the bud-vase centerpiece — all of it smashing against the tiled floor below.

Then she stood up, panting, a little bit of white showing all the way around her eyes' dark irises.

The entire restaurant went dead still, dead quiet.

"I hate you," she said, her voice oddly calm.

She looked at Christoph, then Dean, then

me. "I hate *all* of you."

Christoph said, "Darling . . ."

She swung a fist at her chair, knocking it over sideways onto the floor. Then she stalked away, her footsteps the only noise in the silenced room.

No one spoke for several seconds after the street door slammed shut behind her, then dozens of voices swarmed up, buzzing.

Christoph rose to his feet, oddly graceful. "Please accept my apologies. My wife has not been well, and I must see her home."

We said of course, and asked if there was anything we could do to help.

He shook his head. "Thank you for being such good friends to both of us. It means a great deal to me."

Then he turned to placate the approaching headwaiter, wallet in hand.

Dean pressed his knee against mine. I watched the last stained corner of tablecloth slip down and away, a white flag surrendered to gravity.

There was soy sauce all over my cast.

Astrid called me at work.

No hello, no apology, just launching right in with, "I have to leave him," the moment I pressed line three.

"Did you hear me?" she said, blowing

373

smoke across the mouthpiece of her receiver.

"Yes."

"Well?" She took another drag. "Aren't you going to say anything?"

"I don't know where to begin."

"You have to help me, Madeline. You don't know what it's been like."

"You're right. I don't."

I heard the click of a lighter. Her next words were mumbled a little, around the fresh cigarette. "He's having me watched."

"Christoph?"

She exhaled again. I could hear the echo of hard-soled footsteps against parquet. She was pacing.

"Astrid," I said, "are you serious?"

"I swear to you."

"Well, I mean, how exactly?"

"He's hired people."

"What do you mean, people?"

"In the apartment across the street. With telescopes."

Oh, fuck.

She was quiet for a moment.

"I'm going crazy, aren't I, Maddie?" she said, her voice soft.

"Yes." I didn't know what else to say.

The pacing stopped. "How bad?"

"Um, you sound like my father."

374

"Oh, God. That bad?"

"I don't know. Are you worried about the KGB reading your mail?"

"So I'm pretty much fucked then, aren't I?"

She sounded almost relieved.

"Astrid, I'm so sorry, but I can't help you with this. We need to get you some pros here, okay?"

"Yeah," she said.

"What does Christoph say?"

She started to cry. "He really did push me down the stairs."

"Shhhh," I said. "Don't worry, I believe you."

"I don't know what to *do*."

"You want me to come over?"

She was quiet now. She stopped sniffling. I just listened to her breathe for a while.

"I think I'm just going to go lie down right now. I haven't been getting a lot of sleep."

"You sure?" I asked.

"I'm okay," she said, "really. Not entirely lucid, obviously, but I pose no danger to myself and others."

I believed her. She sounded saner than she had in a long time. Her old self.

"Anything you need, call me back, all right? I'm only over on Fifty-seventh. I could, you know, bring you soup or something."

"Love you," she said. *"Ciao, bella."*

I replaced the receiver in its cradle. "Happy holidays."

■ ■ ■ ■

Manhattan
February 1991

■ ■ ■ ■

When will our consciences grow so tender
that we will act to prevent human misery
rather than avenge it?

— Eleanor Roosevelt

42

I slogged up out of the subway stairs into the knife-edge of February on Queens Boulevard. A bitter cold wind barreled straight at me with a Bessie Smith moan, snapping a star of grit into my right eye.

Blinking didn't work. I had to pull my gloveless left hand from the warmth of an overcoat pocket to rub it clear.

I'd be getting the cast off in two more weeks. They'd told me at St. Vincent's that the pin appeared to be doing the trick, holding the bones together.

I leaned forward into the blast, squinting at the ground. We hadn't had any fresh snow in a week. The existing piles shoved to the edges of the boulevard were glazed brownish black with a glittering, filthy crust of ice.

Wind bulled its way inside my coat, making it balloon out behind me. By the time I reached the courthouse steps I felt like Doctor fucking Zhivago.

The cheese-grater sculpture out front was whipping around so fast it looked primed for takeoff.

I stepped into the line to get inside, which was long and slow this time of morning. There must have been twenty people in front of me just waiting to reach the doors. A few standees gripped steaming cups of take-out coffee. Nobody talked much. It was still cold as shit, but at least we had a little protection from the wind.

The line crawled onward, slowly up one stair at a time. It took maybe ten minutes to reach the doors, and I was grateful when they finally swung closed behind me.

It took some concentration not to fall on my ass, since the lobby's floor was slick with tracked-in snowmelt and little chunks of ice. The line inched toward the metal detector. I thought back to my first time here, when I'd had Skwarecki waving at me in greeting.

I wasn't likely to see her today. And even if I did, talking to a homicide cop once your case has reached trial is like running into your favorite teacher from elementary school. There's so much you still want to tell them but their hearts belong to new children.

Bost had said I could sit in the back of the courtroom and watch the trial, but not until after I'd testified myself.

Cate would be up first, then me.

We'd been told to report by 9:30 A.M., and it was just after nine o'clock now, but trials in Queens were reputed to grind exceedingly slowly.

Cops here to testify waited in a basement hall a couple floors down from the prosecutors in the building's courthouse-to-jail connector. Skwarecki said she'd often been stuck down there for upwards of twelve hours, and her personal best was seventeen and a half.

"At least we got restrooms," she'd said, "unlike those miserable fucks coming out of the cells."

"So you guys just have to sit there?" I asked.

"We bring lawn chairs."

"Lawn chairs?"

"The kind that fold up. Low to the ground is good, in case you get stuck overnight."

"You have to be there a lot?"

"We got up to 2,246 homicides in New York City last year. Any one of mine goes to trial, I'm there. I know that basement like the back of my fucking hand."

That's a lot of dead people, 2,246.

I'd made it up through the line as far as the X-ray's conveyor belt and started emptying my pockets into a plastic tub, then took off my new cheapo-drugstore watch and tossed it in. The metal detectors seemed slightly less exacting than the ones they had in airports, since my underwires hadn't set off any alarms the first few times I'd been here. With any luck I wouldn't have to get wanded and groped this morning, either.

I looked across the room at a huge mosaic mural. It was crammed with allegorical figures, but I couldn't quite follow the intended narrative other than it seemed to have something to do with the figure of Justice.

I'd have to remember to ask Kyle about it. He'd always been good on the art history stuff back in college. He'd said he'd try to join us by lunch, but couldn't be in the courtroom observing beforehand. He was due to attend the funeral of a co-worker, instead, that morning.

The doors behind me swung open again, to let a cold shot of air and few more lucky people inside.

I turned to look behind me before getting waved through the detector gate, just to check if Cate was anywhere back in the line. I didn't spot her, but I couldn't see down the steps once the condensation-fogged doors closed. She'd told me she wanted to be here early, anyway, so I figured she was probably inside.

I walked through the white security portal and the thing started beeping like crazy.

I raised my hands and stepped toward the tall dark matron armed with a wand.

"Feet apart, honey," she said.

Being a rather buxom person herself, she gave me a nod and a wink when I confided, "Underwires. New bra."

Or maybe the metal in my wrist.

The courtroom was huge compared to where the grand jury had met.

I'd spent the entire morning waiting in a stuffy little room with a bunch of other witnesses. Cate and I had chatted for a while until she was called. I'd sat there for another long stretch before we broke for lunch.

Kyle caught up with us in our now habitual booth, across Queens Boulevard, and then Skwarecki walked in too, which made me happy.

"How'd it go?" he asked, scooching in after she did.

"I didn't get to see anything this morning," I said. "But I think I might be up after lunch."

Cate smiled. "But it went fine. My stuff, anyway. Not that I had anything dramatic to share."

"How was the funeral?" I asked, turning to Kyle.

"*Un*believable," he said. "And it went on for fucking hours."

"Schmidt's thing today?" asked Skwarecki. "I went to the wake Sunday. His *gumar* went *meshuggene*."

Mayor Dinkins might refer to the city as a "Glorious Mosaic," but the next time I heard the term "melting pot" being dismissed as politically incorrect, I'd cite a Polish cop's Sicilian-and-Yiddish rundown of the dead German attorney's mistress having lost her shit during the traditionally Irish party thrown to honor his passing.

I spent another hour sitting around the witness green room before the bailiff called my name, saying it was my turn to take the stand.

He opened the door and motioned me toward the courtroom.

I glanced up at the judge as I walked across the floor toward the witness box. He was a stately looking silver-haired African American guy with powerful shoulders under the robes. IN GOD WE TRUST was writ large on the wall above His Honor's balding head.

I thought a better sentiment might be "God Help Us All, Every One," but it's not like anyone had solicited my opinion.

I'd been expecting to get sworn in with my hand on a Bible, having watched my fair share of after-school *Perry Mason* reruns, and wondered if anyone still believed that a few seconds' manual contact with Holy pebbled-black leatherette could override self-interest in late-twentieth-century New York.

In the end all I had to do was hold my hand up, which seemed plenty, not least since the judge looked like a sufficiently omnipotent hard-ass that he wouldn't require divine backup.

Having been sworn, I surveyed the courtroom.

Bost's outpost was next to the jury. Kyle had explained that this was to shorten the distance defendants were required to walk between the side door and their attorneys' table.

Four people were seated at that defense table today, none of them looking at me just yet.

Albert Williams had the outside chair.

It was the first time I'd ever seen him. He was a big guy, thick necked, even more broad shouldered than the judge.

His hair was cut in a high fade, a little boxy on top. He had on a brown jacket, and I could see the scoop of his undershirt outlined below the spread of white collar and knitted black tie.

Williams held a pencil in his left hand. He wasn't writing anything on the legal pad in front of him, but he didn't raise his eyes from its yellow expanse.

I presumed the tiny woman to his right was his public defender. She had very pale skin and curly hair so dead-black she might have been a midlife-crisis Goth in her spare time. I knew from Kyle that her name was Galloway. He'd said she was good.

Galloway faded into the background beside the bright plumage of Marty Hetzler, his blue-white mane a stark contrast to her own dull black curls.

Marty sported a Floridian complexion and a scarlet pocket square to match his tie. Even from this distance I could pick out the hand-stitching along the edges of his navy lapels: Pierre Cardin by way of Kowloon.

I shifted my gaze to the woman seated closest to the room's central aisle: Angela Underhill.

Teddy's mother wore a demure flowered dress with a lace collar and a row of pearly pink buttons down its front.

She was staring straight back at me, and she had to be eight months pregnant.

43

Angela Underhill continued to glare at me. I glanced pointedly at her belly and then raised my eyes back to hers.

No backs, no gives.

Getting knocked up by the guy who beat your first kid to death didn't strike me as anything to cop a fucking attitude about.

Bost stood up, walking around from behind the prosecution table.

She was arrayed in nubby pink bouclé, with a string of pearls, expensively sheer stockings, and a great big fluffy hair bow. I wondered whether she'd gone Hello-Kitty femme to undercut Angela's church-choir maternity frock.

"Good afternoon, Ms. Dare," she said.

I bent down to the microphone in front of me. "Good afternoon."

"We've heard testimony this morning from Ms. Cate Ludlam, about her involvement with the renovation of Jamaica's Prospect

Cemetery. Could you tell us how you first came to be there last September?"

She led me through Sophia's introduction at that long-ago party, Cate's and my familial relationship, and everything else leading up to me getting out to Jamaica that first time.

I glanced out into the gallery, and Cate and Kyle flashed me discreet thumbs-up from the second-to-last row.

Bost continued, "So the afternoon of September nineteenth was the first occasion on which you visited the cemetery?"

"It was," I said.

The questions continued on for a while, in the same sequence Bost had posed them during my grand jury testimony.

We'd gotten to the point where I was standing just outside the thicket, having taken Cate's gloves off.

"And what did you see when you leaned down to pick up that bottle, Ms. Dare?"

"Another headstone," I said.

Now her questions were a lot more detailed than they had been during the grand jury testimony. I presumed she was trying to get me to establish specific points that might negate questions she expected the defense attorneys to bring up later. But I couldn't figure out what those would be.

"Did you see anything besides the head-stone at first?"

"No, but then I jumped to the side a little."

"Why was that?"

"There was a dead rat on the ground."

"What did you see then?"

"Something white. My first thought was that it might be an egg." My throat was really dry. I would've given anything for a glass of water.

"Did you crawl in further?"

"Yes. When I'd gotten about a foot closer, I knew exactly what it was."

"What was this object, Ms. Dare?"

"A child's skull." I looked at Angela Underhill, who appeared to be fascinated with the blank wall off to her left.

"How could you tell the skull was that of a child?" asked Bost.

"He still had his baby teeth."

The jury was saddened by that, especially the women.

Albert Williams just looked bored. He started playing with his pencil, spinning it on the surface of the defense table.

A male juror was watching him too — as pissed off as I was, from the expression on his face.

Good.

"Could you see anything else?" asked Bost.

"By that point, the rest of the bones as well," I continued. "They were the remains of someone very, very small."

"Did you touch or move anything?"

"I didn't," I said. "The moment I realized what I was looking at, I backed out of the foliage and ran to find Cate."

"And were the bones completely intact when you found them?"

"No," I said, glancing at Teddy's mother again.

She had both hands on her belly now, looking down with a little smile on her face. Maybe the baby was kicking.

Jesus, you dumb bitch, the least you could do is fake a tear for the jury.

"What sort of damage could you see?" asked Bost.

"The child's rib cage had been smashed in. I didn't think that it could have —" I looked over at the defense table again as Albert picked up the pencil and started tapping it against the table, clenched in his big fist.

Imagine getting slammed in the chest with that.

Galloway stilled his hand, and he looked unhappy about it.

391

"Could have what, Ms. Dare?" prompted Bost.

"It just didn't look like something that could have happened there, at Prospect," I said.

Tiny black-haired Galloway leaped up to object. "Objection, Your Honor. Lack of foundation. Ms. Dare has no professional expertise in these matters —"

The judge cut her off with a basso "I'll allow it."

He turned to me. "Continue, Ms. Dare."

I nodded. "I'm not trying to offer any sort of expert opinion, it's just that the foliage surrounding the little skeleton was extremely dense and close to the ground. I immediately thought that it would have been impossible for someone to have caused that much damage *after* the child's body had been dragged inside the bushes. That's all I wanted to say."

"All right," said Bost. "Let's move on."

I went through the aftermath point by point until we were all waiting inside the chapel for Skwarecki.

"Did any of you go back out into the foliage that afternoon?" asked Bost.

"No, we didn't. The police took over."

"When did you and Ms. Ludlam first return to the cemetery after that?"

"The following week," I said.

We went through the Quakers, et cetera.

"Had Detective Skwarecki asked you to look for anything in particular?"

"Items of clothing, or any scraps of fabric," I said.

"And did you find any items like that?"

"Not personally, no."

"Did someone else find an article of clothing?"

"One of the other volunteers found a child's shoe," I said.

"When did *you* first see this shoe?"

"It was after the rest of the group had gone home."

"Was the detective with you at the time?" asked Bost.

I explained about Teddy's vertebra, found by the Quaker woman.

"What happened once the detective had left the cemetery?"

I explained Mrs. Underhill showing up.

"Was this before you saw the shoe, or after?"

"Before," I said.

"Did Mrs. Underhill come inside the grounds at *any* point during this time?" asked Bost.

"No."

"Did you notice anything different when

you'd taken your seats on the ground that second time?"

I went into the sneaker stuff, and one of the jurors gasped about the whole Club Melmac thing, which was probably good.

"Thank you, Ms. Dare," said Bost.

She walked back behind her table and shuffled through papers for a moment, then looked up at the judge.

"Your Honor," she said, "as the hour is getting late, I'd like to continue questioning this witness tomorrow morning?"

The judge agreed to that, and I was sprung for the day.

I gave Cate a quick hug when I found her out in the hallway.

"You were great," she said.

"I'm sorry I couldn't be there for you. How'd it go?"

"All right, I guess. Want to go across the street and have a drink?"

"Can't," I said. "I'm late for work."

It was dark enough outside that the Catalog's windows were casting squares of light on the air-shaft bricks. At five of eight I had the day's last customer on the phone. Yumiko was already putting on her coat.

I hadn't wanted to miss any of the trial, so

Yong Sun put me on the schedule to work every day afterwards until now, when we shut down the phones officially.

"Yes sir, we have that in stock," I said. "Would you like the hardcover edition or the paperback?"

My arm itched inside its cast, but I was getting better at the one-handed typing.

Another line rang.

Yumiko rolled her eyes and picked up. "The Catalog. I'm sorry, but our office hours are finished for the day."

I started closing out my order. "Yes, sir, you should have that in plenty of time by regular mail. With the plain red gift wrap."

Yumiko hit the Hold button.

"Some fucking rude guy for you, line three," she said, dropping the receiver back in place.

"Your total will be twenty-two ninety-seven, with shipping," I said.

"Don't forget to turn the phones off," said Yumiko.

She grabbed her purse and walked out into the front office.

"Certainly, sir," I said. "You're very welcome."

The hallway door banged shut in Yumiko's wake.

I killed the final work call and hit line

three. "This is Madeline. Sorry to keep you waiting."

No answer, but there was some noise in the background so the line wasn't dead.

"Dean?"

Nothing.

Maybe he'd put the phone down for a second, thinking he was still on hold. I said his name again, louder.

"No need to yell." A young man's voice, though deep.

"Hi," I said. "Sorry about that."

"That's all right," he said with a little chuckle, mellow, relaxed.

And nobody I know.

"You having a good time at your job today, Madeline?"

"Who's this?"

"Two-fifty West Fifty-seventh Street. That's where you work, right?"

The office suddenly felt really big around me. And empty.

"By yourself now," he said. "Thirteenth floor and all."

My head whipped toward the windows.

Oh, right, like he's levitating in the air shaft.

"Who the fuck *is* this?"

"Might want to lock that door, you know? Keep the boogeyman away."

I heard something tapping softly in the

background. Like a pencil.

"Albert?"

Tap.

But don't prisoners have to call collect?

Tap.

It's an 800 number.

Tap.

Too quiet for jail.

Another little chuckle and the line clicked dead.

I dialed Skwarecki, shaking.

"You're sure it wasn't somebody just fucking with you as a joke?"

"He knew my *name,* Skwarecki. He knew I was alone in the office. What floor this is."

She got serious. "You lock the doors?"

"Of *course* I locked the doors. What d'you, think I'm an idiot?"

I didn't mention having locked all the windows, too. Just in case the boogeyman had climbing gear. Or a helicopter with a rope ladder he could hang off, down the air shaft.

"You got any kind of building security," said Skwarecki, "someone you can call right now?"

"I don't know. Probably. But I don't have the number."

"Okay, just stay put. Don't let *anyone* in

until it's me, all right? And I mean not Little Red Riding Hood. I can be there in twenty-five."

"You are a total goddess, Skwarecki. Thank you."

I hung up the phone and sat there shaking.

"Okay," I said, to the empty room. "Worst case, I can probably bash someone over the head with my cast."

That wasn't exactly comforting.

I looked at the phone room's doorway, toward the front office.

The dash out to flip the locks had scared me so much I still felt a little like puking.

"Stop being such a chickenshit, Madeline," I said aloud. *"Jesus."*

Skwarecki got there exactly twenty-three minutes later. My cowering, wussy ass was still firmly planted in the same chair when she started banging on the outer office door.

"You find a number for Security?" she asked when I let her in.

"Actually? No. I was too busy trying to figure out how to dig a safe boogeyman-proof hidey-hole in the carpet. And not throw up. In terror."

"Pussy," she said.

"Kiss my ass. And the next time there's

398

an election for mayor? I'm voting Libertarian."

"What the hell is *that* supposed to mean?"

"They think we should legalize assault weapons *and* drugs. Tonight is the first time I ever wanted them simultaneously."

"Brilliant. And then whoever it was could've just walked up behind you and blown your head off with an Uzi instead of running you down with a car."

"Not if I saw him first," I said.

"You trying for humor there?"

"No."

And then I leaned over and barfed into the wastepaper basket.

"Cheap date," said Skwarecki.

My "Fuck off" echoed weakly up out of the metal bucket.

"Try not to get any on your cast."

Skwarecki and I walked into the courtyard of my building. She was tense, scoping out all the dark corners, which didn't calm me down any.

Some graffiti butthead had tagged the bricks next to our front door — the paint was still wet, dripping down into the mortar.

"*Four* of you live here?" asked Skwarecki once we were inside.

"It's a two-bedroom," I said.

"What d'you pay — six, seven hundred?"

"Eleven fifty."

"You know you could get a whole house for that out where I live?"

"See, that's why I'm happy to pay so much, Skwarecki. Just to make sure I don't end up with a view of *your* sorry ass out my bedroom window."

She got me in a neck-lock and roughed up my hair. "G'wan, admit it. You *worship* my sorry ass. You'd pay *extra*."

I thunked her in the ribs with my cast. "Get the hell over yourself."

"Make me."

"Piece of cake. I'll scream 'Police harassment!' and puke on your jacket."

She let go and I turned on the living-room lights.

"Jesus Christ," she said, squinting against the onslaught of orange paint. "Who's your decorator? Ray Charles?"

"If you're giving me shit just so I stop being scared, it's not working."

"That paint color? I'm scared myself."

"Maybe you should get a carry permit," said Skwarecki.

She and Pagan crossed their arms and looked at me.

Sue was in Vermont skiing. Dean was back

in Houston.

"What the fuck would *I* do with a gun, you guys? I have a goddamn cast on my shooting arm. My *third* goddamn cast, by the way."

"Might turn out to be handy, someone comes after you," said Skwarecki. "You could just whack 'em over the head with it."

"Don't think that didn't cross my mind tonight," I said. "And I sure as shit wasn't reassured."

"Do you think someone *is* gonna come after her?" asked Pagan.

Skwarecki looked back at me. "You took the call, you know what he said. The guy mention anything made you think he was for real?"

"He knew my *name*, Skwarecki. He knew where I worked."

She shrugged. "Might just be some perv, though. You guys ever get that kind of call — bunch of young chicks, working a switchboard?"

"Some guy wanted to know about my underwear last July," I said.

"You ever tell anyone your name on the phone there?" she asked. "Get to chatting a little?"

"I might have. I don't know."

"Or maybe that other girl told him?"

"Yumiko? She said he asked for me," I said.

"He seem like he knew anything *else* about you?"

"Other than how the boogeyman's gonna get me? No."

"Nothing connected to the trial, this case?" she asked.

"No," I said. "Nothing to indicate it was anything but a prank."

She leaned forward, elbows on her knees. "You're sure? Play it back through in your head one more time."

I did, and still came up with nothing. "All I know is he fucking *scared* me, Skwarecki. Bad enough to make me call you."

"Scares the hell out of me," said Pagan, "and I don't have shit to do with this trial. It's not like we know for sure it *was* a prank, either. There could be a boogeyman climbing the fire escape as we speak."

"I'm sorry," I said.

"It's not your fault," she said. "But that doesn't make me any less freaked out."

"You guys know I've got your back, right?" asked Skwarecki.

"Oh, like you had my sister's when she got run over?" asked Pagan.

"Hey!" I said. "She did her best."

"You could've been fucking killed, Maddie," Pague continued. "And you *don't* know it was random. None of us do. Isn't that right, Detective?"

"How would anyone have known I was going to be at the cemetery that morning?" I asked. "Or even what I looked like?"

"And did you finish testifying today? Or do you have more to go?" asked Pagan.

Skwarecki didn't answer that.

"You never traced that car, right?" I asked. "I thought someone gave you guys a partial plate number."

"Wasn't enough. Two letters."

"They say what it looked like, the car?" I asked.

"Big thing," she said. "American."

"I figured that from the sound of the engine. And it sure as hell didn't *feel* like a Datsun."

"Don't kid yourself," said Skwarecki. "Pedestrian versus car? Japscrap'll kill you just as dead."

I shivered.

She shook her head. "Fucking bicycle will, it's going fast enough."

My bones remembered the gunning engine, the *smack* that punched me out of my shoes.

"What color?" asked Pagan.

Skwarecki looked at her, puzzled.

"The *car*. If someone got a partial plate number, they had to see what color it was, right? At least Maddie'd know what to look out for next time she's stranded alone at a bus stop."

"Guy said it was some kinda gold," said Skwarecki. "With a white roof."

That's right. A flash of white, then pain and sky.

I hunched forward, bile climbing my throat.

Skwarecki touched my shoulder. "Yo, you okay? Gonna puke again?"

I bolted for the bathroom.

44

"If getting run over is connected to this case, how'd they know you'd be back at Prospect the morning you got hit?" asked Pagan once I'd brushed my teeth and returned to the living room.

"Someone overheard us in the restaurant across the street from the courthouse," I said. "There were these guys at the next table —"

"Bost talking about it all pissed off right after the grand jury," said Skwarecki. *"Fuck."*

"How'd they know you'd be in the restaurant, though?" asked Pagan.

"Only place to eat," said Skwarecki. "Lunchtime, you kidding? *Everybody's* there: lawyers, cops, witnesses, jurors, any perp who's made bail."

"Did your perps make bail?" asked Pague.

"No," I said.

"Doesn't mean they don't have friends on the outside," said Skwarecki. "Albert's got some gang crap on his rap sheet. Witness intimidation's practically the entire point of gangs."

Pagan looked at me. "Like maybe those two guys at the cemetery the morning you got run over?"

"Jesus," said Skwarecki. "You tried to convince me in the hospital, Madeline, and I blew you off. You think maybe those two were in the restaurant the day before?"

"Doesn't matter," I said. "They still would've known it was me."

"How?" asked Pagan.

"They took my picture." I looked at Skwarecki. "After you and Bost left they started messing around with a Polaroid camera. I remember the flash going off, right in my eyes. They took my fucking *picture.*"

"You guys have lunch there again today?" asked Pagan.

"Like I told you," said Skwarecki. "Only fucking ziti for twenty blocks."

"But how would they know where I *work?*" I asked.

"The address was your work address on all your witness statements," she said. "Anybody could've sat behind Bost today and seen it."

"This is really getting creepy," said Pagan.

"Creepy, but still weird," I said.

"Weird how?" asked Skwarecki.

"Well, it's not like anyone actually threatened me about testifying *specifically,* right?" I said. "I mean, the guys at the cemetery, the phone call tonight. If they're trying to intimidate me as a witness, shouldn't somebody have come right out and said so? Like 'Go to court and you'll sleep with the fishes' or some shit?"

"Maybe they thought they'd killed you the first time, with the car," said Pagan. "And then when you showed up today, they realized they'd only winged you."

"Even so. The guy on the phone tonight scared the crap out of me, but he *didn't* tell me not to get back on the stand tomorrow."

Maybe it was *just a prank call after all.*

"They don't have to come right out and say it," said Skwarecki. "Shit like this? They figure you'll know."

"But I *didn't* know. Even you didn't, really," I said.

Pagan crossed her arms. "It's still fucking scary."

"Look," I said, "on the bright side? They know where I work, but they don't know where I live."

Skwarecki nodded. "Is your home number unlisted?"

"No," I said.

"Is it in your name?"

"All our names," said Pagan.

"Any of you ask Ma Bell not to publish the address?"

"Shit," I said.

Skwarecki glanced at the security grate over our fire-escape window. "Not to mention someone just tagged your building. Paint was still wet, right?"

"What?" said Pagan.

"Fresh graffiti by the front entry," said our friend the detective. "*There's* your overt threat."

Pague went pale. "You got a gun, Skwarecki?"

"I'm a cop. Of course I've got a fucking gun."

"*On* you?"

Skwarecki peeled back her blazer, revealing the holstered pistol at her hip. Then she put her right foot up on the table and lifted her trouser cuff so we could see the smaller one strapped to her ankle. "Any more questions?"

"Yeah," said my sister. "Want to sleep over?"

Not like any of us actually *slept,* really. Pague and I both went to bed a while after we'd made up the sofa for Skwarecki, but I'd moved from Dean's-and-my bed to Sue's an hour later, apprehensive in the dark.

Around midnight, Pague reached her foot across the space between the beds to poke me in the calf.

"You still awake?" she whispered.

"Yeah."

"Is it *worth* it, going through all this?"

"Yeah," I said. "I just can't believe I'm putting you through it."

"Look, if you think it's important I've got your back."

"Thank you."

"You should probably be glad Dean's out of town, though. He'd freak."

"Hey!" said Skwarecki out in the living room. "Simmer down in there or I'm gonna have to separate you."

Before I could answer, the phone rang.

I threw off the blankets and climbed out of bed.

"You think it's the guy?" whispered Pague. "Calling *here*?"

"My luck, I bet it's Astrid."

I answered it in the dark kitchen, and shut the door behind me.

"Bunny?"

"Hey there," I said softly. "How's Texas?"

409

"Not bad," he said. "One of the sales reps took me out to dinner at his favorite restaurant tonight."

"How was it?"

"Chicken-fried steak so big sumbitch hung off both sides of the plate."

"We'll have plenty of Szechuan waiting soon as you're home."

He cleared his throat. "It's going to be a little longer than I thought."

"Everything okay?" I asked.

"Actually, everything's great. Christoph just promoted me to sales — raise *and* a commission."

I could hear the pride and relief in his voice, and I was incredibly happy for him after the rocky plains of the last year and a half.

Hardly the right moment to come clean about the armed cop camped on our sofa. Pagan was right; he'd totally lose his shit.

"Dean, that is *awesome.* Congratulations. And it makes me like Christoph a whole lot better, that he knows what a good thing he has in you."

"Well, I have to go to Canada as soon as I'm done here. Quebec, to a paper mill. My first sales call."

"Will you be back in time for Mom's nuptial event?" I asked.

"I've got five more days here, then La Tuque. I'll do my best."

"I could use the moral support, you know?"

"I just want to see you," he said.

"Me too you. I'm really glad things are going so well, but it still sucks to have you on the road."

And I'm scared.

"How's the cast?"

"Itchy."

"When does it come off this time?"

"Another couple of weeks," I said.

"I can't wait to see your naked arm again."

"Yeah."

"You okay? You sound kind of sad."

"Just tired," I said.

"I love you, Bunny."

"Me too you," I said, and we hung up.

I walked back to the bedroom.

A car drove by in the street below, schussing through the slush.

"You didn't tell him," said Pagan from across the darkened room.

"This kind of news? I figured I'd better do it in person."

If I'd told him all the details of my day, he would've come running home on the first prop-jet out of Amarillo. Just when things were starting to look up for him.

I didn't care about the paycheck, just his pride. He had something to excel at now — as he so very much deserved.

God knows holding back a few details from my intrepid spouse to protect *that* wouldn't be the hardest thing I'd ever done.

And then I jumped back out of bed and ran to the bathroom again.

Dry heaves, since I hadn't touched a bite of dinner.

"You okay?" Pagan stood in the bathroom's street-lit doorway.

"I'm fucking terrified."

"It's one more day. Skwarecki takes you to court, then you're done, right?"

"I guess," I said.

"You know what?"

"What?"

"It *is* worth it. What you're doing."

"That means a lot."

"Nobody stood up for that kid when he was alive. Somebody has to now."

"I know."

"Don't back down."

"I won't. Thank you."

"Just don't get us all fucking killed, okay?"

"I'll do my best," I said.

"That's all we *can* do. Any of us."

"Yeah."

"You done puking?"

412

"Let's hope."

"So brush your teeth. Come back to bed."

45

I still felt like dog shit when I woke up the next morning, so queasy with nerves I didn't even have coffee.

"You gotta eat something. Settle your stomach," said Skwarecki.

"I'm not hungry," I said. "Feels like I'd just puke if I tried food."

"We could stop at a deli on the way, get you a bagel."

I grabbed the Nutella out of the cupboard and ate three big spoonfuls. "Happy now?"

She shrugged. "How do you feel?"

"Better," I said, surprised.

In fact I was kind of hungry now. Enough to scrape the jar empty with my spoon.

Skwarecki looked at her watch.

"Let's hit it," she said. "When you're up first they always start on time."

Skwarecki stayed with me right up to the

door of the witness room back at the court-house.

"You gonna be okay?" she asked.

"I guess."

"Meet you right back here at lunch, okay? By that point you're probably done with testifying."

"What've you got planned for the morning?" I asked.

"Ah, the usual — couple hands of canasta, maybe run a few license plates. Then maybe drive around, see if I can find any gold Lincolns."

"Thank you," I said. "For all of this."

"Protect and serve, right?"

"Above and beyond. Staying over, making me eat something this morning?"

"Hey," she said. "Who's your buddy, who's your pal?"

As soon as I sat back down in the box, I saw Kyle in the back row of the gallery right next to Cate.

The swearing-in from yesterday still counted, I guess, because Bost got right into the questions from where she'd left off.

I was more nervous, though. I kept looking at the sea of faces behind the two lawyers' tables, trying to see if anyone looked like they had an ax to grind. Literally.

We were quickly in new territory, though, Bost and I. Not just rehashing what I'd already told the grand jury. I had to give up playing Spot the Boogeyman so I could concentrate on her questions.

Bost had led me up through when she asked us to find the second sneaker.

"So you and Detective Skwarecki agreed to return to the cemetery that same afternoon?" she asked.

"We *discussed* it that afternoon, but we planned to meet each other at Prospect the following morning."

"And did you do so?"

"No, we didn't."

"Why not?"

"Detective Skwarecki was late," I said, wondering if she'd discussed last night yet with Bost.

"Did you enter the cemetery grounds before she arrived at any time?" asked Bost.

"I did not," I said. "I'd been told to wait for the detective — and told specifically *not* to undertake any sort of search without her being there."

"Were you still there at the front gates when she arrived?"

"No. I'd moved to the corner of the larger street."

"What happened then?"

"I got hit by a car. Right before she arrived, I guess."

"You guess?"

"The car knocked me unconscious."

"Did you return to Prospect Cemetery that day, Ms. Dare?"

"I had a broken arm, a black eye, and a bunch of stitches in my scalp. I don't even remember most of the ride home from the hospital."

"Your arm hasn't healed yet?" she asked.

"They rebroke it twice," I said. "I'm really hoping the third time's the charm."

A couple of people laughed at that.

"I can imagine," said Bost, smiling at me. "And have you returned to Prospect Cemetery since that morning?"

"I have not," I said. "I didn't think I'd be much use clearing brush."

"Thank you, Ms. Dare."

Bost looked at the judge. "I have no further questions for the witness at this time, Your Honor."

At the defense table Marty Hetzler stood up and shot his cuffs.

46

Angela Underhill crossed her arms above her massive belly as her attorney slipped around behind her.

He paused to button up his blazer before stepping forward toward me.

"Good morning, Ms. Dare."

"Good morning, Mr. Hetzler."

He gave me a little nod of approval for knowing who he was.

"I only have a few questions for you today," he said. "I'm sure we'd all like to break for lunch as quickly as possible."

He moved a couple of steps closer, which was a good thing as I was then no longer blinded by the gloss of his shoes. These were black, buffed to such an acme of luster that they might have been patent leather, or smeared with shellac.

"My first question pertains to your professional background, all right?"

"Certainly," I said.

418

"What is it that you do for a living?"

"I work for a book catalog at the moment."

"What other kinds of job experience do you have?" he asked.

"I've worked as a teacher at a boarding school for disturbed kids, and as a journalist for a couple of small newspapers," I said.

"So you have no training or professional experience in pathology or law enforcement?"

"I do not."

"Ms. Dare, I'm just asking about this to remind our jurors that your speculation yesterday about the condition of the remains you discovered was exactly that, *speculation* —"

"As I said at the time, Mr. Hetzler, I have no professional background or expertise in the fields of forensic science and criminal justice. I just wanted to say that the bushes in which I discovered the child's remains were thick and extremely low to the ground."

"I think we all understand that, thank you."

"You're most welcome," I said.

"This isn't the first time you've stumbled onto a crime scene, though, is it, Ms. Dare?"

"Unfortunately, it is not."

He nodded, smiling at me and then at the jury. "In fact, over the last couple of years, you've been involved with two separate murder investigations, haven't you?"

"Not by choice," I said.

"Really?"

"I beg your pardon?"

Hetzler looked at the jury. "It just seems to me that someone who stumbles across *three* suspicious deaths in as many years might be something of an aficionado."

His body count was low, but why quibble?

He turned back to me. "So what are you, Ms. Dare, some sort of murder *groupie?*"

"No. And I'm appalled by the highly inappropriate flippancy of that characterization."

"Just a habitual witness, then?"

"I worked as a journalist, Mr. Hetzler. As such, I was given information about an unsolved double homicide — which ultimately led to the murderer's apprehension."

Hetzler raised a hand to his flashy tie. "But you then turned up even *more* crime, at a *boarding* school?"

"Objection — relevance?" Bost stood up. "Your Honor, could you please remind Mr. Hetzler to stick with the matter at hand? I see no point in this line of questioning."

His Honor backed her up on that.

Hetzler turned away from me, consulting

420

some notes on the defense table.

When he faced me again his lips were pursed. "I'd like to return to your earlier statement, Ms. Dare."

"Fine."

"Since we can't establish an accurate time frame for the number of months — or *years* — the child's remains might have been at the cemetery," he continued, "how could you have known that the damage to the rib cage you saw was not inflicted *after* the remains had been placed inside the grounds?"

"Because of the bushes," I said.

Hetzler smirked. "The *bushes.*"

"The space beneath them was about this high," I said, holding my left hand less than two feet above my right, stationary in its plaster.

"It's *impossible* that anyone could have accidentally stepped on the child's ribs while walking upright. Furthermore, I can't imagine how someone could have inflicted a blow of sufficient force to crack the bones given the restricted size of the space."

"In your non-expert *opinion,*" said Hetzler.

"Yes sir, in my non-expert opinion. Not least because that foliage had been untouched since the mid-nineteen-fifties."

"Despite the *considerable* homeless population known to camp inside the cemetery?"

"All I can tell you, Mr. Hetzler," I said, "is that they seemed to have done a great deal more camping than gardening."

Someone on the jury stifled a laugh.

"Nonetheless, you offer this opinion on the basis of your *own* expertise as — what, a volunteer gardener?" he shot back.

"Yes, and why not? My initial impression of the vegetation struck me as pertinent to bring up here because what it all looked like originally might not have been apparent to the investigating police officers. It was greatly altered by the time they arrived at the scene."

"And why is that?"

"Because I'd chopped the bushes up with a machete and hedge clippers. That foliage was six large lawn-and-leaf bags *less* overgrown by the time the police arrived. That was the whole point of the afternoon. We weren't there for a tea party on the lawn."

Hetzler looked at the judge. "Your Honor, I have no more questions for this witness."

Galloway passed as well.

I was instructed to step down, the judge dismissed us for lunch, and everyone who could bolted for the lobby.

I waited until the room had emptied out

enough that I could glom onto Kyle and Cate before I would brave the exit doors myself. Even then, my heart rate was manic until I saw Skwarecki waiting outside.

47

"Any news?" I asked Skwarecki.

"Nothing yet on the car," she said. "I've got a couple guys on it again."

"What car?" asked Kyle.

I laid out the previous night's events for Kyle and Cate as we headed once more to the restaurant across the road.

"You guys ever feel like you've been marooned on Gilligan's Ziti Island?" I asked, shivering in the snow as we waited for the light to change.

"Five days a week," said Kyle, blowing into his cupped hands. "Right around now."

Despite my bitching I practically licked my plate, then batted cleanup on Cate's.

"Stomach settled?" asked Skwarecki when I asked if we had time for dessert.

"Making up for yesterday," I said.

My testimony was finished. I didn't figure there was anything else to worry about — outside whether the jury convicted Angela and Albert.

About that I worried a great deal.

Kyle left first, after throwing a ten and a five on the table. "Bost wants to run something by me. See you back inside."

He was waiting for us in the gallery's back row by the time we returned ourselves.

Taking the seat between him and Cate, I knew I'd have a much better view of the judge and jury than I'd had on the stand, but I already missed being able to check out the facial expressions of Angela, Albert, and the three attorneys head-on.

The five of them were already seated at their tables up front, separated from the rest of us by a low railing, but I noticed an extra head next to Bost's. "Who's the new guy?"

"Assistant," Kyle whispered back. "She's got some display stuff to set up."

There were maybe thirty other people scattered throughout the gallery in front of us, most sitting solo, buffered by unoccupied chairs to either side.

The jury box was still empty, as was the judge's high-backed black leather chair. We were quiet but for the occasional rustle of papers or muffled February cough. The clerk and bailiff sat beneath the judge's dais, heads bent over some sort of desk work.

The jurors filed in and took their chairs, two rows of six. The bailiff announced the judge.

Knees and chairs creaked around the room as we all rose to our feet, and for just a second I thought we might sing the national anthem next, or at least turn toward the flag, hands over hearts to pledge allegiance.

The judge twitched his robes and sat down. The rest of us followed suit, sneaking in a few last sniffles and throat-clearings.

Someone nearby crinkled a bit of cellophane, and I caught a sharp hit of mentholated cough drop.

The judge brought things back into play with a gavel rap, and Bost called Skwarecki to the stand at long last.

I looked around the audience while she did the whole swearing in, but couldn't tell much from the back of anyone's head.

Boogeyman, boogeyman, fly away home; leave me and all other children alone.

Bost got to her feet. "Good afternoon, Detective Skwarecki."

"Good afternoon."

Bost walked closer to the witness stand. "I'd like to return to the afternoon last September when you were first called to Prospect Cemetery."

426

"September the nineteenth," said Skwarecki.

"Exactly, thank you. Can you tell us what you found there, Detective, when you first arrived at the scene?"

I zoned out a little as they ran through the preliminaries. The room was getting stuffy now, as though the heat had just kicked up a notch. I unbuttoned my jacket and took it off, laying it across my lap.

I'd forgotten about Bost's assistant until he stood to set up a tripod easel, about twenty minutes in. He walked back to her table and picked up a stack of what looked like posterboards, then settled the first one into the easel brackets so that it faced the jury.

From our corner we had a decent view: a large black-and-white shot of Prospect, from just inside the front gates.

"Detective Swarecki," said Bost, "is this the cemetery as it looked when you arrived that afternoon?"

"Yes. You can see the crime-scene tape running along the outside of the bushes, to the left of the path there."

The assistant replaced shot number one with a view taken from the path into the bushes.

"This is the area where Ms. Dare had

been working that afternoon?" asked Bost.

"Yes."

"She testified earlier that the area of foliage she'd been working on was particularly dense," said Bost. "Would you agree?"

"Yes," said Skwarecki.

Bost nodded to the young guy, who switched out the path image for shot number three: a wall of vines and branches with a low, dark space at the bottom.

"Can you describe what we're seeing here, Detective?"

"This is the area where Ms. Dare stopped clipping branches. You can see the white ends of those she'd just finished cutting."

Bost stepped up to the easel. "Here and here, for instance?"

"Exactly."

"And what is this area?" asked Bost, pointing to the shadowed area at the base of the image.

"That's the opening she crawled into after spotting a headstone."

The fourth shot was a close-up of the tunnel with a yardstick measuring its height: nineteen inches. You couldn't see into the darkness beyond.

"Could you say how this little passageway was made?" asked Bost.

"Animals, most likely."

Bost motioned to her assistant. "And inside that tunnel you saw this?"

The next photo had obviously been taken with a flash. I heard someone in the jury box gasp. You could see Teddy's tiny skull clearly, and his little smashed rib cage.

"Yes," said Skwarecki as Bost's assistant displayed two more photos of the bones from different angles. "We wanted to make sure that we'd recorded the site where the remains were discovered exactly as it was when Ms. Dare found it, before any further effort was made to clear the surrounding brush."

The next shot showed the skull in more detail: Teddy Underhill's big eyes, and baby teeth.

The flash had illuminated part of the headstone behind him so you could make out a piece of its spidery inscription: *Beloved Son, Departed This Life . . .*

I hoped they hadn't shown it to Mrs. Underhill. I'd lied about the cherub.

I turned to look at the jury in time to see one lady crossing herself. The men looked angry, the women on the verge of tears.

Good.

"Could we return to the previous photo?" asked Bost.

Her assistant complied and she thanked

429

him before stepping closer to the image.

"In your opinion, Detective Skwarecki," said Bost, pointing to the broken ribs, "could the damage we see in this photograph have occurred *after* the child's remains had been placed here?"

"No, it could not," said Skwarecki.

"Why is that?"

"Given the amount of force necessary to inflict that kind of damage," she said, "it couldn't have occured in such a confined space. I'm sure the pathologist can explain that in more detail, but I can tell you based just on what you see in this photo that there's no way someone could have done that while inside the tunnel, even if they used some sort of instrument."

Bost nodded. "But could it have been done by an animal, or someone who stepped on the child's body after it was placed here?"

"No, it could not. For the same reasons."

"Thank you, Detective," said Bost.

Her assistant gathered the photos and returned them to the prosecution table, but he left the easel in place.

48

"I'd like to jump ahead a bit, here, Detective," said Bost, "and ask you about how you came to identify these remains as being those of little Teddy Underhill."

"All right," said Skwarecki.

Bost turned to the jury box. "Now first of all, as Ms. Ludlam told us yesterday, Prospect Cemetery has been in use as a burial ground since the mid-sixteen-hundreds. I'm sure we all might wonder whether it's extremely unusual to find human bones in a graveyard, yet it seems that the investigating officers immediately decided that this was a suspicious death which had occurred relatively recently. Can you tell us what first led you to that conclusion, Detective?"

"Two things," said Skwarecki. "The first is that Ms. Ludlam was so familiar with the state of the grounds as a whole. She knew that none of the graves had been disturbed, beyond some vandalism to the memorial stones over the years. The second indication was the state of the bones themselves."

"Can you describe what you learned from your own inspection of the bones on-site that first day?"

"It was immediately apparent that the victim was a child, of course," answered Skwarecki. "But I could also tell right away that these were the remains of someone who'd died within the previous six months."

"How so?"

"Most importantly, the ends of the bones change over time with exposure to the elements. It would be impossible to pinpoint an exact day of the victim's death from skeletal remains, but forensically, we can establish a slightly broader time frame with a good deal of accuracy. The color of the bones themselves also tells us something. They grow whiter over time when exposed to the elements. These bones weren't white. Given those observations, I knew this was not a child who'd died a hundred years ago, or even two years ago."

"So you estimated that the boy had died within the previous six months?"

"Yes," said Skwarecki. "And I was backed up by the pathologist's report, as I expected to be."

"But there were things you couldn't tell

about this victim because of the state of his remains, weren't there?"

"Yes. A number of them."

"In fact, the boy's age made the likelihood of identification more difficult?"

"If the child had been found sooner, of course we might have had more to go on — his blood type, his hair color, his facial features — and had he been older, we might have expected to confirm his identity with dental records."

"With none of those details, you're still certain that the boy found in the cemetery was Edward Underhill?"

"Yes."

"Can you tell us why?"

"First of all, none of the information the pathologist was able to give me on the basis of his examination ruled out that identification."

"Such as?" asked Bost.

"This was a child, aged just over three years, of African American descent."

"Were you aware that Teddy Underhill was missing when these remains were discovered?"

"Not personally, no."

"And yet you found the report that listed him as missing rather quickly, didn't you?"

"Within a week," said Skwarecki.

"Is there some sort of database you consulted?"

"No. It turned out that one of Teddy's relatives had been very active in keeping the attention of some fellow officers on his case."

"Was that the boy's mother, Angela Underhill?" asked Bost.

"No, it was not."

"So Teddy's mother didn't seem to care that he was missing?" asked Bost.

Hetzler leaped up. "Objection!"

"I'll withdraw the question, Your Honor," said Bost before Hetzler could even specify what he was objecting to.

The judge nodded and Hetzler sat down again.

"Which relative kept in contact with the police?" asked Bost.

"Teddy's great-grandmother, Elsie Underhill. She came to the station on a weekly basis."

"Detective," continued Bost, "on these occasions did Angela Underhill accompany Mrs. Elsie Underhill when she visited the officers in your precinct house?"

"Only on the first occasion, when they came together to file the missing-persons report."

"Can you tell us anything else about the

circumstances of that report having been filed?"

"Yes," said Skwarecki. "Teddy's mother waited for two weeks before contacting the police to report him missing."

"And was there a reason why she waited so long?"

"I know why she *stopped* waiting."

"And why was that?"

Skwarecki leaned in, a little closer to the mike. "Angela Underhill went to her grandmother for money the day that report was filed."

"*Objection!*" said Hetzler, on his feet again. "Hearsay."

"Sustained," said the judge. "The jury is instructed to disregard the answer."

"On what date was the report filed?" asked Bost.

"May the second," said Skwarecki.

"And it was something listed in that report that allowed you to identify the remains found at Prospect as Teddy Underhill's, wasn't it?"

"Yes," said Skwarecki. "The little boy's sneakers."

Bost's assistant returned to the easel and fitted a new photo enlargement into its brackets, a shot of Teddy's sneaker, the words CLUB MELMAC clearly legible even

435

though it was smeared with dirt.

Bost pointed at the shoe. "This is the sneaker one of Ms. Ludlam's volunteers found on the afternoon of September twenty-sixth, isn't it?"

"It is," confirmed Skwarecki.

"Ms. Dare testified earlier that she could tell the sneaker matched your description from these words printed on the side."

Skwarecki nodded.

"But can we know for sure that this sneaker belonged to Teddy Underhill?" asked Bost. "It was found some distance from the remains, wasn't it?"

"About a hundred feet away."

"And did you find any other item of the boy's clothing that had been listed in the report?"

"Yes."

"What did you find?"

"The second shoe," said Skwarecki.

Bost's assistant put another photo up on the easel. This one was printed with the aardvark-faced character ALF, waving.

"How can you be so sure that *these* shoes belonged to Teddy Underhill? Isn't it possible that finding them at Prospect Cemetery was a coincidence?"

"We know when and where they were purchased," said Skwarecki. "All the clothes

436

Teddy was wearing when his mother last saw him had been birthday gifts."

"From whom?"

"From Elsie Underhill."

"You're certain about that?" asked Bost.

"Mrs. Underhill still had the receipts," said Skwarecki.

"Detective, can you tell us anything else about that missing-persons report?"

"Such as?"

"Well, how did Angela Underhill say her child had gotten lost?"

"Objection," said Hetzler. "Calls for hearsay."

"Sustained," said the judge.

"In the missing-person's report Angela Underhill filed with the police," said Bost, "Miss Underhill stated that while her boyfriend Albert Williams was babysitting her son, Teddy, Mr. Williams fell asleep and Teddy wandered out of their motel room, isn't that right?"

"It is," said Skwarecki.

Cate leaned toward me, whispering, "Do they know yet what happened?"

I shrugged. "Skwarecki didn't mention anything."

"And *is* that what happened, Detective?" asked Bost. "Did Angela Underhill tell the truth in her report?

437

"No, she did not," said Skwarecki.

"How do you know that, Detective?"

"Following her arrest," said Skwarecki, "Angela Underhill confessed to having sat on that same bed and watched as Albert Williams punched her three-year-old son, Teddy, in the chest repeatedly, until the boy died."

49

I expected a burst of noise in the courtroom following Skwarecki's description of Teddy Underhill's murder.

I leaned over to Kyle.

"Nobody makes a peep," I whispered, "with a bombshell like that?"

"You and Cate are probably the only people here who haven't heard it already. It would've been the backbone of Bost's opening argument unless she's an idiot. And she's not."

The judge smacked his gavel down three times and glared at us, looking righteously pissed.

Bost addressed the judge. "Your Honor, I have no further questions for Detective Skwarecki at this time, but I may want to call her back to the stand later tomorrow morning."

"I'll agree to that, Ms. Bost," he said. "And ask that the defense address its questions to the detective at that time."

Even from behind Hetzler looked like he'd bristled at that, but he didn't put up any argument.

"As it's getting rather late in the day," continued the judge, "we'll recess until tomorrow morning."

"Thank you, Your Honor," said Bost.

Cate and Kyle and I walked out into the front hallway. She had to leave so we hugged good-bye, but Kyle held back with me.

"You have a minute?" he asked as we watched her go out the front doors and back into winter.

"Sure, what's up?"

He put his hand on my left arm and looked around the hallway. "Let's go get a coffee or something."

"Are you done for the day?"

"Yeah."

"Then screw coffee. Let's go back to the city and get a drink."

He seemed preoccupied in the car.

"You're not going to ask me about stealing state secrets or anything, right?" I asked, after we'd driven a number of silent blocks.

"I'm sorry," he said. "I'm just trying to figure out how much I should tell you."

"The number of times we all played Truth

or Dare over tequila, back in college? I wouldn't have thought we had any secrets left."

He didn't answer that.

"Kyle, it's *me.* You can tell me anything. You know that."

"It's not personal, it's about the trial. And I'm not sure about the ethical implications."

"I've kept other secrets. We've all been through some shit since the last time you and I hung out."

"I'm an officer of the court. It's different."

"I wouldn't do anything to jeopardize the outcome of this trial."

"I know."

"So talk to me."

He was quiet, pulling up to the tollbooths for the tunnel.

"Kyle?"

"It's about Mrs. Underhill," he said.

I grabbed his arm. "Is she okay? My God, I should have called her last night."

"She's fine, physically. I didn't mean to scare you."

"Then *what?* What's wrong?"

"Let's wait until we have some cocktails in front of us, okay?"

We ended up at a crappy Irish place on

441

Third Avenue.

Kyle ordered a Jameson rocks. I asked for a pint of Guinness, girding my taste buds for disappointment.

We slid into a booth and the bartender put some quarters in the jukebox.

"Clancy Brothers," I said. "Gag me."

"You used to *love* Irish dives."

"I used to love Irish *guys*. Thankfully, there's a cure for that."

"What?"

"Penicillin."

I took a sip of the Guinness, then pushed it away. Someone had obviously dissolved a urinal cake in it despite the crappy head.

Kyle winked at me over his Jameson. "Pickled egg?"

"You first."

He put down the drink.

"Truth or Dare, Kyle."

He ran a fingertip along the edge of his glass. "Truth."

"Why are we here?"

"Mrs. Underhill's waffling on her testimony. Bost needs her to step up."

"She testified before the grand jury, right?"

Kyle didn't answer. I guess he wasn't allowed to.

"If she changes her story now it's perjury,"

I said. "Can't Bost threaten her with jail time or something?"

"The woman's ninety years old, or close to it. Juries don't want to see someone like her being grilled — elderly, polite, vulnerable. She's lost her daughter, her great-grandson, her husband — and she's old enough to get away with saying she's confused, or forgets things."

"She's sharp as a tack."

"You know that," he said. "The jury doesn't."

I looked at my Guinness.

"Look, Bost mentioned that you'd spent some time with the woman, bonded a little. Maybe you could check in with her. Give her some encouragement. That's all I'm saying."

"How could she back *down?* After what happened to that boy, everything she knew? Jesus, we *cried* together. . . ."

"Families are strange."

"Yeah," I said. "Tell me about it."

"Just call her. It can't hurt."

"If she wants to shut down there's nothing I can do."

"Try anyway."

"I will. Of course I will."

He was quiet again for a minute.

"What?" I said.

"Truth or Dare."

"Truth."

"What happened that makes this matter so much to you?"

"This boyfriend of Mom's molested my little sister. When she was eleven. I just found out about it."

He nodded, sadly.

"It's not — I mean, compared to the stuff you're dealing with, Kyle? It was bad, but let's just say he never achieved penetration."

"Doesn't matter," he said. "It's about the destruction of trust. The physical details aren't predictive of how much damage that will do."

No. They sure as shit aren't.

I tried calling Mrs. Underhill seven times that night. She didn't have a machine and she never picked up.

Bost called the pathologist to the stand the next morning. He looked different in a coat and tie. I hadn't recognized him at first.

"In September of last year you examined the skeletal remains which had been discovered in Prospect Cemetery, did you not?" she asked.

"I did," he said.

"Can you describe your preliminary findings relating to the victim's identity?"

"The remains were those of a child, roughly three years old and of African ancestry."

"And could you determine the child's sex?" asked Bost.

"It's difficult to ascertain the gender of skeletal remains in prepubescent victims. Secondary sexual characteristics aren't apparent before an individual reaches the teenage years."

"And yet you're confident that these are the remains of Teddy Underhill?"

"I am," said Dr. Merica. "Absolutely."

"On the basis of what evidence?"

"A comparison of the child's skull with a photograph taken of Underhill."

Bost's assistant set up another photograph on the easel. It was a head-and-shoulders close-up of a tiny little boy, smiling broadly, the same photo I'd seen on Mrs. Underhill's piano, only ten times bigger. There was a gap between his upper front teeth I hadn't noticed before. I could see the big patch of red behind him: the suit of the Santa whose lap he was sitting on.

"And is this the photograph you used for comparison?" asked Bost.

"It is," answered Merica.

Bost motioned to her assistant. The next

photograph showed Teddy's face superimposed over the image of a ghostly skull. Every feature synced with the structure of the bones beneath: eyes and eye sockets, cheeks and cheekbones, the point of his chin, the gap in his smile.

The jurors looked shocked. I was impressed. Maybe we hadn't needed the second sneaker after all — even without a blood sample.

"And was it possible for you to determine any approximate time frame for when the child's death occurred?" asked Bost.

"The state of his remains indicated that he had died somewhere between three to six months before his remains were discovered."

"What else could you determine from your examination?"

"This was a battered child," said Merica.

"How can you tell?"

"Teddy Underhill suffered extensive physical trauma on a number of occasions before his death."

"What sort of trauma, Dr. Merica?" asked Bost.

"The injuries to his bones," he said. "There were six fractures in various stages of healing."

"Which stages?"

"Technically, we'd call these localized, asymmetrical areas of subperiosteal new bone formation. They were consistent with the types of fractures we associate with extreme, systematic physical abuse in children — injuries to the forearms, cranial vault, ribs, and legs. In addition to periosteal lesions."

"What causes a periosteal lesion?" asked Bost.

"They can be caused either by blows or by the child's arms and legs being used as 'handles' by the abuser. They're a sort of damage caused by actually bruising the bones themselves, evidence of the surface of the bone being stripped away by such trauma, or of bleeding caused below the periosteal layer of the bone by the force of a blow."

One of the jurors brought her hand up to her mouth, her eyes clenched shut.

Bost's assistant placed a new photo on the easel, a shot of two long bones with a thick lump in the middle of one of them.

I felt my own stomach lurch and looked away.

"Can you describe what this photograph shows us?" asked Bost.

"This is a photograph of the bones in Teddy Underhill's forearm — the radius and ulna," said Merica. "The lumps you see in the middle of each are what we call a 'callus' of bone."

"What does that indicate, Doctor?"

"This child's right forearm was broken and never treated or immobilized. It healed on its own, hence the thickening you can see in this image."

I covered my own right forearm's cast, remembering how painful my first break had been — without anesthesia.

Teddy lived through that six times.

Seven.

No painkillers. Not even an X-ray.

Those fuckers.

I looked over at the jurors, hoping they saw Angela and Albert in the same nasty light. Most of them were wincing, and none were looking in the direction of Bost's easel. The woman who'd covered her mouth was crying.

Good.

"And could you tell from Teddy's remains what it was that killed him?" asked Bost.

"I think it's safe to say that the massive blunt-force trauma to his chest could easily have caused the child's death."

"Can you tell us whether that trauma was inflicted *before* his death?" asked Bost.

"It was certainly inflicted when his bones

were still elastic," said Merica. "Either before — or very close to — the time of his death. What we would call ante- or peri-mortem trauma."

"So this damage couldn't have happened later on, when his remains were in the cemetery?"

"No," said Dr. Merica.

"And would the trauma be consistent with someone having punched the boy in the chest repeatedly?"

"Yes, and with a great deal of force."

"Thank you, Dr. Merica. I have no further questions at this time."

Bost returned to her table, and the curly black head of Galloway bobbed up for the defense.

50

Galloway strode over toward the witness stand. "Dr. Merica, I'd like to ask you a few more questions about the trauma inflicted on the boy's ribs."

Merica nodded, his bushy eyebrows casting deep shadow over his eyes when his head tipped forward.

"You say you can tell that these bones were fractured before the boy's death, but can you tell us what *caused* the fracture?"

"Well," said Merica, "blunt force indicates that the injuries weren't caused by anything sharp."

"Such as a knife?"

"Exactly," he said.

"Because a sharp object would have caused different kinds of damage to the bones?"

"Yes. We'd expect to see nicks or other marks made by the sharp edge of such an instrument."

"And those kinds of marks can sometimes indicate what sort of instrument was used, can't they?"

"Yes," he said.

"But with blunt force you can't know that, can you?"

"Know what?"

"What sort of object caused the trauma," said Galloway.

"Not really, no."

"You really can't tell whether the injuries to the boy's rib cage were caused by a fist, can you?"

"No."

"Or any of the other injuries? Could you tell us *what* exactly inflicted them?" she asked.

"No."

"And you certainly can't tell us *who* inflicted them, can you?"

"There are certainly some individuals who wouldn't have had the strength."

"But those injuries could have been inflicted by Teddy Underhill's mother, am I right? You have no way of knowing?"

"That's right," said Merica.

"Thank you, Dr. Merica. I have no further questions."

The judge looked over to the defense table. "Mr. Hetzler?"

"Nothing at this time, Your Honor."

The judge adjourned for the day.

I met up with Skwarecki in the hallway again. "You hear anything back about the car?"

"Nothing like it registered to anyone near Prospect," she said. "I sent a patrol car up to drive around the neighborhood — in case maybe someone's driving it without a registration. They didn't see it."

"I don't feel really relieved."

"You've given your testimony. There's no reason to come after you now."

"Thank you for staying over that night."

"Don't mention it," she said.

"No, seriously. I should at least cook you dinner or something, okay? I'll take off work early. Name the night."

"How you gonna cook with that cast on?"

"Maybe I'll order pizza."

"Everything but anchovies," she said.

"You're on."

The clouds over Queens Boulevard brimmed with mid-winter's gloating certainty that there was nothing between right now and your own death but a thin membrane of iron-poor blood and lonely nursing homes.

I dreaded going back to work at the Catalog.

I wanted to hash out the meaning of the day's testimony over a couple of beers with Cate or Kyle or Skwarecki, instead.

And I couldn't shake the feeling that someone was watching me.

Cars fishtailed homeward through slush. It was already dark enough that their brake lights cast hot bright points of blood-spatter along the hissing street.

I saluted Fat Boy with my uncasted hand and jogged downstairs toward the subway.

The platform was crowded, all of us turning like a school of minnows toward the approaching train, braced to shoulder our way inside.

I got stuck near the door without a handhold. There was one empty seat nearby, but some recent occupant had filled its shallow orange-plastic bowl with a souvenir pint of urine.

It was one of the newer cars, the kind supposedly impervious to graffiti. Frustrated taggers had etched their marks into the Plexiglas windows or scrawled indecipherable fat-marker glyphs on ad posters in lieu of actual walls.

Someone had gouged out the cardboard eyes of every Kool-smoking, condomtouting model pictured — damage as signature. We were years beyond Keith Haring's glowing dogs and babies, the helium-bouncy colors of Fab 5 Freddy.

We screeched into a turn and all the lights went out for a long moment.

Jammed up against strangers in the fetid dark, I wondered if Galloway and Hetzler could succeed in shoveling enough suspicion onto one another's clients that in the end they might both go free.

The apartment was empty when I got home. I ate cold Chinese food and dialed Mrs. Underhill every fifteen minutes.

51

I'd now spent enough hours in the court-room to have made its protocol morph from mystical to boring. It was stuffy and stale the following morning, quiet but for the rustle of papers and creak of chairs as onlookers settled in for the morning's program.

By the time the bailiff sang out the all-rise order as the judge swept in, I felt like we'd been waiting forever.

I wanted to be here, I wanted to watch the testimony unfold, and God knows I wanted to see justice done. It was just that I had discovered the verity of how very, very slowly the mills of justice do actually grind.

Like reading Dickens. At the DMV.

The judge started leafing through some papers.

Cate cleared her throat and reached into her purse. I watched her pull forth a pep-permint, which she tried to unwrap without making any noise. This is, of course, a physical impossibility.

Forget DMV, the whole thing smacked of church: same robes, same enforced solemnity, same inevitable urge to cough.

We lacked only fold-out red-velvet kneelers, stultifying dirges, and a fifth of Episcopal Manischewitz.

At long last, His Honor looked up and gave Bost the go-ahead.

She rose to her feet and squared her shoulders. "The prosecution calls Stephanie Keller."

Cate smiled. "I guess the chemo worked."

The side door opened and there was another long pause, until finally one of the guards conveyed a tiny woman across its threshold in a wheelchair.

Keller's eyebrows were penciled in, her head swathed in a royal-blue scarf knotted low at the nape of her neck. The bailiff took the helm of her slender green oxygen tank, walking beside her chair.

If Skwarecki hadn't said they were both forty-three, I would've presumed this was a woman at least twice the detective's age. She was hunched over, her narrow body swimming in a long-sleeved dress.

The guard backed Keller's chair into place beside the witness stand and set its brake.

"Ms. Keller," said Bost, "I want to thank you for coming here today. I know it can't have been easy for you."

Keller spoke in a soft but clear voice. "I felt it was important. Teddy Underhill was a very sweet little boy."

"Can you tell us when you first became concerned that he might be a victim of abuse?"

"Shortly after Teddy and his mother moved into Albert Williams's apartment, in my building. I would say within the space of a week."

"And when was this?"

"August before last," said Keller.

"Where were your two apartments, in relationship to one another?"

"I lived directly beneath them."

"And what was it that first made you concerned for Teddy's welfare?"

"Both apartments had windows on the street, and side windows opening onto an air shaft towards the rear. When it's nice out, you can't help but learn a great deal about the neighbors. I'd seen Teddy in the stairwell with his mother often enough. We spoke occasionally. I knew his name, how old he was."

"And what was Teddy's age at that time?"

"He was a few months past two," said

Keller. "That's one reason I worried when I heard him getting screamed at within the space of a week or so."

"Could you tell who was screaming at him?"

"Certainly. Albert Williams."

It was Galloway who objected this time. Hetzler didn't so much as twitch.

"Your Honor," said Galloway, "I'm not sure how Ms. Keller could have distinguished one voice from another in the general din of a crowded air shaft."

Keller couldn't see the judge from where she was sitting, so she addressed Bost. "May I answer that?"

"Please do," said Bost.

Keller turned toward Galloway. "I recognized Albert Williams's voice for two reasons: he has a slight lisp, and among the residents of all five apartments in our building, there was no one else named Teddy."

"It wasn't just screaming that worried you, though, was it?" asked Bost.

"I worked as an emergency-room nurse for twenty years, Ms. Bost. I had a good idea what I was hearing, sadly."

"As a nurse, were you expected to act as what's known as a mandated reporter?"

Keller said she was, and they discussed further reporting details.

"Can you tell us what, exactly, you told the hotline?"

Keller pulled a small notebook from the side pocket of her dress. "I'd like to refer to this for specific dates, if I may?"

"Please," said Bost. "By all means."

Keller opened the little book and held it up before her face. "On August twenty-third, I heard Albert Underhill berating the child for not finishing his dinner. I heard the sound of several slaps, and I believe he then smashed Teddy's plate against a wall in the kitchen."

She turned the page. "Two weeks later — September sixth — Williams was upset because Teddy had left a toy on the floor. The child had a black eye the following morning. His mother told me that he'd run into a corner of the couch."

She looked up at Bost. "I'm sorry to say that I was gone from the building for the next two weeks after that. When I returned, I saw Teddy and his mother in the front entry. The boy was limping, trying to walk on a swollen ankle."

A broken ankle. Bone grinding on bone.

My stomach lurched and contracted. I climbed over Cate and burst out the door for the hallway, hoping like hell I'd make it to the ladies' room in time.

52

The ladies' room was less stuffy than the courtroom and my nausea went away, but I still felt light-headed and dizzy, with little dark flea-spots crowding in at the edge of my vision.

I had to be coming down with something. Stephanie Keller's testimony had hardly been uplifting, but I'd heard worse details from Skwarecki and the pathologist.

I looked into the mirror above the row of sinks, noting the dark puffiness beneath my eyes, my winter-greenish pale skin. If hardly Astrid's equal in looks, I matched her on all the earmarks of sheer exhaustion.

The room smelled of damp paper towels and cheap pink liquid soap, and for a moment I wished it actually *were* a "restroom," with a chaise longue or even an army cot I could've curled up on for a few minutes. The trial would be breaking for lunch soon, but the thought of food made me queasy.

Grinding bones.

The phrase roiled my stomach further. I didn't want to go back into the courtroom, but I had to find someplace to sit down. I left the bathroom and shuffled slowly down the hallway, but didn't see anywhere to sit except for some benches downstairs, in the front lobby.

I chose one alongside a wall so I'd see Cate when they broke for lunch.

I closed my eyes and leaned back, hot and flushed now, my upper lip damp.

Great. Probably flu.

I stayed like that for maybe ten minutes, listening to footsteps and voices moving past me, feeling the occasional blast of cold air as people came inside with a breath of winter as chaser.

"Miss Dare? Are you all right?" A woman's voice. "I saw you through the window."

I felt a light touch on one shoulder, and fluttered my eyes open.

Mrs. Underhill stood before me, her forehead wrinkled with concern.

She was sitting beside me on the bench now, holding the back of one hand against my cheek. "You don't have a fever, dear. How's your stomach?"

"Not so good," I said.

461

"Have you eaten anything this morning?"

I shook my head.

She reached into her purse and gave me a peppermint. "This will help."

She was right — it did.

And now that she was sitting beside me, I didn't want to confess that I'd been calling her dozens of times a night for the last few days, like a smitten stalker.

"Are you testifying today?" I asked.

"Not yet. I came with some things for Angela, to leave next door."

At the jail.

"Can I get you a cup of water, dear?" she asked.

"No, thank you."

We were quiet for a minute, but it wasn't quite a companionable silence. I watched her fiddle with the clasp on her purse, then stop. She seemed to be trying to work up her nerve toward something.

"Is everything all right?" I asked.

She gripped the purse tighter.

Making up her mind.

"Miss Dare," she said at last.

"Please," I said, "call me Madeline."

"This might not be the time, but there's something I've been wanting to talk with you about."

"The trial?"

"In a way, I suppose," she said. "Nothing to do with your testimony, of course."

"I've already finished with that."

"And I don't need to know anything you said. It's just . . ."

I waited.

"I so want to do the right thing, Miss Dare. And I'm not sure what that is."

Cate was walking across the lobby, toward us.

"Would it help to talk about it?" I asked.

"It would," said Mrs. Underhill. "I was hoping that you might come by to visit again. When you're feeling better."

Maybe it was the peppermint, or just getting some fresher air, outside the courtroom's stale closeness, but my queasiness had passed.

And maybe Cate could give us a ride.

"How about right now?" I asked.

We pulled into a parking spot right out front, chez Underhill. The noon sky was phlegm-colored, with tracer-bullets of sleet zipping down at a hard slant. We got out and Cate opened the front gate, holding her arm out for Mrs. Underhill to grip as they picked their way along the icy front walk, chatting about recent doctor's appointments they'd had.

I followed along behind them, considering again the block's bizarre aesthetic, each split dwelling a study in Manichaean duality.

If you'd picked the fifty most disparate houses on the planet, chainsawed them in half clean down the middle, and shaken them all up like ginormous Yahtzee dice, you still couldn't have jammed the pieces back together this randomly without the aid of blindfolds *and* secret-CIA-mind-control-experiment-quality hallucinogens.

To me, the discordance acted as a mild nauseant, but each whitened yard was neat, every house in good repair, and Mrs. Underhill knew her neighbors. Here was community, and pride of ownership, while I was but an hourly-wage transient in a rental apartment riding the coattails of someone else's lease.

I ducked my head against the sleet, bits of cold wet grit sliding down to melt between the collar of my overcoat and the back of my neck. Ten paces ahead was a haven of sustenance and sympathy — the exact things for which I'd spent a lifetime yearning — and I wondered if Teddy hadn't felt the same every time he came up this walk.

It was a long way from here to a welfare motel, but I didn't wonder how his mother got there.

Entropy nips at all of our heels, and my own family's descent had been no less spectacular, or rapid. The same forces that pulled Angela's toward LaGuardia took my mother from deb parties to the verge of food stamps, my father from the floor of the Stock Exchange to a VW camper behind the Chevron station in Malibu.

The thesis-statement lyric of our family anthem: *Papa was a rolling stone; wherever he parked his van was his home.*

Any difference between me and Teddy was one of degree, not substance. The margin for error was thinner here, and he didn't get a scholarship to his mother's boarding school.

I flipped up my overcoat's collar, shivering at the foot of the stoop as Mrs. Underhill's keys jangled against her front door.

When the neighbor boys' curtains twitched apart for surveillance, I smiled, raising my unbroken arm to wave hello.

Mrs. Underhill got the door open, and I followed her and Cate into the front hallway once I'd stomped the sleet off my shoes and wiped them clean on the doormat.

"Well, dear, I'm lucky," I heard Mrs. Underhill saying, as she and Cate moved into the kitchen after hanging up their coats. "Dr. Wilson gave me a clean bill of health again just last week. Now my friends, they all have cholesterol pills and heart pills and who knows what-all for their blood pressure. The only medicine in this house is aspirin and Band-Aids, but I don't even use *those* more than once a year."

I found a free hanger for my overcoat in the hall closet, picturing my own Prozac, Excedrin, Advil, and Alka-Seltzer Plus stockpiles back on Sixteenth Street — not to mention the boatload of painkillers I'd happily scarfed down for my busted arm, *and* the communal bong — feeling like a total wuss.

I'd probably blow every penny I ever earned on over-the-counter crap from Duane Reade and die young anyway.

I looked out the kitchen window, past the frilly white net curtains. The sleet had turned to snow, falling thick and fast. I decided I should tell Cate to go on home before the roads got too bad, but now she and Mrs. Underhill were exchanging notes on home remedies for stomachaches.

Before there was a pause in conversation, the feisty old lady turned to me. "Now you said back at the courthouse you hadn't eaten anything, speaking of digestion. I'm going to fix you a sandwich, unless you'd rather have some soup? I have tomato or chicken noodle."

"That's okay, Mrs. Underhill," I said. "I'm really not that hungry. Thank you anyway."

She crossed her arms and shook her head. "Hungry or not, you *look* downright peaked. And it's wintertime."

"I don't want to put you to any trouble," I said.

"Don't be silly — it won't take me but a minute. I made the chicken soup yesterday, and the pot's in the Frigidaire. I just have to heat it up. We'll all three have a nice bowl, with some crackers."

"That sounds lovely," said Cate. "May we help you with anything?"

"Why don't you both just sit down right here and keep me company?" said Mrs. Underhill, motioning toward her kitchen table and chairs.

The old red wall-phone rang as she was putting the soup pot on the stove. She lit the burner and then asked us to excuse her for a moment so she could take the call. "Hello?"

I turned to Cate, worried that maybe Mrs. Underhill wanted to talk to me in private. "I don't want to keep you. It looks like that snow's getting pretty bad. I'm fine getting the train home."

"This is she," said our hostess, into the phone.

Cate said, "I wouldn't mind a little soup. Unless you need privacy?"

"Hello?" Mrs. Underhill jiggled the phone's hook twice, then replaced the receiver. "Must be the storm."

I suddenly had to pee, desperately. "May I use the bathroom?"

The doorbell rang.

"Grand Central *Station,*" said Mrs. Underhill, smiling at us. She asked Cate to mind the soup, pointing me toward the staircase in the front hall. "First door on your right, dear."

I jogged upward, footsteps muffled by the shag carpeting. I turned right past the open door of her bedroom, catching a glimpse of a neatly made four-poster.

The door's chimes went off again and Mrs. Underhill's muttered "Goodness' sakes, hold your horses!" echoed up the stairwell as I reached the landing.

I heard her say, "I'm sorry, Donald, but I have company right now," as I closed the door behind me.

The bathroom was all powder-blue and frilly, with a bowl of apple-pie-smelling potpourri on the windowsill. I peed for like, forever — which was weird as I'd only had a glass of water since my morning coffee — then tried to figure out how to wash my hands without mucking up the perfectly folded little hand towels, or the flower-shaped guest soaps displayed in a curvy glass jar beside the sink.

I rinsed my left hand in hot water, then waved it around.

Maybe a little air-dry, over the heating vent?

I walked toward the room's small, high window, hoping for a blast of warmth from the register beneath it, and glanced outside at the backyard below.

There was a triangular trail of bootprints along the whitened ground, each dark oval already blurring under fresh snowfall. Someone had walked from the neighbors' side of the house to a sagging old garage at the lot's rear, then back to the house directly below me.

The outbuilding's door wasn't closed all the way, and a burst of wind pushed it wider, in a swirl of snowflakes.

I gripped the windowsill, damp knuckles of my left hand going white. Before the door had swung closed again, I'd caught a flash of dull gold: the prow of a huge old American sedan, front bumper hanging crooked, chrome grille smashed in. The car's roof was white vinyl.

My right arm gave a twinge of recognition inside its cast.

No tire tracks. Why would someone go out to the garage in a blizzard, and what did they want with *this* side of the house afterwards?

I leaned my forehead against the cold glass, trying to peer straight down Mrs. Underhill's brick siding.

The window's outer sill blocked my line of sight down the wall itself, but there was something on the ground about a foot away from the house: a twist of colored wire, lying bright against the snow.

The toilet cistern finished refilling, its ballcock float rising to shut off the flow of water. The echoing tiled room went quiet.

I exhaled, then pushed gently off the windowsill with my left hand to stand up straight again, careful not to shift my weight too suddenly.

My breath had fogged the glass, but I didn't need to see anything else.

The guy wearing those boots had cut the phone line.

And if the murmur of voices I could hear through the floor was any indication, he was now directly below me, inside the kitchen with Mrs. Underhill and Cate.

■ ■ ■ ■

I crept along the edge of the tub toward the bathroom door, weight on the balls of my feet so I wouldn't make the floor creak.

It seemed like an hour before I was close enough to reach for the door handle, holding my breath and listening for another long moment before twisting it slowly open.

I tried to picture the view up the stairwell from the hallway below.

Will he see this door moving if I open it?

No, Mrs. Underhill's bedroom was at the top of the stairs. I was safely down the hallway, out of sight.

The voices got a little louder.

And he's definitely in the kitchen. Straight down.

I eased the door outward a few inches, willing it not to squeak.

The murmurs became voices, distinct.

"Donald, I've told you there's no one else here." Mrs. Underhill. "Miss Ludlam drove me home today, after I went to see Angela."

"Angela's in court."

A man's voice. One I knew.

Might want to lock that door, you know? Keep the boogeyman away.

"Yes, that's right." Mrs. Underhill again.

The man said, "You can't go in yet. Not your turn to testify."

"I took some vitamins to the jail so she'll have them tonight. For the baby."

I opened the door farther and slipped out into the hallway, my back to the wall beside the staircase.

"There's *three* of you in this house," said Donald.

Had she told me the names of the neighbor boys? Was he wearing boots?

"Donald, you're scaring me now," she said, voice quavering. "My *heart* . . ."

"Where's the other one?" he asked.

"I don't know what you're talking about. And I need my *medicine.*"

"The one with the busted arm, she was out front with you before," he said.

"Madeline went home," said Cate. "She's not feeling well."

"Not out the *front* door," he said, "and I can see she didn't go out the back way. Only one who walked on that snow is me."

Fuck.

"I'm having a spell come on. I need my pills from upstairs." Mrs. Underhill's voice sounded weak and dizzy.

"I can get them," said Cate. "Just tell me where they are."

I heard her chair scrape back along the

472

kitchen's spic-and-span old linoleum.

"Don't you *move!*" Donald's voice again.

I heard something slam down, and the walls vibrated.

Had he hit one of them?

"All right," said Cate, calm and steady. "I'll just stand right here."

"Donald, let her just go upstairs. I need my pills from my bedside table. The doctor says, if I get excited —"

"The *other* one's upstairs, that what you mean?" he asked, his voice much louder now.

"Madeline went home," said Cate. "We told you that."

Mrs. Underhill's bedroom door was open, three feet away. I edged along the hallway, thankful for its thick shag carpeting.

The bedroom floor was bare hardwood, except for a braided rag rug beside the old four-poster bed. If I made the joists squeak, we were all fucked.

I held my breath and stepped across the threshold, then stopped to listen.

"Donald, please, I just need one pill. Then I'll talk to you about whatever you want." Mrs. Underhill started panting, sounding as though she were on the verge of tears.

I took three more steps, then opened the drawer of her bedside table.

There weren't any pill bottles inside. She'd told me and Cate the truth, earlier, about not needing medication.

The drawer contained a small white prayer book instead. And a Luger pistol her husband must have brought back as a souvenir from the war.

I blew off God and took the gun, relieved as hell to discover that she kept it loaded, though I couldn't imagine someone her size firing a nine-millimeter without getting knocked down by the recoil.

"Donald," said Mrs. Underhill, "how dare you bring a gun into this house when I practically raised you up?"

Smart woman: now I knew what I was up against, below.

"You just be quiet, now," said Donald. "I don't want to have to hurt you."

"I should think not."

"We need to have a little talk, is all," he said.

"We can certainly do *that* without any guns."

"We will, soon as Dougie gets back. We'll bring your friend downstairs and get everything straightened out. She's not going anywhere, and I'm not leaving *you* two alone."

I had to get down the stairs before Dougie

arrived, then, whoever he was. I wished to hell I had X-ray vision so I could approach the kitchen when this Donald wasn't looking.

I moved out of the bedroom and back into the hallway, crouching down beside the staircase.

How long did I have before there'd be two of these guys?

Get your ass down the damn stairs.

I crept forward, trying to peek at the kitchen through the banister, but the angle was all wrong. I could smell the chicken soup now, perfuming the whole house.

I moved down three stairs, the Luger held straight out in front of me.

I knew my way around guns but didn't trust my aim left-handed. If I hadn't had to stay so quiet, I would've shot the damn cast off.

Mrs. Underhill spoke again. "Why don't you tell me what's on your mind, Donald, while we're waiting?"

"We need to talk over what you want to say in court, about Angela," he said. "But that can wait."

"Why is it any of your business?" she asked.

"It's our business as much as yours."

I climbed down three more steps, out in

the open now if he looked up the hallway from the kitchen.

"It is *not,*" said Mrs. Underhill. "Not yours, not your brother's."

"We came up with Angela, since she was a baby. And you're going to make certain she doesn't have *this* baby while she's inside, for real."

"Of course I will," said Mrs. Underhill. "I protect my family."

I was on the bottom stair now, and hoped to hell she was lying about protecting Angela from jail time, the same as she had about needing pills.

"We gonna make sure," he said. "Be certain about *that.*"

I stepped onto the hallway carpet, gun steady, ready to storm the kitchen.

Behind me I heard the click of the front-door latch, and I spun around.

There wasn't any window in the front door, so Dougie wouldn't see me before I saw him, at least. I turned sideways with my left arm out straight like an old-fashioned dueler, making a smaller target.

The door swung wide and I caught a flash of leather jacket and jeans. Dougie lifted his head and saw me, eyes narrowing.

He didn't have time to raise his own pistol before I fired, nailing him straight in the

476

chest, the first slug knocking him back against the door frame.

The Luger ejected the spent cartridge, then chambered another round before I loosened my finger off its trigger.

I heard a woman's guttural yell from the kitchen and the slopping noise of a splash.

Dougie's eyes were still open. But he didn't lift his gun.

I stepped closer.

Bang.

And then Donald's voice shrieked, higher and higher. "I'm burned, you fucking bitch. I'm fucking *burned."*

I held the pistol on Dougie as he twisted to one side and crumpled, leaving a smear of blood all down the flocked wallpaper as he slid to the floor.

His eyes were shut now, but his gun hand twitched.

I stepped closer and pulled the trigger a third time.

Bang.

Donald was still screaming, behind me. No words now, just incoherent whipped-dog shrieks and whines.

Blood bubbled out of Dougie's mouth, and his fingers relaxed on the gun in his hand: a Glock.

I used my toe to move it away from his

477

open hand, then kicked it into the living room, watching it spin under a sofa and out of sight.

Turning away, I jogged toward the kitchen.

Cate and Mrs. Underhill stood over a writhing man I presumed was Donald, each of them armed with a large carving knife.

He rocked on the floor, moaning, surrounded by a still-steaming puddle of chicken soup, eyes swollen shut in his blistered face.

So much for lunch.

Mrs. Underhill looked over at me, steady as a rock.

I nodded.

"Did Angela send you here?" She poked Donald in the ribs with the sharp toe of her little shoe.

He just moaned.

"Answer me, Donald," she said. "Your brother's lying shot dead in my front hall, and I can take you *right* out of this world the same way. Lord knows even your mama wouldn't hold that against me, after what you boys tried here today."

Donald started crying. "I'm burned so bad. I need a doctor."

Mrs. Underhill was unmoved. "You tell me whose sorry idea this was, maybe you'll get one."

My rush of adrenaline was wearing off, and I started shaking.

"Who sent you here, Albert or Angela?" Mrs. Underhill motioned me over, then took the Luger from me and pointed it at his face.

"I don't know if you can see well enough to tell," she said, "but I've got my husband's pistol aimed straight at your sorry forehead."

Donald flinched.

The sight of his face was sickening, and the chicken-soup fumes seemed to be getting stronger.

Cate prodded him with her foot. "I think you'd better tell us, Donald."

As for me, I'm ashamed to say I took one more inhalation of soupy air and passed out cold, right in the kitchen doorway.

"Do you still want to talk about anything?" I asked Mrs. Underhill.

Cate and she had brought me into the living room and helped me lie down along the sofa after I came to.

The kitchen was full of cops and paramedics, with Skwarecki giving orders. I watched Donald getting wheeled down the front hall handcuffed to a gurney.

Mrs. Underhill smiled at me. "Thank you,

479

dear, but my mind is pretty clear on the matter, after today."

"I'm sorry to be such a wuss," I said. "I think I'm coming down with the flu."

Mrs. Underhill gave me a knowing smile, the tiny gap between her front teeth exactly like Teddy's. "You'll be just fine, dear, soon as you get a bite to eat. And I need you in court tomorrow morning, for when I testify."

"Did he tell you whether it was Albert or Angela?" I asked.

"Shhhh," she said, stroking my hair. "Close your eyes for a minute and get some rest. No need to worry about that now."

"Mrs. Underhill, I'm so sorry about everything that's happened."

"You have absolutely nothing to be sorry about," she said. "And I want you to call me Elsie."

She patted my head one more time and told me to rest.

I closed my eyes, drifting off for a minute until Skwarecki's voice brought me sharply back to the present.

"Yo, Dare," she said, "you and me need to have a little talk."

53

"Listen," said Skwarecki, "we have to run you down to the station for a little while."

I sat up on Mrs. Underhill's sofa. "Figured you might."

Someone had taken off my shoes, placing them neatly side by side under the coffee table. I reached down for them and got hit by another wave of dizziness.

"You okay?" asked Skwarecki.

"Sure. Just give me a minute." I took a deep breath and waited for the black spots to swim back out of my vision a little, then got my feet into my shoes.

"You want a hand up?" asked Skwarecki.

"No, thanks. But you might want to look under the sofa. I kicked the dead guy's Glock in there somewhere, before I passed out."

"You pick it up at all? Touch it?"

"No. Should be just his fingerprints. He pulled it on me when he came through the front door. I kicked it in here, after."

"It was a righteous shoot. We know that."

"Even so," I said, "I'd feel better if I watched you bag the thing up personally, you know?"

I leaned down to tie my shoes as she pulled on a pair of gloves.

They had a couple of patrol guys take me down to the One-Oh-Three, where they swabbed me for gunshot residue and took my fingerprints. I started feeling a little queasy again, replaying the day's events in my head, and one of the guys got me a Coke to sip, which helped a lot.

Two detectives I'd never seen before interviewed me, which wasn't surprising. I hadn't expected them to put me with Skwarecki, since we knew each other outside work pretty well by this point.

It was all pretty low-key. They took me into a nice big interview room and their questions were gentle, all things considered.

The older cop even looked a little embarrassed when he asked me why I'd shot the dead guy three times.

He fiddled with his tie and looked down at the table between us. "I understand about the heat of the moment, but we have to follow up."

"Well, I guess the first two shots were

482

because I'd never fired a Luger before. I didn't know it was semiautomatic, so that just kind of happened."

The younger cop was still standing up, leaning against the wall to my left. "And the third time?" he asked.

"He twitched," I said. "And his eyes were still open. So, you know . . . I guess I just wanted to make sure."

"And then you took his gun?" asked the older guy.

"I kicked it away. Into the living room."

"That was before you went into the kitchen?"

"I didn't know the other guy was completely out of commission at that point. I wanted to make sure he didn't have access to another gun."

"But you never picked it up?" asked the young guy.

"The Glock? No. Just moved it with my foot."

"Why didn't you take it with you?" he asked.

"I had a gun already. And I knew by that point that it worked pretty well. I didn't think I needed another one."

"And then you went into the kitchen," said the older guy.

"Yeah. I mean, it all probably happened

faster than I'm telling it, but it seemed pretty slow at the time."

They both nodded.

"And what happened next?" asked the young guy.

"Well, I stepped into the kitchen doorway, and Mrs. Underhill took the Luger from me, and then I pretty much looked at the burned guy's face and fainted."

I took another small sip of Coke, willing it to stay down.

"You okay?" asked the older guy, reaching his hand across the table toward mine.

"Not really," I said.

"You did the right thing today," he said. "Kept your head in an ugly situation."

I nodded. "Thank you."

"Can we get you a ride home?" he asked. "I think we're done here."

"Is Skwarecki back yet? I'd like to talk with her a minute."

"She was down at the hospital talking with the other guy," said the younger detective. "Let me go check if she's here."

He left the room, and the older detective gave me an encouraging smile.

"Can I ask you something?"

"Sure," he said.

"Why'd these guys even do this? I mean, run me down with a car, threaten me at work . . . then today, after I'd already testi- fied? Not to mention that all I had to say in court was that I found the little boy's remains in the first place, back at Prospect. It all seems pretty pointless."

The guy looked me in the eye and shrugged. "Some people are just assholes."

Skwarecki gave me a ride home half an hour later. All I could think about was sleep by that point.

It was dark out, and snowing again. I watched her windshield wipers clearing the flakes off the glass as they melted, making all the taillights ahead of us blur into scarlet stars and ribbons.

"You hanging in there?" she asked, slow- ing down for a stoplight.

The car fishtailed a little in the slush.

"I asked the other detective why this all happened," I said.

"Brodsky?"

"The older guy."

She nodded. "What'd he say?"

I told her, and his assholes comment made her laugh. "Yeah, got that right."

"I'm serious," I said. "What were they thinking?"

"Donald and Dougie?"

"No, Liddy and Haldeman. Of *course*

Donald and Dougie. Was it really a gang thing?"

"Yeah," said Skwarecki. "They were looking out for Albert Williams."

"Not Angela?"

"Her too," she said. "But on Albert's say-so."

"I still don't get what they thought they'd accomplish going after me."

The light turned green and Skwarecki hit the gas again, soldiering on through the slush.

"According to Donald," she said, "it wasn't about you as much as Mrs. Underhill. Albert didn't want her to testify. You, they didn't care a lot."

"They were harshing out on me to scare her vicariously?"

"She practically raised the two brothers, and Angela wouldn't have wanted her hurt."

"Did Angela know about any of this?"

"Donald said they kept her in the dark, but the rest of them knew you were spending time with the old lady."

"So they fucked me up just to send a message?"

"Something like that."

"What," I said, "you people never heard of Western Union out in Queens?"

54

Bost stood up. "The prosecution calls Elsie Underhill."

The courtroom's side entrance opened, and Teddy's great-grandmother stepped forward into the courtroom. She had a little halo of hat perched on her head, dark red, with a greenish black feather pinned to one side.

Elsie took her seat, gripping the upright purse in her lap with both hands.

I watched her glance at the jury, then at her granddaughter.

Bost approached the stand. "Mrs. Underhill, to start off, I'd like to ask you to tell us a little bit about your great-grandson, Teddy. Was he an outgoing boy, or more shy?"

"*Out*going, definitely," she said. "He was the most cheerful little person you can imagine."

"Can you tell us a bit about your plans

for Teddy's third birthday?"

"I was planning to cook Teddy his favorite lunch. Spaghetti and meatballs. And a chocolate cake with vanilla frosting. The weather was supposed to be fine that day. We were going to visit the zoo after lunch. Up in the Bronx."

"When was the last time you'd seen your granddaughter, Angela, before that day?"

"The day before."

"What happened during that meeting?"

"I gave her money. And a new outfit of clothes for him to wear — matching shirt and little overalls, with those shoes he had his heart set on."

"What was the money for? To buy presents?" asked Bost.

"No, dear." Mrs. Underhill shook her head. "That money was for drugs."

"Why would you give your granddaughter money for drugs?"

"Because she told me she'd let me have Teddy, for the right price. And I knew I had to get him away from her, and Albert Williams."

"And how much money did you give her?" asked Bost.

"A thousand dollars."

"I see," said Bost. "And did Teddy come to visit you with his mother the day you gave

488

her that money?"

Mrs. Underhill clutched her purse tighter. "Yes. Teddy came with Angela that day."

"How long had it been since you'd seen him?"

"A little more than six weeks."

"How did Teddy seem the afternoon before his birthday? Was he excited about it?"

"He wasn't feeling very well."

"Was he sick?" asked Bost.

Mrs. Underhill looked down, fiddling with the catch of her purse. "No. He wasn't sick."

"Can you tell us why Teddy wasn't feeling well?"

"He'd gotten hurt."

"Hurt how, Mrs. Underhill?"

"Burned. On a hot iron."

"Did you see this burn?"

"I did. I took him upstairs and put some ointment on it, and some gauze."

"Where was the burn, Mrs. Underhill?"

"In the middle of his back."

"Mrs. Underhill, Teddy didn't do that himself, did he?" asked Bost.

Elsie Underhill raised her head. "Of course not, Ms. Bost."

"And was this the first time you'd come across evidence of such a serious injury to your great-grandson?"

"No." She raised a fist to her mouth, pressing the knuckle of her index finger against the center of her lips.

"Can you tell us about any other injuries you'd seen before finding the burn mark on Teddy's back that day?"

Elsie covered her mouth and wept.

Bost tried again. "Had Teddy been hurt when you'd last seen him six weeks earlier?"

Cate gripped my hand, her fingernails digging into my palm. It hurt but I didn't care.

Bost's voice was quiet. "I know this must be incredibly painful for you, but you have to answer the question."

Mrs. Underhill dropped her hand from her mouth and hugged the black purse tight to her chest with both arms. "I *begged* her."

"Angela?" said Bost.

"I told her, 'I have not raised my hand to a child. Never to your mama, never to you. Don't let this boy get hurt again. Leave him safe with me.' "

Bost waited.

"I got down on my knees." Elsie turned in her seat, addressing her granddaughter directly. "Honey, you *know* I did — just the same as when I begged your mama to let me keep *you*."

"When did you ask Angela to let you have Teddy?" asked Bost. "Was it during their

490

visit to you, the day before his third birthday?"

"That was the last time."

"But not the only time?" asked Bost.

Elsie shook her head. "You asked whether I'd seen the boy injured before that day."

"Yes," said Bost. "I did."

"The truth is, I had seen him hurt over and over again."

"How had Teddy been hurt on those other occasions?"

"One time he had a black eye. One time his little arm was all swollen. Then his leg was too sore to walk. It was always something."

"When did Teddy's injuries first come to your attention, Mrs. Underhill?"

"After Angela and Teddy moved in with Albert Williams," she said.

"Did you ever ask your granddaughter about what had happened when you saw Teddy with a black eye, or a swollen arm?"

"I didn't have to. I knew."

"And when did you first ask her to let Teddy move in with you?"

"When she met that man." Mrs. Underhill pointed at Williams.

"Albert Williams?" asked Bost.

"Yes. When Angela told me she planned to live with him, I asked her to leave Teddy with me. Just for a while. Let them get on their feet together."

"Did she agree to do that?"

Mrs. Underhill shook her head, looking like she was going to cry again. "I was so afraid."

"Of what?" asked Bost.

"That I'd lose her, just the same way I lost her mother — because I didn't fight hard enough to keep her safe when she was a little girl."

"You were concerned about how Williams might treat Angela?"

"I saw that man, and it was like the whole thing starting up again. I *knew* him, all the ones like him. Won't look you in the eye, won't even bother to come up the front steps — just sit in the car out front. Waiting to be waited upon, and angry about it. You don't let a man like that around your baby."

I wondered which baby she meant: Teddy, or his mother, or *her* mother. Probably all three.

"But Angela took Teddy with her, didn't she?" asked Bost.

Mrs. Underhill dropped her head and nodded, in defeat. "And then, when I saw how he *was* being hurt . . . so soon after?"

"You asked her again to let you have the boy?"

"That man got Angela on the drugs. I'd ask her to let me see Teddy, and she'd only come for money. If I told her no, she'd steal it. I knew it was the only way I'd get to spend time with him, so I let her do it."

"But you gave her a thousand dollars, that last day before Teddy's birthday?"

Elsie dropped her chin to her chest, eyes closed.

"Mrs. Underhill?" asked Bost.

The woman's voice was just above a whisper. "She said she'd let me keep him."

"In exchange for the money?"

"She was so filthy — nothing but rags and bones. All she did was pace around, scratching herself. Teddy just lay on the davenport, staring. They smelled like animals. When I tried to pick him up, to take him for a bath, he started screaming. That's when I saw the burn mark."

"What happened then?"

"I gave her the money. I took it out and got on my knees right there, laid it out on the floor in front of me. I told her, 'You take this, and you leave the boy with me.' "

"What was her response?" asked Bost.

"She snatched up the money and counted it."

"Did she say anything?"

Mrs. Underhill's face crumpled up. " 'This

all you got?' "

"Then what happened?"

"She pulled Teddy to his feet and dragged him to the front door."

"And did she speak again before she left?"

"She looked at me and said, 'Give me more tomorrow, maybe I let you have him for real this time.' "

"What happened the next day?"

"The next day? The next day was too late. They'd killed him."

"Thank you, Mrs. Underhill," said Bost.

Then she looked up at the judge. "Your Honor, nothing further."

55

Galloway was up next.

She got right to the point. "Mrs. Underhill, did you ever actually *witness* Albert Williams hitting your great-grandson, or harming him in any way?"

"I saw the results."

"Yes or no, Mrs. Underhill. Did you ever see Albert Williams hit Teddy?"

"No."

"Did you ever see him cause any *other* injury to the boy?"

Mrs. Underhill raised her chin.

"Answer the question, please," said Galloway. "Yes or no?"

"No."

Galloway nodded. "And did you ever see him taking drugs with your granddaughter, Angela?"

"I know a junkie when I see him."

"Yes or no?" asked Galloway.

"No."

"You do know that for the entire time he and your granddaughter lived together, Albert Williams held down a full-time job?"

"I'd heard that. From Angela."

"She was alone with Teddy all those hours that Albert spent at his job, wasn't she?"

"I only know that the times she came to see me, it was always when he was working."

"So it was when Albert Williams was *working* that you saw your great-grandson had been injured, every time?"

That got an objection from Bost.

"Withdrawn," said Galloway. "Angela always wanted money on those visits, is that right? Money you presumed she would spend on drugs?"

Mrs. Underhill bowed her head. "Yes."

"In fact, your granddaughter as much as offered to sell you her own child for drug money, didn't she, Mrs. Underhill?"

"I don't —"

"And isn't it true that Teddy's injuries first appeared when his mother, *Angela,* began using drugs?"

Mrs. Underhill didn't answer.

Galloway kept on. "In fact, you have no idea *who* hurt Teddy, do you? For all we know, Angela beat him just to soften you up whenever she needed more cash."

Hetzler jumped up this time. *"Objection!"*

"No more questions, Your Honor."

Hetzler waited for Galloway to get back to the table and take her seat.

He stood up slowly, taking time to button his jacket before he approached the witness stand.

His first question surprised me. "You're a widow, Mrs. Underhill?"

"I am."

"How long were you married?" he asked.

"Twenty-five years. Edward passed just after Angela was born."

"Did you and your husband know who Angela's father was?"

Mrs. Underhill dropped her eyes. "We suspected."

"Your husband was greatly displeased when he found out your daughter was pregnant with Angela, wasn't he?"

"He was *disappointed*. We raised our daughter in the church."

"In fact, when he found out he threw her out of the house, didn't he?" asked Hetzler.

Mrs. Underhill looked away.

"How old was your daughter at the time?"

"Seventeen."

"Seventeen years old. Pregnant. Living in the street. Is that when she started using drugs?" he asked.

"She wouldn't do that to her baby."

"As far as you *know*," said Hetzler.

"She *loved* that child."

"But she got into drugs later?"

"It was with that man, Butchie. He got her started."

"A lot of families have been ravaged by drug abuse, haven't they?"

Mrs. Underhill nodded. "In those days, it was heroin. Now it's the crack."

"How old was Angela when she came to live with you?"

"She was nine years old."

"What kind of impact did her mother's death have on her?" asked Hetzler.

"She was devastated. She didn't speak for two months. I kept her home from school."

"Do you think she ever fully recovered following that tragedy?"

"Would *you* have recovered, Mr. Hetzler, if you'd lain with your dead mother's body all night in the dark, wondering whether her killer was going to come back gunning for you?"

"No, Mrs. Underhill," he said. "I can't imagine that I would have."

Elsie nodded. "My granddaughter was a gentle child. She never meant anyone any harm. But that man didn't just kill her mother, he killed a part of Angela, too.

Something inside her was gone after that. Butchie died in prison, but his damage still had her by the neck, and it wasn't ever letting go."

"I'm so sorry for your loss. Mrs. Underhill. I have no more questions."

Hetzler walked back to the defense table.

Bost stood up. "The prosecution rests, Your Honor."

"Court is adjourned for the day," said the judge. "We'll hear from the defense starting tomorrow morning."

It was dark in the living room at home. I was curled up on our sofa this time, talking quietly to Dean, long distance.

"How's Texas?" I asked.

"Actually, I finished there early. I'm in Canada."

"Okay, then how's the great white north?"

"Cold," he said. "Boring. Not so great."

"I miss you."

"I miss you, Bunny. I wish I could come home."

"Yeah," I said.

"Well, I'd better go forage for dinner before they roll up the sidewalks here on the *boulevard Ducharme*."

"What's the cuisine in fashionable La Tuque? Escargots à la Gretzky?"

He sighed. "PFK."

"PFK?"

"Poulet Frit Kentucky," he said.

Given my yelp of laughter, it was a profound blessing that I did not happen to have a mouthful of beverage at that moment. It would've shot straight out my nose.

"That's what I treasure most about you, Bunny," said Dean. "Your compassion."

Yeah, like you've asked me anything about the trial. Or even remembered it's happening.

I shook that off. I didn't want him to know. Or ask. He had too much at stake to worry about me.

"Dude," I said, trying to sound lighthearted, "you know my sympathies are *totally* with you in this dark time of culinary sorrow, but it's still fucking hilarious."

"It would be way funnier if it weren't the only restaurant in town, or at least the only one open within sight of Le Motel Ranch."

"Le Motel Ranch? What, no vacancies at Le Motel Chunky Blue Cheese?"

"Vey iz mir," he said. "Don't get me started."

"You've been gone so long it feels like forever. . . . When do you get home?"

"They want me up here at least a week. We're doing a trial run with one of the BOD machines on their wastewater as part of the

500

sales call. Christoph really wants this account."

"A week?"

He didn't answer.

"Not even home for the weekend, you mean?"

"No."

"Wow."

"I miss you so much, Bunny. You know I want to be home."

"What about the wedding?"

Valentine's Day.

"I'll do my best," he said. "I can't promise at this point."

"Hey," I said, "you should probably go get dinner. I don't want to keep you."

The phone rang again an hour later. I picked it up, hoping it would be Dean again, après-PFK.

"Hello?" I said.

"Mad?"

Astrid.

"I'm leaving," she said. "Tonight."

"Leaving for where?"

"Wherever. Just leaving Christoph."

"Okay," I said.

"Okay?"

She was pacing again. I could hear her

501

heels clacking back and forth across the floor.

"Astrid, I've had a long shitty day and a long shitty week. You want to leave your husband, fucking leave him. I don't care. Why do *you* even care about my opinion?"

"I have my clothes packed up," she said, as though I hadn't spoken. "And I want you to promise me something."

Getting packed was new, but it didn't make me any less exhausted with the whole thing. "Sure. Fine. Ask away."

"I want you to promise me that Dean will quit tomorrow."

"Quit what?"

"His job."

"Astrid, wait a minute —"

"You're *my* friend, aren't you?"

"Of *course* I'm your friend, but that's not my decision."

And I didn't trust that she wouldn't change her mind and then report back anything I'd said to further her own advantage. God knows I'd been a pawn in enough breakups to know how often that happened.

"If he doesn't quit tomorrow, I'll never speak to you again."

"Astrid, please —"

"This is it, Maddie. Dean quits or I'll know I can never trust you again."

"I can't promise you that."
"Fine," she said, and hung up.

56

The phone's ring woke me up the following morning. I looked at the clock-radio.

Eight A.M.? Infidels!

"Hello?" I croaked.

"Maddie, a very good morning to you." It was Christoph.

Excellent. Not.

"Same to you," I said.

Was she gone? Did he think she was hiding out here?

"I am hoping I might ask you for a favor," he said.

Here we go.

"When Dean calls home could you ask him also to ring me?"

"Um, certainly."

"I have a new home number, if you could take it down."

"Did you move out?" I asked.

"Yes, just this morning."

Why did he sound so happy?

"I must say it's lovely here — I finally have room for my little horses, and Astrid is really quite pleased with our new place."

"She *is?*"

"Surprising, no?" He laughed. "Who would have thought she'd like New Jersey?"

I refrained from comment. The whole thing just made my brain hurt.

Angela Underhill was wearing another flowered dress, this time with a pink cardigan over it that stretched across her enormous belly. She walked slowly and flat-footed to the witness stand, one hand pressed to the small of her back.

Sworn in, she smiled down at Hetzler. I wondered if she thought her impending nativity could possibly sway the jurors in her favor.

Marty Hetzler didn't strut as he approached the stand this time. Instead he walked up until he was within arm's reach of Angela Underhill, circling in quietly as though she were a wounded bird he hoped to catch.

She put her hand over the microphone so he could lean in to pat her on the hand and offer some words of encouragement, his good side angled toward the jury.

"Mr. Hetzler?" prompted the judge.

"Yes, Your Honor," Marty said, backing away. "We just needed a moment."

He squared his shoulders a little. My view of him was now straight on from the back, but I pictured him raising a hand to check the knot of his tie before he spoke again.

"Angela, I'd like to talk to you about something Ms. Bost mentioned earlier, all right?"

"Yes, sir."

"Ms. Bost talked about you being raised by your grandmother, but that wasn't always the case, was it?"

"Only from the time I was nine on."

"Before that, who did you live with?"

"My mother."

"And when you came to your grandmother, did your mother come with you?"

"No. I come alone."

"Can you tell us why?"

"My mother passed."

"When you were nine years old?"

"Mm-hm."

"And your father?"

"Don't know."

"Angela, how did your mother die?"

"The man she with then, Butchie? He shot her."

How was it possible that this woman was related to Elsie? It boggled the mind.

506

Bost stood. "Objection, Your Honor. Relevance?"

"It goes to my client's state of mind," said Hetzler, "at the time of her son's death."

The judge said, "I'll allow it."

"Angela," said Hetzler, "you saw Butchie kill your mother, didn't you?"

"Yeah."

"They'd been arguing?"

"What woke me up. I come out to see."

"From your bedroom?"

"Just the corner. Behind the sofa, you know. I slept out there when Mama have a boyfriend."

"What were your mother and Butchie fighting about?"

"Me."

Hetzler waited.

"It was winter," she continued. "Mama axe Butchie could she buy me a coat, you know."

"What did he say?" asked Hetzler.

"Not my *daddy,* not *his* fault I don't have no coat."

"And then?"

"Mama said, 'Give me back just a little money, Butchie. Enough for that and you know I want you to have the rest.' "

"What did he say?"

"He didn't say nothing, just grab her by

the throat and start knocking her head up against the wall — left a big hole in it, with cracks all around."

"And what happened then?"

"I run out to grab his arm, try and make him leave off."

"You were such a little girl," said Hetzler, holding his hand waist-high from the courtroom floor. "Could you stop him from hurting your mother?"

"He let go her neck and start hitting me instead. Broke out my side teeth, knock me down."

"What did your mother do?" asked Hetzler.

Underhill looked away, forearm draped across the top of her belly so she could pick at a loop of yarn on her pale-pink sweater's cuff.

Hetzler leaned in, gentle. "Angela?"

Her voice was quiet. Flat. "Mama screaming: 'Don't you *hurt* my baby,' and all like that, you know."

"Did Butchie listen?"

"Listen?" Her shoulders twitched beneath the pink sweater. "Butchie have a *gun.*"

"Did he have to go get it?"

"He pull up his shirt and I seen it then, stuck in his belt."

"So he pulled the gun out of his belt?"

She nodded. "Smack Mama once with it right off, real hard in the face."

"How hard?"

"Smashed her nose flat. He hit her again and she fall over acrost me — like this." Angela raised both hands, making an X with her slender wrists.

Hetzler didn't say a word.

She let her hands drop.

"What happened then?"

"Butchie step close and lean down. He say, 'Shut up' and shoot my mama twice in the head. Then he walk out."

"He left you there?"

"After he reach back in to turn off the lights, you know. Close the door after him, before he go."

Hetzler let those words sink in for a moment.

Angela resumed picking at her cuff, as though she'd just reminded him they needed eggs and milk, at home.

"You were there a long time, weren't you, lying in the dark with your mother?"

A quick glance at the jury told me I wasn't the only person in the room substituting *under* for that euphemistic *with*. His slick bait-and-switch of a single word rendering Hetzler compassionate, and his client worthy of our sympathy.

509

Underhill didn't look up from her sweater. "Till morning. I slept some, right there."

"Do you remember anything else about that night?" asked Hetzler.

Underhill pursed her lips, thinking. "First Mama felt warm. Then she cold."

"And who found you?"

She lifted her chin toward Mrs. Underhill, seated in the gallery's front row. "Someone call my grandma. She come."

"Angela," said Hetzler, "when your mother tried to protect you that night, she was killed, wasn't she?"

Her pink shoulders twitched again. "Mama passed. That's all."

Hetzler patted her hand. "No further questions, Your Honor."

"Ms. Underhill," said Bost, "I'd like to ask you about your boyfriend, Albert Williams."

Underhill nodded.

"Was he Teddy's father?"

"No." She placed her hands high on her jutting belly, protective.

"And how long have the two of you been together?" asked Bost.

"Two years, something like that."

"When you and Albert Williams first moved in together, you were living in Brooklyn, is that right?"

"That's right," said Underhill.

"Why did you leave that apartment and move to Queens?"

"The social worker," said Underhill.

"Why was that?"

"That woman downstairs. She reported us."

"For what, Ms. Underhill?"

Underhill said nothing.

"Ms. Underhill? What did the neighbor report you for?"

"Said we hurt Teddy."

"And did you?"

"Not me," said Underhill, raising her chin.

"But Mr. Williams *did* hurt your son?"

"When Teddy act up."

"Can you tell us what you mean by 'act up'?"

"Maybe eat too slow, or complain about things."

"So if your three-year-old son ate more slowly than Mr. Williams thought was appropriate, what would he do?"

"Sometimes."

"Sometimes what?"

"Only sometimes. Not every time," said Underhill.

"On those occasions when Teddy's speed at meals was of concern to Mr. Williams, what might he do in reaction?"

"Punch him, you know. Or lift him up and shake him."

"What would Teddy do?"

She shrugged. "Cry."

"And what did *you* do, Ms. Underhill, when your boyfriend would punch your son with his fist?"

"I tried to stop him one time."

"And what happened?"

"Albert had a knife. He cut me."

"Where did he cut you?" asked Bost.

Underhill pushed her pink cardigan sleeve back along her right forearm, up toward her elbow. "Here."

"And after that, did you ever try to protect your son again?"

Underhill looked away, over all of our heads, toward the distant wall of the courtroom behind us.

"Ms. Underhill?" asked Bost. "Was that the last time you tried to intervene, to stop your boyfriend from hurting your son, Teddy?"

"Yeah. The last time."

"And is Mr. Williams the father of the child you're carrying now?"

"Yeah."

"Do you have any worries that he might hurt the child you're carrying now, after it's born?"

512

Angela's hands rose to the high sides of her belly again. Her right hand moved slowly, stroking the mound of flesh as though offering reassurance to the being inside it. Or herself.

"Albert wouldn't do that," she said, shaking her head once from side to side. "Hurt his *own* baby."

"But you had no problem with Albert Williams hurting a little boy who *wasn't* his, Ms. Underhill? Even though that child was your son?"

"Albert work hard. He took good care of me and Teddy. Buy us food, pay the rent."

"Albert took good care of you and your son until he killed Teddy, isn't that right, Ms. Underhill? And you did nothing to stop him?"

"Objection," said Hetzler. "Argumentative."

The judge nodded. "Sustained. The jury will disregard that last question."

How could anyone disregard it? It was the reason all of us were sitting here in this room.

"Ms. Underhill," said Bost, "on the afternoon of April fourteenth, can you tell us where you were?"

"In my room. At that motel by the airport."

"And who was with you?"

"Teddy. And Albert."

"And did your son do something that day that upset Mr. Williams?"

"*You* know," she said.

"I'd like you to tell us all anyway. What did Teddy do?"

"He wouldn't listen."

"Listen to what?" asked Bost.

"Albert say he should go to sleep. Take his nap."

"And did he take his nap?"

"No. Wouldn't lie down and be quiet."

"What were you doing?" asked Bost.

"Watching TV."

"What did Mr. Williams do when Teddy wouldn't settle down?"

"Yell at him, first. But Teddy didn't listen to that."

"Why not?"

"Said he's thirsty."

"What happened then?"

"Albert get angry."

"What did Mr. Williams do after he got angry?"

"Hit Teddy."

"With his fist?"

"Yeah."

"*Where* did he hit him?"

"Here," said Underhill, patting her breastbone with her right hand.

"How many times?"

"I don't know."

"More than once?"

"Yeah."

"Five times?"

"Yeah."

"More than that?" asked Bost.

Angela looked away, but she nodded.

"Teddy was very small, wasn't he, Ms. Underhill?"

His mother shrugged.

"Did he get knocked down?"

"The first time."

"But Mr. Williams kept hitting him, didn't he, even though Teddy was already down on the floor?"

"Yeah."

"Could you see how many times Teddy got punched?" asked Bost.

"Albert in front of him, then, but I seen his arm come up."

"How many times?"

Angela mumbled something.

"Can you speak up, Ms. Underhill?"

"Twelve," she said.

"Twelve times?"

Angela nodded.

"Answer the question, please," said the judge.

"Yeah. Twelve."

Bost leaned in closer. "And what happened after Albert Williams punched your son in the chest twelve times, Ms. Underhill?"

"Albert sit on the bed with me."

"What did the two of you do then?"

"Watch TV."

"For how long?"

"Until the end of the show."

Bost let that answer hang in the air.

I looked over at the jurors. The church ladies were pissed.

Good for them.

Bost waited one more beat, then asked, "You didn't check on your son?"

"He quiet, then."

"Teddy wasn't just quiet, Ms. Underhill. He was dead, wasn't he?"

"I didn't know."

"But you didn't check, did you? After watching a grown man punch your three-year-old son full force in the chest a dozen times, you didn't check to see if the boy was all right? If he might need medical attention?"

Underhill started stroking her belly, again.

"Please answer the question," said Bost.

"I didn't check."

"And when you discovered that your son

had been beaten to death by your boyfriend, what did you do?"

"Nothing," said Underhill.

"What happened to his body?"

"Albert take care of it."

"What did Mr. Williams do with your son's body? Did he take Teddy to the cemetery?"

"Later."

"So what did he do with Teddy's body that afternoon?" asked Bost.

Underhill mumbled again.

"Please speak up, Ms. Underhill. We can't hear you."

She leaned in closer to the microphone. "Put him in the mini-fridge."

Bost walked two steps closer to the stand. "Teddy's body fit *inside* the refrigerator in your motel room?"

"He small," said Angela, nodding to herself, eyes not focused on anything in the room.

"How long did you and Mr. Williams keep your son's body in that refrigerator, Ms. Underhill?"

"A week."

57

The immediate response to Angela Underhill's admission that she'd left her son's
body in a motel-room refrigerator for a
week was not uproar, but a sudden *absence*
of sound. Like that final hush of menace
before you get slammed by a hurricane, or
a tsunami: no birdsong, no breath of wind,
just the turncoat hiss of tidewater sluicing
away from the beach beneath your feet.

And then the room burst into noise and
motion. No one yelled or even said any
specific words loudly enough to be intel-
ligible — we just all had to jostle around in
our seats, muttering and sighing, desperate
to shake that hideous picture out of our
heads.

The judge called us to order.

Bost waited a moment before she spoke
again. "Ms. Underhill, what did you do during that week?"

"I don't know," she said, her voice broken

and slight.

"Did you and your boyfriend talk about what to do with Teddy's body?"

"Don't know."

Bost tilted her head to the side. "You don't remember?"

Underhill hunched forward, dropping her eyes to the floor. "We got high."

"Did you tell anyone what had happened?"

"Didn't leave that room."

"You and Mr. Williams stayed inside the room for a week?"

Underhill said, "Just me," then muttered something else that sounded like "baby dead."

"Was it your idea to hide Teddy's body at the cemetery?" asked Bost.

"Don't know."

"The cemetery's in your old neighborhood, isn't it?"

Underhill shrugged.

"Where your grandmother raised you?" asked Bost.

No response.

Bost stepped closer. "Your grandmother's apartment is only a few blocks away from Prospect Cemetery, Ms. Underhill. You walked by it every morning on your way to school, and every afternoon when you came home."

"Objection," said Hetzler, more quiet than strident, for once. "I'm not hearing any question here, just a lecture."

Bost turned to the judge. "I'll withdraw it."

His Honor nodded.

Bost looked back at Underhill. "Who took your son's body out of the refrigerator?"

"Albert."

"What happened then?"

"Put Teddy in a gym bag."

"Albert did this?"

"Yeah."

"And after that?"

"Took him. Went away."

"To the cemetery?"

"I said, 'Don't tell me. Just you treat my baby decent.' "

"And do you think he did?" asked Bost.

"Did what?"

"Do you think Albert Williams treated your son's body with decency?"

Underhill dropped her eyes again, mumbling.

"I'm sorry, Ms. Underhill, I couldn't hear you," said Bost.

"He lie about it."

"About what?"

Underhill looked up, straight at Bost. "Say it was a proper grave, where Teddy laid to rest."

"But it wasn't?"

"My baby dead and Albert leave him on the ground. Wouldn't even dig no hole."

"And that upset you?" asked Bost.

Underhill nodded, perhaps expecting sympathy.

Bost played at giving her some. "In fact you're *angry* about that, Ms. Underhill, aren't you?"

"Yeah."

"Angry that Albert Williams just dumped your son's little body in the bushes after beating him to death, without any attempt at a proper burial?"

"Yes."

"I'd say that's made a lot of people in this room angry, too," said Bost. "But there's one thing I'm still confused about, Ms. Underhill. Maybe you can clear it up for me?"

"What?"

"Are you angry because Albert's treatment of your son's body showed his utter lack of respect for the life of your child, or because dumping Teddy in the bushes like a sack of garbage was so damn sloppy that the two of you got caught?"

Hetzler shot to his feet, shrieking, *"Objection!"*

"Withdrawn."

Bost waited for quiet. "I have no further questions for this witness, Your Honor."

58

After lunch, it was Galloway's turn at bat.

"Ms. Underhill," she began.

I had moved up to a middle row in the gallery, near the right wall, for a better view of the jury.

Galloway paused and looked toward them too, as though to emphasize further her distance from the familiarity of Hetzler's "Angela."

She turned back toward the witness box. "What you've *already* said here today is very different from what you first told the police, isn't it?"

Underhill made no response to that.

"In fact," Galloway continued, "you lied to the police — and your grandmother — about your son's death, didn't you?"

"Because of Albert," said Underhill. "What he might do."

"You were frightened of Albert Williams?"

"Yeah," said Underhill.

"And that's why you blamed your son's disappearance on him, when you *did* finally file a report with the police? Because you were so *frightened* of Albert Williams?"

"No, I just . . ." She stopped, giving a little head shake.

"Can you remind us how long you waited before you went to the police at all, Ms. Underhill?"

"I don't exactly know. After what happened."

"And why was that, Ms. Underhill?"

"I was so shook up."

"Were you shook up, or just *high?*" asked Galloway.

"I was . . ." Underhill's voice trailed off again.

"You remember what day your son died, though, don't you?"

"Yes."

"What was the date?"

"April."

Galloway stepped to the defense table and picked up a sheaf of papers, then turned back to face the stand. "Which day in April?"

"Fourteenth."

"And why is that date easy for you to remember?"

Underhill made that tiny head shake again.

Galloway stepped closer. "April fourteenth is more than just the day your son died, isn't it?"

"His birthday."

"*His* birthday?" asked Galloway.

No answer, just a small nod.

"Speak up, Ms. Underhill."

Another nod, and Teddy's mother lifted her hands to the sides of her swollen belly.

Galloway zeroed in. "Tell us *whose* birthday fell on April the fourteenth."

Angela slid her arms up over the top of her belly and hugged them to herself — balled-up hands crossed, protecting her collarbone. "Teddy's."

There was a rustle of movement from the jury box, muttered exhalations and creaking seats. They were looking at Galloway now, eyes averted from Underhill.

"Your son, Teddy, turned three years old that day, didn't he?"

Underhill's chin dropped into the vee of her wrists. "Yeah."

"That's why Teddy was wearing the new clothes your grandmother bought him, isn't it?" asked Galloway.

The barest of nods and a whisper, "I dressed him all up."

"So that's why Teddy was wearing his new clothes when you put his body in the refrigerator?"

"Objection!" said Hetzler.

"Move on, Ms. Galloway," said the judge.

Galloway nodded, turning back toward Underhill. "So Teddy died on the fourteenth of April, but you don't remember how long it took you to file the report that he was missing?"

"A while. Because I was upset."

"Can you take a look at this?" asked Galloway, walking up to hand her a sheet of paper. "It's the first page of the report you filed. Can you read the date on the top?"

"It's blurry," said Underhill.

"Just the month, then."

"May."

"So at least two weeks, then, would that be correct?"

"I guess."

"Your grandmother, she loved Teddy?"

"She do."

" 'She *did,*' " corrected Galloway.

Underhill closed her eyes.

"In fact," continued Galloway, "your grandmother wanted Teddy to have more than just a new set of clothes that day, didn't she?"

"I don't —"

"What *else* did she give you, for your son's birthday?"

Hetzler stood up. "Your Honor, I don't see how this —"

Galloway gave a fine impersonation of not having heard him. "She gave you *money*, didn't she, Ms. Underhill?"

Hetzler threw up his hands. "Your *Honor*."

"Sit down, Mr. Hetzler," said the judge.

Hetzler sank to his chair, telegraphing his great injury from the weight of the world's oppression.

The judge turned toward the witness box. "Answer the question please, Ms. Underhill."

"Yeah."

Galloway clarified with "*Yes*, your grandmother gave you money for your son's birthday?"

"Yes," Underhill repeated.

"What was the money for?"

"To buy him things. You know."

"But you didn't use that money to buy anything for your son, did you?" asked Galloway.

"He didn't know."

"What did you buy with the money?"

"Wasn't that much," said Underhill. "There was things we needed."

"How much money did your grandmother

527

give you?"

"Fifty," she said.

"Your grandmother testified that she gave you a thousand dollars that day."

"No," said Angela.

"What did you spend it on?" asked Galloway.

Angela gave her a shoulder-twitch, guiltier this time. "You know."

"I don't know, Ms. Underhill," said Galloway. "That's why I'm asking *you*."

"We get high, but not right away."

"Not right away?"

"Wasn't like, soon as we leave Grandma's *house,* you know?"

"Did you spend any of the money on your son?"

"It was for Albert. He told me."

"And what did he tell you to buy?"

"Some rock, you know."

"I see, so you spent all that money on crack cocaine because Albert Williams told you to?" asked Galloway.

"I was afraid. What he do. Hurt Teddy, if I don't do like he says."

"Did you go to purchase the drugs yourself?"

"Yeah."

"With Teddy?"

"No."

"You left your son with a man you were *that* afraid of?"

"Albert made me," she said, then added, "I don't know, maybe Teddy with me. That whole day, it's not like I remember. I was so afraid."

"In fact, if you were so afraid of Albert Williams, there was no reason you had to be in that motel room at all. Your grandmother had asked you and Teddy to move in with her many times. Even the previous day, hadn't she?"

"It wasn't like that."

"Wasn't like *what*, Ms. Underhill? Wasn't like you were actually afraid that Albert Williams might harm your son?"

Angela dropped her head.

"Or it wasn't like you wanted to have your benefits cut if you left the motel and moved in with a family member?"

Angela mumbled something.

"I beg your pardon?" said Galloway.

"Albert say he kill me if I left."

"But you told him where the motel was, didn't you, after you moved out of his apartment in Brooklyn?"

Underhill shrugged.

"The caseworker couldn't find you there, but Albert could?"

No answer.

"Tell us the truth," said Galloway. "You didn't care *what* happened to your son, as long as it meant you could stay high, isn't that right, Ms. Underhill?"

Hetzler sang out with "Objection!"

Galloway held up her hand before the judge could speak. "Let me rephrase that question, Ms. Underhill. You could have moved in with your grandmother, or let Teddy stay with her by himself — she asked you to do at least that, the day before his death — but instead you kept your son with you in that motel room, and you allowed Albert Williams to stay there too, isn't that correct?"

The judge had to tell Angela to speak, once again.

"Only because I was afraid," she said.

"Of what?" asked Galloway.

"I told you. Albert say he kill me."

"If you left him?"

"Mm-hm."

"Did Albert Williams ever hurt *you*, Ms. Underhill, or did he just hurt your son?"

"Albert cut me," she said. "I told you."

"On the arm, wasn't it?"

"Like I told before."

"Was it a bad cut?"

"It hurt real bad, yeah. Lot of blood and everything."

"But you didn't need stitches?"

Silence.

"And was that the only time?" asked Galloway.

"I said already."

Galloway nodded. "Just the once, then. And could you tell us again *why* Albert cut you?"

"*Because.* I try and stop him from beatin' on Teddy."

"Just the once, then," repeated Galloway.

"I was too afraid."

"So as long as you kept Teddy with you, though, you had it pretty good, didn't you?"

"What's that?"

"You told us all earlier that Albert had a good job, right?"

"Security guard."

"Decent paycheck, since you called it a 'good' job?"

"I guess."

"See, now that's what *I'd* call a pretty sweet deal, Ms. Underhill: Let your boyfriend use your son for a punching bag, and you get more money for drugs."

"*Objection!*" Hetzler popped up, livid.

"I'll withdraw it," said Galloway.

The judge nodded.

"Ms. Underhill, let's just run through the timeline, here," said Galloway, looking again at the papers in her hand.

"Okay."

"You took money from your grandmother, but you didn't let her have your son because you wanted more?"

"Objection, leading the witness," said Hetzler.

"I'll rephrase," said Galloway. "Did your grandmother offer you money in exchange for Teddy?"

"Yeah."

"But you kept your son and bought crack with that money because you were afraid your boyfriend would kill you?"

"Yeah."

"But when — according to you — he *did* kill your son, you stayed with him in a motel room for another two weeks instead of reporting him to the police?"

"I didn't —"

"Even when he went to his job and you were *alone,* you didn't report him?"

Hetzler looked ready to get back to his feet.

"Oh, that's right, you were *high,* weren't you, Ms. Underhill, smoking away with your son's body jammed into the fridge right next to your bed, right?"

"Your Honor," said Hetzler, not even getting all the way upright.

"Fine," said Galloway. "Let's say you just waited for two weeks so we can move on, okay?"

Hetzler sat again.

Galloway continued, "So it was *after* that two weeks, when you went to your grandmother for more drug money? And when she wouldn't give it to you, you lied to her *and* to the police about your son's death, isn't that right?"

"Because —"

"Because *what,* Ms. Underhill?"

"Albert. I told you."

"And was Albert with you at your grandmother's house, two weeks after Teddy died?"

"He wasn't, because of work."

"And was Albert there with you and your grandmother when you went to the precinct house and lied to the police?"

Angela just shook her head, and Galloway let it pass.

"You lie an awful lot, Ms. Underhill, don't you?"

"If I'm afraid. Only then."

"Tell us, Ms. Underhill," said Galloway, "you're sitting in the witness box, facing a charge of murder. And your son's bones can't tell us anything about *who* killed him — or even who beat him, over and over again, while he was still alive. It's your word against Albert Williams's, about what happened on April fourteenth. Are you afraid right *now?*"

Underhill stood her ground. "It was Albert killed Teddy. *That's* the truth."

Galloway let Underhill's assertion hang in the air while she walked back to the prosecution table, squaring up her sheaf of papers so she could set them down neatly on its surface.

She turned to face the box again. "I see you're expecting, Ms. Underhill. And you mentioned that Albert Williams is the father?"

"Yes," she said, hands to belly again.

"When's the baby due?"

"Three weeks."

"So you conceived, when, around July?"

"I guess."

"You and Mr. Williams were still living together at the motel when you were arrested last September, weren't you?"

"You know I was."

"It's funny, though, Ms. Underhill."

"What?"

"Well, you were getting a family voucher from the borough, but you didn't *have* a child anymore, once Teddy was dead."

"They give vouchers for when you pregnant," said Underhill.

"So you lied and lied and lied because you were so *afraid* of Mr. Williams, but he sure turned out to be handy when you needed to keep your free housing, didn't he?"

Hetzler's *"Objection!"* was his loudest yet.

"Nothing further," said Galloway, turning to walk back to the prosecution table.

She stepped behind her client, tucking the back of her skirt primly smooth before taking her seat.

It was after seven and I was stuck alone at the Catalog, staring at the non-ringing phone on my desk, too tired and disgusted after Angela Underhill's testimony to have my heart in much of anything.

After another five minutes of staring at the wall, I picked up the phone and dialed Kyle at home.

"How's everything going?" I asked.

"Marty's yakking it up to the press," he said.

"Why?"

"I guess he figures his argument isn't going to stick. The whole Hedda Nussbaum thing."

"*What* whole Hedda Nussbaum thing?"

"I keep forgetting you didn't hear his opening," he said.

"I hadn't testified yet. You were supposed to be my spy, remember?"

"I'm a terrible spy. That's why I went to law school."

"If I'd known they accept carbon-based life-forms, I would've taken the LSATs myself. What about Hedda Nussbaum?"

"You know who she is, don't you?"

"Her psycho-crackhead-lawyer boyfriend Joel Steinberg beat their illegally adopted daughter Lisa into an ultimately fatal coma," I said, "and even though Nussbaum didn't do a thing about it until they took the poor kid to the hospital twelve hours later, she got off anyway because her face looked like Steinberg'd smashed it flat with a veal mallet and/or because she's a white chick who used to work at Random House," I said. "That the one you mean?"

"I take it you've done some recent cramming?" he asked.

"Dude. I was merely Upstate, not living under an assumed name in Algeria."

"Did you know that Steinberg left Lisa lying on the bathroom floor?"

"And what did he do after that, just piss directly on the child because it was too much trouble to lift his feet?"

"He went out to dinner with friends."

"I think that might actually be worse," I

said, "if such a thing is possible."

"Yeah."

"So Nussbaum was *alone,* and she still didn't call nine-one-one? I thought they just sat around smoking rock until he'd get high enough to attempt a resurrection."

"That was later," said Kyle. "Hedda was by herself for eight hours or something."

"So, like, what'd she do that whole time? Just sit in the living room reading old *New Yorker*s?"

Kyle sighed. "She said she used the time to organize Joel's files."

"For eight hours."

We were quiet for a minute.

"Jesus," I said.

"Right?"

"And she fucking got *off?*"

"Well, she testified against him," said Kyle. "Plus there was the whole veal-mallet makeover thing. She got all the movie-of-the-week *Burning Bed* sympathy, you know?"

"I don't care. That shit ain't right."

"*Talk* to me," he said.

"I mean, do you buy that? She was too pummeled to know right from wrong, anymore?"

"Are you asking me to respond in my capacity as a prosecutor or as a carbon-based life-form?"

"Is there a difference?"

"Not when it comes to that."

"And?"

"And I thought the bitch should fry. With every fiber of my entire being."

"Attaboy, Kyle."

"We aim to please," he said.

I looked at my wan reflection in the airshaft window. "Is that bullshit going to work this time, too?"

"For Marty and his client?"

"Yeah."

"Well, he's got some guy from the *Times* sitting in."

"In the gallery?"

"That's what I hear. Marty knows from PR, you've gotta give him that."

"So what did he actually say in his opening?" I asked.

"That given Nussbaum's deal, it's obvious the only reasons Angela Underhill was charged in her son's death are that she's poor and she's black."

"The boyfriend never even hit her, Kyle. She says he cut her in the arm once, but otherwise she just sat there and watched."

"And they finished up with her today?" he asked.

"I guess. At least Bost's go-round. The

defense might bring her back for more, right?"

"Batting cleanup."

"So does it make me a racist, that I hate this woman so much?" I asked.

"Maddie," he said, "I come from a nice liberal Jewish family. When I told them I was giving up my white-shoe corporate gig to become a prosecutor, my father gave me a ton of shit about how it meant I was going to be busting poor black and Hispanic people, 'for the man.' "

"What'd *you* say?"

"That he had it totally backwards: I was going to speak out on behalf of poor black and Hispanic victims — mostly women and children. And take a seventy-thousand-dollar pay cut."

I tried digesting that.

"Look, sweetie," Kyle continued, "you're angry on behalf of a three-year-old boy. How can that be racist?"

"Because I was born racked with guilt?"

"How is that even *possible?* You're a god-damn Episcopalian."

"Fuck if I know. Some sort of genetic mutation."

"So go home, get some sleep. And pick up a copy of the *Times* tomorrow morning. You'll probably know the outlines of Marty's

539

closing before you get on the subway."

"Hey, Bunny," said Dean's welcome voice two hours later.

I was curled up on the sofa with the phone. Pagan and Sue were out for the evening.

"It's so great to hear your voice," I said. "I thought it was going to be Astrid again."

I'd given him the new home number for the happy newlyweds out in New Jersey.

"Nutty Buddy getting you down?"

"I just wish she'd make up her mind. I mean, stay married or don't, just stop whining about it, you know?"

"I can't understand what her problem with Christoph is. He seems like a helluva guy to me."

"Who knows what evil lurks in the hearts of men?" I asked.

"Could she be happy with *anybody?*"

"Probably not. Not even you."

"Perish the thought."

"Oh come on, you wouldn't want to be married to a gorgeous titled Euro-chick? Imagine the possibilities."

"Imagine Thanksgiving dinner at the farm," he said. "Especially when my mother brought out the Jell-O salad."

"I *love* your mom. Jell-O and all."

"Of course you do. That's why I married you."

"And you told me it was because I'm such a buxom heifer."

He laughed. "That too."

"Ooo la la," I said, and we told each other good night.

59

There was an article on page three of the next morning's *Times*'s "New York and Region" section:

MOTHER TELLS OF BEATINGS THAT LED TO HER SON'S DEATH

In a whispered monotone, Queens resident Angela Underhill testified yesterday that her male companion had inflicted horrific beatings on her 3-year-old son in the months before the boy's death in 1989. . . .

. . . The case has drawn wide attention because the lawyer for the child's mother, Angela Underhill, 25, and advocates for battered women contend that she also had been a victim of these assaults. The case has also raised questions about the response of child-welfare authorities to a complaint that the boy was a victim of routine abuse.

Hedda Nussbaum rated three mentions. Teddy Underhill was called merely "the boy" throughout.

I figured Hetzler would be going for broke.

Cate was standing on the courthouse steps when I got out to Queens.

"I couldn't get out of work yesterday," she said. "You have to catch me up on what happened on the stand."

We got in line for the metal detector and I ran her through the narrative each lawyer had conjured forth: how Bost teased out the appalling choreography of both Teddy's death and his mother's nonchalance, Hetzler deployed Angela's own harrowing childhood as a get-out-of-jail-free card, and Galloway limned the proportions of a mendacious greed that was more powerful than a locomotive and able to prove her own client's innocence in a single bound.

Cate placed her purse in a plastic bin for the X-ray machine. "The Three Faces of Teddy's Mother?"

"Angela Underhill: bitch, victim, or money-grubbing crack ho? *You* decide." I dumped out a pocketful of nickels and

543

subway tokens.

"All of the above," said Cate.

"Yahtzee."

I stepped toward the metal detector's victory arch.

Cate and I sat down directly behind Bost once we got inside the courtroom. I gave her the article I'd ripped from the *Times* and then turned in my seat, trying to spy out its author. It had to be either the balding blond guy in a linty blazer or the tweed-bedecked ringer for Trotsky, but I couldn't decide between them. Both had notepads at the ready.

Bost had Teddy's poster portrait back up on the easel as backdrop for her closing argument.

She looked at it for a long moment before saying a word. The jurors gazed along with her.

When she turned toward them, she let her hand rest along the top of the image.

"We've heard a lot of testimony in this room over the last two weeks," she said. "Testimony from a variety of experts and regular citizens who were drawn into the horrible, gut-wrenching circumstances of this little boy's death, and its aftermath."

She dropped her hand from the photo and walked toward the jury box. "We can tell you how Teddy's body was discovered. We can tell you how he was identified, and how the homicide investigation was conducted, once his identity was known. We can describe the series of horrific injuries he suffered over the course of his three years on this earth — injuries so severe that their impact is still literally *mapped* in his very bones, even after his death."

Bost looked toward the defense table. "His mother described the beating which caused his death, and the indifference with which she and Albert Williams treated his tiny, broken body when it was all over.

"Stephanie Keller told us what it was like to hear his screams. She could give us some sense of what it must have been like to suffer the violent fury of a full-grown man for transgressions as slight as not finishing a bowl of cereal fast enough."

She looked back to the jury. "What we cannot know is what it was like for Teddy Underhill to be *alive*. We cannot know what it was like to live in that much pain, and fear — wondering when the next blows were going to come, when the next bones would be broken. He can't tell us. He can't tell us anything at all. Angela Underhill and Albert

Williams made sure of that, made sure he would never know anything more of life than his short, desperate glimpse of this earth as a place filled with fear, and pain, and suffering.

"We cannot know what he dreamed of, the hopes he cherished . . . what he might have become. The only things left to mark this boy's short, horrible life are the photograph you see before you, and his tiny, ravaged bones."

She turned back to his picture once more. "Take a look at that little face, ladies and gentlemen of the jury. That moment captured when he was overjoyed to be sitting on Santa Claus's lap in a department store, smiling with gratitude because he got to have at least one normal childhood afternoon — secure in the love of his great-grandmother, safe from harm for just a few precious hours.

"What Angela Underhill and Albert Williams did to this child goes beyond homicide. They didn't merely rob him of his future, they took his *entire* life, stripping away all vestiges of his childhood even before he was so brutally slaughtered.

"Albert Williams's lawyer would like you to forget the testimony of Stephanie Keller, who knew full well what sort of abuse Teddy was suffering at her client's hands. Keller, a medical professional with twenty years' experience, knew exactly what she was seeing and hearing. Stephanie Keller *fought* to live long enough to come here and tell us all that, in person, to prove that someone in this world cared enough about Teddy to seek justice for him. She offered to help Angela Underhill save her son from this life of pain, and she did her best to make sure the state would step in to protect him, if his mother wouldn't. Think about that, ladies and gentlemen: a *stranger* cared more about the welfare of this child than his own mother did.

"But Albert Williams's lawyer didn't manage to shake Ms. Keller on this stand. She knew exactly what happened, and she told her story clearly, and convincingly. Because of her, we know what sort of life Teddy was forced to lead, and we know the kind of violence that ultimately led up to his death. We know that Albert Williams killed him, as Ms. Keller feared he would.

"And here's the thing that's most sickening, of all the sickening things you've had to think about, here in this courtroom: none of this had to *happen.* There was a safe, nurturing place for Teddy to live, with a beloved family member who cared for this child and who loved him dearly. Teddy's great-grandmother offered him a home, but his mother was too selfish to let him go. Teddy's suffering was Angela Under-hill's ticket to independence — a free place to live, free food, no need to work. If only she could put up with the nuisance of raising a child, she had no one to answer to. Ultimately, that free ride was worth more to her than her child's very life. And now that he's gone, she's got another meal ticket on the way, fathered by the same man who beat her little boy to death.

"Angela Underhill's lawyer will tell you that she was so damaged by the violence she saw in her own childhood that we could not have expected her to safeguard the life of her son. He wants you to believe that she was not responsible for the actions of Albert Williams, and that she was powerless to stop him from battering her child to death."

She looked at the photograph again. "Take a look at this boy's face and tell me that you wouldn't have tried to save him from a life of pain. Take a look at his great-grandmother's face, here in this courtroom, and tell me she didn't love him enough to give him a loving home. Angela Underhill knew that full well, but she was too selfish to keep her child safe, or even to keep him alive.

"We know how Teddy Underhill died: Albert Williams punched him in the chest a dozen times, until the damage to his tiny ribs was so severe it stopped his heart. That is a horrible, excruciating, and absolutely sickening way to die. Teddy Underhill's life ended with fear, and pain, and suffering. And his mother sat on a bed four feet away watching television while it happened. She didn't protect him, she didn't comfort him, she didn't even get up off the bed to *look* at him once the beating had stopped. She sat by as Albert Williams stuffed her son's body in a refrigerator. Then she spent a week in the motel room with her son's corpse, doing drugs.

"Her lawyer has argued that the only reason Angela Underhill is facing charges in her son's death is that she's 'poor and black.' He's argued that she feared for her life, and that her judgment was so distorted by an abusive childhood that she was incapable of protecting her son. He's argued — and I'm sure *will* argue further — that this means you should declare her not guilty on all counts.

"But I'm asking you, today, to think about the fate of Teddy Underhill when you weigh your decision concerning the guilt of *both* Albert Williams and Teddy's *mother,* Angela Underhill. A three-year-old child is dead because of their cruelty, their selfishness, and their depraved indifference. Nothing can bring him back, but it's within your power to demand justice in his memory.

"Stephanie Keller came here at great personal cost, asking you to do just that. She battled cancer with tremendous courage for a long, long time, and willed herself to survive long enough to testify before you.

"Stephanie Keller was a warrior. She fought to save the life of Teddy Underhill even as her own life ebbed away. She fought to *make* us comprehend this little boy's pain and fear and suffering, knowing full well it meant spending her *own* final hours in crushing physical agony. She fought to be wheeled into this room because *nothing* could stop her from asking all of us — with her *last* ounce of strength, her *last* breath of life — for justice."

Bost dropped her eyes to the floor for a moment, hands clasped at the small of her back.

"I'll say it again: Stephanie Keller was a warrior." She looked up, taking a step closer to the box of jurors.

Cate said, *"Was?"* beside me.

I countered with an unvoiced *"Fuck."*

Bost said, "When you think about Teddy Underhill, I want you to think about what this woman — a *stranger* — willingly sacrificed on his behalf."

She turned, pointing toward the defense table. "Weigh *her* compassion against Angela Underhill's cruel indifference. . . . Weigh *her* courage against Albert Williams's cowardly brutality. . . ."

She faced the jurors once more. "Make *her* strength your touchstone as you consider the facts of this case."

Bost stepped toward Teddy's picture. "Teddy Underhill was murdered."

She gripped the side of the poster firmly with one hand and pointed to the boy's joyous face with the other.

"Angela Underhill *knew* how the ravages of physical abuse build inevitably, until they culminate in murder. Albert Williams *knew* he was smashing the fragile rib cage of a three-year-old child into shards, just as he *knew* that his final blows punched through to crush a tiny, beating heart.

"They are *both* murderers," said Bost.

"Yes," said Cate, under her breath but vehemently.

Bost looked at Teddy's picture one more time, then let her gaze linger on the face of each juror in turn.

"Hold them accountable."

Please God.

"Thank you."

60

Hetzler took his time getting up, each motion distinct, a sort of gestural stop-motion. Chair pushed back. Hands on tabletop. Chest tipped forward. Feet braced. Legs straightened to full height. Jacket patted smooth and buttoned closed. Three strides to the center of the floor.

It was like watching a sniper assemble his favored rifle, click by click.

"The facts of this case . . ." said Hetzler.

His nostrils flared, once, as though he were testing the air to ensure that even the *fragrance* of Bost's closing had dissipated entirely before conjuring forth his own.

"Here's the *main* fact of this case: Teddy Underhill's death was a senseless tragedy."

Teddy's portrait remained in place on its easel. Hetzler gave it a look of sad appraisal.

"This beautiful, innocent boy? Just barely three years old?"

He raised his hand to the pixels of Teddy's cheek.

"Horrible, what happened to this little angel . . . *heart*-rending. . . . No one with a shred of human decency could call his death anything less.

"But" — he looked up from Teddy, toward the jurors — "as tragic as it was, what happened to little Teddy Underhill was *not* murder, ladies and gentlemen.

"To find either Angela Underhill or Albert Williams guilty of murder, the prosecution would have had to prove that their actions were undertaken with the *intent* to cause Teddy's death. The prosecution would have had to prove that the defendants sitting before you actively *planned* to kill this child, which is what we call premeditation."

He nodded, sagely. "The defendants did *not* intend Teddy's death. No one has testified otherwise, here in this courtroom, and rightly so.

"The *facts* of the case," said Hetzler. "You've been told that Albert Williams injured this little boy repeatedly — finally battering him to death. Angela Underhill described witnessing him inflict those injuries. Stephanie Keller testified that she heard Williams yelling, heard him strike the child, heard the boy's own screams as Williams beat him. Mrs. Elsie Underhill told you that she saw the mark of a clothes-iron burn on the boy's back, the day before he died."

Hetzler dropped his hands, taking a few strides closer to the jury box. "Were they telling the truth, those three women?"

He looked at one juror, then another. "*I* think they were. *I* think these injuries were inflicted on Teddy Underhill by one person: Albert Williams."

Here, he pointed an accusing finger at Teddy's killer, bouncing his hand angrily to underline each emphasized word to follow.

"*I* think that the man you see seated before you — a man who weighs two hundred fifteen pounds and who measures six feet two inches in height — battered the body and soul of a three-year-old child without mercy, whenever the spirit took him. *I* think Albert Williams is a vicious man, a coward, and a bully."

He paused.

"The facts of the case — here's another one: the medical examiner estimates that at the time of his death, Teddy Underhill weighed thirty pounds and stood three feet tall. We all know that he had no hope of defending himself against the violent attacks of Albert Williams.

"But we all have to wonder why Teddy's

mother didn't step in to defend him, don't we?" asked Hetzler, looking over his shoulder briefly at Angela. "Well, here's another fact: Angela Underhill stands five feet two inches tall. And before her pregnancy, she weighed roughly one hundred five pounds. Physically, she is no match for Williams."

Hetzler crossed his arms. "The sad truth is that she was no match for him emotionally, either. We can hate her, we can *despise* her, for not protecting her son, but we all *must* take into account the *fact* that she suffered irreparable, horrifying, profound damage during the course of her own childhood. Mrs. Elsie Underhill told us that, didn't she? She said that the man who killed Angela's mother killed something inside Angela, too."

Hetzler clasped his hands behind his back, looking thoughtful. "Angela was forced to take a terrible, crushing, and *flawed* lesson to heart during that long dark night when she lay pinned beneath her mother's dead body: she learned that if you speak up in defense of your own child, you will *not* survive. She learned that the *only* possible result of attempting to deflect the violence of a lover's rage is death."

He nodded again, raising his eyes above the heads of the jurors. "We can hate her. We can despise her. We can smugly assure ourselves that *we* would have been strong enough to act differently. But we *cannot* blame her. Angela Underhill sustained such devastating psychological damage when her mother was shot to death before her nine-year-old eyes that she was rendered *wholly* incapable of defending her child from Albert Williams.

"Three years ago, another child died at the hands of a vicious, cowardly bully named Joel Steinberg. The dead child's name was Lisa Steinberg, and her adoptive father battered her into a coma, then left her body lying on the bathroom floor for twelve hours. Steinberg went out to dinner with friends for several hours, and his common-law wife, Hedda Nussbaum, did nothing to help little Lisa. She *didn't* call nine-one-one. She *didn't* call the pediatrician. She didn't even *try* to make the little girl more comfortable — with a blanket, or a pillow.

"Hedda Nussbaum waited until Joel Steinberg told her it was time to take Lisa to a hospital, but all charges were dropped against Hedda Nussbaum, in exchange for her testimony against Steinberg."

Hetzler unclasped his hands. "Here's what I find fascinating about that case. Do any of you remember what Nussbaum and Steinberg did in the hours before they carried Lisa's body to the emergency room?"

Several of the jurors nodded.

"They smoked crack cocaine together, didn't they?" he said. "For seven hours, according to Nussbaum. So that means Hedda Nussbaum was alone in that apartment with little Lisa for five *hours* — five *hours* in which she could have called an ambulance, or a friend, or a doctor. But she didn't do any of those things. And the State of New York decided that she wasn't *responsible* for Lisa's death because she had been battered herself to the point that she was no longer *capable* of exercising the sort of judgment necessary to saving the life of her own adopted daughter.

"Ms. Bost, the prosecutor, asked you to weigh the character of Stephanie Keller against that of Angela Underhill. I ask you now to weigh something *else:* the State's treatment of Hedda Nussbaum against its treatment of Angela Underhill."

Hetzler started pacing slowly, as though considering the import of his thoughts for the very first time himself.

"Two women *equally* ravaged by domestic brutality, two women *equally* damaged, *equally* overwhelmed by the violence inflicted on their children, *equally* incapable of normal human response in the face of that tragedy. One white, one black. One privileged and highly educated, one equipped with a high-school diploma."

He'd reached the empty witness box so he spun on his heel to pace slowly back toward the gallery.

"Both of them agree to testify against the men who battered their children to death, and yet only *one* of them gets charged *alongside* that man, only *one* of them is held responsible for *his* actions."

Hetzler stopped, midstride, and looked at the jurors.

"Guess which one of those women was shown mercy by the State of New York, ladies and gentlemen."

He turned toward Bost, and glared.

"Go ahead. *Guess.*"

Galloway didn't bother with Hetzler's prolonged theatrics when she got to her feet. She jumped right in, bristling with indignation on her client's behalf.

"You've heard Angela Underhill's version of her son's death. You've heard the testimony of a woman who was both racked with the pain of cancer surgery and stupefied by powerful drugs. You've heard the words of a woman suffering from three generations of tragedy, desperate to save the life of her last remaining descendant."

Here she paused. "What you have *not* heard is the testimony of Albert Williams, in his own defense. And it's important that I remind you, right now, that you cannot hold this against him. His having chosen *not* to take the stand is no admission of guilt, or of innocence. You were told this, ladies and gentlemen of the jury, at the outset of this trial. It is no less true now. The fact that Albert Williams has not taken the stand to speak to you directly can*not* factor into your decision, at the culmination of this trial.

"And now I'm finished with what you are not allowed to consider. Here is what you *can* —"

She held up one finger. "First, consider that Angela Underhill has everything to gain by convincing you she had no hand in her son's abuse, or in his death. We have *only* her word that the injuries inflicted on her son, Teddy, were inflicted by Albert Williams. She is the *only* so-called eyewitness produced by the prosecution, the *only* person who told you that she *allegedly* saw Williams beating her child. Can we take her words at face value, can we take them as the words of a disinterested party? No, we can't."

Up went finger number two. "Second, we have the testimony of Stephanie Keller, the former emergency-room nurse. Ms. Keller *never* saw Albert Williams mistreating Teddy Underhill. She *never* saw him hit the child, she *never* saw him cause the boy even the slightest *discomfort*. And when Ms. Keller asked the boy's mother how these injuries had occurred, what did Angela Underhill do? She ran from the building, and refused to speak with Keller further. What was the basis of Keller's claim that Albert Williams had harmed Teddy Underhill? Disembodied voices in an air shaft, ladies and gentlemen, the vague echoes of voices she heard while under the influence of the most powerfully intoxicating, mind-altering *drugs* known to medical science. Nothing more than that."

Galloway lofted finger number three, a benediction.

"Third, you heard the testimony of Mrs. Elsie Underhill — a widow, an upstanding member of this community — who raised her granddaughter following the murder of the girl's mother, her *own* daughter. Think about that, ladies and gentlemen — think about what's at stake for Mrs. Underhill, the powerful loyalties that must have informed her testimony. She's lost her husband, lost her daughter, and lost her great-grandson. The only family member she has left in the world is Angela Underhill — and the unborn child Angela now carries."

Galloway gave her three-pronged hand a little bounce in the air. "*Think* about that, ladies and gentlemen. *Think* about the tragedies suffered by Mrs. Elsie Underhill, and then ask yourself whether she could have brought herself to condemn the last living member of her own family — whether she could have taken that stand and told us the *truth* about who hurt little Teddy — when by so doing Mrs. Elsie Underhill would lose her granddaughter, Angela, on top of everything *else* she's been made to endure.

"Mr. Hetzler just urged you to consider the facts of the case, ladies and gentlemen," she continued. "*The facts of the case.*

"Angela Underhill. Stephanie Keller. Mrs. Elsie Underhill" — she looked at her raised trio of fingers. "You've heard the *testimony* of these three so-called witnesses, ladies and gentlemen —"

Galloway's hand fell like a slingshot-struck songbird. "But they did not tell you even a single *fact.*"

She shook her head.

"My colleague Mr. Hetzler urged you to consider the facts of the case, but *are* there any facts in this case?" she asked. "Only one: Teddy Underhill is dead."

Galloway stepped closer to the jury box. "But we *cannot* know who killed him. We have no hard evidence — no *facts* — to consider, just the word of three women whose testimony is tainted by self-interest, by the ravages of disease, and by the unbearable burden of misplaced familial loyalty. The homicide investigation offers nothing else, the pathologist's report offers nothing else — and yet Mr. Hetzler and Ms. Bost just stood up right here in this courtroom and told you to drop a noose of circumstantial evidence — of bushwah and *hearsay* — around the neck of Albert Williams, and they want you to pull that noose tight.

"They want you to convict Albert Williams on the basis of a *drug* addict's testimony. A woman so amoral, so inhuman, she was willing to *sell* her own child for crack money. A woman who lied and lied and lied, whenever it suited her purpose."

Galloway paused, chin high. "Don't you let them get *away* with it."

61

When Galloway returned to her seat at the defense table, the judge began his instructions to the jury.

I didn't catch his opening words because Cate leaned over and whispered, "Was Galloway actually trying to imply that this is some kind of *lynching?*" into my ear.

I shrugged. "Hell if I know."

"To find the defendants guilty of murder in the second degree," said the judge, "you must —"

Cate interrupted with a whispered "What happened to *first?*"

The bailiff glared in our general direction, but we weren't the only source of noise competing for His Honor's airtime. The crowd fairly brimmed with hisses and grumbles.

"Order!" The judge smashed his gavel down.

"I *will* clear this courtroom," he said, "if

those of you in the gallery do not immediately contain yourselves."

Chastened, we all shut right the hell up.

His Honor started up again where he'd left off.

Cate reached into her purse and pulled out a pen and a piece of paper.

"With malice aforethought," continued the judge, "which means that you *must* find —"

Cate poked me in the knee and I looked down.

She'd scrawled *I still don't get why they can't charge them with murder in the first degree* across the back of a crumpled receipt.

I took the pen from her, writing *First's only for special circumstances. Like if you killed a cop, or more than one person.*

"To find either or both defendants guilty of manslaughter," said the judge, "you must —"

Cate grabbed the pen back out of my hand, scrawling *How can the death of a child not be considered a special circumstance?*

I wrote *I know!!!* beneath that, as the judge started explaining that only Angela Underhill faced a charge of filing a false report with the police.

The judge's charge to the jury was over

far more quickly than I thought it should have been, given the eight counts each against Albert and Angela. How could anyone drive the enormity of all that evil home in under ten minutes?

The bailiff said, "All rise," and Cate dropped her pen and receipt back into her purse before we got to our feet.

I watched the judge leave, then the jury.

The room filled with pent-up commentary in their absence.

I looked at Cate. "What happens now?"

"I guess we wait."

"Fuck that," I said. "Let's go pester Bost."

The prosecutor very kindly allowed us to tag along behind when she returned to her office.

"I just want to dump my papers on my desk and make a phone call or two," she said. "Then I'm taking off these damn heels and putting my feet up."

Bost waited while Cate and I signed the guest register and stuck name-badge stickers onto our lapels.

"Is Kyle here?" I asked.

Bost turned to the receptionist. "Have you seen him, Therese?"

"Five minutes ago," the woman replied.

"Stick your head in his office on the way by."

Kyle looked up and nodded when we reached his doorway, pointing at the phone held to his ear before holding up a pinched thumb and forefinger to let us know he'd join us shortly.

Bost nodded and continued down the hallway, Cate and I trailing in her wake.

"So now we just wait for the jury?" asked Cate when we'd all kicked off our shoes in Bost's office.

"This is the tough part," she replied. "Never gets any easier."

"Do you have any sense of what they're going to decide?" I asked.

Bost leaned back in her chair. "You never *really* know what a jury will do. That's what makes it so tough."

"They can't believe Galloway's whole lynching speech, though," said Cate, "can they? I mean, that was absolutely *appalling.*"

"I have no idea whether she swayed anyone with that specific part of her closing," answered Bost. "But she did a good job of pointing out the weaknesses in the state's case against Williams."

"Was her implication that this is a lynching supposed to convince the African American jurors?" I asked.

"Sure," said Bost. "Or any of the jurors."

I felt awkward about my next question. "Okay, but, um . . . does it not occur to Galloway that she's, like, white and you're —"

Bost laughed. "Not?" she said. "Galloway's willing to pull anything out of her ass she can when it comes to slamming the honesty of the prosecution."

Kyle rapped the doorway with his knuckles. "Is someone calling Louise racist again?"

"I don't get it," I said.

"Honey," said Kyle, "you should have heard all the church ladies rank on this poor woman during her *last* case."

"I was going after a young guy who'd shot a Korean storekeeper and his wife to death during a robbery," said Bost.

"Every time she walked down the hallway, outside the courtroom," continued Kyle, "some righteously indignant bunch of grandmas would start the chorus up again."

"*Just* loudly enough for my ears," said Bost. " 'Call herself a *black* woman, cutting down that flower of young African manhood the way she do.' "

Cate's eyes went wide. "That's absolutely —"

"*Fucked,*" I finished for her.

"Yeah," said Bost. "Tell me about it."

568

"So who was it this time, Marty or Galloway?"

"You have to ask?" said Bost.

"Galloway. What a peach." Kyle rolled his eyes.

" 'Peach' is not the first word that springs to mind," I said.

"I'm pretending to be professionally objective," said Kyle. "Give me a break, here, Maddie."

"Break given," I said.

He looked at Bost. "How'd your closing go?"

"Fingers crossed," said Bost.

"Knock wood," added Cate, reaching toward Bost's desk to do just that, "but *I* think Louise was magnificent."

"How long will this all take?" I asked. "The jury and everything?"

"Nothing's going to happen today," said Kyle. "But I'm betting this one will take them a good long while."

"And how long is 'a good long while,' usually?" asked Cate.

"I doubt they'll come back before the weekend," said Bost.

Kyle consulted the ceiling, lips pursed. "My money's on Wednesday morning."

"From your lips . . ." said Bost.

"Longer is better?" asked Cate.

"Longer means they're really trying to do the right thing," said Bost.

"*Next* Wednesday morning?" I asked.

"You've got someplace better to be?" asked Kyle.

"I just have this wedding coming up."

"Anyone I know?" asked Kyle.

"My mother."

"*Mazel tov,*" he said.

62

I was back at the Catalog the next morning. I didn't know what else to do. The idea of waiting for the jury to come in at home in the apartment drove me crazy. All I could think about was the dead guy, and how much my arm itched inside the filthy cast.

Yumiko picked up the phone around ten o'clock.

"Some guy for you," she said, punching the Hold button. "Kyle. Line Two."

I thought about what Bost had said yesterday, how the jury taking a long time meant they were serious.

Not good.

I picked up the receiver and pressed the blinking cube beneath it.

"This can't be good," I said. "You told me Wednesday."

"It's not the jury," said Kyle.

"You just called to say 'I love you'?"

"I just called to say Teddy's mother went

into labor last night."

I sucked in my breath.

"A little girl, Maddie," he said. "Six pounds."

I burst into tears.

"Maddie?" he said. "Are you okay?"

"No."

"Honey . . . I'm so sorry."

I sniffed. "I can't stand it."

"I know."

"What happens now?"

"With the jury?"

"With everything," I said.

"I don't know. They probably won't wait for her."

"To recover?"

"It was a C-section. I don't know how long that takes."

"Me either," I said.

"They'll give the verdict when they're ready."

"What happens if she's not there?"

"Depends on what they decide. If they don't convict her, it doesn't matter."

"And if they *do* convict her?"

"I don't know. I've never had this happen during a trial."

We were quiet for a minute.

"A girl," I said. "That's just so horrible."

"I have to go. Louise will call you later, okay?"

"Okay," I said. "Thank you."

"Sure you're okay?" he asked.

"I'm alive," I said. "It doesn't get better than that, right?"

"Sweetie. Just know I'm thinking about you, okay? Go home early. Call me if you need anything?"

"I will," I said. "Thank you."

I put down the phone, then looked out the window into the air shaft.

It was snowing. Again.

I turned in my chair to face Yumiko. "It's just that trial thing."

"Out in Queens?"

"Yeah."

"What happened? They let those fuckers go?"

"Worse," I said.

"What's worse than that?"

"The mother had another baby. Last night."

"Wow," she said. "That *sucks*."

"Yeah. It does."

Pagan walked in. "You have plans for lunch?"

"Not really," I said.

"Hey," she said, "are you crying?"

"I think I'm done now. Maybe."

573

"What the hell happened?"

"The woman in that trial, she had a baby," said Yumiko.

Pagan gave me a pained smile of commiseration. "And I've just come to ruin your day even further."

"I'm not sure that's possible," I said.

"We need to pick up our bridesmaid dresses from Laura Ashley," said my sister, wincing.

"Wow," I said. "You were right."

"Who the fuck is Laura Ashley?" asked Yumiko.

"Trust me," Pagan told her, "you so do *not* want to know."

"Some white chick," said Yumiko.

"Pretty much the whitest chick who ever *lived*," said Pagan.

"And then some," I said.

"Better you than me, then." Yumiko shivered.

"Laura fucking *Ashley*," said Pagan. "You believe this shit?"

We were standing just inside the entrance of the aforementioned store's Upper East Side location.

Looking around the frothy, luxuriously fitted boutique, none of it quite seemed real. Even the sound of footsteps here was silenced by the thick, expensive carpeting.

Are these my people? Do I even have *a people?*

"I'm still struggling with the concept that we've been conscripted as bridesmaids for our own mother's wedding," Pagan said.

"*Fourth* wedding —"

"And that the new stepsisters we have not yet *met* had the unmitigated chutzpah to pick out our fucking dresses."

I nodded.

"Do you feel like we died and got relegated to tufted-chintz hell?" she asked. "Seriously. Maybe we got hit by a bus out on the sidewalk. Maybe this is our punishment for all of fucking *eternity.*"

"I don't know," I said. "What are the chances Satan reeks of rose petals?"

"I think they call it brimstone."

"Brimstone is sulphur. It smells like rotten eggs."

"How do you even fucking *know* shit like that?" she asked.

"I spent three years in Syracuse," I said. "Trust me, hell is Upstate. And it smells like rotten eggs."

"I'm getting this creepy feeling that someone wants to reincarnate me as an overstuffed love seat."

"Let's just get it over with. Find a sales chick."

"How can you tell who works here and who's just shopping?" she asked. "They're all remote-controlled zombie-assassin Stepford-pod androids enslaved by the receiver units tucked inside those humongous plaid hairbows."

"Pagan, we can take these bitches. We're still in the goddamn *Social Register*."

"No fucking way. They can smell fear. They'll turn on us with their capped zombie *teeth*."

"Oh, for chrissake," I said. "We survived the *Granta* Bitches. Don't *make* me slap you."

I walked over to the nearest counter, Pagan trailing behind me.

"Hi," I said, addressing the zombie Stepford-pod android directly in front of us.

"My name is Courtney, how may I help you today?"

Courtney. God help us.

"We're here to pick up two bridesmaid dresses?" I said.

"Mm-hm," said Courtney, head bobbing. "What's the name of the wedding party?"

"McClintock," said Pagan.

"Mc*Cormack*," I said.

Pagan shrugged. "Like it will matter six months from now."

The woman ignored us. "Here we are — let me just go to the back and bring those out for you to try on, all righty?"

"Thank you so much," I said.

"This is going to suck," said Pagan, the minute she walked away. "I bet you they picked something yellow. Or pink. Floral monstrosities with fat sashes and great big foofy sleeves. Big and foofy and lame."

"We're going to look like a pair of fucking cabbage-rose armchairs," I said. "Mark my words."

I saw Courtney coming back with a big fat pair of dry-cleaning-bag-encased dresses draped over her arms.

"Um," I said. "You may want to close your eyes."

"Fucking *plaid?* You have got to be kidding me."

"It's a nice *dark* plaid. Be grateful for small mercies."

"Small mercies my ass. What next, they beat us to the ground with haggis and light us on fucking *fire?*"

"Yes. If we're lucky."

Courtney gave us a capped zombie-pod Stepfordian smile.

"I'll get you set up in a dressing room, all

577

righty?" she said.

On the bright side, the damn things fit us like big, fat, foofy-sleeved plaid gloves — even with my cast.

There was a polite little knock on the dressing room door. "It's Courtney? I forgot to give you something?"

"Come on in," I said. "We're dressed."

The door swung outward and she stepped into the plush little cell with us.

"These are your headbands," she said, holding up a pair of the damn things. "In matching tartan."

I started laughing so hard it made me choke.

"Is everything all right?" asked Courtney.

No longer able to inhale, I waved my hand, helpless, and collapsed onto the room's tufted little cabbage-rose chaise longue over in the corner.

I beat the thing's femme-y down-filled upholstery with my left fist, positively *gagging* with laughter.

Alarmed, Courtney tossed the headbands in Pagan's general direction before scuttling out backwards and shoving the door firmly closed behind her.

My sister stared down at the pair of big padded-plaid horseshoes that now lay at her feet, centered akimbo on the room's lushly carpeted floor.

"Shoot me," she said. "Shoot me right fucking *now.*"

Dean called that night, a few hours after they cut my cast off.

"Can't wait to see you, too, Bunny. I'll miss the rehearsal dinner, but I should make Bar Harbor by midnight if I drive your car straight up from New Jersey."

"I can't believe it's not possible to come from La Tuque direct."

"It's four hundred bucks to change my flight. I can't ask Christoph to cover that."

Right, like Astrid doesn't tip more than that for cocktails she doesn't actually consume.

"It just seems crazy," I said. "You sure you don't want to blow off Maine?"

"It's your mom's *wedding.*"

"So you'll catch the next one. No biggie."

"How's your arm look?" he asked.

"Pale. Kind of skinny."

"Can't wait to see it," he said. "Sucked having twenty pounds of plaster between me and your fine buxom self."

"Yeah," I said. "Don't I know it?"

63

I was packing for Maine when the phone rang Tuesday morning out in the living room. My entire closet's dispirited contents lay spewed across our unmade bomb crater of bed, a sartorial nuke-test-detritus cacophony.

But at least my right arm was free of plaster.

I jogged away from the textile-explosion's epicenter, relieved.

Pagan tossed me the receiver. "Your buddy Kyle."

"Hey," he said as I sank down into the sofa.

"Hey back," I replied. "What's up?"

"The jury."

"How soon?"

"An hour, tops. Hit the subway right now and you'd be here in time."

"I don't know if I can," I said.

"Bullshit," said Kyle. "Get on that train."

No good-bye, no chance to tell him our rental car was already parked out front — just *click* and then dial tone.

Pagan gave me the hairy eyeball, arms crossed. Her bag and Sue's stood at parade rest in the front hall, ready for deployment.

"Listen," I began.

She shook her head, pissed. "Madeline, do not even *think* about fucking with me."

"We're making a pit stop."

"No."

"It's on the way."

"No."

"The car's on my Amex and I'm driving," I said. "You don't like it, go stick out your thumb on Sixth Avenue — see how fast *that* gets your ass to fucking Bangor."

I heard her say "Bitch," but I was already sprinting to grab my toothbrush and the stupid plaid dress still veiled in its dry-cleaning plastic.

Pagan called shotgun, but Sue was the better co-pilot so I sent her grumbling to the backseat instead.

"You're bitch-at-the-switch as consolation," I told Pagan, handing her my pile of CDs.

I started the car and she tossed me some Hendrix.

Sue took one look at the dashboard clock, said, "FDR," and we shot uptown like a Roman candle through gift wrap.

"Bridge or tunnel?" I asked, as we streaked past Twenty-ninth Street.

"Tunnel," said Sue. "No question."

Sliding down toward the narrow tube's eastern mouth, I hit the exact-change toll-bucket with a fistful of quarters, through so fast we set off the scofflaw buzzer — nothing but net.

Twenty minutes later I parked next to Kyle's car outside the courthouse.

"I am so fucking carsick," said Pagan, telescoping her legs out of the backseat. "You drive like shit."

I could see Kyle's head craning, anxious, from behind the crowd inside.

I pointed him out to Pagan. "He'll get us through fast. There's a decent bathroom pretty close."

My adrenaline was contagious by that point.

"No worries," she said, taking a deep breath. "I'm cool, so let's boogie."

Boogie we did.

The courtroom felt different that morning. Like there was some kind of low-grade, sub-auditory buzz infecting everyone inside.

"That's her up there?" whispered Sue. "The mother?"

I nodded.

"What is she, our age?" she asked.

"Younger," I said.

Kyle leaned forward to quiet us, warning finger to his lips.

The bailiff stood up to say, "All rise."

We got to our collective feet, the room filling with muffled clatter.

The judge's door opened slowly outward behind his empty chair, and then the man himself strode in, broad shoulders proud beneath his robes' black yoke.

"Hear ye, hear ye," intoned the bailiff. "The Supreme Court of the County of Queens is now in session, Judge Malcolm Arthur presiding."

Someone coughed behind us.

Another door opened and the jury filed into its box.

Pagan leaned in close. "This is *intense.*"

I nodded and grabbed her hand, glad to have her and Sue beside me.

Another cough, and Judge Arthur turned toward the jury. "In the case of the State of New York versus Albert Williams, has the jury reached a verdict?"

One of the elder church ladies stood up. "We have, Your Honor."

The bailiff walked toward her and she gave him a folded slip of paper, which he ferried back to the judge.

The judge unfolded this missive and looked down at it, taking a moment to digest its contents.

Pagan clenched my hand harder.

The judge raised his head slowly, handed the paper down to the waiting bailiff, and then shifted his gaze back toward the jury's elected captain.

When the bailiff had carried the printed verdict back to the solemn woman standing in the jury box, the judge cleared his throat.

"Madame Foreperson," he asked, "how do you find?"

I held my breath and closed my eyes.

"On the count of murder in the second degree," she read, "we find the defendant Albert Williams not guilty," she said.

My eyes snapped open, tears already pricking at their corners.

"On the count of manslaughter in the first degree," she continued, "we find the defendant —"

Here Pagan gave my hand another squeeze.

"Guilty."

I exhaled with relief, ducking forward to catch Kyle's eye.

He mouthed "Yes," giving me a new thumbs-up when each of the next six counts came back guilty, as well.

Pagan hadn't let go of my left hand yet, but as the bailiff carried the leaf of paper inscribed with Angela Underhill's verdict toward the judge, Sue threaded her fingers through my own on the right.

Judge Arthur unfolded this second sheet, again taking a moment to absorb its contents before looking toward the jurors in turn.

"In the case of the State of New York versus Angela Underhill," he said, "has the jury reached a verdict?"

"We have, Your Honor," replied the woman to whom he'd addressed his words.

"Madame Foreperson," asked the judge, "how do you find?"

I closed my eyes, gripping Pagan's hand even harder, and all I could hear was the woman's voice saying "Not guilty, not guilty, not guilty . . ." over and over again, until she reached the very last count and paused.

"On the count of filing a false police report," she said, as Sue gripped my other hand, "we find the defendant *guilty.*"

The room exploded.

I watched Elsie reach across the railing

between herself and the defense table, in order to hug her no-longer-pregnant grand-daughter close.

Good God.

When she turned around and saw me, she dropped her eyes.

I felt comforting hands settle on my shoulders, but I shook them off.

I looked over at Kyle. His eyes were clenched shut, and he shook his head slowly back and forth.

"What does that mean?" Pagan asked him. "They're just going to let her *go?*"

"They'll set bail first," he said. "She'll probably get probation."

The judge banged his pointless gavel, calling for order.

My voice was hoarse. "I can't *be* here anymore."

Pagan tugged at my wrist, her hand gentle.

"No," I said. "I just can't fucking *stand* it."

"Maddie," said Kyle.

"She got off, Kyle. She fucking got *off!*"

There was a glitter of shared pain in his eyes, but I bolted out of that room all the same.

64

I didn't stop until I reached the rental car out in the parking lot, and then I just let my body go slack against the driver's-side door — head down, hands thrown loose across its cold blue roof.

I didn't shut my eyes or anything, just lay there staring into the tweed-covered crook of my elbow.

I watched my steamy breath unfurl against the overcoat's wrinkled warp and weft until the fuzz escaping its married threads of black-and-white wool bowed down, burdened with tiny beads of exhaled moisture.

I didn't move or even look up when someone sat on the hood beside me, making the car's body dip beneath the added weight.

"Dude," said Pagan, "that *sucked*."

She insinuated the point of an elbow into my exposed rib cage.

I leaned over and threw up all over the asphalt.

■ ■ ■ ■

Northeast Harbor, Maine
February 13, 1991

■ ■ ■ ■

65

So of course we showed up thirty minutes late to the rehearsal dinner, and I was dressed like shit besides.

That we'd only stopped twice to piss during nine otherwise-straight hours of incredibly fast driving didn't count in our favor, nor had I expected it to.

I looked around for Dean, hoping maybe he'd gunned the Porsche and created a rent in the fabric of the time-space continuum in order to have beaten us there. No such luck.

It wasn't like anyone had started sitting down already once we got to the party. The guests were still milling around a hunter-green-painted clubhouse bar, swilling gin but disdaining the offered platters of shrimp, baked morsels of Brie *en croûte,* and bacon-wrapped water chestnuts.

"Slightly better food than I was expecting," said Sue. "For a WASP wedding. I practically starved to death at yours, Madeline."

"I don't think we're allowed to bitch about anything," said Pagan, "when we show up this late."

"Who's bitching?" asked Sue.

At least I'd remembered to tuck Dean's and my wedding gift into the rental car. It was a rather elegant Chinese-red lazy susan, fitted out with a series of blue-and-white glazed bowls — the perfect delivery system for those garnishes with which one hoped to enliven suppers of Minute Rice and indifferent Episcopalian curries.

"There's Mom," said Pagan, grabbing my arm. "Let's go say hello."

"I am sorely in need of some ice water," I said.

"What, no gin?" she asked.

"Maybe later. Right now I'm just thirsty."

"Call yourself a WASP?" Sue shook her head. "No pain, no gain."

"Are you sure *you're* not an Episcopalian?" I asked.

"I'm just good with the blending," she said.

"*Big* smile, bitches," said Pagan. "Time to make the proverbial effort."

We snaked our way through the drinking crowd toward Mom, single file.

"Oh *fuck* me," I said, halfway there. "Larry's wearing a kilt."

They'd split the three of us up at dinner, scattering our place cards around the room to ensure that we'd have no actual support from one another.

"You're the bride's *daughter?*" The woman beside me pulled her head back, further exaggerating the cords of her tennis-leathery neck.

"The eldest child," I said. "Yes."

She peered at me, squinting with distaste at my outfit. Had there been a pince-nez handy, she'd have landed the part of "opera-bound matron" in a *New Yorker* cartoon circa 1934, hands down.

"I had a court date this morning," I explained. "In Queens."

"You're an attorney?" she asked.

"Witness," I said. "Homicide."

With that, she abandoned me for conversation with the dining partner on her right.

Fine.

Whatever.

Rescued from ignominy by the delivery of a paillard of chicken in taste-free cream sauce, I turned toward the tiny octogenarian man seated to my left.

"I couldn't help overhearing what you

were just discussing," he said.

"The sorry excuse for my appalling tardiness?" I asked.

"Just so," he said, blue eyes twinkling beneath an unkempt white hedge of eyebrows. "I believe you mentioned a homicide."

"I'm not sure it's a topic you'd appreciate my going into, over dinner."

"Try me," he said, patting my hand. "For an old coot, I'm surprisingly tough."

"I first got involved last September."

"Who'd been killed?"

"A little boy," I said, "the day he turned three years old."

"Did you see it?"

I shook my head. "I found his bones five months later, in a cemetery. That's why I had to testify."

"And who did it?"

"The mother's boyfriend. I wanted to hear the verdict this morning. That's why we got here late."

"Did they get him?" my companion asked.

"Manslaughter," I said. "I'll miss the sentencing, I guess."

"New York State?"

I nodded.

"Fifteen years," he said. "Probably out in seven."

I winced and took a sip of my water. "His mother as good as got off scot-free."

"Fuckers," he said.

I choked.

My new friend gave me a sturdy clap on the back.

"I beg your pardon," he said. "No doubt that editorial comment caught you rather by surprise."

I laughed, eyes still watering.

"What are your thoughts concerning your own mother's impending nuptials?" he asked.

I hedged. "Larry strikes us all as a very nice man."

"Well played," he said. "But don't worry, I have no dog in this hunt. I'm only here because I'm old as hell and I don't go south for the winter."

"In that case, I give him six months."

"Generous," he said, resting his gnarled hands on the white tablecloth so they bracketed his untouched plate of chicken.

"You're not going to eat?" I asked.

"One gets tired of nursery food. Creamed chicken and peas, a dab of wild rice."

"Innocuous, at least."

"I'm saving up for dessert," he said, as people started clinking their water glasses with random cutlery.

I lifted a miniature slice of rye bread from my butter plate. "A toast."

"Witty girl."

"Thank you," I said.

A bunch of old Yalies started singing about losing their lambs.

My dinner partner flexed his fingers, and I noticed that he wore a gold crest ring on each pinkie. They didn't match.

"Tell me about those," I said, pointing.

"Sharp eyes."

I shrugged. "They look interesting."

"They are," he said. "I inherited them, one from each grandfather."

"Did you like your grandfathers?"

"Never met them," he said. "Only their widows, both of whom I loved a great deal."

"That's quite a story," I said.

"There's more," he said.

"Tell me."

"My grandfathers went down with the *Titanic*," he said. "Each of them took off his ring and gave it to his wife once he'd made sure of her place in a lifeboat."

The Yalies sat down.

"I'm going to have to stand up and say something," I said.

"You're the daughter relied upon for a good toast?"

"Indeed," I said.

"You look as though you're about to ask me for a favor."

I nodded. "Would you mind terribly if I mentioned your rings?"

"I'd be delighted."

"Thank you," I said. "By one's mother's fourth wedding, it's tough coming up with fresh material."

My new friend started dinging his water glass with a dessert spoon.

I downed a hopeful slug of water and stood up.

The room grew quiet, all eyes on me.

"I promised our mother that I would not mention the monogrammed towel we kids gave her last Christmas," I said, "so I won't. Except for the part about how we had to put a hyphen at the end of her initials, so people would know they continued around on the back."

General laughter, with one hearty basso *Hear, hear* from across the room's expanse.

"We're already tremendously fond of Larry," I continued. "How can one help but admire a potential stepfather who introduces himself over lunch at 'Twenty-One' by imploring his fiancée's gathered children to join him in a shrimp cocktail?"

Someone called "Attaboy, Lawrence!" from the bar.

I nodded. "I'd like to offer two bits of advice to my dear mother, Constance, the first of which runs as follows: Mummie, when that special time arrives, during the course of your wedding night, remember the advice Queen Victoria gave each of her daughters: 'Just close your eyes and think of England.' "

Brays of laughter, all around.

I dropped my eyes, waiting for quiet.

"My second bit of wisdom has more serious import," I said, "though I learned it only this evening, from my charming companion at dinner."

I held my glass with both hands and looked across the room at my mother.

"A good marriage," I said, "is when you know the other person will always make sure you have a place in the lifeboat."

I dropped one hand, lifting my glass high. "My wish is that you and Larry will enjoy that loving confidence in one another, throughout all the many-splendored years to come."

I sipped my water, all those around me reached for their cocktails, and I sat down amidst a round of hearty applause.

"Or for the next six months," said my new friend.

"Whichever comes first."

The old man clinked my glass with his.

"Hear, hear," he said. "Hear, hear indeed."

I looked up and saw Dean across the room, standing in the doorway to the bar. He hadn't caught sight of me yet.

I wondered which piece of news I should tell him first: that I'd killed a man, or that I was pregnant.

I got up and started walking toward him.

"You made amazing time," I said, standing on tiptoe to kiss his cheek back in the bar. "I thought you wouldn't get here until midnight. You must've broken the sound barrier in the Porsche."

"Bunny, I didn't drive."

"You came straight from La Tuque after all?"

"No," he said. "Look, let's go sit down, okay?"

His face was ashen.

I felt cold, ominous fingers of angst twining like briars around my heart. "I don't want to sit down. Tell me here."

Tell me standing up, so it doesn't hurt as much. So I can run.

He pulled me close, pressing my cheek gently to his chest. "Astrid's dead."

"No she's not," I said.

"She took the Porsche — stole the keys

599

out of my desk. They think she was doing about a hundred and twenty when she hit the concrete. She aimed straight for it — didn't swerve, never hit the brakes."

No she's not. No she's not.

66

Pagan pulled me out behind the church the following morning to savor a last bit of fresh air before the full catastrophe got under way.

Our headbands were firmly in place, our plaid taffeta gowns pressed within an inch of their tartan lives — but we'd donned overcoats and Bean duck boots before stepping outside to brave the cold.

I couldn't feel anything.

"I'm sorry about Astrid. And that whole thing with the trial," she said.

I didn't answer.

"You okay?" she asked.

I started to cry again.

"That poor little kid," she said. "Jesus Christ."

I couldn't answer her.

"Kyle said yesterday that the only way we can stomach it is if we ask the universe to protect his new sister," she said.

"Like she has a chance in hell."

"Maybe she does."

You don't believe it either.

Pagan spread her arms and looked up at the white Maine sky, a plume of breath rising from her mouth.

"Come on," she said, kicking me in the ankle with the rubber edge of her duck boot. "We need to do this."

We joined our hands, then bowed our heads.

"Dear Universe," she said. "It's really important that you take care of that little kid. Because she's going to need it so damn much."

And Astrid. And Teddy.

If there's anything out there resembling a lifeboat, they both deserve seats.

"Thank you, Universe," said Pagan. "You're totally the best."

We stood for a while in silence, then stomped through the snow back to the church doors.

"Why are we even here?" I asked.

"At the wedding?"

"On the *planet.*"

"To seek enlightenment, I guess," said Pagan.

"Which is what?"

My sister thought about that for a moment.

"Enlightenment," she said at last, "is not being an asshole."

And she opened the door.

Summer 1978
Carmel,
California

■ ■ ■ ■

. . . From different throats intone one
  language.
So I believe if we were strong enough to
  listen without
Divisions of desire and terror
To the storm of the sick nations, the rage
  of the hunger-smitten cities
These voices also would be found
Clean as a child's. . . .
    — "Natural Music," Robinson Jeffers

Surely this bond of common faith, this bond of common goal, can begin to teach us something. Surely we can learn, at least, to look at those around us as fellow men and surely we can begin to work a little harder to bind up the wounds among us and to become in our hearts brothers and countrymen once again.

— Robert F. Kennedy
Cleveland City Club
Cleveland, Ohio
April 5, 1968

67

Mom was at the wheel of our Pacer and we'd just crested the big hill after Odello's artichoke fields, headed south out of Carmel on Highway One. The white shoulders of Monastery Beach sloped away toward Point Lobos on our right. Above the monastery to our left, black cows dotted honeyed pastures across Stuyvesant Fish's mountain.

I heard the throaty buzz of a motorcycle swooping downhill in our wake. It had been a week since the carving-knife debacle in Fassett's kitchen.

"I've always thought Stuyvie should invite me to lunch up there," said Mom. "We'd have spinach salad and a cheese soufflé."

"Linen napkins," I said.

"Decent flat silver."

The monastery itself looked vaguely Tuscan: pale clotted-cream walls and a single tower rising from a stand of celadon eucalyptus, capped in roof tiles the deep brick-orange of Mom's favored tanning unguent, Bain de Soleil.

There was a car in front of us, a rusty yellow hatchback. It slowed with a flash of brake lights just before the creek bridge, turn signal on for the monks' long gravel driveway.

The motorcycle couldn't see why we were slowing down and so swung around us to pass, doing a solid fifty. There were two shirtless young guys on it, long hair streaming.

Their bike T-boned into the yellow car with an explosive crack of metal and glass and I watched its rear wheel shimmy up in slow motion, pitching both riders into flight. The driver soared thirty feet, smacking headfirst into a WPA-steel bridge railing. His passenger caught a boot on the car roof and bounced once, high, before plummeting earthward to skid down the asphalt on his bare chest.

And then everything speeded up again and Mom and I were running toward them, the Pacer astride both lanes behind us with its doors winged open.

The guy who'd hit the bridge had a bloody half-softball lump swelling on the side of his forehead. He was trying to sit up but I put my hand on his shoulder. "Don't move, okay? You've hit your head."

He looked up at me, eyes out of sync. His left pupil was huge and black, drifting wide of its mate.

"It hurts," he said.

"The other car's going fast to the monastery. They'll get an ambulance."

He closed his eyes. "Okay."

I heard Mom say, "Madeline?" and turned toward her.

The guy who'd skidded along the road was standing up. She had her arms around him, trying to get him back on the ground again.

"You have to lie down now," she said.

I touched my guy's shoulder. "Don't move."

I ran to Mom and put my hand on her charge's bare back. "She's right. Just lie down for a minute until the ambulance comes."

I helped her lower him to the ground. He curled up on his side and started crying. Mom sat down next to him, Indian-style, one hand gentle on his pale shoulder.

"It's okay . . . it's okay . . ." she said, stretching out each "oh" long and melodic, the way she always had when we were little and sick, her cool hand testing our foreheads for fever, holding our hair back while we threw up.

Mom's white shirt was sopping crimson with the guy's blood now. There were bits of gravel stuck in its lacy weave.

He shivered, and then the force of a sob made his mouth go wide.

"Shhhhh," she crooned. "It's okay."

I looked up and realized we were surrounded by people, their trail of emptied cars stopped behind ours on the highway.

First an ambulance and then a fire truck came wailing over the top of the hill, lights flashing, and then I couldn't see them above the wall of bystanders.

The crowd parted for a pair of gurneys, and then they had both guys in neck-braces and everyone melted away until it was just Mom and me, standing by the side of the road all pale and shaking.

There was a bank of fog paused off the coast — sun low enough now to tip it with apricot and lavender.

"I think we're in shock," I said.

"Hm?" Mom's eyes were unfocused, shiny in the soft light.

"We should go home."

"Yes," she said, peeling the blood-tacky shirt slowly from the flesh of her belly. "Of course."

■ ■ ■ ■

It was ebbing twilight by the time we pulled into our driveway: *l'heure bleu.*

Our house was old for the West Coast, and Spanish — a humbler version of the monastery, embraced by Brothers Grimm cypress trees, green fading to black.

Mom's hands trembled, keys jingling in her lap long after she'd pulled them from the Pacer's ignition.

The fog sidled in, wicking up darkness like ink-thirsty cotton wool.

The car stank of blood so I opened my door, but Mom and I both just sat there, quiet, our seat belts still fastened.

"We need a drink," she said.

"Wine?" I grimaced, knowing the raw-but-sweet whites she favored. At fifteen I already had a taste for the stuff — just not *that* stuff.

Mom shrugged. "There's Scotch. Or maybe it's bourbon."

That dusty half-gallon of Old Crow, another spot of flotsam bobbing abandoned in the S.S. *Pierce Capwell*'s sloppy wake. *Sucks ahoy.*

"I suppose that's what they'd call medicinal," I said.

She climbed out of the Pacer and I followed, each of our steps making the drive-way's gravel crunch underfoot like breakfast cereal.

Mom lifted the garden-gate latch. The stout portal swung outward, sighing on its hinges, and we picked our way single file across the moss-slick bricks beyond.

I hooked a left once we were inside, shouldering open the kitchen door and slid-ing my hand up the wall until I'd flipped the light switch.

Mom stepped in behind me, squinting at the glare.

She didn't say a word, just grabbed her fouled shirt at the waist to yank it up and over her head. She tossed it in the sink and turned on the cold-water tap, then turned back toward me.

Mom's shoulders were slack and the overhead light made her eye sockets blackly hollow. Brown flecks tattooed her bra and the skin of her belly in a faint floral pattern — blood stenciled through lace.

I wet a fistful of paper towels and pressed them into her hand. She closed her fingers around the sodden mass but didn't move again.

I opened the dishwasher, picking out a pair of glasses. "Where's that bourbon?"

"Top of the broom closet," she said.

The Old Crow bottle was half-empty, furred with dust. I pulled it down by its seamed jug-handle and filled our glasses about a third of the way up.

I handed one to Mom and raised my own. The brown liquor gave off fumes: kerosene cut with nail-polish remover.

"Just swallow it fast," said Mom. So I did.

The stuff made my gag-reflex stand at parade attention, and I suddenly understood why Jack Nicholson made all those Road Runner–esque "neet-neet-neet *swamp*" noises whenever he took a nip off his pint of rotgut in *Easy Rider.*

"Jesus," I said, wincing at the burn in my throat. "They should call it Old *Festering* Crow."

Mom tipped her glass back and swallowed a bit herself, then coughed.

"People really drink this shit on purpose?" I asked.

"The first sip is the hardest."

"I should fucking well hope so," I said.

We tipped our glasses back once more.

"It's still putrid," I said.

Mom swirled the bourbon in her glass, smiling at me. "Don't be a chickenshit."

I finished mine off with a third swallow, not wanting to face the prospect of another mouthful after that.

"Old Festering Crow in Mold-Riddled Sneakers," I said when I could breathe again.

Mom took two more sips to finish her own glass, then giggled.

"Yeah, okay," I said. "The aftereffects are decent."

I'd been hooked up to a nice BenGay IV — the burgeoning glow in my belly seeped into every sore muscle and made it go slack. The world was a cozy old place, our kitchen was my spiritual homeland, and the motorcycle guys were going to be okay.

Mom was still holding the wet paper towels. They were probably cold by now, so I took them out of her hand and tossed them in the kitchen garbage.

"I think maybe you need to take a bath," I said.

She shook her head. "I'm tired. I want to lie down now."

I pointed at her bloody stomach.

Mom cleaned herself up with a sponge and some dish soap, standing at the sink. She tossed her bra on top of the shirt already in its deep basin and pulled the tap across to run cold water over them for a moment, then threw away the sponge.

The ship's clock out in our living room chimed eight bells, marking the end of some distant deck-crew's watch.

Mom wandered off to her bedroom.

I watched the dregs of blood-rusty water meandering across white sink porcelain and down the drain, then headed down the unlit kitchen stairs to my own bed, sloppy and loose on bourbon-wrought sea legs.

I lay on top of the covers for maybe half an hour, listening to pop tunes on my clock radio — something new from the Eagles and then Boz Scaggs, Elton John, and Fleetwood Mac — all interspersed with the deejay's chipper patter about mattress sales and the occasional warm flicker of a passing car's headlights across my ceiling.

My bourbon swoon was sneaking away like a soft tide, and then I was just hungry. I stood and started back upstairs, wondering whether Mom would want to eat, too, if I could find anything to make in the kitchen cabinets.

I navigated back through the unlit kitchen and across the dining room, sure of my way even in the dark.

In the hallway outside Mom's bedroom, I raised my hand to knock — softly, in case she'd drifted off to sleep — but I heard soft laughter just before my knuckles touched wood.

"I miss you too," she was saying, and then

615

there was a phone-conversation pause before she laughed again.

I lowered my hand from the door and turned away.

"Why don't you come over right now, Pierce," said my mother. "I can't wait to see you."

There was a sleeping bag tucked in our downstairs hall closet. I took that and my pillow and left the house. No need for a flashlight; the fog had cleared.

I crossed the night-blue driveway, silent and barefoot, then slipped away down trails I'd blazed as a child, on into the moonlit woods.

ACKNOWLEDGMENTS

I am blessed to have Amy Rennert as my agent, and doubly blessed to have Les Pockell and Celia Johnson as my editors at Grand Central Publishing. Thank you all so much for having my back, and for making sure this book became the best I could make it. A fond farewell to the inimitable Susan Richman — you will be greatly missed.

I owe many lifetimes of gratitude to the members of Mysterious Writ, my writing group: Charles King and Marilyn MacGregor (emeriti), Karen Catalona (New Karen), Karen Murphy (Karen Classic), Daisy James ("We're gonna need a bigger moat . . ."), and Sharon Johnson.

Sharon and Julianne, thank you for the Diet Pepsi with Lime, the *Big Love* on demand, and the most excellent hours of procrastination.

To dearest Rae, Janine, and Maggie — you guys are fabulous!

Andi, Ariel, Muffy, and MBH — death to our enemies, O excellent ladies.

BRANCH

DATE DUE

LIGHTNING
TIME

A NOVEL

by Douglas Rees

A DK INK BOOK

DK PUBLISHING, INC.

NEW YORK

A DK INK BOOK
2   4   6   8   10   9   7   5   3   1
DK Publishing, Inc.
95 Madison Avenue
New York, NY 10016
Visit us on the World Wide Web at http://www.dk.com

The text of this book is set in 13 pt. Cloister.
Manufactured in the United States of America.
A catalog record is available from the Library of Congress.
ISBN 0-7894-2458-4

To Dennise,

book aunt

CONTENTS

Part One   *A Man of Many Names*   1

Part Two   *The Invisibles*   109

The Raiders   163

Historical Note   165

LIGHTNING
TIME

PART ONE

A Man of Many Names

ONE

Winter was mounting one last attack on Boston, an army of small, hard flakes that melted when they hit the ground. The road to Concord was a swamp of ice and mud. The horses threw up clumps of the stuff against the underside of our cab, and our wheels were covered to the hubs with it. There was a crackling crunch as our carriage lurched through another patch of rotten ice and into the rut below. The coach tipped crazily, and my mother, my father, and I were all jerked out of our seats.

The coachman got down from his perch and rapped on the door with his whip. "Excuse me, gents, you'll have to help me," he said.

"What is the problem?" my father replied, though that seemed obvious enough to me.

"The horses need a little help."

Grumbling, my father got down from the coach. I jumped out after him.

The front wheels were half-buried in a trench of mud.

"It appears to me you could have gone around this," my father said.

"Yep," the coachman agreed. "Now, here's what I need you to do. Each grab a spoke and pull backwards. This ain't a bad hole, and Dolly and Bill will have us out of it in a minute if you bear a hand. Then, I promise you, sir, we will drive around it."

Swearing under his breath, my father took off his coat and laid hands on a muddy spoke. I went to the other side and gripped mine. The coachman jumped back into his seat and cracked his whip over Bill's and Dolly's heads.

"Now, heave!" the coachman cried.

We heaved. The coach didn't budge.

"Again!" shouted the coachman. "Put your backs into it."

I pulled with all my strength but felt my feet sliding out from under me. I stumbled, caught myself, and heaved again. There was a sucking sound, the wheel turned, and I rolled down with it into the mud. The horses' rear hooves threw more muck as I lay there, splattering me on the only clean places left.

I got up laughing and trying to brush myself off. I looked at my father. He was as muddy as I was. Unlike me, he wasn't laughing. "Not an ideal night to go to a lecture, is it?" I said.

"Come along, gents, it's getting late," the coachman urged.

"Indeed it is not, Theodore," my father snapped. "And we are not going. Turn this cab around, sir," he called to the coachman.

"But Father, we're almost there," I said.

"That is enough, Theodore," my father said.

My mother leaned out of the cab. "Thee are angry,

my love," she said soothingly, "but we must go to the lecture, even as we are."

Mother was a Quaker and still spoke in the old-fashioned way, using "thee" with everyone but God. It was thanks to her that I was there at all, instead of at home with Amy and Talitha, my seven-year-old sisters, and an unwritable Latin composition.

"If we go into the Concord Congregational Church looking like this, we will become a topic of gossip all over Boston," my father said.

"My dear, what people may say does not matter," my mother told him. "What we do does. Thy great-grandfather was at Bunker Hill. Was not he dirty by the end of the day?"

"So was everyone else," my father growled.

"Many people are coming tonight. Many will have walked," my mother said. "And many who came in carriages may also have had to get out and push them. Please, my love. It means much to me."

"Which way would you like to go, sir?" the coachman called down.

"Please, dearest," my mother said.

"Concord," my father called to the coachman.

My mother smiled. "Thee will be glad, Hale," she said. "What we hear tonight will be important."

"Caroline, my love, I deplore what is happening in Kansas Territory as much as any man in Boston," Father said. "But I am not sure that what happens out there matters to Massachusetts."

My parents were at it again, arguing in their politest way over slavery. It was almost all they ever argued about. They adored each other and seemed to agree on everything else. They even said they agreed on slavery. But when it came down to what to do about it, they went around and around and got nowhere. As for me, I was curious. All I knew was what I'd been told, which was what everyone knew.

Once, slavery had been found only south of the Mason-Dixon Line. Then an exception had been made for Missouri. Massachusetts then gave up Maine to raise the number of free states. After that, the number of free and slave states was kept equal. That had been the "Missouri Compromise." It had stood for forty years. Then several new free states came into the Union. The South demanded, and got, a new policy. They insisted that the voters in each state should decide the slave question for themselves. Kansas was the first test of that policy.

Now North and South were each sending armed men there to insure that the new state would be their kind. War had begun last year, and now, in 1857, Americans were still killing each other in "Bleeding Kansas." This was what we were seeking to learn more about. I was glad to be going. Our speaker had taken part in the fighting. It ought to be exciting.

We lurched into Concord at last, and the ruts widened into cobblestoned streets. We clattered up to the doors of the Congregational Church.

There were several other carriages there, and many people hurrying to the church on foot. They were nearly as muddy as we were. Clearly they must have thought that what happened in Kansas mattered to Massachusetts.

My father cheered up a little when he saw so many others in our condition. "Perhaps I ought to go about like this more often," he said. "Looking as I do, no one with a manuscript under his arm would be likely to approach me."

My father was a publisher, and writers often sought him out. His firm, Worth House, was small but well thought of. He published novels mostly, but they were good books. No one looked down on my father for specializing in fiction.

As we shouldered into the church, a tall, sharp-nosed man with a black beard forced his way down the aisle toward us.

"Hello, Hale. I want a word with you in private," he said.

"About what, Mr. Howe?" my father replied as formally as possible. Although my mother and Julia Ward Howe were friends, my father never addressed her husband as anything but "Mister." Dr. Joshua Gridley Howe had been knighted a chevalier by the king of Greece and liked to be called "Chev," but my father refused to do it. "If 'Mister' was good enough for George Washington," he told me once, "it ought to be good enough for Howe."

"As I said, it is a private matter," Dr. Howe repeated.

"Perhaps after the lecture," my father said. "At the moment I am occupied in trying to find three seats together."

"Right this way," insisted Dr. Howe. "I took the liberty of keeping some seats in the front in hopes that you would be coming."

"Indeed," said my father.

But my mother smiled. "We thank thee, Dr. Howe."

He led us up to the front of the church. Mrs. Howe and my mother embraced, as they always did.

When we were seated, I couldn't help looking at the people around us. Nearly everyone who was known for anything in Boston or Concord was there.

Just behind us were Theodore Parker and Bronson Alcott and his family. Alcott, a believer in women's rights, had brought his wife and all his daughters. Mr. Emerson was there with his handyman, Henry Thoreau. Just in front of them were the Reverend Thomas Wentworth Higginson and a man I didn't recognize.

The man soon rose to speak. "Good evening, ladies and gentlemen," he said. "My name is Franklin Benjamin Sanborn. As many of you know, I conduct a school here in Concord. And I am an abolitionist."

There was a scattering of applause when he said this.

"The man whom I am about to introduce to you is also an abolitionist, a far greater one than I. For he has put his principles to the test in the fiery furnace of battle on the windy plains of Kansas. Neither the man nor the principles have been found wanting." Mr. Sanborn brought his fist down on the lectern.

This time the applause was louder.

"I am not free to name this man, though he is known now across the country. There is a price on his head. Our government wants him for crimes it says he has committed, crimes that were carried out in the name of liberty. There may be agents of that government among us tonight, ready to seize him. For that is what it has come to in the land of the free and the home of the brave, my fellow citizens. It has become a crime to fight for liberty. Thus, ladies and gentlemen, I have the honor to introduce to you a criminal. A man without a name. Almost, a man without a country. A wanted man. A hunted man. A patriot and a freedom fighter. A captain of men like himself. Ladies and gentlemen, I give you—"

And Mr. Sanborn sat down.

A few people clapped uncertainly.

In that moment of confusion, a tall, thin, gray man with a fierce jaw strode out from the back of the church to stand before the pulpit. His black suit was worn. His pants were stuffed into high boots that had seen a lot of travel. He looked us over slowly with sharp, dangerous eyes.

"My name is John Brown," he said. His voice was deep, his accent pure old-fashioned Yankee. With his granite face and his broad vowels, he might have been anyone's great-grandfather come back from the dead to address us.

"Praise be to God for the avenging of Israel," a woman called from the back.

Brown put up his hand. "Is there anyone here who would like to arrest me? I am worth two hundred fifty dollars to you."

I looked around. No one moved.

"As my friend Mr. Sanborn says, I am lately come from Kansas. I have done some fighting out there. I mean to go back and fight again. That is why I am here with you tonight. To ask your help for the next campaign. I imagine all of you know that there are really two Kansases now. There is a free Kansas, with its capital at Lawrence, and a slave Kansas, with its capital at Lecompton. The free Kansas is being settled by your friends and neighbors from New England and Ohio. The other is being settled by packs of slavery-loving ruffians and murderers from Missouri and Alabama."

He went on to tell us how his sons had gone out to Kansas Territory first, with fruit saplings and seeds. They had settled farms along Pottawatomie Creek.

But the Border Ruffians from Missouri had kept threatening them, trying to force them to leave. The Missourians didn't intend to stay in Kansas. They were there to make sure that Yankees didn't stay either.

Armed companies of Southerners came in from other states. Finally, some of them from Lecompton marched up to Lawrence and burned it to the ground. They destroyed everything, even the big stone hotel, which had been built to serve as a fortress. Brown, his sons, and their militia company had been marching to save the town but had arrived one day too late.

"And as we stood on that hill and looked at that twisting smoke and those still-rising flames, a messenger arrived. He told us that on the day Lawrence was burned, your own senator, Charles Sumner, had been beaten nearly to death with a cane by a Southern congressman who didn't care for what he had to say about slavery."

A shudder ran through the crowd. Sumner was still not recovered from the attack. And the Southern congressman had received hundreds of canes to replace the one he had broken across our senator's back. The South approved of such behavior. All New England believed it.

"From that time, from that place, I have been an active-duty soldier in the fight for freedom and Kansas," Brown said.

He came a step closer to us and held out his half-opened hands. He looked from one to the other. "Now the one thing all agree on is that two Kansases are too

many. We and the South each reckon that there shall be
only one. The question is, shall it be the free Kansas or
the slave?"

"Free! Free!" some of the people shouted.

Brown put up a hand again. "I wish I could tell you
that it will be so," he said. "But it may very well not be
so. The Southern slavery men understand as well as we
do what is at stake. Not only the future of Kansas, my
friends, but the future of our entire republic. Under the
government's policy, each new state is likely to become
another Kansas. The old promise that slavery would be
confined below the Mason-Dixon Line is dead. The slaver
insists on his right to take what he considers to be his
property—that is to say, another human being—into any
state in the Union. He claims the right to pursue that
property wherever in this land it may attempt to flee from
him, and to compel anyone to help him do it. And the
Congress of the United States has agreed that he has
those rights. That is why there is war now in Kansas."

All around me, people were shifting in their seats.
They were murmuring in agreement. One man across the
aisle stood up, opened his mouth, clenched his fists, and
sat down again.

"Now I have not told you anything you do not already
know," Brown said. "The Fugitive Slave Act and the
Kansas-Nebraska Act have been law for some time. I am
only here to point out that if you do not agree with these
laws, you must do something to oppose them."

"Tell us, tell us!"

My father harrumphed and crossed his arms over his
chest.

"I do not ask you to return with me to Kansas and

fight," Brown said, looking straight at Father. "There are men enough for that. I have five sons waiting for me there—"

We broke into applause.

"—and we have friends enough to do the job. What we need is money for good weapons. In a few more weeks, it will be spring on the prairies again. The fighting will likely start early. Will you not, for the sake of a free Kansas, for a free country, for the sake of the slave yearning for freedom, give what you can?"

The man who had stood up before now rose again. He waved his tall hat over his head and shouted, "I propose we fill this hat with money unless someone here has a bigger one."

There were cheers and applause. The hat started bobbing up and down the pews while people sang hymns and talked.

When it finally reached us, my father took the hat and handed it on immediately.

"One moment, please, Hale," my mother said. She reached into her reticule and took out a silver dollar. I was amazed. Mother's reverence for thrift was profound. Brown must have touched her deeply. I felt in my pocket and found fifteen cents. It was all the money I had for the rest of the week, but I thought of the widow in the Bible who gave all she had, and put it in proudly. I was surprised to see that, although the hat was so heavy it was nearly falling apart, most of the money was nickels, dimes, and pennies.

The hat made its way up past Mr. Emerson and Mr. Thoreau and into the hands of Mr. Sanborn.

"Thank you, thank you, my friends!" Mr. Sanborn

shouted. "This money shall be consecrated to the liberty of man and the honor of God."

"I thank you, my friends," Brown added.

People started singing hymns in different parts of the church. Gradually, they settled on one, and sang it over and over. It made no particular sense, but it was one everybody knew, and it gave release to our feelings.

> *Praise God, from Whom all blessings flow;*
> *Praise Him, all creatures here below;*
> *Praise Him above, ye Heavenly host,*
> *Praise Father, Son, and Holy Ghost.*

While we were singing, Brown disappeared.

People began to file out of the church. We waited with Dr. Howe. When the building was empty, he bent his head close to my father's.

"See here, Hale," Dr. Howe began. "Our friend has a problem. That federal marshal who's followed him here from Kansas is across the street. We need a place to put Brown up for a couple of days. Preferably with someone who is not known to be an active abolitionist. Will you do it?"

"No," my father replied.

"It would only be for a day or two," Dr. Howe said. "We have another house ready to take him. But we fear it may be being watched. We know yours is not."

"That can only mean, sir, that your people have been spying on us," Father snapped. "Thank you for your solicitude, but it was unnecessary. I will never give houseroom to an assassin."

Dr. Howe reddened. "John Brown is no assassin," he answered. "He is a Christian and a fighter for freedom."

"He murdered four men on Osawatomie Creek the night after he failed to save Lawrence, and the whole country knows it," my father replied. "Dragged them from their homes and butchered them with broadswords."

Dr. Howe glared at Father. His jaws worked. At last he said, "There is no proof of that, Worth."

"And what is your marshal waiting to arrest him for if not those murders?" my father said quietly.

"That's true," said a voice behind us.

Father and I turned.

"I am wanted for murder in Kansas. I understand that the charge is not quite accurate, since I did not kill anybody that night myself. But I organized the killing. And I put one bullet into one man to make sure he was dead. Which he was." John Brown turned to Dr. Howe. "It is all right, Chev," he said. "Any place will do for me tonight. It doesn't matter so much, since I won't be taken alive in any case."

Now my mother was standing beside us, her hand in my father's.

"But what had these men done, Mr. Brown?" she asked.

"Done?" Brown said, smiling at her. "Not much. Only threatened other folks who lived along the creek. They promised to kill some Free-Soilers who had the bad sense to live nearby. One old man ran away and froze to death on the prairie because he knew they meant what they said. But I don't reckon there's any great crime in that. The murder of an abolitionist is no crime in Kansas. Had those four men I ordered killed come and killed me instead, there'd be no federal marshal after them."

"But why those four, sir?" my mother insisted.

"Well, ma'am," Brown drawled, "after the slavers

burned Lawrence, I was mighty hot to get back at them any way I could. Those men were well known in our district. I reckoned killing them would have a good effect."

"The effect it seems to have had is to turn Kansas into a war ground," my father said.

"That is so, sir," said Brown. "But I do not apologize for my part in it, since we fight for freedom against slavery. What I did forced every man to choose his side."

"I think our government's policy in Kansas is a scandal," my father said. "I despise its weakness. But I think you seek to split this country in two over slavery. I can never agree to that."

"And what do you propose instead?" Brown asked.

"I detest slavery as much as any man in Boston," my father replied. "But if you destroy the Union, the South will still have its slaves. It is only within the Union that the abolitionist has any hope of victory."

"And what hope is that?" Brown said. "Tell me, sir. I am anxious to know. I have a wife and children I yearn to go home to. If there is some hope of freeing the slaves without fighting, I want to know about it. What hope do you see?"

My father was silent.

"You may be right, sir," Brown agreed. "Perhaps it is better to live in a country where the slaveholder has all the rights and the free man none. I can only say that I have heard the cry of the slave in his chains and it has pierced my heart. This being so, I can only follow my conscience where it leads me. And it has led me to war."

Everyone was silent then.

Mother put her hand on my father's arm. "I believe we should take him in, Hale," she said.

"Indeed?" said my father.

Dr. Howe stared. He was known to be a supporter of women's rights, but he was no more used to seeing a wife disagree in public with her husband than most people.

"If we turn him away and he is captured tonight, then everything that follows from that will be our doing. If we keep him safe for a night or two, we have done our part to preserve his life. That, I think, is our duty." My father started to speak, but my mother went on. "Thee are right, my love, but so is Mr. Brown. He is wanted for his part in murders. But specifically for his part in murdering slavery men. Thee and I know that this is true. Thee say that thee hate slavery, and I know that this is true. Do thee hate it enough to risk something for thy beliefs?"

"I won't risk you and the children for anything," my father said.

"I want to help," I blurted out. "He can have the spare room, after all."

"This is not your decision, Theodore," my father snapped, but my mother said, "And I will answer for Talitha and Amy, as well as myself."

"And if this marshal comes to our door with his warrant and enters our house and Mr. Brown makes good his promise to kill or be killed—" my father began.

"We must pray it will not come to that," my mother replied.

Father stood with his fists clenched like stones for a moment. Then he turned to Dr. Howe. "We are leaving," he said. "We will be home within two hours. Bring him to the back door after that time."

"Not I," said Dr. Howe. "Mr. Sanborn will convey Mr. Brown tonight."

"I thank you, sir," Brown said.

"I do not thank you, Mr. Brown," my father declared. "But you will be as safe as we can make you."

"It will be an honor, sir," I said, ignoring my father's scowl.

And as quickly as that, we, my own ordinary family, were suddenly doing something exciting. I hoped Brown would tell us some war stories.

On the street, our carriage was standing by itself, the horses drowsing under their blankets.

My father jerked open the cab door. The driver was asleep in one corner, wrapped in his cape.

"We are leaving, sir," Father nearly shouted.

"Right," sighed the coachman, stumbling out past us. I smelled whiskey on his breath.

"This night—" my father grumbled.

The coachman tried to climb into his box but slipped. I went to steady him.

"Thanks, boy," he said with an amiable grin. "Want to ride up with me?"

I agreed at once.

"Theodore, come down," my father ordered.

I bent as close as I could to his face. "I think I'd better," I said. "He's been drinking—"

"I know that, Theodore."

"—and up here I can watch for any more large holes. We don't want to get stuck again."

My father thought that over. "Very well. See that we do not," he said, and climbed into the cab with Mother.

The coachman took the reins and got us back onto the muddy road to Boston. Then he settled down into his cape and pulled his hat over his eyes.

"Sir—" I said.

"Nothing to worry about. Dolly and Bill know the way home. Just wake me up when we get back to pavement." He pulled a bottle out of his coat and offered it to me.

"Oh, no thanks," I said, feeling flustered.

The coachman winked at me, took a long swig, and closed his eyes with a happy sigh.

" 'This night,' " Father had said in disgust. It seemed like a fine one to me. Before we left Boston, my mother had said, "Theodore is fourteen, Hale, and should hear this lecture. He is old enough to begin taking part in the country's business. Even when it is bad business. Perhaps he can help better it." Now, suddenly, I was a part of it.

I picked up the reins that had fallen from the coachman's slack hands. I liked the feel of them in mine.

TWO

"We must refer to him as Hawkins. Nelson Hawkins," my father said. "Howe whispered it to me as we were leaving."

The three of us were standing in the kitchen, looking into the backyard. The room was dark except for the low orange glow of our iron stove. I could hardly see my parents. They stood facing each other, shadows against the windows.

"He will be safe here, Hale," my mother said, touching Father's shoulder.

"Safe," my father repeated. "May we all be."

Our maid, Mary, put her head in at the door. "I've got the room ready, ma'am," she said.

"Thank thee, Mary, for thy trouble," my mother said. "Please set one more place at breakfast tomorrow."

Mary nodded, spun on her heel, and marched out. She didn't approve of guests at this time of night. If she had known what kind of man was coming, she would have approved even less.

"Will thee want anything else?" my mother asked.

"No, thank you," my father said.

"I will say good night, then."

"We shall be very quiet when he comes, I assure you," he replied as my mother slipped out of the room.

The storm was rising. A stinging cloud of snow galloped south now, blown by a shrieking wind. The barren branches of our oak trees clawed at the sky. I had the fancy that they'd torn down the stars.

"You may go to bed also, Theodore," my father said.

"No, sir," I said, "I want to stay with you."

"Well," my father said after a moment, "I suppose you are in no more danger downstairs than upstairs."

I moved closer to him. It was strange. I was in our own kitchen, in the house where I had spent all my life so far. But now everything seemed different; precarious and vulnerable. It was the other side of excitement.

The wind blew; the house groaned a little. My father and I waited. At last, I saw two dim shapes detach themselves from the dark and come slowly toward the door. There was a quiet knock.

I picked up the fire poker. "Just in case our visitors are not whom we expect," I said.

"And what good will that do if they are not, Theodore?" my father asked, and opened the door.

I heard Mr. Sanborn's voice. "Have I the honor of addressing Mr. Hale Worth?"

My father agreed that he did.

"Permit me. I am Franklin Benjamin Sanborn. This is Mr. 'Nelson Hawkins.'" I could hear the quotation marks around the name.

"Come in, gentlemen," my father said.

I put down the poker.

"It is all right, sir," Mr. Brown said. "We weren't followed."

We all shook hands, and my father introduced me.

"How d'ye do, young man?" Brown said to me.

"Very well, thank you, sir."

Mr. Sanborn turned back to the door. "I must go. Mr. Hawkins will require your hospitality for only two or three days. We have his next refuge arranged for, as soon as we are sure that no one is watching it."

"So I understood," my father said.

"I will bid you good night, then," Mr. Sanborn said. I let him out.

Here in our kitchen, John Brown, in snow-pelted black coat and broad-brimmed hat, carpetbag in one hand, seemed more a part of the night than ever.

"Would you care to go to bed, Mr. Hawkins?" Father asked, lighting a candle.

"Yes, thanks," Brown said. He followed my father to the stairs.

"May I take your bag, Mr. Hawkins?" I offered.

He handed it to me. It was surprisingly heavy. "Take care with it, young man. If you set it down hard, it might go off," he said.

Intrigued and a little frightened, I followed them up the stairs and down the hall.

I lowered the bag softly onto the bed in the room next to mine.

"Will you need anything else tonight?" my father asked.

"Nothing," Brown told him. "I thank you again for giving hospitality to a wanted man."

"We breakfast at seven," my father said. "Good night."

He and I left the room. I heard Brown turning the key in the lock behind us.

I undressed quickly and pulled my cold flannel nightshirt on as fast as I could. My bed was like ice, and as I lay curled into a ball while my body slowly warmed it, I heard a series of thumps and scrapes come from Brown's room. He was moving the furniture. I could tell exactly what he was doing by the sounds. First he pushed the bureau against the door. Then he shoved the bed against the bureau.

The racket wakened Amy and Talitha in their room across the hall. "Marmy," they called. "Marmy, what is that noise?"

I went in to them, shivering.

They were sitting up in bed, looking like frightened owls.

"Hush," I whispered. "It's only Mr. Hawkins getting settled."

"Who is Mr. Hawkins, Theodore?" Talitha asked.

"A man who will be staying with us for a few days."

"Why, is he a friend?" Amy asked. She pulled the blankets up higher under her chin.

"Yes. A very great friend," I said. "But don't tell anyone at school that we have a guest."

"Why not?"

"Because it would be impolite." That was a good answer for Amy. She was very concerned these days with what was polite and what was not. This was especially true when she could accuse someone else of impoliteness.

But Talitha said, "When aunts and uncles come to visit, we tell everyone. That's not impolite, is it?"

"No," I told her. "But Mr. Hawkins is different. He is not a relative, you see. So just be careful to say nothing about him, or the other girls will laugh at you behind your backs for not knowing better."

"Why is he moving our furniture?" Talitha wanted to know.

"Mr. Hawkins is not from Boston," I said. "Where he comes from, they arrange furniture differently."

"But he's pushing things up against the door," Amy pointed out.

"Mr. Hawkins has been living in the West," I said. "Where he is from there are bears."

"No bears around Boston, Theodore," Talitha said wisely.

"Well, perhaps he can't get used to a place without bears."

"I think you are making up a story," Talitha replied.

"You're right," I said. "I'm only guessing about Mr. Hawkins. Let's ask him tomorrow."

That satisfied them. They lay down and allowed me to tuck them in.

I got back into my own bed, but I couldn't sleep.

There were no bears in Boston, but there was a federal marshal who wanted the man I had called Hawkins. There was a price on our visitor's head. The national government had put it there. And he thought the threat was real enough that he had barricaded his room.

I lay awake remembering what my father had feared. I imagined the marshal, a thick, ugly man with two

Colt's revolvers in his belt and a shotgun. He had a squad of our Boston police behind him. When Mary opened the door, he thumbed his badge at her and pushed his way in.

My mother was standing in the mudroom, blocking his way to the rest of the house. She barely came up to his shoulder. "What does thee mean to invade my house this way?" she demanded.

The police sergeant took off his cap and said, "Begging your pardon, ma'am, but we're here on most official business."

"Not official enough," I said, coming to stand beside Mother. "You have no warrant."

The marshal yanked a paper out of his coat pocket and thrust it forward. "Here you are, boy. A warrant for the arrest of John Brown, also known as Nelson Hawkins. Wanted for murder in Kansas, as I expect you know. Now stand aside."

What would I do at this point? What could we do in the face of guns, police, the power of the government?

Suppose I tried to block the marshal from going up the stairs? Would he shoot me? And what would John Brown do? Would he attempt to escape, or would he appear at the landing with weapons in his hands, blazing at the marshal and police? What would happen to us then?

The wind struck the house a sudden blow and I jumped.

I had known since I was old enough to understand that there were great winds in the world. Men struggled over mighty questions like independence, abolition, and democracy, and these struggles made history. Tonight I had learned that there were dark things deeper than the winds that flowed in secret and came to light only a little. And they were as fierce as any storm.

Now these things were trying to get into my house. No, they had got in. Something deep and dark was in the next room, and its enemies were seeking it. And I greatly suspected that none of these things cared much what happened to one man and his wife, two little girls and a boy.

It was hours before I slept.

THREE

 I woke to the sound of the furniture in the next room being moved again. The light came in through my windows clear and gray. Feeling very tired, I rolled out of bed and dressed. I met John Brown on the landing.

"Good morning, young man," he said.

"Good morning, Mr. Hawkins," I replied.

He was dressed as he had been the night before. I spied the butts of two revolvers sticking out of his boot tops. When he saw that I had noticed them, he smiled and shoved them out of sight. Then we went down to breakfast.

Mary had laid on a company meal, with plenty of ham and eggs, as well as fresh bread and fruit. We were the last ones at the table. My father introduced Mr. Hawkins to Talitha and Amy. I sat down. John Brown remained standing.

"I beg your pardon, Mr. Worth," he said after a minute. "Have you already said the grace?"

My father led grace at dinners. We rarely said it any other time.

"Would you be so good as to lead us, Mr. Hawkins?" he said.

John Brown turned his chair around backwards and tilted it toward himself. He leaned his arms on the back of the chair and prayed, "Lord, bless this food to our health and Your service. Bless our work, and grant that we may recollect to thank You for it in the business of the day. Above all, bless this family, and my own. Keep all the children safe, and make them good. Grant that this day may bring us all one step closer to that Heavenly City where we may dwell forever in Your presence. Amen."

"Amen," we all agreed.

John Brown turned his chair back around and sat down.

"Are you frightened of bears, Mr. Hawkins?" Talitha asked.

"Somewhat," Brown said. "Have you got many bears in these parts?"

"No," said Amy. "So you don't have to push the furniture against the door at night."

Then John Brown did something I thought he would never do. He laughed. His whole body shook, but he never made a sound. Finally, he said, "I am very relieved to hear it, child. But I rather suspect one or two large bears may have followed me from Kansas. So perhaps I had better do it anyway, for those Kansas bears make a terrible mess, and I shouldn't like them to spoil your mother's pretty little room."

Then he turned to my father. "I had no opportunity of saying so last night, Mr. Worth, but I greatly admire a book you published two years ago. *Stilicho; or, The Barbarian of Rome.* I read it through three times."

"I fear you were the only one who read it at all," Father

said. "Sales were disappointing. Still, I am pleased to hear that you enjoyed it. I will inform the author if you like."

"A very improving novel," Brown said. "It is a great pity that more people did not see the value in the book."

"That is the way with most novels," my father observed.

"Most novels are not of such a quality," Brown replied.

My father put down his fork. "Tell me what you found so praiseworthy," he said.

"Stilicho is a great warrior who tries to save Rome by compromising his principles, but he fails; he is poisoned, and the barbarians overwhelm the empire," Brown said. "*Stilicho* teaches us not to compromise."

"I don't believe that was the meaning the author intended," Father said. "Nor is it what I saw in the book when I edited it. We saw it as Stilicho's undoing by his own pride. Had he remained loyal to the government he had sworn to defend, he might have lived. He would, at least, have kept his honor."

"Then I suggest the author did not completely understand his own work," Brown said. "Stilicho's tragedy is that there is no longer anyone worthy of his loyalty."

My father poured himself another cup of coffee. "Frankly, Mr. Hawkins, I had not thought of you as a great reader."

"I mostly read books on scientific farming, military subjects, and religion, but I am very fond of any improving literature I can get," Brown replied. "When I lived in Ohio, I kept a library and a boarding school in my home for a time."

"Really," my father remarked. I could tell Brown had surprised him.

"And did thee teach girls, or only boys in thy school?" Mother asked.

"Only boys for pay, since it was a boarding school and there was no room for girls," Brown told her. "But I have taught my own daughters somewhat."

"Do little girls not have to go to school in Ohio?" Amy asked.

"It was a rough, new place then," Brown said. "I hope there are schools for them now."

"Remember thy grandparents live in Cincinnati, Amy," my mother said. "And it is a fine, modern city with many schools."

"Oh," said Amy, losing interest in Ohio.

"Do you have many little girls?" Talitha asked.

"God has given me twenty children, though he has taken some of them back to Heaven," Brown said.

"Thee did not mention any daughters in thy talk last night, Mr. Hawkins," my mother remarked. "Are any of them in Kansas?"

"All are at my farm in New York State, ma'am," Brown said. "I hope to visit them before I go west again."

"Why did you turn the chair around to say grace?" Talitha asked.

"It's an old custom of the Scots Presbyterians," Brown explained. "When there is no pulpit, a man makes his own. I favor the practice, though I am a Congregationalist myself."

"We are Friends," Amy informed him, using the proper, formal word for the Quakers. "All except Father."

"I greatly admire the Friends," Brown said. "They were the first church to call slavery wrong, a hundred years ago. I wish all churches thought so."

"Friends also believe that war is wrong," I said, wondering what response I might get.

Brown fixed me with his dark eyes. "War is wrong. Slavery is wrong. On these points the Friends and I agree," he said. "We disagree only on which of them is the more wrong."

Father passed the bread around the table. I offered Brown the butter.

"No, thank you," he said. "Have you any molasses?"

I handed him that. We all watched as he sliced off a great wedge of bread and smothered it in thick brown molasses.

"Is that how people eat bread in Kansas?" Amy asked.

"I have eaten bread this way since I was a boy," Brown told her. "But I have eaten stranger things than this in Kansas."

"What sorts of things?" Talitha asked.

"Oh, skunk drumsticks, snapping turtle soup, rattlesnake pie when I can get it. It's mighty good with fried grasshoppers mixed in." Brown's eyes were twinkling.

"Did you ever eat a lion?" Talitha asked wonderingly.

"Only a little one," Brown said.

"But there ain't no lions out West," Amy exclaimed.

"There are mountain lions," I offered.

"I reckon it was one of those," Brown said. "There was a small mountain close by."

"But little girls in Kansas don't eat rattlesnakes, do they?" Talitha asked.

"Oh, no," Brown said. "Little girls are too delicate for that. A Kansas girl has to be ten years old before she's allowed to eat rattlesnake."

Talitha squealed.

Amy said, "But do they put molasses on their bread?"

"No," said Brown. "I believe they don't."

"Then I don't believe they eat rattlesnakes, either."

"Well, child," Brown said, "you never did ask me if they put molasses on their rattlesnakes."

"Now I know you are telling a story," Amy said, in such a way that all of us laughed.

"You have caught me, child," Brown said, once he had stopped his silent shaking. "But I have eaten some mighty strange things in Kansas."

When breakfast was over, the girls and I got up to start for school. But my mother said, "How would thee children like to stay home today?"

Father gave her an odd look yet said nothing. The girls yelped with delight. I looked out the window at the cold, gray sky and the thin coat of icy snow and smiled. If Brown's presence would keep me away from Mr. Weems's School for Boys, he could stay for a year.

"I, in any case, must go in to the office," Father announced.

"Of course thee must, Hale."

Then I understood. Mother was afraid that the girls had liked Mr. Brown too well. They might go to school and tell their friends about our visitor. But how could she think that I would be so foolish?

Father put on his coat and left. He had a long, cold walk to the shop on Chester Street. I watched him hunch into the wind and set off down our hill, leaving the family he didn't want to leave, going into work as if everything was normal, because that was the best way to help a man he did not want to help.

After he left, the rest of us went into the back parlor.

"Have you any chores that I might do for you, Mrs. Worth?" Brown asked. "I don't love to be idle."

"Thank thee, Mr. Hawkins," my mother replied. "But we have a man who comes. Perhaps thee could keep company with the children this morning while he is here. He does not come into the house."

"I would be pleased," Brown said.

Now it came to me why I was being kept home. My mother did not want to entertain a strange man while her husband was away. I was standing in for my father. I liked the feeling.

And so my sisters and mother and I passed the morning in the back parlor playing children's games with John Brown. His hair was iron gray and his skin was deeply wrinkled, but I have seen few men who were spryer or stronger. After we had played puss-in-the-corner and ring-around-the-rosy and everything else the girls knew, he and I took them on our backs and played horses. Afterwards, he bounced them on his knee together and sang to them.

What he did at the end of the morning was hard to believe, even seeing it. He had Amy and Talitha each stand on one of his hands and lifted them up toward the ceiling. Watching, my mother gasped and covered her mouth, but the girls cooed. John Brown held his arms straight out from his sides. They barely trembled. "Some day, little girls, you can tell people that J— Mr. Nelson Hawkins did this with you," he said.

He set them down slowly.

That afternoon, when the girls had been sent upstairs for naps, Mother, Brown, and I returned to the parlor. Mother asked if he wanted coffee. He asked for tea. When Mary had brought it, he carefully removed his two big pistols from his boots and laid the weapons out beside the tea things. Slowly, as Mother watched in silence, he pulled a smaller pistol from his pants. He set out two knives along with them. Then he began to clean the weapons, one by one. He began with the knives, sharpening their edges with a small whetstone, then sliding them back into their scabbards. He set the small pistol's bullets in a straight row, then took it apart and cleaned it. When it was put back together and reloaded, he went on to the next, humming one of the hymns he'd sung to the girls. Finally, when he was working on the last pistol, he said, "I am glad to see that you aren't nervy, ma'am. Many women would object to a man cleaning his pistols in the parlor."

My mother said nothing.

"Oh, this is only the back parlor, Mr. Hawkins. You may do as you like here," I joked.

He smiled and snapped the cylinder of the revolver back into place. Then he held it out to me.

With a glance at my mother, I crossed the room and took it. It felt heavy, but not as heavy as I had expected. I didn't know how to hold it. I cocked the hammer and snapped the trigger. It had a good, crisp, hard sound.

"Have you ever held a pistol before?" Brown asked me.

"No," I admitted. At that moment it seemed as though I had been shirking my duty, as though I ought to have been carrying guns all my life.

"Let me show you something," Brown said. He stood, took the weapon from me, and held it out straight in front of him with both hands. He spread his feet wide apart. "This is the best stance for a pistol. In this position you can kill a man at fifty yards if you're good," he said. "But sometimes you are in too much of a hurry."

He handed it back to me, and I copied what he had done.

Brown nodded. "Right smart."

My mother's face was grim. When I gave back the weapon, she let out her breath.

"Would you like to try it, Mrs. Worth?" Brown asked.

"No, thank thee," my mother said. "I have no love for carnal weapons."

"I felt so once," Brown replied. "Before I went to Kansas, I could never see the use of them. Now, carnal weapons and the money to get them are almost all I think about."

"Thee fight against an evil thing," my mother said. "I wish thee did not do it in so evil a way."

Brown stuffed his weapons back into his clothes as he spoke. "When I was a boy younger than your son, I used to drive cattle a hundred miles to sell to the army. That was back during the 1812 war. What I saw in the camps turned me against soldiering. Crime, corruption, and villainy was all the soldiering our militia knew. When I became a man, I never would serve. I paid the fine instead. But I have come to think there are some things a man must fight for."

"War is an evil thing always," Mother declared. "Persuasion is the only sure way to end slavery."

"I wish all men could be convinced so," Brown said. "But what remedy is there for those who will not be?"

"There are prayers," said my mother.

"I do pray for the end of slavery," Brown said. "And so, I know, do you, ma'am. And so, I'm sure, does every slave. But these millions of prayers rising to Heaven every day have not yet made one master free one soul from slavery, so far as I know."

"Killing leads only to more killing. As thee know well from experience," my mother said.

"That is so," Brown replied. "But my inner light shows me that slavery is a greater evil than war."

"Thy answers are so good, Mr. Hawkins, it is hard to remember that thee are wrong," my mother said.

Mary came into the room. "Beg pardon, but a message has come for Mr. Hawkins," she said, and handed him a folded sheet of paper.

"It's from Howe," Brown said. "They are sure now that my next hideout is safe. I will be leaving tonight."

"Will he be staying to dinner?" Mary asked.

"Yes," replied my mother.

"Thank you, ma'am," Brown said.

Mother stood up. "I must help Mary in the kitchen for a while," she told us. "Perhaps Mr. Hawkins would be interested to see thy telegraph, Theodore."

"Would you be, Mr. Hawkins?" I asked.

"I should be grateful," Brown said.

We went up to my room. I kept my telegrapher's key on a small table in the corner. It had no wires. I used it only to practice.

"Do you know the Morse code?" Brown asked.

"Yes, of course," I said. "And I even know a lot of the abbreviations and shortcuts real telegraphers use. Bob Gibbons down at the railroad station is teaching me."

"It's a fine thing to see a young man improve his mind with such useful knowledge," Brown said. "Do you mean to work at it when you're older?"

"Oh, no," I said. "This is only my hobby. My father doesn't like me to do it."

Brown looked surprised. "Why?" he asked.

"He thinks it's beneath me," I said. "He thinks I'll meet the wrong sort of people. And he wants me to spend more time studying for Harvard. He wants me to go there before I join him at Worth House."

"And what do you want?" Brown asked me.

His question surprised and flattered me. "Well ..." I shrugged. "I love books. And it's exciting to meet the people who write them. I suppose I will."

Brown stroked his chin. "Time is our most precious gift from the Almighty. We ought not to waste it," he said. "Your father is right about that. But I think you have made a fine choice of a hobby. A fine choice." He clicked the key up and down a couple of times. "When I was your age, this thing did not exist. Now it seems we cannot exist without it. A message flies from one end of the country to the next in seconds. Who could have imagined it? Lightning itself carries our thoughts now. Yes. Our times are lightning."

He turned back to me. "What do you think, young Worth? Are some things to be fought for?"

"I don't know," I replied.

"A man ought to have an opinion," Brown said.

"Then I shall think about it," I told him.

"The time is coming when we shall all need to know our minds," Brown went on. "It did not trouble your mother much when I cleaned my guns. It was when I handed one to you she became Quaker-minded."

I nodded.

"How did the pistol feel in your hand?" Brown asked.

"I liked it," I said.

"Then remember that feel, and remember the look on your mother's face," Brown said. "They will help you to decide."

"Is my father right?" I asked. "Do you want to start a civil war?"

"I am only one man," Brown said. "I cannot even raise the money to arm one company of men with good guns."

"Will there be much more fighting in Kansas come the spring?"

"I reckon so," Brown said. "Or if not in Kansas, somewhere else."

"Where?" I asked.

"It may be one place; it may be another. Every time a new state is added to the Union from now on, there will likely be a new war there. Maybe in the older states, too."

"Mr. Hawkins, I have something I want to give you," I said. I went over to a box on my bookcase. Inside was a five-dollar golden eagle my grandmother Evans had sent me for my last birthday. "This is for your work. I am sorry it is all I have."

"No one can give more than all."

"You might call me Theodore if you care to," I said.

"Then I thank you, Theodore," Brown said. He tapped the key again. "Could we not spend an hour or so at this key?" he asked. "I should like to learn a little."

So we spent the time until dinner in my room. I taught John Brown that day all he ever knew of the Morse code. By evening, when my father came home, he was tapping out his name, .—————....—. —....—.———.———. , over and over.

Father arrived home with his mouth still set in a grim

line. It vanished when Mother told him that Brown would
be leaving that night. Smiling, my father said, "I was able
to locate a copy of *Stilicho* in the shop today, Mr. Hawkins,
if you would care to have it."

"Indeed I would," Brown said. "My old copy is far
away from here."

Every time the door to the kitchen opened, I caught
the smell of my mother's spice cake. That was what she
had been doing in the kitchen with Mary. I looked forward to dessert more than usual.

But dessert came and went and was not spice cake.

It was not until Mr. Sanborn arrived to take our visitor
wherever he was going next that my mother brought the
cake out. It was wrapped up for Brown alone.

"This is my best baking," she said. "I would not have
thee leave my house remembering only the words that
passed between us this afternoon."

"They were good words to hear, ma'am," Brown said.
"I thank you for this cake, and for all besides. Including
the words."

Talitha and Amy lined up to kiss him.

I shook his hand and said, "Good-bye, Mr. Hawkins.
I will think about what you said."

"Good-bye, Theodore." Brown put his firm hand on
my shoulder. Perhaps Chev Howe had felt the same when
the king of Greece knighted him. "Thank you for teaching
me to write my name in lightning. And for the other
thing. It was a noble gift."

My father raised an eyebrow, and I explained: "Morse
code."

My father handed two books to him. The first was
Stilicho. The second was a small, handsome book from a

set in his own library. *"Julius Caesar,"* my father said. "It is very informative on the fate of conspirators."

"Was not one of those conspirators 'the noblest Roman of them all'?" Brown remarked.

"Yes," my father replied. "He was called so because he fought to preserve his republic, not to destroy it."

"And he failed," Brown said. "The Roman republic lived by slavery. That's a bad thing for a republic to do, seemingly."

"The Roman republic fell, and the slaves were still slaves," my father said.

"Well, sir, your ideas and mine differ materially on what is best for our country," Brown said. "But I thank you for the book. I've never seen a better."

My father did not answer, but I felt the anger behind his silence. I could not understand it. John Brown was defending his country, not betraying it. Why couldn't he see that?

"We must be going," Mr. Sanborn said. "We are expected at Judge—excuse me. We are expected."

The two of them left by the back way. We watched until once again Brown became part of the night. The wind had shifted at sunset and was blowing warm again. I noticed that only Mr. Sanborn had left footprints in the melting snow. Even with no one after him, Brown had been careful where he stepped.

FOUR

Father was different for weeks after Brown's visit. It was as though, having let someone from outside into his careful life, even for one night, he was afraid something else might happen to upset it.

One evening, he came into my room. I was studying my geometry, trying to prove something pointless about the section of a cone. I looked up, grateful to be interrupted.

"Theodore, I have been thinking," he began. "I have decided that the time has come for you to put away your telegraph. I have given the matter careful consideration, not overlooking the fact that telegraphy is, in its way, useful knowledge. But your toying with it has gone on long enough. It is a skill you will never need, and it distracts you from what ought to be your real pursuits."

I flushed.

"I am sure I have your agreement."

"No," I said. I was not going to give up my key.

"The sort of people who engage in telegraphy, Theodore, are frequently disreputable and are never the sort of people with whom our sort associate. There is no point in continuing."

Our voices had started to rise, and brought my mother to the door. When she heard what the matter was, she took my part.

"We cannot keep Theodore at home forever," she said. "And he cannot spend all his time studying. As for telegraphers being persons of low worth, I think thee are wrong, my love. It is true they are poorly paid, but they are decent. Remember that this is one of the few things a woman may honestly do to support herself."

She had my father there. Like Dr. Howe, he was a strong believer in women's rights.

"This thing has done him no harm, and like any learning, it is good in itself," she went on. "Theodore should be allowed to continue."

My father paused, calculating his chances against Mother's arguments. Finally, he nodded. "Reluctantly, Theodore, reluctantly. And as long as your school marks remain acceptable."

My marks were always acceptable, if no more than that. Weems's school was exclusive, expensive, and run on the highest principles of dullness. Knowledge was presented in such a way as to mummify the brain in the shortest time possible. Mr. Weems intended to prepare us for Harvard or kill us. He seemed to feel that one end was as good as the other. I hated it there.

To be fair to Weems, the other students seemed not to mind, or even to notice. They were all from old Boston families like me. Unlike me, they were pure Boston, running back to its founding on both sides. I had a Quaker mother who had been born in New Jersey. This made me close to a foreigner. My classmates were not unfriendly, exactly. They simply preferred their own company.

But this was the place my father had chosen to send me to become a proper Bostonian. "I know that many of these boys lack your mind and spirit, Theodore," my father had told me. "But you must learn to get on with people like that. They will become the men among whom you will pass your life. The mere fact of your having been at school with them will be an advantage to you, whether you were popular or not. And as for Weems's dullness"— he shrugged—"school is supposed to be dull. You should not expect to be exempt from what every well-educated boy has suffered."

We heard from our abolitionist friends that Brown had not done well on his speaking tour. Everywhere he went, people had come to hear him and cheered what he had to say. They had promised thousands of dollars to his cause. But they had given him pennies. It seemed that my five dollars had been real money after all.

"Julia Ward Howe told me that he had over thirty thousand dollars in pledges when he left New England," my mother said. "But she believes he got only a tenth of what was promised."

"Three thousand dollars are three thousand too much for that man," Father snapped. "No sensible person would give him a nickel."

"I gave him a dollar," my mother said quietly.

"And you protected him. You gave him books," I protested.

"I gave him protection because my wife made me see that I must," he replied. "I gave him books that I thought might make him see his error. As for the man himself"— he measured his words out slowly—"he is dangerous and untrustworthy. He is a fanatic, with grandiose notions of himself. I confess that I should probably want John Brown for a neighbor if I were a frontiersman trying to raise a family in the wilderness. But it will take more than one old farmer with delusions of grandeur to end slavery in this country. He should leave these things to his betters."

"But his betters are doing nothing," I replied.

"Then it may be that there is nothing to be done."

Nothing to be done. In the months after John Brown hid in our house, I thought more than once, *We can put that on Father's tombstone. Here lies Hale Worth. Nothing to be done.*

The fall of 1857 came, and a financial panic, the worst in our history, crept across the country, closing businesses and throwing men out of work. Sales of Father's books fell to nearly nothing. Many other publishers went under. But nothing changed in my life except in measured, predictable ways, as my father expected. I ground out my days at Weems's school.

At least Father didn't try to interfere with my telegraphy again. Whenever I could after school, I slipped away to see my one good friend, Bob Gibbons, at the Western of Boston Railroad.

Bob had never told me where he came from, and I thought I should not ask. He'd never mentioned a family. He'd mentioned working in Baltimore and Brooklyn before Boston—"All the *B*'s. When I'm done with the *B* towns, I'll get onto the *C*'s. I'll never stay put. I know the inside of a barroom better than a schoolroom," he said with a laugh, "and I learned more there, that's for sure. Learned the Morse. If you can learn the Morse, you can learn anything you want to know. I can outfight any

man my size and outtalk the rest. I haven't been afraid
since I was nine years old, and I was wrong then. Been
on my own since I was twelve, and I'll be on my own till
the day I die.... They always need operators. I can pick
up and go whenever I feel like it. That's what you call
freedom."

I kept our friendship secret. I never brought him home.
My father and mother would see Bob as a threat to their
precious son.

I'd met Bob when I'd wandered into the depot looking
for someone to teach me the Morse. He'd been rapping
out messages with a little half-smile on his face and hadn't
noticed me at first. When he did, he asked me my business
in a friendly way. When I told him what I wanted, he'd
tipped his hat back and said, "Sit down, buddy. Any guy
can teach you the Morse, but nobody can teach you as
well as I can. And you look smart. I bet you can teach
me a few things, too."

He'd just arrived in Boston—"Blew in off the track and
thought I'd sit down. Guess I'll stay till the wind blows hard
enough to move me again." And we'd started teaching each
other what we knew. "Listenin' to you is better than reading
the books'd be, Ted. I can ask you just what I want to
know. Don't have to bother with the rest of it."

I flattered myself that Bob hadn't been blown down
the track again because he liked me. I hoped he'd never
leave.

He was only about a year older than I was but had
been a telegrapher for three. He walked fast and rolling
everywhere he went. He spent his time at work, though,
with his feet up on his desk and his eyes closed.

"Not sleeping, only just dozing. Eyes closed, ears open. Ever alert for the summons to action," he said.

That was true. When a message that concerned him clicked over the wires, he swung his feet down, reached for his key, and rapped out dots and dashes as though his hand had become electrified. However ordinary the message was, Bob treated it as if he were about to learn the secrets of the universe.

"Whatever comes across the wire, I'm the first fellow in Boston to know it," he said. "That's the reason why I love this job so much. Makes me feel spry."

I understood perfectly. The depot was an exciting place to work. Trains came and went all day, clanging their bells and shrieking their whistles, scattering cinders and smoke. And news of the trains came clattering over Bob's key. It was like seeing all the vastness of America come to life, and the telegraph was its voice.

A paper tape with the dots and dashes recorded on it came spooling off a reel whenever a message was sent or received, but no real operator looked at it. He knew what it said just by listening. Rattling out at over thirty words a minute at its fastest, the voice spoke of trains delayed or derailed, events and emergencies up and down the line.

Once, when Bob had stepped out for a few minutes and left me alone in his office, a message came over the wire that had to be answered immediately: TRAIN FROM NEW YORK DELAYED ONE HOUR STOP ADVISE STATIONMASTER STOP ACKNOWLEDGE IMMEDIATELY STOP

I went over to the key and tapped out, ACKNOWLEDGED STOP. Then I waited for Bob to come back. "Message came while you were out," I said. "It's on the tape."

Bob looked at the message and my answer. "Well, better tell the stationmaster." He went out again.

For a second, I had joined the voice. I had spoken to New York. I listened to a message for Hartford go clicking past, and felt mighty. I tried to explain it to Bob without gushing.

"Know how you feel," he said. "Fellow gets to miss it after a while. Time was, I used to work for the Baltimore & Ohio. They fired me. I went west lookin' for a job. One day, walkin' along beside the wires, I got so lonely for some news I cut into them and just listened for a bit."

"How did you do that without a set?"

"Put the ends of the wires on my tongue," Bob said.

"You're joking!" I shouted.

He bent over his key and disconnected it. Then he stuck out his tongue and placed the wires on it. "Train from Springfield's right on time," he said after a moment. He held out the ends to me.

I placed them gingerly against my tongue and felt a message from Albany coming in!

I kept thinking that one day I'd hear some news of John Brown over the wire. But Kansas was nearly quiet now. The Free-Soilers had won. The Congress had accepted their government at Lawrence as the legitimate one for the state, and the army had enforced peace. Most of the Border Ruffians had gone back to Missouri. So far, no state seemed ready to follow Kansas into bloodshed. I wondered what Brown would find to do now.

Then, one morning in early 1859, we had word of him. The whole country did.

My father opened his paper and exclaimed, "Well, I—" Brown was staring at him from the front page. A steel-cut engraving showed him with a long beard, looking very different now, wilder and fiercer. He did not seem like a man who would ever laugh, except, perhaps, at the death of an enemy.

At my mother's request, my father read the story aloud.

Back in Kansas, Brown had started calling himself Shubel Morgan. He had recruited a few men and raided into Missouri around Christmas. He had attacked one plantation, killed the owner, and freed eleven slaves.

In the dead of winter, he had led his band north across the blizzard-driven plains toward freedom. They had hidden in freezing barns, traveling at night when they had to. Sometimes a farmer gave them a little charity. Finally, after eighty-two days and eleven hundred miles, he delivered the former slaves to the Canadian border. They had crossed that magical line and become free men and women in an instant. Not one person died on the way.

After giving the interview, Brown had disappeared into Canada himself.

My father studied Brown's picture closely. I saw his face tighten into the expression it had had the night Brown came up to us in the Congregational Church.

"I see Farmer Brown has undertaken to resemble Moses in looks if not in powers," he said. "No doubt his friends will be greatly impressed."

I put down my fork. "Who have you ever heard of who has freed eleven slaves?" I said.

"This business was not about freeing slaves," my father replied with a scowl. "It was about Mr. Howe and his crowd. Mark my words, Brown will be back in New England next, looking to raise more money for his next scheme."

"Brown is willing to risk his life for his beliefs," I said. "Next to that, money seems little enough."

"Money is no little thing, Theodore, as you will discover when you are responsible for making it," my father said. "And sending your son to school."

"Money is little enough when it is given for the right cause," I said.

My mother put her hand on my arm. In my head a voice cried, *You've never done anything in your life to free a single slave, Father. What right have you to sneer at those who have?* But I held my tongue.

"Excuse me," I said, and stood up.

"Sit back down," my father snapped.

"I prefer not to," I said, and headed out the door.

"Theodore, come back, please," my mother said.

"No," I said stiffly. "John Brown is a man I consider to be principled and heroic. I do not want to hear him insulted."

"Thee must not leave angry," she continued. "Thee and thy father must make peace."

I was too furious to answer. I grabbed up my books and headed for school.

The thought of it seemed more sickening than usual as I strode off down our hill. I was sure I'd finally throw an inkwell at Mr. Weems. I imagined doing that. I imagined what might happen to me if I did. Then the thought struck me—why go? Why not simply head for the Western of Boston depot and drop in on Bob?

It had never occurred to me to cut school before. Now

it seemed like an amazingly good idea. If I liked it, I might never go back. Why did I need Harvard if I had the telegraph? It struck me in that instant that I could simply walk away from my life with my key under my arm. I saw myself with a hat like Bob's, and a life as free as his. In an instant, I was whistling.

I heard Bob's voice in my head as I sauntered down the street. *Been on my own since I was twelve, and I'll be on my own till the day I die.... They always need operators. I can pick up and go whenever I feel like it. That's what you call freedom.*

I had the depot in sight when I saw two men walking toward me from that direction. I could not believe it. John Brown himself was coming up the hill, with Mr. Sanborn stuck to his side.

Brown's hand swooped up to his hat and waved it at me. Mr. Sanborn called out, "Young Master Worth," and ran to take my hand. "I was not aware you came this way to school."

"I have other business this morning," I told him.

"A very happy accident," Mr. Sanborn chirped. "You remember Mr. Morgan, of course?"

"Theodore, I am happy indeed to see you again," Brown said, grasping my hand and putting his other on my shoulder. "I want you to know, young man, that your five gold dollars were particularly well spent."

It was strange to meet him unexpectedly. The beard, although it did not hide his face, made him look like another man. The John Brown we had sheltered had looked dangerous but knowable. This man looked as though there was something inside that nobody knew.

But the deep voice was the same. The granite handshake was the same. I was glad to see him again, very glad.

Mr. Sanborn beamed at me. "Mr. Morgan told me that story. That is how I know you are a true friend."

"And how are all at home?" Brown asked.

"All fine, thanks," I said. I was hardly willing to say more. "I was very happy to hear that your—your adventure went so well."

"Oh, it was more than an adventure," Mr. Sanborn said. "He has proven himself all over again. I am telling you this only because I know you are one of the true ones." He looked around and dropped his voice. "But there are those here in Boston who were thinking of withdrawing their support. Important men. They thought Mr. Morgan was not reliable. That his plans were too extreme—beyond even his ability to carry out. Now they see differently. Now they know he can do whatever he sets out to do. First he must make another try at fundraising. Then things will begin to happen. You will see."

"That's enough, Frank," Brown said, nodding his head in the direction he wanted to go.

"Yes. We must be leaving," Mr. Sanborn agreed. "There are those about who—well, you know Mr. Morgan's situation." He winked at me.

"I hope that we will meet again, Theodore," Brown said. "My best respects to your family."

He and Mr. Sanborn strode away through the crowd. I looked after them, before turning back toward the depot. If Mr. Sanborn had had a tail, it would have been wagging.

FIVE

Bob was surprised when I came into his office. "Why ain't you off in school learning something I can ask you about?" he said.

I told him of my words with my father. "I guess it must seem like pretty mild stuff to you," I said. "But I couldn't believe he said such small-minded things about Brown."

Bob shrugged. "Come on. If you're playing hooky, I reckon I can, too."

"You have your job," I said.

"Just watch the key for a minute," Bob said. He went out but was gone for much longer than a minute. A few messages came through, yet nothing that needed more than a short answer, which I could give. Soon something important would have to come over that key, though. I began to pace the crowded little room.

At last, the door opened, and Bob shoved back into the office with a tall, sleepy-looking man in his grasp.

"This is Wilson. He's coming in early to finish my shift. Ain't you, Wilson?"

Wilson didn't look all that happy to do it, but he sat

down at the key, put his hat over his eyes, and seemed to go back to sleep.

"Owes me a couple of favors," Bob said. "Glad to pay me back for one of them, aren't you, Wilson?"

Wilson shrugged and snored elaborately.

"Let's go, buddy," Bob said to me.

"Just like that?"

"Sure, just like that. You look like you need a friend today."

We hurried out of the depot into the bright spring sunshine.

We kicked down the streets that led to the harbor, stopping and looking at every common thing: huge coils of ships' cable, heavy wagons trundling along to the docks. It was all ordinary, and all new because we were doing it together and we were both free.

Eventually Bob took me to his room on the top floor of an old three-story house on a dingy street. It was dark inside and smelled stale, but Bob had paid for it himself and could leave it when he wanted. It seemed a noble place to me, in spite of the unmade bed with its thin mattress and the single oil lamp with its smoke-blackened chimney.

"What are we doing here?" I asked.

Bob grinned. "Getting a couple of things. I figured out a plan for today. Old Bob's going to expand your education." He pulled a spare railroad telegrapher's hat off a nail and put it on my head. I took the hat off and looked at it. The brass plate on the front said *Baltimore & Ohio R.R.*

"Looks good. Now we're both working," Bob said. He fetched a telegraph key from under the bed. It had a short roll of wire attached. "Come on. Remember when I learned you to read the wires on your tongue? This'll be better."

We headed back to the Western of Boston tracks.

"Now I'll show you something," Bob said.

He picked out a telegraph pole and climbed it like a monkey. He unlooped the wires of his telegraph key and twisted them onto the wire strung between the poles. Then he threw the key down to me.

It started to rattle in my hands.

"Pretty slick, eh?" Bob called down. "You can even send messages like this."

"What should I send?" I called back up.

"Nothing," Bob said. "It's something to know how to do, but only a dog'd send a bogus message."

"But then what's the point of showing me?" I asked.

"Well," said Bob. "Suppose you were somewhere else and you needed to get in touch with me. You could just hook up your key and get off a message, and sooner or later I'd get it."

I paid closer attention to the message coming through. It was just a jumble of numbers. It made no sense. "What kind of message is only a string of numbers?" I asked.

"Secret code," Bob said. "Some businessman doesn't want everybody else to know his business. Stockbroker, probably. Or banker."

Bob unwound the wires and shinnied down the pole. "Let's go," he said. We walked on up the tracks till we came to a pole that had a few metal spikes sticking out of it to make a ladder. "Up you go," Bob said.

"Me?" I said.

"I picked you an easy one. You ain't scared, are you?"

I was, but I couldn't let that stop me. I dragged myself up to the top of the pole and leaned heavily on the crossbar at the top. I wasn't very high, but I felt as though I were. I could see back the way we'd come to where the track curved, and up ahead all the way to the depot.

"Okay. Now do what I did," Bob shouted. I did, and threw the key down to him.

That's when I saw a handcar with four men aboard coming up the track. Two of the men, huge fellows, were wearing the uniform of the railroad yard police. When they saw us, they slowed down and stopped.

I thought, *Here's trouble.*

The policemen got off the car and came over to Bob. "What's going on?" the bigger one asked.

"Clarity test," Bob said. "Some of the signals are coming into the office muddy. We don't want that. Trying to trace down the place where the electricity's leaking."

The policeman nodded wisely, but his companion said, "Seen you before, but who's that?" and jerked his thumb up at me.

"Just helpin' me out. Used to work for the B. & O.," Bob said. "Might be able to use him around here. Hey, Jess," he called up, "this wire's all right. Come on down and we'll try up the line."

I detached the wires and hurried down the pole as fast as I could. The handcar went its way.

"That was top-notch lying," I said.

Bob shrugged modestly. "He's happy. We're happy. No harm done," he said. "Let's get something to eat."

It was long after noon, but I hadn't realized I was hungry until Bob mentioned lunch. "Well," I said, "I don't have much money today."

'I never do," Bob replied. "Come on."

Jot far from the station there was a low, dark building

a sign in front that said CHEAP LUNCH. Bob plunked

a couple of nickels, and we fed ourselves at a long

piled high with the remains of platters of beef and

nd bread.

is is a good place," Bob said. "One of my favorites."

ked around. Food and sawdust covered the floor,

re were large damp stains of beer on the tables

e still cluttered with scratched white dishes and

eins. We were almost the only people in the

ept for a couple of knots of men singing loudly

in a language I didn't know. I fell in love with

t once.

to do something to thank Bob. I felt in my

found ten cents. "I'll get us beer," I said.

bought a pitcher. I poured lavishly into the

ng back when they overflowed.

enhorn, now let me show you something."

He refilled the glasses by pouring slowly

s. "See? This way you're not just getting

hefted his drink. "Here's how," he said.

e way he drank and tried to copy it. Some

nt up my nose. I snorted and wiped my

eve.

on," Bob said. "It ain't real hard."

ished the first pitcher, Bob got another.

a glorious haze. I loved Bob. I loved

sic in the corner. I loved John Brown,

and my schoolmates. I almost loved

"We need a secret code," I decided.

"What for?" Bob asked.

"In case," I said. "I mean, suppose one of us really needs the other."

"Kid stuff!" Bob snorted.

"It would be easy," I protested. "All we need is two *Webster's* dictionaries. I'll be Noah and you'll be Webster. That'll be the sign that what comes next is going to be in code. Every word is a three-number group: page number, column number, and number of the word down the column. Like this—" I tapped out, 25–1–6 STOP, on the table.

"And what's that supposed to be?" Bob asked.

"Page twenty-five, first column, sixth word," I said.

"Okay, okay," Bob said. "I ever get a message for Webster, I'll go right out and buy me a dictionary."

I went on tapping out Morse code on the table. BOB GIBBONS IS A GREAT GUY STOP.

Bob tapped back, THANKS ACKNOWLEDGED STOP AND I MEAN STOP.

But I didn't want to stop. I looked over at him seriously as I could, and tapped, I SAW JOHN BROWN OUTSIDE YOUR STATION TODAY STOP.

SURE YOU DID STOP ARM IN ARM WITH PRESIDENT BUCHANAN STOP, Bob tapped back.

"No, really," I said. "It was him sure as I'm sitting here."

"Some guy who looked like him," Bob said.

"I know John Brown," I said. "He stayed with family once. That's a secret, though."

"Tell me another," Bob said. "Your old man Brown—you told me so yourself. So what would doing in your house?"

I told him the story.

"Well," Bob said, shaking his head, "guess if I gave room to somebody like Brown, I'd keep it a secret, too. Man ought to be hanged."

"What?" I was sure I'd heard him wrong.

"Stole eleven slaves according to the papers," Bob said. "Killed their owner. You should have turned him in when you saw him."

"For freeing slaves?" I said.

"Owning slaves was still legal last I heard," Bob remarked. "If he'd stolen eleven horses, what would you call him?"

"But Bob—human beings aren't horses."

Bob laughed. "Hell, I saw slaves all the time in Baltimore. Didn't look so bad off to me. They sure weren't running off to Canada."

"These slaves thought differently," I said.

"How do you know? If a crazy old white man comes riding onto your place with a gang, shoots your owner, waves a gun at you, and tells you to come along, you'd do it, wouldn't you?"

"You—" I stuttered as though I'd made a great discovery, "you're not an abolitionist, are you?"

"Hell, no," Bob replied. "We've always had slaves in this country. Always will have. Hell, Boston needs a few slaves. Folks'd calm down about it if they saw what they're talking about."

"We had slaves in Boston once. We freed them. That's because we saw slavery was wrong. That's why there are abolitionists. That's why I am one."

"Slavery wrong? You never even asked most people what they thought," Bob shouted. "It was just a few of

you swells that decided for everybody. Ask a workin' man
what he thinks about slavery. Like those guys in the
corner. Or those cops we talked to today. Or me. Most
people don't give a damn for abolition, even in Boston.
And those that do don't know what they're talking about.
Like you." Bob was glowering at me.

"And what do you know about it?" I asked, glowering
myself. "You saw slaves, but did you ever talk to any?
Or ask them how they felt? And if they're so damned
happy, why does it need a federal law to bring them back
if they run away?"

"I didn't say they were happy. I said they weren't so
bad off," Bob said. "Slavery suits 'em."

"Bob, you're the freest man I've ever met," I said.
"Can't you see that other people want their freedom as
much as you want yours?"

"Then why ain't they got it?"

"Because—because they'd be killed if they tried to take
it," I said.

"There you go. They'd rather be alive than free. And
that's what they are."

"But in your heart—" I began.

"I've got a white man's heart."

What I did next was unforgivable. Drunken. I tossed
my beer in Bob's face.

He sat there for a second, looking stupid with surprise.
Then he uncoiled his right arm and hit me square on
the eye. The blow knocked me backwards.

By the time I got to my feet, Bob was already on his.

"You want to go 'round, I'm ready," he said, his fists
clenched and cocked. His eyes were red hot.

If I'd been sober, I'd have tried to apologize. But I

wasn't sober, and I was furious. "To hell with you," I said.

The singers had stopped. They were standing up now, watching us and grinning.

"Finish him off," one shouted.

"Give it to him," another said.

"Go on, get out of here," Bob muttered. "And don't come back when you're sober. Damn abolitionist."

I made my way to the door, hardly seeing. A wave of ugly laughter pushed me out onto the street. The light hurt my eyes.

With my head spinning and anger choking me, I staggered off. There was nowhere to go but home, and I couldn't go there. Not as I was. I needed to sober up and to think of a good lie to tell. Bob would have had one at the tip of his tongue. "Clarity test. Some of the signals are coming into the office muddy." I shook my head and it spun. My eye hurt.

Beer, despair, and anger overwhelmed me, and I bent my head over the gutter to retch. I told myself I felt better afterwards, but I didn't.

SIX

 By late afternoon, I had thought of a lie. I had stayed late at school to work on my geometry. My eye was black from a badly thrown ball. I squared my shoulders and marched into the house.

I stopped as soon as I opened the door. Mother was standing in the parlor with Amy and Talitha clinging to her dress. My father had his arms around her. They were all in tears.

"Where have you been, you rascal?" my father roared. He stalked across the room to me.

"At school—" I began.

"I see very well what kind of school you have attended today," my father said. He swept his arm in front of me, and Bob's spare hat flew from my head and bounced against the wall. Somehow, it had stayed on my head all day, until I had forgotten about it. He stared me in the eye and smelled my breath. "Drinking, fighting. A fine education. Exactly what I feared would come of your 'hobby.' And you've brought home a trophy to commemorate your achievements. Tell me, did some low friend give you that hat, or did you steal it? Never mind, this is no time—"

My mother pushed past him, fell on my shoulder, and sobbed, "Theodore, thy grandfather Evans is dead. We have just had the telegram."

I had hardly known my mother's father. He and my grandmother had moved to Cincinnati when I was very small. I had only vague memories of a short, lively man with a sharp nose. Yet I felt as though something had been ripped away from me.

"Your mother and I must discuss the mourning, Theodore. Mind your sisters."

He took my mother into another room while I sat down with Talitha and Amy. They had not met their grandfather Evans, but they had never seen their mother so anguished. They were crying from fear. Nothing I could do would comfort them. They kept trying to jump down from the sofa and follow our parents. Every time I brought them back, they screamed more loudly.

At last, Mary came in to rescue me, with milk and a gingersnap for each of them. When she saw my eye, she brought a piece of beef for that. The girls calmed down enough to eat, and a little later, our parents came back.

"We have discussed what is best to do," my father said. "Your mother must go to Cincinnati for a time to be with her mother. We cannot all go; tickets for that would be too expensive. Therefore, I will stay here and look after the girls. Theodore, you will go with your mother to support her. You will leave as soon as we can find a train going west."

"There's a night train to Albany on the Western of Boston," I said. "It leaves at 9:10."

"Indeed," my father observed. "You are amazingly informative on some subjects, Theodore. One wishes you were as well versed academically. Well, that leaves us very little time. Go and pack one bag. Don't take your good suit; you'll be measured for mourning in Cincinnati."

"Surely I could leave tomorrow morning, Hale," Mother protested. "There is so much to do here."

"You will have to rely on me to see to it, Caroline," my father said, taking both her hands. "Your mother needs you most now. And I will do the best I can."

"Yes, Hale."

Mother went upstairs to pack.

I went to my room with one of our old carpetbags and stuffed it with nearly all the clothes I owned. By the time I was finished, the bag was bulging and I could barely close it.

My mother came downstairs in her black mourning dress. She would wear black for a year from this night.

"Put this on, Theodore," she said, handing me a black armband. "It will serve until thee have thy new suit."

We ate hurriedly. In the middle of the meal, Mary came back into the dining room.

"Beg pardon, but there's a young man to see Master Theodore. He says he'll wait," she said.

It had to be Bob.

My father gave me a hard look. "We will interrupt our meal, Mary. Come with me, Theodore."

Bob stood up when we came into the room. " 'Scuse me, Mr. Worth. I'm Bob Gibbons," he said. "Ted was down at my office earlier and left these." He held up my schoolbooks.

"It was good of you to return them, sir," my father replied coldly. "He will be spending more time with them in the future than he has in the past. He also has something I believe may be yours. Fetch the hat, Theodore."

When I brought it, Bob took it and said, "Thanks. It's mine. Ted, about today, I—"

"Then I believe our business is concluded," my father interjected. "My son is breaking off his connection with you. We are not accustomed in this house to drunkenness, fighting, and lying. I trust it will not be necessary to meet in the future, sir. Good night."

With a sigh, Bob turned and went out. My father looked silently at me for a long time. "This is disgusting and shameful," he said at last. "Have you forgotten who we are? Or do you simply not care anymore?" He held up his hand to cut off my answer. "I have nothing more to say on this subject. We will not mention it again. It goes without saying that you will stop your telegraphical nonsense at once and spend your afternoons henceforth in preparing for Harvard. Now we will go back in to your mother. Try to be a comfort to her, at least."

I sat at the table in misery for a few more minutes. Then a wagon came and took us to the depot. As we jolted away from home, my mother began to cry again.

The depot at night was the same scene of passengers and freight that I had seen scores of times, but somehow it was different now. Details I had not noticed for months stood out boldly under the gaslights.

I was full of sorrow and shame, but I could not help feeling a little excited. I had never left Boston before except to visit Concord or Cambridge across the river. Now in less than two days I would be in Cincinnati.

My mother bought our tickets. They were twenty dollars apiece. No wonder only two of us were going. Even in good times a hundred dollars for such a purpose would have been something to think over. A well-bound novel from our bookstore cost two dollars at the most.

There was little to see as we pulled away from the depot. Only the Charles River stood out, a wide swath of absolute darkness between the dim lights of Boston and the towns across from it.

My mother sat looking straight ahead. At last she said, "I wish so much, Theodore, that thee had known thy grandfather better. I often thought to take thee to visit, but I kept putting it off. I wanted more money in the house, or a more convenient time. Now that there is almost no money, and no time left at all, we go. I have been a fool."

It struck me that my grandfather, who had been a prosperous man, could have come to visit us, but I didn't say so. I simply put my arm around my mother's trembling shoulders.

There were sleeping cars on the train, but we did not pay the extra cost of one. We would spend the night sitting on hard red velvet seats, getting what rest we could. The train jerked and rattled, the engine rumbled and hissed, and the clack of the rails marked time for it all. It was more loud and uncomfortable than I had ever imagined, but we were making a steady twenty-five miles an hour. Tomorrow morning would find us in Albany.

My mother slept at last, but I couldn't. I felt betrayed by Bob, but I missed him. I was angry with my father. I was ashamed of myself. I felt the last of my drunkenness slowly leave my head, and as it lifted, felt the weight of my grandfather's death come down more heavily.

We reached Cincinnati late in the afternoon. At the train, we were met by a staid, middle-aged black man in top hat and frock coat. He had a mourning band like mine on his sleeve.

Tipping his hat to my mother, he said, "Have I the honor of addressing Mrs. Worth and son?"

My mother nodded.

"I am Jacob, ma'am, an employee of your mother's. Please come with me."

Jacob carried my mother's luggage to a fine-looking coach in front of the depot. The horses' harness was draped in black. The coachman was much younger and lighter-skinned than Jacob, but I saw a strong resemblance.

Jacob climbed up beside him, and we started off.

The streets of Cincinnati were crowded with people and wagons of every kind. On all sides, I saw fine new red brick buildings and the steeples of churches. There was a sense of bustle about the city that made me like it at once. Its people seemed to have come from everywhere. I could hear the accents of New England and the South on the streets. And repeatedly I heard German. The signs on the stores were in German almost as often as English.

Then I saw something that stood out even here. A gigantic birdcage of a building with a sort of minaret, the tallest thing on the street. I craned my head back to look at it again and wondered what it could be.

My grandparents' house was an immense place, with a deep porch running all along its front and sides. Perhaps it circled the building—I couldn't tell. There was a similar porch for the second story. The roofline was broken by a squarish six-sided tower. From this, and along the roof, ran a narrow widow's walk with an iron railing.

The house was generously supplied with chimneys, tall windows, and elaborate wooden scrollwork. It would have looked much like a Mississippi riverboat, except that the windows had all been shuttered for mourning. I was impressed, yet I wondered what kind of Quaker my grandfather had been. It wasn't the Friends' way, or Boston's way, either, to spend so much money on show.

But the outside of the house was nothing compared to the splendor beyond the entranceway. Even the vestibule was paneled in some rich, dark wood. The double doors that led into the rest of the house were a deep rose. The parlor to which Jacob showed us was as heavily furnished as a palace. There were so many sofas, tables, thick stuffed chairs, and fire screens that it was almost impossible to turn around.

"Mother, I never realized Grandfather was so rich," I whispered.

"We never were before," my mother said. "Nothing like this. It does not feel like home. I cannot see a single thing that I recognize."

There were two large portraits hanging over the fireplace. One was of a smiling, white-haired woman with her hand on a dog's head. The other showed a dapper little man leaning easily on a bale of cotton. My grandparents.

My mother went to the fireplace and looked up at the painting of her father. "Dearest one," she said, "please forgive me that I did not come before now."

Behind us Jacob said, "Mrs. Evans, ma'am."

I turned. My grandmother looked much like her portrait, but she was bent and unsmiling now. The same dog, old and bony, shuffled into the room after her.

She and my mother clung together.

"I thank God that thee have arrived safely."

"We had a good trip. Mother, this is thy grandson."

My grandmother took my hand and studied me. "A good face," she said at last. "Mostly Worth, but there is Evans enough in it. Thee are a very welcome sight, my boy."

"Thank you, Grandmother," I said, and kissed her lightly on the cheek.

Something pushed against my leg. It was the dog's nose. He wagged his tail slowly.

"Tiger likes thee. That speaks well of thee. He likes only gentle people."

She sat heavily on a chair so tall she almost disappeared into it. "The funeral is tomorrow," she said. "We hear the will afterwards. I have seen it. Thee will be well pleased, I think."

My mother started to cry once more.

Quietly my grandmother told us about my grandfather's death. He had been down on the landing, helping a gang unload cotton bales, when his heart had failed him. "It was a place he loved to visit," Grandmother said. "And the men thought it a good joke that one of the richest men in Cincinnati would play at longshoreman with them. But he was very strong for his size."

I glanced up to see Jacob nod.

After a while, Grandmother said, "Shall we go in to see thy father?"

I couldn't avoid it, of course. This was why we had come.

Jacob helped Grandmother out of her chair and led us into the back parlor. There was a coffin in the middle of the room, set on a catafalque draped in black. The coffin was also solid, shining black, with silver handles. Black candles burned at its head and foot.

I had never seen a dead body. My grandfather looked very small lying on the satin lining. His long nose was bigger than ever in his shrunken face, his skin covered with chalk. He did not really look like a man anymore. It was like looking at a huge, grotesque doll.

We sat on small, hard chairs. Grandmother and my mother were, I supposed, waiting for the inner light to inspire them with something to say. I was conscious only of the heavy heat and the silence in the parlor.

After what seemed to be a long time, Jacob put his hand on my shoulder and whispered for me to follow him. He led me up the stairs to my room, which, with the gas turned all the way up, was brightly lit. I could see through the cracks in the shutters that the sun was setting.

There were three men waiting for me there. Two had tape measures and bolts of black cloth. The third had a large pile of shoes.

"These gentlemen are here to provide you with mourning, Master Worth," Jacob said. "Because the funeral is tomorrow, I took the liberty of making the arrangements myself. These are Mr. Zimmermann and his assistant. The gentleman with the shoes is Mr. Schaeffer."

In a few minutes, Mr. Schaeffer had tried on several different pairs of fine black shoes and found one that fit me beautifully. They had high tops that ran up past my ankles.

Next, the tailors took my measurements and marked up some of the cloth with chalk. They went out of the room. In a few minutes, I heard the whir of a sewing machine down the hall.

"Mr. Zimmermann and his assistant will, I believe, require an hour or so to prepare your suit," Jacob said. "Until then, I will return you to the corpse."

But I didn't want to go back into that hot, still parlor just yet. My curiosity was bursting. "Jacob," I said, "could you tell me something about my grandfather? I hardly knew him."

"I shall try, Master Worth," Jacob said. "What is it that you would like to know?"

I blurted out, "How did he get so rich?"

"Hard work, Master Worth," Jacob answered.

"But in what? What did he do for his money?" I asked.

"Chiefly, he speculated in cotton, I believe," Jacob said. "Cotton and wheat. But chiefly cotton. He also exported luxury goods to the plantations. Iron lawn ornaments and the like."

I remembered the portrait of Grandfather leaning on a cotton bale. No wonder he'd built a house that looked like a riverboat. The wealth that had made him had flowed up from the slave states across the river. I saw it suddenly—this house was built on the labor and blood of slaves.

Quakers were abolitionists. But Grandfather had apparently seen nothing wrong in making a fortune based on slavery. I felt sick.

"But, Jacob—you are free, aren't you?"

"I am, Master Worth," he said calmly. "Is there anything else you would like to know? I am sure your mother and Mrs. Evans will be grateful for your return."

I let him lead me back through the darkened house to the parlor where my grandfather lay.

I don't know how long we sat there. I tried to feel sorrow, but I kept thinking of how my grandfather had made his money. How had he justified it to himself? Had he ever been bothered by what he was doing? If so, when had he changed? His coffin was silent, full of secrets. I was very grateful when Grandmother finally announced it was time for bed.

Jacob woke me early. I got up, feeling I hadn't slept at all. The morning was quiet but hectic. The undertakers came to set out a huge feast in the dining room, and people arrived to pay their last respects and to visit and eat. The tailors came back to make a few alterations to my suit.

I went downstairs and was introduced to dozens of white-whiskered gentlemen who shook my hand and called me a manly chap and told me what a fine man my grandfather had been. At last it was time for the funeral procession.

This was the biggest parade I had ever seen, bar the Fourth of July. Grandfather led off in the hearse with high glass sides, plumes, and black bunting. Four matched black horses drew it. Professional mourners in tall black hats trimmed with crepe marched along behind. A line of carriages came next, with the three of us in the lead. There might have been fifty others, all decked out in black.

The procession looped through the downtown and back again. We interrupted traffic for blocks. Many men stopped to doff their hats as we passed. I felt foolish and exposed sitting in our open carriage. My mother's eyes were dim, and she was hunched over, facing me. Grandmother's veil was so heavy, I couldn't see her face.

At last we returned home. I had thought that we were going to one of Cincinnati's new cemeteries, but I was wrong. Grandfather had had a tomb built for himself and Grandmother on a little hill behind the house.

Twelve pallbearers carried the coffin to a catafalque set up at the door to the tomb. The building was of polished granite with a couple of columns flanking a shining bronze door, and so tall it seemed top-heavy. On the lintel above the door was the word EVANS carved into the stone and gleaming like gold. Below, in smaller letters, ran DEUT. 23:15–16.

Standing waiting for us at the door was a tall, fat man in some sort of clerical clothing. He conducted an elaborate burial service that no Quaker would have approved of, in a heavy Southern accent. It was full of high-flown language and came out of a book. In the middle of it, he preached a long sermon on the holiness of my grandfather's life. What anyone else thought about it, I couldn't tell. My own thought was that, somewhere in his life, Grandfather had ceased to be a Quaker.

At last, it was over. My grandmother thanked "The Reverend Mr. Barnes" for his kindness in preaching, even though Grandfather "had not been of his flock." Barnes smiled and simpered and assured her that it had been his privilege and honor.

Everyone left, and we went back to the house to hear the will read.

The lawyer was a little man with immense muttonchop whiskers and no other hair. He had pale, bony hands with rings on most of his fingers.

"I am happy to be able to inform you that the late Mr. Evans left you all exceedingly well provided for," he said. "It is indeed fortunate that there are so few among whom to divide his generous estate."

He rustled his papers and began: " 'I, William Evans, being of sound mind and body, do hereby bequeath all my worldly goods to my dear wife and companion, Elizabeth Evans, with the following exceptions. To my loving daughter, Caroline, I leave the sum of ten thousand dollars in gold—' "

Mother gasped. Then she began to cry again.

The lawyer went on, " 'And to her son, my much missed Theodore, I leave my best watch and the sum of three thousand dollars in gold, to be paid to him on the day of his graduation from college or at the age of twenty-five, whichever shall come first. I leave as well any small personal item my wife may think fit to give him.

" 'To my dear granddaughters, Amy and Talitha, I leave the sums of three thousand dollars in gold each as dowries to be paid on the occasions of their marriages. Finally, to my son-in-law, Hale Worth, I leave my best thanks for the care he has taken of my daughter and the fine children he has brought into the world.

" 'I regret now that, in my enthusiasm for my business, I never returned to Boston to renew my connections with you, but God is calling me back to a home that is even older than Boston. Farewell, my dears.

" 'Your affectionate husband, father, and grandfather, William Evans.' "

The lawyer left, and we all sat with our thoughts. I had never imagined so much money. And so much of it for me. It didn't seem quite real. I wished I had known him. I wished he had come to visit us.

But perhaps it wouldn't have mattered. I would have been a child, with a child's vision. I would have loved him more but not known him any better. No, I was never going to know what kind of man William Evans, Friend, businessman, and profiter in slavery, had been really. Had he been a hypocrite, or had he simply not been able to see his connection to a thing he knew was wicked? Or had money answered every question for him?

At last my grandmother spoke: "Well. It has grown late. I suggest we all go to bed. Tomorrow will be better. Let us make it come a little sooner."

I did try to sleep. I lay on top of the covers for hours, pretending to ignore the heat and the stale air. I held absolutely still, telling myself I didn't notice the sweat running off me. The air grew worse.

Finally, I drifted into a doze. But on the edge of sleep, I heard the house creak in some far corner. I jerked awake, thinking of ghosts.

There was no point in trying to sleep now, I decided. I got up and raised the window in my room. I pushed open the shutters. No one would know if I mourned my grandfather with the window open.

It was balmy for March, and I held out my arms to the breeze coming up from the river. The moon was half-full but so bright that I could see every detail in the yard below.

I don't know how long I leaned on the windowsill, but

shortly before the moon went down, I saw three figures run across the lawn and disappear behind the house.

A shiver of fear went through me. A moment later, I heard Tiger bark. It was a tired noise, the sound of a dog who didn't really care who was in his yard. Nothing else happened as far as I could tell.

I didn't know what to do. I couldn't wake Mother and Grandmother and frighten them with what I'd seen. Nor did I want to admit I'd opened my window. Jacob and his son seemed to be the only men around the place, but where were they? I didn't even know where they slept.

I lit my candle, pulled on my pants and shirt, and slipped into the hall and down the stairs. The thick carpets muffled my steps. The heavy front door unlocked quietly, and I edged through it, blowing my candle out.

Now I felt well and truly scared. There was no sign of anything in the front yard. I crept around the side of the house where the three figures had gone. There was nothing to be seen there, either. Only a few trees and my grandfather's tomb.

I waited for a while in the shadow of the house, but nothing moved in that quiet place. I decided to go back inside. Then from the tomb I heard a cry.

I froze. There was no mistake that the sound came from behind the brass door, so faintly that in daylight I would never have noticed it. It came again.

Why I didn't run I do not know. Probably I was too frightened. But the third cry, louder than the first two, made me realize what had happened. My grandfather must be trying to get out. He had awakened in his coffin and was trapped in his own monument. Such things happened. I had to rescue him.

I ran to the tomb. The bronze door had a huge leverlike handle so big I needed both hands to move it. But it moved. I heaved on the door and pushed it slowly in.

"Grandfather?" I said. "Grandfather?"

Seven pairs of eyes looked back at me. No faces, only eyes. The cry came again. It was not a man's voice. I took a step back and bumped into the door frame. Then a dim red light glowed in that awful place, and I saw a face I knew.

"Go back to bed, Master Worth," said Jacob. "There is nothing here. You have seen nothing. Go to bed."

Behind him, a baby whimpered. Half a dozen dim shapes were holding their breaths.

"Jacob, my grandfather—" I began.

"Is in Heaven with the just," Jacob said. "But those he has left behind must do his work. Your part is to go to bed. Now." He gently pushed me out the door and closed it behind us. "Allow me to escort you back to the house."

As we rounded the front of the house, Jacob looked up at my open window. "So. Master Worth, I believe your grandmother would be very distressed to know that you had neglected your mourning. I suggest that neither of us say anything of these events to her. Do I have your word as a gentleman?"

"Yes," I said. "Only, what is going on?"

"Good night, Master Worth," Jacob said, and left me.

SEVEN

 I slept little that night. There must be some way, I thought, to warn Grandmother that her faithful servant was up to something behind her back. I had to find it.

When I came down to breakfast, Jacob was standing by my grandmother's chair.

"Thy mother and I have sad work to do this day, Theodore." She surprised me by smiling. "We must go through thy grandfather's things. There is no need for thee to be here. I shall have Jacob's son Joshua show thee Cincinnati."

"Respectfully, ma'am, that will be difficult for Joshua," Jacob said. "He has much work to do with the horses. I should be very glad to escort Master Theodore."

Grandmother nodded slowly. "Very well, Jacob, if thee think best."

When breakfast was over, he and I set off on foot. Our steps took us down broad streets lined with mansions into the center of town.

I felt sure that Jacob was anxious to keep me under his eye. And, since I knew he wouldn't answer any questions about what I had seen last night, I wasn't going to give him the satisfaction of asking them.

I was struck again by how busy Cincinnati was and how quickly it appeared to be growing. The city was not much older than I was. The fine stone houses I saw, decorated in the German style, and the college, churches, and theaters, had not been here when I was born.

Jacob didn't mind how long I took to examine the sights we passed. In fact, he took me out of our way to show me some of them. And he answered any question I asked him about what I saw. But all his answers were carefully considered, and as formal as if they came out of books: "This building, Master Worth, is a *verein* hall. German workmen build them as places to meet and to study. There are several in Cincinnati, each built by men of a different trade. . . . This spot, Master Worth, is where the original fortifications of the town were set up. It was a log palisade with loopholes for guns. I do not believe that it was ever attacked." After a morning of this, it struck me that Jacob would have been a great asset to Mr. Weems.

But even Jacob's pedantry couldn't kill my interest. The finest thing of all, when we reached it at last, was the river. It was a powerful dark gray, with the green hills of Kentucky rising on the far side. There were steamboats everywhere, coming and going and tied up to the wharves in front of us. They filled the sky with their smoke and called to each other with their bells and whistles. They were smaller and rounder than the Mississippi riverboats I had heard about, but they looked grand enough to me.

There were warehouses and stores all along the waterfront, full of goods and buyers. About half of them seemed to have the word *Kanawha* in their names.

I tried it aloud: "Kanawha."

"If I may, Master Worth, we pronounce it Ka*na*wha," Jacob said. "It is a river that flows into the Ohio some miles southeast of here in western Virginia. It is a region united to us by trade."

I looked toward the river, where a gang of black stevedores was unloading cotton from one of the riverboats. They were chanting a work song, only a few words repeated over and over. I wondered, *Are they slave or free?* I glanced at Jacob but could not read his expression.

Somewhere on that noisy wharf, another song started. Low, throbbing, and full of yearning. I had never heard anything like the sorrow in it.

> *Deep river,*
> *My home is over Jordan,*
> *Deep river, Lord,*
> *I want to cross over into campground,*
> *I want to cross over into campground.*

For a moment, the whole waterfront seemed to stop and listen. Then a steam whistle rose over the words and those who had listened turned back to their work.

It was late afternoon now, and Jacob suggested that we should go back to Grandmother's. But there was one more thing I wanted to see first. Something I had noticed on my first day in Cincinnati.

Even in a town full of ambitious buildings, this one stood out. It was three stories tall and crowned with a dome like something from the *Arabian Nights*. There was a deep granite porch in front. It sat on its lot at the corner of Third Street like a toy a giant had put down and forgotten. I wanted to know what it was.

When we reached it, I saw that the doors were heavily locked. Shrieks and wails came from inside. The word ASYLUM was painted over the door.

"What is this place, Jacob?"

"It is a madhouse, Master Worth."

"But why would anybody build a madhouse that looked like this?"

"It was not one originally," Jacob said. "It was, in fact, a museum. Your grandfather told me that an English female writer, a Mrs. Trollope, built it. Have you heard of her?"

I had heard of Fanny Trollope and of her son, Anthony, the novelist. But to come upon this connection with them here was astonishing.

"A museum? What kind of a museum?" I asked.

"She tried various things to attract the local people," Jacob replied. "The one that worked best was the Last Judgment. There were large paintings on glass of Heaven and Hell, and live actors moving among them. There was even a devil with an electrical pitchfork. I have been told that people came back time and again to see it."

To go from a museum of damnation to a madhouse seemed logical somehow, but frightening. It was as if the power of Hell had been tempted to this spot and been made real.

I noticed for the first time that everyone crossed the street to avoid this place.

"Let's go, Jacob," I said.

"Very well, Master Worth."

Three men who had been lounging in the shadows across the street caught up to us as we started toward home. One was a little gray man who barely came up to my shoulder and was bone thin. The other two were much bigger. One had a scraggly black beard, the other pale eyes and oily blond hair.

"Where you goin', boy?" asked the little man in an accent I had never heard before.

"I beg your pardon, sir?" I said.

"This nigger yours?" the little man said.

"We are both free men," I said. "Good-bye."

The three of them laughed.

"Both free, eh?" said the little man. "Well, I reckon we'll take your word—about you."

Suddenly Jacob broke into a run. Before he had got ten yards, the black-bearded man had hold of him and the third man had lifted him off the ground with his arms twisted behind his back.

"Let him go!" I shouted. "Help, murder!"

" 'Tain't murder," the little man said, grinning. " 'Tis returning property to its rightful owner. We're slave catchers, you see."

"But Jacob is free, I tell you. He works for my grandparents."

People were stopping to watch, but no one crossed the street to help. The two big men began hustling Jacob back toward the river.

"This man is being kidnapped," I called. "Someone help us, please."

No one moved. A few laughed.

"See, boy, those folks know the law better than you do," rasped the little man. "It's a mighty serious thing to interfere with a officer of the law in the process of his rightful duty. You could go to prison for it, by the laws of these here United States. But seein' it's your first offense—"

The pain shot up my groin and I bent double, letting out a sad little gasp. Then I felt a knee in my face. A blow pushed me into the dirt.

"Hold on just a minute," cried a big wagoneer with a whip in his hand.

Thank God, I thought, and tried to stand up.

"What proof you-all got?" said the wagoneer.

"All we need," said the blackbeard. But they stopped.

"What proof?" The wagoneer shook his whip.

"Got a paper here for a runaway slave just his height an' age," said the little man. "Want to see it?"

"Can't read," said the wagoneer. "But it don't matter. Probably ten hundred men in Cincinnati like him."

"This is the one we want," said the little man.

The wagoneer turned to me. I could almost stand straight again. "You say he's free?"

"Yes, damn it," I coughed out.

"Let's see his back."

The little man slit Jacob's clothes up the back with his Bowie knife. Jacob's skin was trenched and welted by whips. The scars were old.

"Fancy work," said the wagoneer. "Well, if he ain't your runaway, he's somebody's." He gave me a dirty look. "Lyin's a great sin, boy. For all your fancy clothes, you're less than a man like me. Don't forget it."

The three slave catchers hauled Jacob to the river while I struggled behind, calling for help. A few bystanders looked on; others turned away. No one took a step toward us.

There was a dirty little sailboat tied up at the wharf. The blackbeard leapt aboard and snatched up some chains. Jacob was bound wrists, feet, and neck. He had said nothing all this time. But when the chains were locked onto him, he threw back his head and howled.

"You'll pay for this," I shouted. "I'll rescue you, Jacob. We'll get lawyers—"

The little gray man said, "He's snug now, Burl. You can belt that boy if you want. Don't cripple him none, though."

The big blond climbed back onto the wharf and in one motion lifted me off my feet. I swung at him, and he laughed. Then he sat down on a barrel, turned me over his knee, and pulled down my pants. His hand was like iron.

After he'd had his fun, he threw me to the ground and kicked me.

"Jest you lay there till we're gone," he said. "I see you get up, I'll whup you good." He jumped back into the boat.

I stood up as they pushed off. "I'll have you for this," I shouted. "I'll have you all for it."

Jacob looked back at me, despair in his face.

The slave catchers laughed, and then they were beyond hearing me. I watched as they edged out into the strong current some yards offshore. I saw the little boat swing around, and the men turn their attention to the rudder and sail. That was what Jacob was waiting for. As soon as they took their eyes off him, he jumped.

He made one great splash and disappeared. He'd never had a chance, and he knew it.

The little boat crossed to Kentucky.

EIGHT

It was dusk by the time I limped back to the house. As I came up the street, Joshua was cantering toward me on the bare back of one of Grandfather's horses.

He pulled up when he saw me. "Master Worth, you are hurt," he exclaimed, sounding just as Jacob would have. Then, "Where is my father, Master Worth?"

I leaned against a picket fence for support and dropped my eyes. "Jacob's—*dead*. He . . . we . . . slave catchers near the river . . . I tried . . ."

Joshua whipped his head from side to side like a hunted thing.

I reached up for his hand and clutched it. "I tried. I tried, but . . ."

"No," Joshua said, his eyes glistening with tears. "You're wrong. You must tell me so, Master Worth. Please."

"I'm sorry," I said. "I tried. There were too many for us."

"Slave catchers? Slave catchers killed my father?"

Joshua was on the ground beside me now, hanging on to me.

"No," I said. "He killed himself."

"He would never do that," Joshua shouted.

"They tore the shirt from his back. They saw his scars," I said. "No one would help. When they put chains on him, he jumped in the river."

Joshua collapsed against the side of the horse and wept, pounding his fists into the animal's side. The horse bent its head around and nickered at him. It pushed its nose against his face.

I did not know what to do. At last, I put my arm around Joshua's shoulders.

The door to the house opened.

"Theodore?" my mother called. "Theodore, what is wrong?"

"Joshua," I said to him. "Joshua, we have to tell the others."

Without Jacob, the whole household seemed to collapse. The dignified mourning for my grandfather evaporated. All of the silent and almost invisible servants suddenly appeared and wandered up and down the halls weeping. I cried more for Jacob than I had for my own grandfather. They were tears of rage at the slave catchers, the wagoneer, and at the people who'd stood by and watched. I hated Cincinnati now. I hated my country, where what had happened to Jacob was legal. The slave catcher had been within his rights.

The next day, Grandmother called all the servants into the front parlor. She gave them train tickets to Canada and money to get started there. "There is no safety here anymore for thee," she told them. "There never was. And without Jacob and my husband, there is no keeping their work going. I am too old and too weak in cunning, and Joshua cannot do it alone. Go and find thy true freedom."

There was more crying then, and a great deal was said that I did not understand. Joshua swore that he would never leave. "They can't stop us, ma'am, and you can't make me go. We can keep the work going. Don't send me away."

My grandmother only shook her head.

People began to leave the house later in the day. I felt the life seeping out of the place. Early that night, Grandmother called Mother and me into the parlor in the back. She had a few things stacked on a little table beside her chair.

"I would have thee know about my husband," she said. "Thee have seen how we live. It is not exactly according to how thee were brought up, Caroline. Thee may think that thy father had forgotten who he was. He had not." She stopped, cried a little, and then went on. "Thy father and Jacob were stationmasters on the Under Ground Rail Road. In our years here in Cincinnati, they saved more than one hundred poor souls out of bondage. They used his fine tomb to hide them."

I understood suddenly. Grandmother would have known well enough what old Tiger barked at that night.

"Thee have seen the verses cut over the door of his tomb," she went on. "They were his little joke. Here, read them." She took a Bible from the table and handed it to us.

> *15 Thou shalt not deliver unto his master the servant which is escaped from his master unto thee:*
> *16 He shall dwell with thee, even among you; in*

that place where he shall choose in one of thy gates;
where it liketh him best. Thou shalt not oppress him.

My grandfather had rescued more slaves than old John Brown. He had borne the disdain of other good men and pretended friendship with bad ones, all to save men and women from bondage.

Mother's eyes were shining. "Mother, I thank thee ten thousand times for this," she said. "Thee has given me my old, true father back. He was a better man than I ever knew."

"He was the best man," my grandmother said. "But his work is ended now." She put the Bible back and handed me a leather tube with brass fittings. "This is for thee, Theodore. I am sure thy grandfather would want thee to have it."

I opened the tube and slid out the finest spyglass I had ever seen. No Boston ship's captain could have had a better one. It telescoped out nearly the length of my arm, and when I put it to my eye, the flocking in the wallpaper stood up like wheat.

"It's wonderful, Grandmother," I said. "Thank you."

"I hope thee may find a use for it."

Grandmother quickly hired some white servants to replace the others. But things did not go as smoothly as before. The new help had everything to learn. Mother took over their training, and so we had to stay in Cincinnati longer than she had planned.

I tried to make myself useful, but there was little for me to do. My best help seemed to be to stay out of the way.

I took to sitting with Tiger in the garden or on the steps of the tomb. I brought along books from Grandfather's library, but I didn't finish any of them. I brooded for hours on what had happened and on what I could have done differently. I wondered what I would do now. Only one thing seemed clear to me. If I had had old John Brown's pistol with me that day, Jacob would still be alive.

Brown was the man I should talk to, I decided. He would understand. He could advise me what to do. When we got back to Boston, I would track him down, no matter where he was.

We returned home. My days there were slow and very much alike. The last weeks of school crawled along. A glorious spring went by outside my window, but I barely noticed. I spent my afternoons studying, since there was nothing else to do with them. My telegraph key was locked up in a closet in my parents' bedroom, and Bob was out of my life.

My father announced that he was well pleased with me. I didn't care. After Cincinnati, nothing in my old life seemed to matter. It was too small for me now.

I wrote to everyone I knew who might know where Brown was, asking for his address. Those who answered wrote only to say they did not know. I was sure they were lying, but there was nothing I could do about that. Brown might as well have been on one of the stars I looked at through my telescope at night.

Then Julia Ward Howe came to call on my mother.

Normally, I had nothing to do with visits from my

mother's friends. This time, I found excuses to stay within earshot of the parlor. Mother's version of our trip to Cincinnati left out a great deal. She said nothing of Jacob's death or of the Under Ground Rail Road. Mrs. Howe was all sympathy and courtesy, and stayed exactly the proper length of time.

As she was getting ready to leave, I appeared at the door and said, "May I walk you home, Mrs. Howe?"

My mother smiled. Mrs. Howe thanked me.

When the door closed behind us, I said, "Mrs. Howe, I would like to tell you some more things that happened in Cincinnati. My mother did not mention them, perhaps because she did not see them, but I did. And because I saw them, I need your help, if you will give it. I want you to intercede with your husband for me."

"Whatever can you mean, Theodore?" Mrs. Howe asked.

"I saw a man die rather than be taken back into slavery," I said.

"Dear God!" she gasped. I waited. "And what do you want Dr. Howe to do?" she said finally.

"Only to give me John Brown's address. He has refused to do it already, but perhaps if I could tell him the story, he would relent."

Julia Howe shook her head. "I do not follow you. Why should you need Mr. Brown's address?"

"I want his advice on how to proceed," I said.

Julia Howe looked at me quizzically. "Proceed with what?"

"I want to know my best course as an abolitionist," I said. "I think he is the man to tell me."

Julia Howe regarded me gravely. "Mr. Brown leads a dangerous life. People who are near him may be in danger, too. As you already know."

"You and your husband don't mind it," I said.

"We accept it," Mrs. Howe said. "But the rest of your family does not see things as we do."

"I do not see things as my family does," I replied.

"I am torn, Theodore," she said. "When we reach home, come in. Tell your story to my husband. I think he must decide whether to help you."

I waited while Mrs. Howe found her husband. When at last Dr. Howe appeared, he sauntered into the room, his wife following. He was prepared to be polite to an excitable boy.

"So, Theodore, I understand from my wife that you have had a most terrible encounter in Cincinnati," he said. He made a little temple of his fingers and bent forward. "I should very much like to hear it from your own lips."

"When I was in Cincinnati, I met a man who worked for my grandfather. A free Negro named Jacob," I said. "A quiet man. He seemed unfriendly. The night of my grandfather's funeral, I heard noises outside the house and went to see what the matter was. I found nothing outside, but I heard a wail from my grandfather's tomb. I found the door unlocked, and some people inside. Jacob was with them. He would tell me nothing, but escorted me back to the house and made me promise to say nothing of what I had seen. The next day, he took me walking in the town. Down by the waterfront, slave catchers attacked us. I told them Jacob was free, but they ripped the shirt from his back and discovered whip marks. That was all they needed. They took him aboard their boat and chained him. Then, when they turned their backs for a moment, he jumped into the river and drowned. I had to carry the news home to my grandmother. She immediately dismissed all her servants and sent them to Canada. Then she told us that Jacob and my grandfather had been stationmasters on the Under Ground Rail Road."

Chev Howe's back was straight; his fists were clenched and his eyes burning. Mrs. Howe moved over to the little sofa where I sat and took my hands in hers.

"If I had been there, boy, there would have been blood," Howe snapped.

"Since that day I have been thinking what would have happened if John Brown had been there," I said.

"Ah, Brown. Now there would have been the man to have at your side," he said.

"Dr. Howe, I need to find John Brown," I said. "I have to find my own way to fight slavery. And I think John Brown is the man to tell me."

Dr. Howe did not answer for a long time. Then he said, "Brown is not an easy man to find. And he is at present very busy on work that I will not discuss without his leave to do so. Indeed, I do not know much about it," he said with emphasis. "But knowing what little I do, and knowing your father, I think I must regretfully decline to help you."

"Dr. Howe, I am not my father," I said.

"You are quite right, Theodore," he said blandly. "But you are not quite yet your own man, either."

"Good night, then," I said, getting up and heading for the door.

"If there is any other help or advice I can give you, please come to see me again," Dr. Howe said to my back.

Mrs. Howe came to the door with me. "What you have seen makes me want to do anything I can to help you," she whispered. "But I fear what may come of it if I do."

My heart leapt. "There can be no danger to us in a letter or two," I said.

"There isn't, if it stops with that," she agreed. "If I help you, you must promise me it will go no further than letters. I value your trust, Theodore. Please, for your mother's sake, do not betray mine."

I said nothing. Mrs. Howe bit her lip.

"He stops sometimes at a hotel in Springfield," she said, and gave me its name. "Remember to address your letter to Shubel Morgan."

NINE

To my surprise, I heard from John Brown within the week. His letter lay on the tray by the door, with the rest of the morning mail. The paper seemed to glow in my hand.

>*North Elba, N.Y.*
>*June 15, 1859*

My Dear Young Friend,

I have just received yr. letter and will be most happy to see you again. It fills my heart to think of those events in Cincinnati, and I understand how it is that now you wish to do something against such men. I am home at present on business which I cannot confide here. If you can come to my farm at North Elba, we may talk about it. Come soon if you can, as I do not expect to be here much longer.

>*Your Friend,*
>*John Brown*

P.S. Bring your telegraph. J.B.

I needed to be alone to think. I went out the front
door and jumped down the steps into the street. I walked
around the block three times before I was calm enough
to look at the letter again. Then my brain started to
work.

If I was going to make my way to upstate New York,
I needed to start soon, and I needed money to get there.
My parents would look for me, of course. I must do
something to throw them off my trail, and I must travel
fast. After a long time, I had worked out a plan. I went
back into the house.

Mother was sitting in the front parlor, sewing a dress
for Talitha. The bright fabric spilled across the floor in
the sunlight. She made a happy picture sitting there, but
her face was drawn and pale.

"Thee have had a letter from John Brown," she said.

"How did you know?" I asked.

"Julia Howe told me what name he is using now."

"I wrote to him on a private matter," I said.

"I fear to ask what that matter is, Theodore." She
studied my face for a long time. Then she said, "Theodore,
do not thee remember thy grandfather? Did he not save
more poor souls out of bondage without violence than
John Brown has with it?"

"I think that only John Brown has an answer for the
men who killed Jacob," I said.

My mother closed her eyes and bent her head to her
hand. "That answer is death," she said.

"If John Brown had been with me and Jacob that day,
no one would have died," I said. "Those slave catchers
would not have dared to attack us. Jacob would be with

Grandmother, helping more people to freedom and taking care of her."

"It is a hard thing to reject violence in a good cause," my mother said quietly. "But violence is never just, Theodore, even in the best cause. And it rarely achieves anything but more violence. Mr. Brown is a brave man and a good one, but it was votes, not bullets, that made Kansas a free state."

"It was Brown's guns that protected the voters," I said.

"Have thee prayed for thy inner light?" Mother asked.

"Yes," I lied.

"I hope thee are telling me the truth, Theodore," she said. "But I fear Jacob's death has killed something in thee, too. Dearest one, do nothing from hate."

"I promise," I said, lying again, "if you will promise not to tell Father about this letter."

"I cannot do that," Mother replied. "Thee should talk with him about this."

"No," I said. "He hates Brown."

"He does not hate Brown," Mother said. "He fears what Brown would do if he had the power."

"If Brown had the power, he would free all the slaves," I replied. "Doesn't Father want that? Don't you?"

Mother looked away and shook her head sadly. "It is not like me to keep secrets from thy father. And I am not sure thee are telling me the truth. But I will promise to keep this secret." She sighed heavily.

I kissed her cheek and went out of the room. I had to work quickly.

Money was the first and easiest of my problems to solve. I took Grandfather's beautiful telescope, extended it one last time to its full length, closed it, and slid it into its tube. Then I went down to the waterfront and sold it to a clipper's first mate for ten dollars. Together with the two dollars I had saved, it should be enough.

Now all I needed was my telegraph key.

There seemed to be no way to get it. It was sitting in a locked closet, and I rather suspected my parents wouldn't open that particular closet for me. I wandered around Boston Common, trying to think of how it might be done, and came up with nothing.

Then two words from the past came back to me. "Clarity test," I whispered. One well-told lie could solve my problem.

The next day, about two in the afternoon, I ran into my father's office.

He was busy with his red and blue pencils and some author's manuscript. He looked up and raised his eyebrows at my interruption.

"Father, Mother has misplaced her keys and sent me to borrow yours," I blurted out.

"That is very unlike your mother, Theodore," he said. Still, he reached into his pocket.

"I'm sure they'll turn up," I said. "I'll bring these back shortly."

Father nodded and resumed his work.

It was a hot, heavy afternoon, and Mother and the girls were sitting under the trees behind our house. It was the easiest thing in the world to go upstairs and unlock that closet door. My telegraph key was there, as I had known it would be. It felt good to hold it again. I tapped it twice and smiled.

I returned to my father. "Here," I said, handing him the keys, "and thank you."

"And where was your mother's set?" Father asked.

"They fell out of her pocket when she was hanging out clothes," I said.

He shrugged, and I left, to seek the best way to North Elba.

There were seven railroads leading out of Boston, but not one of them went near the place. It lay at the edge of the Adirondack wilderness. The best way there was by stagecoach to Lake Placid, about three miles beyond it. From there, I would have to walk back. I paid for my ticket on the next day's early coach.

June twentieth dawned hot. I was up before then to leave a note on the kitchen table.

Am gone West to try my luck. Don't worry—I have my key.

T.

Talitha's and Amy's voices followed me downstairs. "Where are you going, Theodore? Why are you up so early? We want to come, too."

"I'll be back soon," I called, reflecting briefly that lying was becoming rather easy for me, with relatively little practice. Perhaps I had a talent for it.

The night before, I had hidden my bag, with my key and some clothes, under a bush in the yard. I snatched it up now and made my way swiftly in the direction of the stage station.

The coach was leaving just as I ran up. The driver

threw my bag on top, and I jumped in. I was the only passenger.

The driver started with a jolt that threw me hard onto the seat, and we were off, bouncing over the cobblestones so that my teeth rattled.

It took three days to reach Lake Placid, and by that time I was heartily sick of stagecoaches. To ride in one was to spend all day being shaken like a rat by a terrier, except that this terrier could shake up to a dozen unfortunate passenger-rats at once, all knocking into each other. By the time we reached Lake Placid, I was as glad to see the place as if I were returning to a much-loved home.

I walked back to North Elba, a small village of five farms on poor soil. I found a room in a house for the night and counted the hours until morning.

While I was waiting, I practiced with my key, getting the rust out of my fingers. It felt good to be tapping out the Morse again. Once or twice a wave of regret rose up in me at what I had done, not so much to my parents as to my sisters. I thought of their bewilderment and fear and longed to go back home and take them in my arms. But these times passed, and I stayed where I was.

The next day, I made my way to John Brown.

A long road ran straight uphill toward the farm. It stood alone at the foot of a mountain, not a high one, but steep. Any marshal or sheriff coming near would be visible a long way off. The farmhouse was low and unpainted, with a chimney at either end and a scraggle of trees behind it. There was nothing unusual about it except for a huge rock leaning against one side.

I knocked. A girl opened the door. She had black hair and froglike eyes. "Good day, sir," she said.

"My name is Theodore Worth," I told her. "Is Mr. Morgan in?"

"You may call me Brown up here," said a voice from the back. John Brown came and stood in the doorway. "Come in, Worth." He smiled. "I expected I'd see you here."

The inside of the house was almost as barren as the mountain. It was dark and drafty, and full of people.

A man with a shotgun and hard eyes came over and shook my hand. "Jeremiah Anderson," he said. "Pleased to know you."

I was sure he had been holding that gun on me as I came up to the door.

Brown introduced me all around. Besides Anderson, there was Brown's handsome son Oliver, who sat close by his new wife, Martha. They were as fine-looking a couple as I have ever seen. The girl who had answered the door was John Brown's daughter Annie. She was a little younger than I, and followed her father adoringly with her huge eyes. Her sister Ellen, next in the circle, looked about four. Their mother, Mary, nodded silently to me. She had a fine, strong face and had cut her hair very short. Last, there was Owen Brown, his shoulders bent, his hands nervous.

As for Brown himself, he looked different again. I noticed for the first time that he was not as big as I had remembered. I recalled him as nearly a giant, but he was almost exactly my height, and I am not tall. His beard was short now and grayer. He was aging. But when he took my hand, I felt the power in the man. Nothing had touched it. I thought he seemed fiercer than ever.

We all followed Brown into the kitchen, like filings after a magnet, and Annie made some tea. Brown told everyone a couple of stories from the time he'd spent with us. He seemed to remember every detail.

"You will eat with us and spend the night," he said to me. "Tomorrow, we will have time for some private talk."

I was given a place at the table next to Brown. When our plain meal was finished, everyone gathered around the fire. The family treated Brown like visiting royalty, I thought. Annie waited on him hand and foot, though she seemed to be everywhere else at once, washing dishes and cleaning up. Oliver stayed close to his wife, but kept his eyes on his father and never made a move without his say-so. Mary Brown sat by her husband and worked on a pile of clothes needing to be mended, talking about things on the farm, but speaking only when Brown spoke to her.

Brown spent most of the time after supper paying attention to Ellen. He took her on his knee and played and sang to her in his strong, flat voice. He was as tender and gentle as a man can be with a child, but Ellen seemed a touch frightened, as though she had seen so little of her father that she didn't really know who he was. Finally, he asked her, "Would you like your old father to lift you up on his hands?"

Ellen gravely shook her head no.

"My dearest little one, you need never be afraid when I am with you. I once lifted Mr. Worth's two little sisters up, one on each hand. Isn't that so, Worth?"

"Yes," I agreed, and added, "they still talk of it."

"Come, I will show you how I do it," Brown said, and lifted Ellen almost up to the ceiling. He set her gently down, and she immediately ran to her mother and hid her face in Mrs. Brown's skirt.

Anderson and I sat together. He stationed himself closest to the door and kept his shotgun by him. I had seen no dog on the farm, but perhaps with Jeremiah Anderson they didn't need one.

"Were you in the fighting in Kansas?" I said, trying to start a conversation.

"Oh, yeah," he said.

"Was it bad?"

"It's always bad," Anderson said.

After that he withdrew into himself and was silent until he announced he was turning in.

"I should, too," I said.

"Wait," said Annie, and lit the stub of a candle for me. It was in an old pewter holder with the handle broken off. "I reckon you'll bunk with Mr. Anderson. Good night."

Our bed was just big enough for the two of us. I blew out the candle and lay down with my back to Anderson. I felt very strange to be sleeping next to a man who hadn't exchanged more than a sentence with me all night.

"Good night," I said.

"Night," Anderson agreed. Then he added, "Don't worry about the fighting. You either do it or you run. Real simple."

I soon heard his breathing change to the long-drawn rhythm of sleep. Then I slept, too.

Breakfast came early and was quickly over. When we were finished, Brown said, "Come with me, Worth. I'll show you a bit of the farm."

The wind was blowing so hard we almost had to shout over it. Even on this sunny morning, the air felt cold. Small clouds came and went swiftly.

"I am sorry about your grandfather," Brown said as we took in the view down the road to North Elba. "I never knew mine, but he was a hero to me. Was and is. He was a captain in the Revolution." He put a hand on my shoulder. "Does your family know where you are?"

"No," I replied. "They think I've gone West with my telegraph key."

"Well," said Brown, "they aren't fools. They will be looking for you here pretty quickly, I expect. No matter. I shan't be here."

"I am sorry to have caused you any trouble," I said.

Brown laughed. "Half this country wants to kill me, and the other half wants to turn me over to those who do," he said. "I reckon you are not much more trouble."

"But that's not true," I said. "You have support all over the North."

"I can always draw a crowd," Brown said. "I suppose that is a kind of support. But it is not what's needed. What did Chev Howe tell you?"

"Only that you were busy at something he didn't know much about."

Brown's body rocked with one of his silent laughs. "That's Chev," he said. "Well, he's right. He knows little enough. And the less he knows, the happier we both are."

"But doesn't he give you money for your work?" I asked.

"Oh, yes. Some. And Sanborn and a few others. But they don't necessarily want to know what I do with it," Brown said. "And I am not inclined to think that they should. It makes some folks nervous to know too much."

Brown shrugged and swung his arms irritably. His face looked grimmer than usual for a moment, and he went on. "I was almost set to go South in '57, but the business panic dried up my money. And a fellow I'd hired to train my volunteers went to my supporters—Chev Howe and Frank Sanborn and the others—and told them that if he didn't get more pay, he was going to run down to Washington City and squeal like a stuck pig. When they wouldn't pay, he went to Senator Sumner and told him all about it."

"And then what happened?" I asked.

"Well," Brown said, "they are all fine gentlemen and are a little worried about being associated with anything that might land them in prison. First, they cut back on the money they'd already promised me. Then they told me that they would have nothing to do with such plans, if they knew about them. So we agreed that, in the future, they would not know about my plans."

"My father thinks you mean to split the Union over slavery," I said. "Is that what you hope to do?"

"I think this country is split apart by slavery already," Brown answered. "And the slave owners know it. Look at the army. Every department but New England is commanded by a Southerner. The Southern secretary of the army is transferring weapons into Southern arsenals. The

Southern secretary of the navy has sent all our ships into far waters. The Southern secretary of the treasury is draining all our money into Southern banks. They know what they are doing. So should we all."

He fixed me with his hunter's eye. "Some of us would split this country to keep slavery alive. Others would risk splitting it in order to kill it. What would you do?"

"Anything I could," I replied. "I hate all slaveholders."

"Careful, youngster," he said. "Don't let hate get a grip on you. Anger yes, but not hate. I never yet killed a man because I hated him."

This answer, so much like my mother's warning, stunned me. "But didn't you hate the men you killed out in Kansas?"

"No," Brown said. He leaned closer to me. "Now, let me tell you a story. My boy Frederick was killed about a year after Osawatomie Creek. Shot on his own front porch one morning by some Missourians. They were taking revenge. We knew who had organized it. We tracked that man to his farm, and one of my men put him in the sights of his rifle. But at that moment I forbade the killing. He did not own slaves. I saw that to murder him would not have advanced our cause. So I let him live. Hew to the one task, Theodore, and you will never go far wrong."

"But what task is that?" I asked. "That's what I need you to advise me on. How can I best serve the cause of freedom?"

"That all depends," Brown said slowly. "Are you a Quaker like your mother?"

"No," I said.

"Then can you kill?"

That stopped me. "I don't know," I said at last.

"That is a thing to know," Brown said. "Do you remember the day I put the pistol in your hand years back?"

"Yes," I replied.

"If you had had it in Cincinnati, would you have used it?"

"Yes," I said. I felt sure of that.

"Then you have the answer to my question," Brown said. "Come along." And he led me in the direction of the barn.

"For twenty years or more I have had a plan," he continued. "I have studied it and researched it. I have visited the fortresses of Europe and read all the books I could find on guerrilla warfare. Do you know what kind of warfare that is?"

"No," I admitted. I didn't know then that there *were* different kinds of warfare.

"It is the war of the weak against the strong," John Brown said. "The war of the ambush and the quick, small raid. It is the kind of war my grandfather fought against the redcoats. We won one war for freedom with guerrilla tactics. We can win another."

"What is your plan?" I asked.

"That is as much as I can tell even a friend," Brown said. "It is better not to know too much of it at once. Besides, plans must change sometimes to fit circumstances. But I will tell you this: I think I have the right to require a few men to be as dedicated as myself to the work, so long as I ask nothing of them that I would not do.

"This fight runs in my family," Brown went on, unlocking the barn door. "Do you know much about the Alton Riots?"

"A little," I said. "Men in Illinois killed a minister for printing an antislavery newspaper. That was in '36, I think."

"Thirty-seven," Brown said. "I was living in Ohio then. My father and I were in church when the news reached us there. I stood up, raised my hand, and said, 'Here before God in the presence of these witnesses, I consecrate my life to the destruction of slavery.' Then my father got up. He had a terrible stammer and didn't love to speak in public, but he said, 'When John the Baptist was killed, his disciples took his body and laid it in the tomb and went and told Jesus. Let us go to Jesus now and tell Him,' and the congregation sang mightily as we went up to the altar, my father and I, and knelt there. That is the kind of men I need, men who have knelt at that altar."

"Captain Brown," I said, "will you take me along when you start your war?"

He cocked his head at me. "Captain? Yes, Worth, you may call me captain now."

In the light from the open door, I could see stacks of long wooden cases. The lid on one case was loose. Brown lifted it up and handed me what was inside.

"Sharps rifle," he said. "Most accurate weapon in the world. Loads from the breech, so it fires five times as fast as a muzzle loader. Here, look at these."

From another case he took out a long pole with a Bowie knife blade attached. He tapped his finger against the blade, and it rang. "Bell metal," he said. "The finest. I have these and five hundred more coming."

I took it from him. "But Captain, are pikes useful in war nowadays?" I said.

"They are as I will use them," Brown said. "For a

brave man who does not know how to shoot, a pike may serve well until he learns. Militia, you see, won't stand up to bayonets. A thousand free men charging with these can scatter their enemies like dust."

The wind keened through the barn, whistling and sobbing.

"This is what it must come to," Brown said. "This is what it must be. Can you do it?"

I thought a long thought. It was a desperate thing, but not impossible. There must be more to this than I could see. More men, somewhere. More weapons to come. Under this man, who had already done so much, we could finish the job. We could shake slavery apart. I was sure of it.

"I will kneel at the same altar," I said.

Brown nodded. "We will leave tomorrow morning."

We started back to the house. We stopped by the immense rock that leaned against it. The name JOHN BROWN was cut deep into its side. I felt something go cold inside me.

"That was my grandfather," Brown said. "Captain John Brown, who served Connecticut in the Revolution. About a year ago, I had the stone moved here and my son Frederick's name carved on the back of it. When I am dead, this stone shall cover all of us." He patted it.

There was a grim smile on his face. A cloud passed overhead, and for an instant Brown and the stone were the same black mass. Then the sun came back.

"It will be a fine thing to lie here when all is done," Brown said.

PART TWO

The Invisibles

TEN

 Two rivers came together, making a point of land as sharp as a spear. Along both banks of the point the arsenal buildings were strung out, in neat red brick. The town filled in the space behind them and ran up the hill beyond. It was as pretty a spot as any in America.

"What rivers are those?" I asked.

"The big one is the Potomac; the smaller one is the Shenandoah," Brown answered.

This was my first look at the valley, though we had been nearby for two weeks now. Brown had spent nearly every day scouting with one or two of the others, but I had been kept at the farm he had rented eight miles away in Maryland. Sometimes I had been the only one there, and I hadn't liked being left behind. But today I was part of the deception.

"How well is the arsenal guarded?" I asked.

"A few night watchmen is all," said big, blond John Cook. "I've made friends with a couple of 'em. Nice old fellows. I would hate for 'em to get hurt."

I had met Cook just that day. He had been living in

Harper's Ferry for a year, spying for Brown. He was an outgoing man, and everyone in town liked him. He had even married one of the town girls.

"None shall be hurt, I hope," Brown assured him. "We want no battle here."

Looking down into the valley below us, I could see why. Its sides were as steep as a bowl's. Only three ways led out of it by land, and only two of those were any good. The third, which we were on, was a rugged track that led into the mountains. It would be easy to be trapped in a place like that. I was glad Brown was an expert raider who always left himself a line of retreat.

"And there are no regular troops in the area closer than Washington City," John Kagi said happily. He was Brown's second-in-command. He had joined us last night at the farm.

"Regulars," Brown snorted. "A few dozen marines, you mean. Guarding ships' stores is all their soldiering. And no militia anywhere. Not that I give spit for militia."

"Still, when the day comes, we must be quick," said Kagi, stroking his fine brown beard. "Once we seize the arsenal, we must begin work at once to get away. We won't be safe until we're up in these mountains behind us."

"Oh, there'll be time enough to get out," Brown said. "There's no one to stop us."

"Still, we must be quick," Kagi said.

Jeremiah Anderson started to unpack the extra horse we had brought. He handed me a rock hammer, while Brown, Kagi, and he set up surveying equipment.

"I thought we were cattle buyers and farmers," I said.

"So we are." Kagi grinned. "But we also drop hints

that we are prospectors. It gives folks a reason why we are out and about scouting so much. And the rumors that we're looking for gold cheer everyone up."

"I like to make folks cheerful," John Cook said.

The sound of horses coming up the road caused us to turn. There were six riders, all carrying pistols and shotguns. Chains clanked at their saddlebows.

"Morning," said their leader, reining up beside Brown.

"Good morning to you," Brown said.

"Seen anything of two niggers go this way?"

"You are the first people we have seen this morning," Brown answered.

The man looked hard at us. "You ain't from around here," he said.

"I rent a farm a few miles north," Brown said.

"The old Kennedy place?"

Brown nodded.

"I heard of you," the man said. "Well, if you didn't spot 'em on the road, check your barn and henhouse when you get home. There's money in it if you catch 'em. Fifty dollars apiece."

"Indeed," said Brown. "And how would we know them?"

The man handed over a poster with two descriptions on it: *CUJO, about twenty-five, medium height and build. Very thick arms. CASSIE, about eighteen, light complexioned, about five feet. If taken, contact the sheriff or Mr. Hiram Harris, Waverly Plantation. $50 reward each.*

"And you gentlemen have hopes of catching them?" Brown asked.

"Oh, I guess we will," the leader said. "We run down five last season, didn't we, boys?"

The boys all nodded, and one let out a long, drawn-out whoop.

"I was not aware that slaves had a season," Brown said.

"Well, you'd better know it if you're goin' to live around here, mister," the leader said. "Fall's the time the owners sell their extra slaves south. Some of 'em don't take to the idea of goin' to Mississippi, and run off. Mostly, though, what happens is one of a pair gets sold and the other one hangs itself. That's what the season is."

"We thank you for the information," Brown said. "If we run into these two ungrateful runaways, we will certainly know how to treat them."

The leader stuck out his hand. "Brannan's the name, Captain Bill Brannan," he said.

Brown took it. "I am Isaac Smith."

"Remember what I told you, Smith," said Brannan. "Fifty dollars apiece, if we don't catch 'em first. Come on, boys." They rode off north.

"I thought you said there were no militia here," I said.

"Slave patrollers. Less than militia," Kagi replied.

Brown was wiping his hand on his pants. "Scum of the South," he said. "Scum of the earth."

Brown and Kagi passed a telescope back and forth, arguing quietly about which route to take into town, where to post guards, and other things. I eased myself off my horse for a short rest. I wasn't used to riding yet.

The arsenal turned out as many as ten thousand rifles a year and stored them there. That made it important in our plans. It was reassuring to know that Brown needed tens of thousands of weapons. I could not see how we were supposed to transport them up this muddy ditch and into our mountain fortresses, but I was certain that Brown knew. Soon, soon, I told myself, men like Captain Brannan would be running for their miserable lives.

That July day was the last time I was outside in daylight and good weather for three months. When we got back to the farm that afternoon, Brown said to me, "You will have to stay in the attic now, except at meals. There will soon be too many of us to come and go as we please."

The thought of being confined in that place seemed almost like being buried alive. I spent nights there already, and that was not bad, but never to leave it, except to go downstairs? "But what about Kagi and Cook?" I protested. "What about Owen and Anderson?"

"Kagi's going back to Pennsylvania tonight," Brown said. "As for Cook, you know he lives in town. I and a few others must be able to move about and spread false stories of what we're doing here. But you and those who are coming must hide. If the local people get a hint of what we're up to, they'll burn us out."

So I nodded and climbed the stairs to the long, dark attic.

Anderson and Owen spent their nights there, but I was alone much of the time at first. I saw the others at breakfast, where Brown led the prayers and the discussion. Then they would go off on their scouting trips, and I would be left alone with a drill manual and a Sharps rifle for company until night. When Brown didn't want Anderson with him, he and I would drill together. Anderson taught me how to use the Sharps, as well as he could in an attic. Sighting at a shiny penny nailed to the far wall, I would click the trigger and tear through the motions of opening the breech, sliding in a cartridge, and sticking on a new percussion cap. I learned to fieldstrip my rifle and clean it. Soon, I was an experienced Sharps-shooter in everything but the one thing that counted.

I was running through the manual of arms one day when a new man climbed into the attic. He was a gaunt-looking mulatto well into middle age. He had a thin bedroll on his back and one of our Sharpses.

"Dangerfield Newby," he said. "The captain sent me up."

I put down my rifle and stuck out my hand. "Thank God for some company," I replied.

Newby's face creased into a smile, and we shook hands. He put down his bedding next to mine.

"Captain Brown said you'd show me how to handle this," he said, lifting his rifle.

"As much as I know about it," I replied, and as quickly as that I was converted from recruit to veteran.

No one ever had a better pupil. Newby watched every move I made and copied me perfectly the first time. His concentration was amazing.

"You've done this before, I would guess," I said. "You're very good."

"I have to be," was all he replied.

That night, Owen and Anderson came back, and I introduced them.

"Know anything about when we start fighting?" Newby asked us.

We shook our heads.

"Can't be too long, can it?"

"I suppose not," I replied.

"You from around here?" he asked.

"No, from Massachusetts," I said.

"Ohio, mostly," said Owen Brown.

Anderson shrugged. "Indiana for a start."

"So far away," Newby mused, as though we had said "Mars." Then he took each of us by the hand, taking ours in both of his. "Thank you," he said.

"For what, Mr. Newby?" I asked.

"For coming down here." He picked up his rifle again and stroked it. "I'm free," he went on. "My father freed me when I grew up. But my wife's a slave, so my children are slaves. Their master means to sell them into Louisiana. He'd sell them to me if I had the money. That's a joke. Where am I going to get money for a woman and seven kids? So I'm joining up with the captain. If we win, I get my family back. That's my reason to be here. But you others came down to free all the families."

Owen, Anderson, and I couldn't think of anything to say to that, so we all just sat together in the dark, feeling each other's nearness. But that moment was the one that founded Captain Brown's new company.

Other men came in ones and twos in the next weeks and crowded into the attic. We were a strange collection: tough veterans of the Kansas wars, farmers, poets, and a former slave. There were the Thompson brothers, Bill and Dauphin; Charlie Tidd, Francis Jackson, Barclay and Edwin Coppoc. Another of Brown's sons, Watson, came, and we knew that John Jr. would be joining us before we went into action. There was Albert Hazlett, who had fought under Brown before. An odd bird named Stewart Taylor was a Canadian and a spiritualist.

These men were white, but blacks came, too. Besides

Dangerfield Newby, there was Shields Green, who had worked for Frederick Douglass, and handsome Lewis Leary and his brother-in-law John Copeland, both from Ohio.

We drilled every day. Brown's old military adviser, the one who had gone bearing tales to Senator Sumner, had written the manual we used. When Brown was there, he barked out the commands. When he was away, we took turns giving the orders. "Right shoulder arms! Left shoulder arms! Port arms! Order arms! Right about-turn! Left about-turn!" for hours at a time.

At first I couldn't see the use of so much of this kind of training. In the cramped attic, we couldn't even march. But as we trained together, the spirit that had begun the night Newby came grew stronger, and the drill helped build it.

We were very different men. We argued with each other about everything, and we even teased each other, but always as friends. I had never had so many friends before. I stopped being lonely, and at times was as happy as I'd ever been in my life.

Until the day Bill Leeman came.

I was lying on my blankets studying the drill manual again. Leeman thrust his narrow face up through the floor, sniffed, shrugged, and coiled the rest of his long, thin body into the attic. Then he glared down at me and put his hands on his hips. He had a whip looped through his belt, and a magnificent beard that looked brand new.

"What are you doing here?" he demanded in a strong Maine accent.

"What?" I said. "Studying the manual. Would you like to see it?"

He took it, scowled at the page I'd been reading, and said, "Book soldiering. I didn't need this in Kansas, and I sure as hell don't need it now."

"We're all supposed to learn it," I said. "Captain's orders."

"Don't tell me about the captain," Leeman said with a sneer. "I've rode under him." He threw the book back at me. "See this whip? I made it. I'm a whip maker. Just stay out of my way, boy."

"That's going to be difficult in the circumstances," I said. My voice was steady, but I was shaking. Why was he attacking me?

"Just see you do it, boy," he said, and turned his back on me. "Hey, Hazlett," he said. "Haven't seen you since Lawrence."

From then on, Bill Leeman insulted me at every chance. If I made a mistake at drill, he was sure to smirk and make some crack about "the boy." And he liked to stare at me and stroke his whip.

Although I could tell that the other men didn't like what Leeman was doing, it was clearly up to me to stop him. But how? I didn't understand where his anger was coming from. If he'd been a fat, cowardly bully out of a book, it would have been easy to know what to do. But Leeman was as lean as a snake and really had been a hero in Kansas. I couldn't help thinking that something in his warrior's eye told him I was no good.

I tried to think of what Bob would have done. One thing I was sure of, he would never have stood it. He would have put Leeman in his place with a few smart, tough insults or pitched into him with his barroom fighting skills. But neither of those were talents of mine.

I wasn't the only one Leeman seemed to hate. He hacked on Dauph Thompson and Barclay Coppoc, until Edwin stood up for his younger brother. He ragged on Stewart Taylor, too, but then almost everyone did that.

We couldn't help teasing Taylor. He was such a pompous little fellow that he may not even have realized we were doing it. Perhaps that's why he never seemed to mind. And pompous or not, he was one of us. In fact, in a way, he was the one who gave us our name.

We were dipping our rifle barrels in a mixture Cook had learned about at the arsenal. The stuff turned them brown, which minimized glare when aiming. Taylor wiped off his barrel, slid it back into the stock, and announced, "Men, I have been thinking."

"Thought we'd made you promise to stop that," someone drawled.

"Our company needs a name," Taylor went on. "A name as glorious as our cause. What do you say to 'The Liberty Grenadiers'?"

"I say *haw* to 'em," Bill Leeman replied. "That's as mush-mouth a name as I ever heard."

"There's a militia company back home calls itself the Invincibles," Dauph Thompson offered.

"Invincibles?" I said. "Hidden up like this, we ought to call ourselves the Invisibles."

We all laughed except Taylor. "You lack seriousness of purpose," he told us, but from that time on, we called ourselves Captain Brown's Invisibles.

The question was whether we could stay invisible as our numbers grew. Some of the local people began to suspect there was more happening at the farm than Farmer Smith was letting on. One old woman was especially troublesome. She was a toothless, ancient-looking crone with a company of greedy children. Hardly a day went by that they didn't come by to poke around and ask to "borrow" things.

Brown couldn't both keep watch on the place and come and go as he needed. Besides, with the attic full of men, the house was in chaos. So Brown sent for Annie.

The day she came, she bounced into the attic, looked around, sniffed, and declared, "You men had better give me your bedding and clothes quick. And don't hold anything back if you know what's good for you."

We did as we were told. We knew what was good for us. She was. Annie became our housekeeper, cook, laundress, and watchdog. Very often in the middle of one of our drills, Annie's head would suddenly thrust up through the trapdoor and hush us. We would all jump for our bedrolls and lie there, barely breathing, with our rifles held tightly along our legs while she dealt with the old woman.

Later, Oliver's wife, Martha, joined us and Annie had some help. It seems ridiculous now, but all John Brown's great plans depended on the courage and brains of two girls in their teens. We Invisibles relied on them for everything, from our breakfasts to our lives. In all the weeks we hid there, we never missed a meal, and we were never discovered. If there were any invincibles on that farm, they were Annie and Martha Brown.

That stinking attic was becoming hard to bear. There was no privacy at all. We breathed each other's air. The days dragged by, and our sense of danger grew.

Leeman became more and more morose. "I don't like

being cooped up like this" became his constant complaint. "I'm used to Kansas. See forty miles and sleep under the stars. When are we goin' to start fighting?" Albert Hazlett always chimed in with him, and the two fed each other's gloom.

One hot, sodden day, when the temperature in the attic must have been over one hundred and the walls were dripping wet, we were going through drill as usual. Brown had left Owen in charge of us, and Owen was giving us turns at commanding. At last my turn came. I fell out of ranks, took my place in front, and shouted, "Attention!"

Everyone jumped to the order but Bill Leeman. "Why can't we find some *men* for this company?" he sneered. "Damned if I'll take orders from you, girly." He threw down his rifle, yanked his coiled whip off his belt, and hit me across the face.

Instantly I was back on the riverfront in Cincinnati. I pitched into him as if he were one of Jacob's killers come back. "Here's a man's fight for you!" I shouted.

Leeman could have taken me apart if he'd known I was coming. But before he could react, one wild swing had found his nose and made it bleed. He fell back against Dauph Thompson and hit the floor. Then my hands were around his throat and he was on his back bucking like a wild colt and punching me, but I wouldn't be thrown off.

It must have lasted less than a minute. Then the others pulled us apart.

"You damned little Quaker devil," he said. "You broke my nose."

"No, he hasn't," Owen Brown said. "But it would have been fair enough if he had."

We stood glaring, ready to tear into each other again, and then—oh, glory! The thunder cracked right over our heads, and the rain began to pound on the roof like hail.

Dangerfield Newby looked out the little window. "You can't see the road!" he cried. "Come on." And we all ran whooping down the stairs out into the storm. The rain came sheeting down, hiding us as we shrieked and danced all over that hill. The thunder shook the ground, and the lightning scrawled across the sky.

Brown was furious when he heard about the fight. He made a long speech about Cain and Abel and brothers dwelling together in peace. Then he made Bill and me shake hands and apologize. We did, not meaning a word of it.

"I always say it never pays to get a Quaker mad," Newby murmured as we lay down that night.

"I'm not much of a Quaker," I said. "My mother is."

"Well, you fought like one," Newby said. "Took it serious. I think you'll have less trouble now. By the way, have you noticed anything about Leeman?"

"Only that he's a snake," I said.

"It's you and Barclay and Dauph that he rags on most," Newby said. "And they're the only two besides you who look younger than he does. And *you* really are younger."

"What are you saying?" I said.

"Just that Bill's young and scared. Probably more scared than we are. He wants to run, but he won't let himself. You and the others remind him of how young he is, and how frightened."

"You're not just saying that, are you?" I asked.

"Nope. Seems pretty clear to me," Newby said. "But then, he's fought before. He knows what the chances are better than we do."

"What do you think our chances are?" I asked.

Newby closed his eyes and shrugged. "Depends on what we try to do."

ELEVEN

Leeman backed off almost completely after our fight. He and Hazlett began sneaking out of the house late at night, hiding in the bushes until dawn. They almost never spoke, except to each other.

We speculated endlessly on what Brown's real plans were. Brown was in and out all the time on trips. I assumed he must be organizing the forces that would join us for the strike at Harper's Ferry. I knew he was sending a steady stream of letters to his son John Jr. about money and men. I knew several of us had been given commissions and offices in the government Brown meant to set up in the mountains. So things must be going forward. But I was impatient to get on with the business.

At last, one night in early September, Brown assembled us downstairs. Everyone was there, even Kagi and Cook. Brown unrolled a huge map of the slave states and spread it on the floor. It was marked with every arsenal and fort. A note on each state gave the number of slaves there. A tangle of arrows pointed every which way—into Virginia, the Carolinas, even Florida and Texas. But only one pointed north. It ran through the mountains above Harper's Ferry and stopped at the Canadian border.

"Men, the time is close," Brown said. "We must strike soon, and we shall. This is how it will be. We will seize the weapons at Harper's Ferry and spread the word to the slaves to meet us in the mountains west of here. We will establish a republic of free men, under the American flag. It will be a republic like those of the revolted slaves in Roman times. But this one will not be conquered. We will gain strength as runaways flock to join us. Those who cannot or will not fight with us, we will guide north to Canada.

"At first, we may have to retreat into the north from time to time. If we do, we will come back. And each time, we will come back stronger. Success will build on success. We will move farther south, and more slaves will rally to us. We will arm them from the arsenals in each state."

Brown stood back from the map and threw out an arm. "Under such an assault, slavery will collapse. The mere threat of our coming will cause the price of slaves to fall in every Southern state. Men will free their slaves for fear that they will free themselves, our way. I can't say how long it may take, perhaps years. But I hope and believe it will not be so long. One hard blow struck will shake the whole system, or even wreck it. Only strike that one blow and all the rest must follow."

Anderson nodded. Kagi crossed his arms. Stewart Taylor shouted, "Amen."

Then Dauph Thompson spoke up. "Captain, how many more men are coming, and when will they be here?"

"We are likely all," Brown said evenly.

No one spoke then. We looked at each other, looked at the floor. Unsaid words brooded between us.

Finally, Charlie Tidd ran his fingers through his beard and said, "This is the surest way to get us all killed. Damned if I'll throw my life away on this crackbrained scheme." Oliver and Owen Brown growled agreement.

Instantly we were all shouting at each other. We threw around words like "coward" and "madman" and got nowhere. Brown roared louder than anyone, and defended every comma in his plan. It wasn't long before we were split into two snarling camps. Charlie Tidd led one. Brown, of course, led the other. They were clustered on opposite sides of the room, with the two leaders doing most of the talking, while Kagi tried to bring them together.

I hesitated between them. Then I went to the door.

"Where are you going?" Annie said.

"Outside," I replied. "I'll be back soon."

Bill Leeman laughed.

I went as far away from the house as I could. There was a clump of trees up the rise behind the house, and a rock to sit on. The breeze sent the leaves sifting down around me. An owl cried, and another answered it. Light still hung over the western mountains, but the Big Dipper was out, its two guide stars pointing north, showing some runaway the road to freedom, if he could make it. I closed my eyes and tried to find the silent place within me.

My mind kept racing in circles like a frightened rabbit. Brown's plan was brilliant. Brown's plan could not work. I had to run. I had to fight. The sounds from the house rose and fell. I was in despair.

I was realizing for the first time the size of the thing

we meant to do. Slavery was the most powerful force in the United States of America. It selected our presidents and passed what laws it liked. Religions were set up to praise and defend its cruelties. Southern officers controlled the army, and held slaves while they did it.

What did we have? John Brown couldn't raise a thousand dollars at one time. And the only antislavery army on the planet was gathered in one room, at war with itself.

What do thee fear most?

I jumped. It was as though someone had spoken. "To die," I told the night.

Then thee should go home.

"But then I will be a coward," I said to myself.

Are thee sure?

"Yes," I answered.

Why do thee think so?

"Because of Jacob." It was the first thing that came into my head.

Jacob is dead. No one can hurt him now. And thee can do nothing for him.

"But I can do something for the others," I said.

Then thee have faith in Brown's plan?

"Yes," I said. "I don't know why. Maybe it's because it's the only plan there is. But I believe that, somehow, John Brown will free the slaves."

Then thee may choose. Go or stay. Brown will win with thee or without thee.

"Then I am free," I said.

Thee are as free as a man ever is.

Jacob's grave face came into my mind. I looked up at the sky again. The Dipper had wheeled a long way since

I sat down. It was time to go back. I walked up to the house, as free as a man ever is.

Owen Brown was sitting hunched over, bent under his father's eyes. The room was quiet.

"Thought you'd cut and run," Bill Leeman sneered.

I didn't answer him. I just went over and stood beside John Brown. Annie smiled. Brown nodded. Charlie Tidd shook his head.

For the next few days, we went through the motions of being a military company. More drill, more weapons cleaning, and more tense silence when a neighbor came by. But nothing was settled. Charlie and Owen and some of the others were talking about pulling out.

Finally, Brown called another meeting downstairs. It was dark outside, and only one lamp was lit in the big room on the ground floor. The sound of dishes being washed came in from the kitchen. It seemed odd at such a moment.

"Men," he said, "it may be that you are right, those of you who think my plan is not sound. I have decided to resign. I invite you all to choose another leader from among yourselves. Devise something better if you can."

Brown went back into the kitchen. Jeremiah Anderson rubbed his face and looked at the floor. Bill Leeman whispered a curse. Charlie Tidd spat his out loudly.

Then no one said anything, until Dangerfield Newby spoke: "Men, if you have another choice, make it now. Otherwise, come with me to Harper's Ferry," and he walked into the kitchen.

I followed. Shields Green, John Kagi, and Stewart Taylor were right behind me.

We found Brown bent over the table, scratching his pen across a sheet of cheap foolscap. Piles of paper surrounded the single smoking oil lamp. Martha was at the metal sink. Annie was standing behind her father, her big eyes full of fury.

"Captain," I said, "whatever you plan to do next, I want to be part of it."

"So do we all," Taylor announced.

Brown nodded. "Thank you. I seem to have no plan just now. We must await developments."

"Proceed as the way opens," I said. "That's the old Friends saying."

"Proceed as the way opens," he agreed. "I have always done that."

Annie slammed her fist against the wall. "It's a shame and disgrace on this country that there's only one man like Daddy," she said. "If there were a dozen, slavery wouldn't last a year. But there isn't. Every time Daddy leaves here, it's to go to someone who ought to help him but won't. Everywhere he goes, people pray and praise him and treat him like Moses. But will they come to fight? Not likely. You men are all. All in this country."

She put her head on Martha's shoulder and cried the way her father laughed—silently, her whole body shaking.

No one knew what to say. We had always thought Annie was dauntless. We wanted to comfort her but had no idea how.

At last Kagi spoke. "It can still work, even with so few," he assured us. "The essence of the plan is in speed, not numbers."

"If numbers told the tale, you Yankees would have conquered us Canadians in 1812," Taylor said.

"Mexicans had us outnumbered in every battle we had with 'em," Jeremiah Anderson agreed, joining us. "We won 'em all."

Brown put down his pen. "During the great uprising against the British in India two years ago, there was a Scotch parson and his family who were taken prisoner by the rebels," he said. "They were told that they would be killed the next morning. All night long the mother kept putting her ear to the ground and saying she could hear the war cry of a Scottish regiment growing louder and louder. 'Dinna ye hear it?' she kept asking her family. 'Dinna ye hear it?' They believed that she had gone mad, but they assured her that they heard it, too. The next morning when the sun rose, those rebels found their camp surrounded by that regiment. Somehow I feel that that story is for us."

"I hear it, Captain," Taylor said. "Before God, I do."

Annie dried her eyes on her apron. "Who wants tea and who wants coffee?"

We all had cups in hand when Owen Brown came into the room behind me, his shoulders more hunched than usual. He held a folded piece of paper in his hand. "Here, Father," he said, and left.

Brown read it. "It seems the doubters have decided to follow the old man after all. The way is opening."

Annie smiled broadly at her father. "I guess we all hear it, Daddy," she said.

Our doubts did not disappear. Some of us still mentioned leaving. But no one, not even Leeman or Hazlett, ever put a foot off the farm without Brown's permission. The Invisibles remained at full strength, such as it was.

October came, and turned gray. The rain fell cold. Our breaths began to hang in the air. Mold grew on the attic beams. We all were wound as tight as springs. Dauph Thompson started whistling the first notes of "Yankee Doodle" under his breath over and over. Newby took to suddenly punching at the air. Hazlett started wringing his hands. I spent every minute I could staring out our dirty little windows hoping for storms.

Then at last things began to happen. Brown sent Annie and Martha home. He moved most of our weapons to an old schoolhouse a few miles away and sent Owen there to guard them. He drilled us personally in the attic. In between drills, he wrote, wrote, wrote.

Nothing broke in on our concentration now. We worked with our rifles from the moment we woke up until we went to sleep, with only short breaks for a little food.

A few more men drifted in. The last to come was Francis Merriam from Boston. We heard he'd brought more than a thousand dollars with him to buy his place in the Invisibles. "He could have mine for nothing," Bill Leeman said. I wasn't certain he was joking.

Then a letter came from my mother. Most of the Invisibles got mail. It sounds surprising, but it is true. While we kept ourselves hidden, we were telling people all over the country more or less what we were up to. Letters came and went in big packets under the name of Isaac Smith. I never sent any, because I didn't want my family to find me. Now they had.

"How the Devil—" I muttered, tearing the envelope open. The letter was short, but my mother's careful writing told me that she had spent much time over it.

2nd October 1859

My Dearest Son,

I hope this letter may find thee well and in good spirits. We are all well here, but that we miss thee every moment. Thy sisters cannot understand where their brother has gone. Thy father hired a detective to try to find thee, but the man was a fool. He could no more find John Brown than a blind man could. Thy father told him he was sure thee were wherever Brown was, and the man went to the Brown farm, but learned nothing and got no farther.

I have found thee, as I hope, by my own methods. John Brown is not hard to find if one wants to do so. Julia Howe has always been a great friend to me.

Theodore, I do not beg thee to return, though I wish it with all my heart. I know what thee are doing, and, while I can never approve of violence, I must believe thee are proceeding by the light thee have been given. So long as thee do so, I trust thee will be under God's wing.

Could thee not write to me just to let me know that thee are well? I swear I will tell no one, not even thy father, if thee do. But it will ease my heart beyond telling if thee will do only that much.

Bless Thee, My Son,
Thy Mother, Caroline Evans Worth

I felt a rush of shame at worrying my family, and of gratitude toward my mother. I borrowed a pencil from Stewart Taylor and wrote back at once.

October 14th, 1859

My Dearest Mother,
You letter has just arrived. I am well and safe. The others here are good fellows. I wish you could meet them. If you did, I know you would be less worried. Many of them have done this kind of work before and know what they are about. We seem to have everything we need to make a good beginning.

I am glad that you know what I am doing. I am sorry to worry you so much. Thank you for keeping what you know secret. I think you will not have to do so much longer. We have been here so long that either we must do something or give it up, at least for now. Give my best regards to Mrs. Howe.

Your Son,
Theodore

I looked at what I had written. Nothing in it was untrue, but the letter was one lie from start to finish. I took another sheet of paper and wrote the truth.

October 14th, 1859

Dearest Mother,
Thank you for not telling what you know or trying to get me back. I couldn't stand the shame of leaving, even though I expect I will never see any of you again.

We have been here so long that something must happen soon or the men here will start to leave. Brown seems to be trying hard to make a beginning, but there are so many obstacles and so little support, it is a wonder he has got this far. I do not see how we can succeed. Still, he must do something or fail completely. I cannot imagine that he would accept that. He would ride into Harper's Ferry all alone rather than do nothing now.

I will write you again if there is time before we launch our attack. If not, this letter will likely be the last word you ever have from me. Please know that I always loved you.

Your Son,
Theodore

I read both letters over. Then I folded the first one and put it into the big envelope Brown had left for our mail. I looked again at the other and tore it up.

On the night of October fifteenth, John Brown swore us in as citizens of his provisional republic. Those of us who were to be army officers received commissions signed by Kagi.

Since I wasn't one of them, I went to get my gear ready. The attic was empty for once. Everyone else was downstairs watching the swearing-in of the officers. The place looked sad and dirty now. It seemed as though I had been there forever. Now I was looking at it for the last time. Whatever happened, I would never see it again.

I cleaned the breech and barrel of my Sharps. I slipped my cartridge box over my head and made sure it held forty rounds. I hung a bayonet on my belt. I was as ready as I would ever be.

Steps came up the stairs behind me.

"Worth. I missed you downstairs," Brown said.

"I'm anxious to get on with it," I replied.

"So am I," Brown said. "Well, all is going forward now. I'm sending a few of the boys to Colonel Washington's plantation to fetch him and a sword I want. George Washington's sword. It's going to the mountains with us. Owen is at the schoolhouse. The rest of us are heading down to the arsenal in about an hour."

I nodded.

"Worth, I want you to put up your rifle. I've a particular plan for you."

I wasn't sure I had heard him right. "Put up my rifle?" I said. "Where?"

"It doesn't matter," Brown said.

A thought flashed through my mind. "You're not going to leave me behind?"

"No," said Brown. "It's rather different from that. I'm sending you off with your telegraph. I want you to roam up and down the wires, listening in. I reckon that the news of what we're going to do at Harper's Ferry will get out sometime tomorrow. When it does, I want you to pass the messages on to me if you can. I want you, too, to send false messages to confuse our enemies. That will buy us time and help us to know which route to take out of town. It's a job only you can do, and it could make the difference between success and failure for us."

"But Captain, who can read any messages I send you?"

"Oh, Kagi knows the Morse," Brown said. "I expect

he didn't tell you. You will send me messages through him."

I didn't know what to say or what I felt. Relief? Yes, and guilt. And anger. "Captain Brown," I stammered, "I'm as much a member of this company as any man, and I have a right to go into battle with it."

"There'll be plenty of battles later, Worth," Brown snapped. "Slavery won't fall at the first tap we give it, you know; never mind what I said before. Mind me now; after we get away, you'll know about it from the wires. And you'll be able to calculate where we've gone. You'll join us in the mountains, and there you'll likely get all the fighting you want."

"You're not doing this because I'm the youngest man here, are you, Captain?" I said.

"You aren't young anymore," Brown said. "You have not been young since Cincinnati. I would not have brought you if you were."

"What about my rifle?" I asked.

"You won't need it tomorrow," Brown said. "Take this instead, for emergencies." He handed me the little pistol he carried in his pants. I slid it behind my belt.

"I'll need a horse," I said.

"Take whichever one you like best," Brown said.

"When do I leave?" I asked.

"Now," Brown said. "I want you down on the Baltimore & Ohio line as quick as you can get there."

My telegraph was sitting by the head of my mattress. I slung it over my shoulder and put on my hat.

Brown stuck out his hand. "Good-bye, Worth," he said. "We'll make a good fight."

"I'm sure we will, Captain."

I went downstairs. The house was empty. Everyone was in the barn. Kagi was supervising the loading of the wagon they would take with them to Harper's Ferry. John Cook and Dangerfield Newby were sliding a crate of Sharps rifles onto the tailgate.

"Here you are," Dauph Thompson said. "Bear a hand with these pikes."

"Can't," I said. "The captain's sending me off to fiddle with the telegraph."

"Oh, well, so long for now, then," Thompson said.

Since I was no horseman, I threw a blanket and saddle on Frank, the only horse I'd ever ridden before, and led him outside. The night was cloudy, cold, and moonless. Rain was getting ready to fall. I reckoned I would be soaked by morning. I turned and waved into the dark barn. One pale hand waved back. I didn't know whose it was.

"I'll see you in the mountains," I said.

There was no answer. I rode away, and the fog took me in.

TWELVE

I rode almost three miles before I found the spot that I wanted. The trees were thick, and the wires hung conveniently low. It was as good a place as I was going to get.

I tethered Frank. Carefully, I climbed the nearest pole and connected to the wires. The wet made them spark fiercely. I listened. There was no traffic on the line. I hung there and got slowly soaked. After about an hour, I tried sending Kagi a short message. No answer came. I worried if the wet had shorted out the wire to Harper's Ferry. Not likely, but a cracked insulator could have leaked.

I wondered if everything had gone according to plan. It crossed my mind that if, for any reason, the raid was postponed, there would be no way to get word to me. That would be a joke. I might be the only Invisible to go into action. I didn't believe it could happen, but it made me laugh.

Then, as the clouds in the east began to turn from black to gray, the wire leapt to life:

TO PRESIDENT, BALTIMORE & OHIO RAILROAD
SIR STOP ABOLITIONISTS LED BY JOHN BROWN
HAVE SEIZED THE TOWN AND ARSENAL AT
HARPER'S FERRY STOP THEY HELD UP THIS TRAIN
ABOUT FOUR HOURS STOP TELEGRAPH TO
HARPER'S FERRY CUT STOP ADVISE GOVERNOR
WISE AT ONCE TO SEND MILITIA STOP
SIGNED CONDUCTOR TRAIN 42

So it had begun. Brown must have cut the wires for some reason and detained the train until he was ready to escape with the weapons. He must be on his way to the mountains by now. Our war was under way. I wondered if I should leave my perch now and start looking for the Invisibles or wait a while.

"I haven't done any mischief yet," I said quietly to myself. I sent another message:

OSAWATOMIE BROWN AT HARPER'S FERRY
WITH SEVEN HUNDRED MEN STOP ARSENAL
SEIZED STOP OTHER ABOLITIONIST ATTACKS
EXPECTED IN AREA STOP FOR GOD'S SAKE

I left the message unfinished.

That seemed to stir things up. It wasn't long before I heard:

COMMANDING GENERAL MARYLAND FIRST
LIGHT DIVISION NOTIFIED STOP PRESIDENT
BUCHANAN NOTIFIED STOP HELP IS COMING
STOP BE RESOLUTE
SIGNED GOVERNOR HENRY A. WISE

I wondered who the governor intended the message for. Anyway, I sent him a reply: BROWN NOW BELIEVED

TO HAVE AS MANY AS FIFTEEN HUNDRED MEN STOP, and didn't sign it. Then I sent:

> GOVERNOR HENRY A. WISE
> ABOLITIONIST FORCES ESTIMATED AT TEN
> THOUSAND BELIEVED EN ROUTE TO
> WASHINGTON CITY STOP COULD YOU NOT
> REDIRECT FIRST LIGHT DIVISION TO DEFENSE OF
> THE CAPITAL STOP
> SIGNED JAMES BUCHANAN, PRESIDENT OF THE
> UNITED STATES

This had a wonderful effect:

> PRESIDENT JAMES BUCHANAN
> SIR STOP FIRST LIGHT DIVISION NOT
> AVAILABLE FOR FEDERAL SERVICE STOP WILL
> RALLY TO YOU AS SOON AS POSSIBLE STOP
> GOVERNOR HENRY A. WISE

And after a while:

> GOVERNOR HENRY A. WISE
> FIRST LIGHT DIVISION NOT REQUIRED HERE
> STOP PLEASE ADVISE CONCERNING REPORTS OF
> ABOLITIONIST REBELS STOP
> PRESIDENT JAMES BUCHANAN

It kept getting better. Other towns in Maryland and Virginia were seeing abolitionists in the bushes. I read their messages and improved where I could:

> PRESIDENT JAMES BUCHANAN
> SIR STOP ABOLITIONISTS BELIEVED HEADED
> FOR CAPITAL NOW KNOWN TO BE ADVANCING TO
> RICHMOND STOP SEND REINFORCEMENTS OR

Which brought:

> GOVERNOR HENRY A. WISE
> TROOPS ARE NOT AVAILABLE HERE STOP GOD
> BLESS YOU IN THIS HOUR OF CRISIS STOP
> PRESIDENT JAMES BUCHANAN

I was beginning to enjoy my correspondence with the White House:

> PRESIDENT JAMES BUCHANAN
> WE WILL SELL OURSELVES AS DEARLY AS
> POSSIBLE BUT I FEAR THIS MAY AFFECT YOUR
> CHANCES OF REELECTION STOP
> GOVERNOR HENRY A. WISE

Then came:

> ALL OPERATORS AND STATIONMASTERS
> NOT ALL MESSAGES ON THIS LINE ARE TO BE
> BELIEVED STOP ABOLITIONIST RAIDERS MAY BE
> SENDING FALSE WARNINGS STOP REFER ALL
> MESSAGES TO THIS OFFICE FOR VERIFICATION
> STOP
> GOVERNOR HENRY A. WISE

It looked as though my game was nearly up, but I would wait a little longer. I might hear something good to take to my friends in the mountains, something we could laugh at tonight.

The next message was:

> BROWN SURROUNDED NOW IN ARSENAL
> BUILDINGS STOP MILITIA HERE HAVE SITUATION

IN HAND BUT DECLINE TO STORM STRONG
POINTS STOP SEND REINFORCEMENTS AT ONCE
STOP
SIGNED JOHN D. STARRY MD

Militia? My stomach turned over. But there were no militia around Harper's Ferry. Was someone else playing tricks on the wires? The Invisibles had got away into the mountains hours ago.

After a while, another message clacked through:

MARINES UNDER COLONEL ROBERT LEE EN
ROUTE FROM WASHINGTON CITY STOP EXPECT
THEM BY TONIGHT STOP
SIGNED GOVERNOR HENRY A. WISE

The Washington marines. If the Invisibles *were* still at Harper's Ferry, if they *were* surrounded by militia, that militia could only be a scratch force of volunteers with hunting weapons and no training. We could probably fight our way through men like that. The marines were another matter entirely. If we were still in Harper's Ferry by nightfall, we would never get out.

I sent another message:

GOVERNOR HENRY A. WISE
SIR STOP WE HAVE REPORTS THAT JOHN
BROWN IS TRAPPED AT HARPER'S FERRY AND
THAT MARINES ARE GOING THERE STOP CAN YOU
VERIFY STOP
CAPTAIN JOHN H. KAGI

The answer came back quickly:

TO ALL ON THIS LINE
RUMORS THAT JOHN BROWN IS SURROUNDED
AT HARPER'S FERRY ARE TRUE STOP FEDERAL
MARINES EXPECTED THERE BY TONIGHT STOP
GOVERNOR HENRY A. WISE

How could Brown, Osawatomie Brown, have been so stupid? He was an old guerrilla fighter; he knew he had to have his retreat planned out. But it had happened. There was no reason to hope for him, or anyone with him. And if anyone suspected I had been with him, I was as good as dead. The best thing for me to do now was to get north as fast as I could.

And yet, I was an Invisible. I couldn't leave without knowing for certain what had happened. So, against all common sense, I rode back toward Harper's Ferry.

I could hear wild tides of noise coming from the town as I neared it. A chant rose and fell in the midst of the babble, but I couldn't quite make out the words. When I reached the middle of the bridge across the Potomac, I stopped and looked down. Something was waving at me.

It was Bill Leeman. He was bent nearly double against the piling. His body was pocked with bullet holes, and half his head had been shot away. His one eye was turned up in what was left of his face. His upstream arm was cocked over his head. His hand floated limply in the swift current. He looked as though he were still trying to run.

I went cold. I got down and held on to the railing to steady myself. This was nothing like my grandfather's death. "Oh, Bill" was all I could say. "Oh, Bill."

If there had been one of us whom I would have wanted dead, it would have been him. But all I felt was pity, horror, and a kind of loyalty.

As I neared the end of the bridge, I saw another body floating face up at the edge of the water. It was what was left of Bill Thompson. His face was hideous.

I could hear the chanting clearly now. "Kill them, kill them, kill them, kill them" was coming from hundreds of throats. Newly minted militia men were waving their weapons drunkenly.

As I turned down the street that led to the armory, a ragged double file of men approached me. The man at the head of the column ordered it to halt and came over to me with his pistol out.

"Who might you be?" he demanded.

I forced myself to look straight into his face. It was the leader of the slave catchers we had encountered that day above Harper's Ferry. I said the first thing that came into my head.

"Name's Bob Gibbons. Telegrapher. Looking for work. What's going on?"

"You talk like a Yankee," he said.

"I am," I said. "Is there a crime in that?"

"There might be," he said. "There just might be."

Then a voice behind him called out, "Hey, Cap Brannan, ain't he one of them we saw up in the mountains that day? Back when we was slave-catchin' them two last summer?"

"Who's that, another one?" some of them called out. "We'll finish him now."

"My name's Bob Gibbons. I'm a telegrapher. I'm looking for work," I said.

Frank and I were surrounded by drunken men with rifles. Somebody grabbed Frank's bridle. Another man cupped his hands under my stirrup and threw me to the ground.

I got to my feet. "What is all this?" I said. "Isn't there anybody here who can tell me what's going on?"

"Oh, there's a lot goin' on," someone shouted. "He look familiar to you?"

I was shoved along the street until we came to a body lying in the gutter. It had been shot through the throat and torn by animals. Its ears were cut off. Dangerfield Newby.

"Oh, my God," I said.

"Put up your hands," Brannan ordered.

I did. He yanked my little pistol out of my belt and smelled the barrel. "Ain't been fired," he said. Then added, "Lately." He called over his shoulder, "Corporal Wallace."

A little man with a potbelly came over and tried to salute.

"Corporal, you are to escort this here prisoner back to Harper's Ferry and put him with the others," he said. "Take two men with you. If he tries to escape, shoot the Yankee bastard in the back."

"Aw, Captain, I want to go up to Pleasant Valley with you," the new corporal said.

"Follow your orders, Corporal," Brannan said, waving his pistol at him.

Corporal Wallace shrugged and called to two men who were as reluctant as he was to return to town. Brannan swung up onto Frank.

"Hey," I said. "That's my horse."

Brannan laughed. "I requisition this horse in the name of Brannan's Company, Maryland Militia," he said. "You can have him back when the war's over. If you ain't hanged first." And that was the last I ever saw of Frank.

They hustled me along down the street a short distance. Then a new knot of drunks surrounded us.

"Who's that? Is he one of them? We'll string him up," they shouted.

"My name's Bob Gibbons," I said. "I'm a telegrapher looking for work."

"The only work for your kind is rope stretchin'," someone shouted. "Give him to us."

"If we let 'em have him, we can still catch up with the company, Corp," one of my guards said.

"You're thinking good today, Randall," the corporal said.

In seconds, I was lifted off my feet and passed along to a building with a high-roofed porch. I felt a rope around my neck.

Then there was a tall, handsome man in a blue uniform in front of me. He had a squad of marines with him.

"Gentlemen," he said, "I accept this prisoner from you in the name of the United States." And he lifted the noose off me.

"Kill him, kill him, kill him," the chant started. But the man who had rescued me silenced it with a look. "There has been enough killing," he said. "Sergeant, convey this prisoner to the engine house."

The marine sergeant snapped a salute, and the militia parted for us like water.

The officer walked along beside us. His uniform told me that he was a full colonel. He must have been the man who led the troops that overcame us.

"Sir, I'm just a telegrapher," I said. "My name's Bob Gibbons. I came down from the North looking for work. I don't know anything about what's going on here. I've had my horse stolen and nearly been lynched. Please, let me go."

The colonel smiled gently under his fine moustache. "I'm afraid that won't be possible, sir. At present, Harper's Ferry is under martial law. And under my command. I fear I must hold you, at least for the moment. In any case, it hardly seems safe to release you just now, even if what you tell me is true. Believe me when I say that I regret this sorry necessity. This is a terrible day for our country."

We had reached the engine house. A ring of marines stood guard around it. A line of bodies lay along one wall, with their faces covered.

"But I haven't done anything wrong," I said.

"I fear that may be said of many who have died here," the colonel said. "Believe me, I will do my best for you. But the civil authorities must hear your case."

"What case?" I said.

The colonel led me to the door of a small attached building. The marines there came to present arms. "There has been an abolitionist raid on the arsenal here," he said. "Numbers are dead on both sides. We expect more trouble. But here comes a sheriff to take charge of you." He saluted me. "I regret your trouble, sir," he said, then turned on his heel and left.

"In here with you," the sheriff said. "I reckon you know most of these fellows well enough."

Shields Green raised his head from his hands, looked at me, and said, "Who's that?"

"What are you putting him in here for?" Edwin Coppoc demanded.

There was a body lying on the floor at the back of the room. A head turned slowly toward me. "Who are you, boy?" Watson Brown groaned.

They were trying to save me. "I'm supposed to be an abolitionist raider," I said.

"Let him go, sheriff," Watson said slowly. "We came here to free slaves, not to rob cradles."

The sheriff locked the door.

I sat between Shields and Edwin and held their hands. I knew now why I had come back. There were no words for how I felt. Live or die, I was one of these men.

When I could trust myself to talk, I whispered, "Are we all?"

"Don't know," Edwin said. "A few may have got away. But I know John Jr.'s dead. So are Taylor, Dauphin, and Jeremiah Anderson. The captain's wounded—badly. I don't know about the others. We weren't all in the engine house."

"I saw Bill Leeman's body in the river," I said. "And Bill Thompson's. Newby's lying in the street. He looked like something had eaten him."

Watson groaned terribly, and Shields Green looked up. "That's hard," he said. "All us good men, and the bad ones thundering right over us."

"Thanks for lying for me," I said.

"We'll do it again if we get the chance," Edwin said.

"I tried to get away myself," Shields said. "When they broke into the engine house, I got rid of my gun and bullets. Said I'd been a prisoner of the old man. But the real prisoners all told on me. Ain't no disgrace not to want to die."

"If they do let you go, you can tell our story," Edwin said to me. "It would be something not to be forgotten."

Watson spoke. "My heart tells me you will live," he said. "You will live for all of us." He licked his lips. "Do we have any water?"

We didn't. I went to the door and knocked. After a while, it cracked open. I looked into the face of a marine over his bayoneted rifle. "We have a dying man in here," I said. "Can we get some water?"

"He can get a drink in Hell when he gets there," the marine said, and the door slammed.

We sat listening to Watson dying all night long. The next day, someone brought him one cup of water and lifted him up onto a bench when he asked for it.

Later that day, they marched us all under heavy guard to the train heading eight miles down the track to Charlestown.

When I got onto the car, I saw John Brown lying in the aisle on a stretcher. Watson was lying at his feet. Aaron Stevens was next. Besides Brown and Stevens, the only survivor I hadn't already seen was John Copeland. He was sitting next to Stevens.

"They got me when we tried to make a break from the rifle works," he told me later. "Kagi and Leary were with me. None of us made it."

If Brown recognized me, my chance of being released

was gone. But he seemed not to recognize any of us just then. In spite of the heavy jolting of the train, he was almost asleep. Only when we hit a hard bump or went around a sharp curve did he say anything, and then it made no sense.

Charlestown had a strong county jail. They kept us there under heavy guard. The marines and the handsome colonel were gone. We were Virginian property now. I shared a cell with Watson for a little while. Then he died and I was alone.

Brown came back to himself later that day. He looked at me through the bars that divided our cells and said, "So, Worth, I thought you had got away."

"Beg your pardon, mister," I said, "but my name is Gibbons. Bob Gibbons. I'm a telegrapher."

"I see," he said.

There was a guard in front of each cell, so at least two men had heard us. I felt my last hope go.

I sat waiting for what would happen next. When two men in fine suits came to examine me that afternoon, it was almost a relief.

"I am Mayor Charles C. Green," the older one introduced himself. "This is Judge Richard Parker. We apologize for not having come to see you sooner."

"How do you do, gentlemen," I said. "My name is Bob Gibbons."

"So we have been given to understand," Judge Parker said. "And that is what we are here to ascertain. Your case is an unusual one. You may or may not be who you say you are. You may or may not be an abolitionist raider. At present there are no charges framed against you at all. Perhaps there should not be. You may be an innocent

victim of circumstance. On the other hand, one of my
bailiffs informs me that today, in his hearing, John Brown
addressed you as 'Worth' and said that he thought you
had got away."

"That's right, your honor," I said. "And I told him,
I'm Bob Gibbons, just like I'm telling you."

From his cot, Brown said, "There was a man named
Worth with us. I do not know what happened to him.
When I saw that young man there, I thought at first he
was Worth. Then my head cleared and I saw I was wrong."

"Have you any identification at all?" Judge Parker
asked.

"Only my word and my telegraph key," I said.

"Hardly conclusive," said Mayor Green.

Judge Parker looked through a thin sheaf of papers.
"I have a communication here from the officer who took
you in charge that you were recognized upon the bridge
at Harper's Ferry by himself and another man as one
who had been seen in the company of Brown several
weeks previously. Can you account for your whereabouts
in the last months?"

"That would be the man who stole my horse," I said.

Judge Parker raised his eyebrows. "Horse?"

"I had a horse named Frank and he stole it," I said.
"Maybe if I were a horse thief, I'd want people to think
the man I'd robbed was a criminal, too."

Judge Parker put his hand to his eyes. "This case is
vexing," he said. "I have men who must be put on trial
for treason and murder. I do not have time just now to
deal with horse thievery as well. Surely there must be
some way to determine your identity."

"Who was your last employer?" the mayor asked.

"The Western of Boston," I said.

"You are a very long way from Boston," the judge said.

I shrugged. "I like to travel."

"I believe the thing to do is to contact the Western of Boston and inquire of them," the judge said. "Who was your superior there?"

I thought fast. "Mr. Webster."

"First name?"

"He was always 'Mr. Webster' to me."

"I shall send a message with your physical description and the particulars of your circumstances today," the mayor said. "If you are who you say, to hold you any longer is a flagrant miscarriage of justice."

"That will be all for now, I think," the judge said. "We shall return either to release you or to charge you properly."

There was a small rectangle of sunlight on the floor of my cell. I made a great study of it for the rest of the day. I watched closely as it changed shape, moved across to the wall, and at last disappeared.

My mind kept dancing in a mad circle that wouldn't stop. Would Bob be in his office? Would he remember our code that we had never used? Would he recall me naming him Webster that day in the bar? Would he still be working for the Western of Boston? And would he help me if he could?

It was long past dark when the door down at the end of the line of cells opened again. The mayor, a bailiff, and a man I hadn't seen before were there. The mayor had a jaunty new bounce in his step.

"This is the one," he said.

The bailiff came into the cell and clapped irons on my wrists.

"Come along," he said.

They led me out the door and into a courtroom. Judge Parker was there. "Well, you have led us on a merry chase," he said. "And it is very late. But we Southerners love the chase. Mr. Harding, show the prisoner the evidence against him."

The man I didn't know turned to me. "Permit me," he said. "I am Charles B. Harding, county attorney. It is my duty to acquaint you with the evidence against you."

"All right," I said. "Whatever I did, I did for reasons that seemed good to me and still do. Do what you have to."

He shoved a telegram under my nose. I felt my jaw drop as I read it.

> HONORABLE CHARLES C. GREEN
> THE MAN YOU HOLD ROBERT GIBBONS IS
> WANTED BY US IN THE MATTER OF THE
> EMBEZZLEMENT OF TWO THOUSAND DOLLARS
> STOP CHARGE HIM AND HOLD HIM UNTIL WE CAN
> COLLECT HIM STOP WE ARE COMING AT ONCE
> STOP
> SIGNED NICHOLAS WEBSTER, VICE-PRESIDENT,
> WESTERN OF BOSTON RR

"Small wonder you like to travel, Mr. Gibbons," Mayor Green said. "But I fear your next journey will be back to your old haunts."

I stood with my head hanging and tears of joy falling

onto the courtroom floor while they formally charged me with being an embezzler, and being Bob Gibbons.

I had three days to wait for my deliverance. In that time, two more of the Invisibles were brought in. John Cook and Albert Hazlett had both been taken in Pennsylvania, where they had thought they were safe. They were at the opposite end of the line of cells from me, so I saw them only once. "Hello again" was all Cook said.

On the third day, the guard on us was lifted somewhat. Just two bailiffs were kept in the block. It gave me my last chance to speak to John Brown.

I sat on my bunk as close to him as I could. I kept my hands folded and my face down. I looked, I hoped, like a very guilty man. He was still lying on his bed.

"Captain Brown, what went wrong?" I murmured when the afternoon had made the guards a little drowsy.

"Everything, maybe. Or maybe nothing," Brown answered. "It is not over yet. Everything that happens now has been ordained. Or so I believe."

"You mean you never meant to leave Harper's Ferry at all?" I said.

"I meant to begin what has begun," he said. "The means are not so important." He turned on his side a little. "Let me tell you what happened in that engine house. I had everything I wanted in there. Even Washington's sword. Washington's sword in my hand. I had pushed the fire engine against the doors, and it gave them a devil of a time breaking in. They used a ladder as a battering ram. They opened a small hole in the bottom and started to crawl through. That was hot work. But then the doors fell back against the engine, and they swarmed up and over. They used their bayonets on us.

"Their officer saw me and jumped down on me from the fire engine. He tried to stab me with his sword. But he'd brought the wrong one, Worth. It was his shiny little dress sword, not a real blade. Still, he might have finished me with it. But he stabbed me in the breastbone, right where my two leather cartridge belts crossed. His blade bent. All he could do was beat me with the hilt. God has taken the sword into His hand now. I have been spared for the work to come."

Even so, Brown had very nearly died of those blows.

"Spared?" I said. "But what can you do now?"

"I can proceed as the way opens," Brown said.

"But what about me? Did you mean to—" I began.

"Look, Worth," Brown said, "it is no good brooding about the past. Especially not for you. We must go forward. All of us. By different ways. Now I am tired. Goodbye, if I am asleep when you leave." And he turned away from me.

Later that night, the bailiffs came and led me out. I looked back over my shoulder, but the cells were all dark. My friends were truly invisible now.

They took me back into the courtroom. There were three men waiting for me. One was a giant in a loud suit flourishing a pair of handcuffs and some papers. He almost hid Bob Gibbons from sight.

When I came into the room, Bob whirled around and shouted, "That's him! He's the one who did it. See, Mr. Webster, I told you we'd run him down sooner or later."

"Indeed. You were right, Worth. I never should have doubted you," my father said.

Mayor Green smiled. "I took the liberty of informing this gentleman that you had already confessed."

"Though with the evidence this faithful employee has provided me, your admission is hardly necessary," Father said, and he clapped Bob on the shoulder. To me he said, "It's back to Massachusetts for you."

I was signed out of the jail and into the custody of the detective my father had brought. He slapped the handcuffs on me and led me out.

"I must advise you to say nothing more concerning your case," my father said. "You are in trouble enough."

"Wait till we're on a train headin' north," Bob muttered.

There was a carriage waiting for us. The detective drove us north as fast as he could. The road took us through Harper's Ferry. It was quiet tonight, just as it must have been the night John Brown came into it to—do what? Start a war? Split the nation? Offer himself up to his fierce God? To free the slaves?

Yes, that was for certain if nothing else was. To free the slaves.

The Potomac rolled dark below us as we rattled across the bridge to Baltimore.

AFTERWARDS

They hanged John Brown on a hill near Harper's Ferry with three thousand militia surrounding his scaffold. All for one old man with his hands tied and a noose around his neck.

It was a windy, bitter day when his body came home. About twenty of us were waiting for it. I helped to dig the grave under the huge rock carved with his name. The clouds went racing south like an army of ghosts.

I was the only one of the Invisibles there. Most of us, of course, were dead, or waiting to be hanged. A few, like me, had got away and were in hiding. I did not need to hide, since I had never come near the battle or fired a shot. Officially, I had never been there. I was the most invisible of us all.

The women were a terrible sight. Martha hung on Mrs. Brown as if every bone in her body were broken. Mrs. Brown was quiet until we lowered the coffin into the ground and started to throw dirt on it. Then she howled. But Annie frightened me the most. She stared straight into the grave without trying to wipe away her tears, and smiled.

Afterwards, she came over to me and took my hand.

"I'm glad you could be here," she said. "It's right that one of you should see the beginning."

"Thank you, Annie" was all I said, wondering what she was talking about. But she was right. It was the beginning. Just as he had at Osawatomie Creek, John Brown had forced every man to choose his side.

The Harper's Ferry raid shook the cage where the South kept its deepest fears locked up. Almost a year to the day after John Brown was executed, South Carolina seceded from the Union. Six more Southern states joined her. No one in the North knew what to do. Then, in April of '61, the South fired on the American flag flying over Fort Sumter, and we knew. We marched away to our training camps, singing,

> *John Brown's body lies a-mold'ring in the grave,*
> *John Brown's body lies a-mold'ring in the grave,*
> *John Brown's body lies a-mold'ring in the grave,*
> *But his soul goes marching on.*

I left Harvard and volunteered as an army telegrapher. Bob came with me.

"If the army's hard up enough to take you, then I'd better come along to keep an eye on your work," he said.

We get less pay than soldiers, and every once in a while somebody shoots at us, but whatever comes over the wires, we're first to know it. Makes us feel spry.

We sing a new song now. One Julia Ward Howe wrote because she loved John Brown and thought the words we had did him no justice.

> *Mine eyes have seen the glory*
> *Of the coming of the Lord,*

He is tramping out the vintage
Where the grapes of wrath are stored,
He has loosed the fateful lightning
Of his terrible swift sword,
His truth is marching on.

She is right. Brown wrote his name, and our fate, in lightning.

There is so much I still don't know. I will never know if Brown meant to stage his raid as he explained it to us or if he intended to sacrifice himself and us to bring on this war. I know now that he cut the wires to Harper's Ferry before he even reached it. He held up a train for hours, then identified himself and let it go on to Baltimore. He let a man from Harper's Ferry gallop off to spread the alarm. What was in his mind?

I will never know if he intended for me to live. I asked my mother point-blank if she had given Brown money to buy me a chance to get away. "There is not enough money in all the world to buy thee, Theodore" was all she said.

My friends from the Invisibles are close to me in a way I can't explain. I try to live for us all, as Watson said I would. I never feel John Brown. Wherever he is, it seems a long way from here. Oddly, though, I sometimes wake up dreaming that I have heard him. It is always the same dream, a dream that makes no sense. I hear him singing in his flat, hard voice the song I heard on the docks at Cincinnati the day that Jacob died. It is soft but persistent, and absolutely real.

Deep river,
My home is over Jordan,

Deep river, Lord,
I want to cross over into campground,
I want to cross over into campground.

John Brown may have his peace. We have his war.

THE RAIDERS

Jeremiah Anderson *Killed in action*
Osborne Perry Anderson *Survived; fought in Civil War*
John Brown, Jr. *Killed in action*
Oliver Brown *Killed in action*
Owen Brown *Survived*
Watson Brown *Died in prison from wounds received in action*
John Cook *Escaped Harper's Ferry; caught later, tried, and hanged*
John Copeland *Hanged*
Barclay Coppoc *Survived raid; died in Civil War*
Edwin Coppoc *Hanged*
Shields Green *Hanged*
Albert Hazlett *Escaped Harper's Ferry; caught later, tried, and hanged*
John Henry Kagi *Killed in action*
Lewis Leary *Killed in action*
William Leeman *Killed in action*
Francis Merriam *Survived; fought in Civil War*
Dangerfield Newby *Killed in action*
Aaron Stevens *Hanged*
Stewart Taylor *Killed in action*
Charles Tidd *Escaped*
Dauphin Thompson *Killed in action*
William Thompson *Taken prisoner and shot*

John Brown *Hanged*